SAVAGE KINGS
BOOK FOUR

WICKED SAVAGE

LILIAN HARRIS

Editing/Interior Formatting: CPR Publishing Services

Proofreader: Judy's Proofreading

Cover Design: Wildheart Graphics

TO ALL MY READERS, NEW AND OLD, THANK YOU SO MUCH FOR READING THIS SERIES.

RUTHLESS SAVAGE TOOK OFF MORE THAN I EVER IMAGINED, AND TO HAVE YOU STILL HERE MEANS SO MUCH TO ME.

I HOPE YOU STICK AROUND BECAUSE I HAVE SO MANY MORE STORIES TO TELL, WITH OUR FRIEND KONSTANTIN BEING NEXT.

TRANSLATIONS & PRONOUNCIATIONS

- Fionn – "Fee-yun"
- Eriu – "Air-ooh"
- Iseult – "Ee-salt"
- Tynan – "Tie-nan"
- Cillian – "KILL-ee-in"
- Bratva – Russian organized crime or Russian Mafia
- Suka. – bitch
- Moya milaya. – my darling
- Maladets. – atta girl
- On suma saydot kakda on uznayit. – he's going to go nuts when he finds out.
- Hvatit. Ti nekhochesh problemy s bossom. – Stop it. You don't want problems with the boss.
- Moya lubimaya sistra. – my darling sister.
- a ghra. – love
- leannan. – sweetheart
- Tha thu bòidheach. – You are beautiful.
- Taim i ngrá leat. – I'm in love with you

PART I

ONE

DINARA
AGE 18

"So, how far is this place?" my cousin Natalia asks while checking her reflection in a compact mirror and reapplying a bold layer of red lipstick.

"About an hour," I tell her, looking over at her as I adjust my dress in the limo.

"Damn." Alisa, my best friend, sighs from across the seat, tugging at the hem of her black minidress. "That's pretty far."

"Yeah, and Konstantin always changes the location because it's so hush-hush."

"Ooh, mysterious." She grins. "Is it always in Jersey?"

"Not always."

"I can't believe he let us come." Natalia slips her black lace mask into place. "Think we'll meet any hot guys there? Maybe a sexy athlete?"

I laugh. "I don't know, but let's stick together tonight, okay? Even though Konstantin tracks people with their masks, we don't wanna talk to anyone sketchy."

"These have trackers?" Alisa stares at her mask in disbelief.

"Yep. Oh, and before I forget, no bags or phones are allowed inside."

"No phones?" Natalia looks horrified. "What the hell? I didn't know that."

"Well, duh." I wave a hand dismissively. "Imagine the scandal if someone snapped photos or took videos."

"Shit," she mutters. "I hadn't thought of that."

"We can just leave our bags in the limo."

"Damn, now I'm really nervous." Alisa's foot starts bouncing.

"Hopefully, once we're inside, we'll forget all about the nerves."

I'm not sure if I'm trying to convince them or myself. But I wanted to do something unforgettable for my birthday. Something few people ever get to do.

When Konstantin, my oldest cousin, said it was okay, I was ecstatic. Getting out of my comfort zone is good sometimes.

As the conversation shifts to college and the guys we like, I feel my excitement growing despite the nerves.

Soon, we pull up to a nondescript industrial building. The parking lot is crowded, and a few people are already heading for the entrance, all dressed to the nines.

One would think this was an elegant party if they drove past. But looks can be deceiving.

"I'll be here whenever you're ready to leave, Ms. Marinova," Pavel, Konstantin's driver, says in his thick Russian accent as he opens the limo door.

"Thanks."

He nods as he rounds the vehicle to head back to the driver's side, while we approach a man standing by the entrance, his red devil's mask barely concealing his piercing gaze as he uses a wand to scan the crowd.

I stride past the others in line, Alisa and Natalia close by. A few curious eyes follow us, probably wondering who we are. If they only knew.

When the devil man sees my mask, his expression shifts. He recognizes me immediately. Mine's unique, designed especially for me by Konstantin.

"Mozhete voiti," he says in Russian after scanning us. *You can go in.*

"Spaseba." *Thanks.*

We head for the entrance where a woman in a sleek black gown with a dramatic feathered mask steps aside, silently signaling for the elevator. She presses the button once we're inside, and we rise in silence.

"I'm gonna need a drink," Natalia whispers in my ear.

"Same." I nod.

Konstantin did warn me that anything goes at his club and told me to be careful or he'd have a big mess to clean up. Of course, I knew what he meant. I'm not some naïve little girl who doesn't know what sort of family she belongs to. They kill, and they do it easily.

I should know. I watched my father do the unspeakable when I was sixteen, and I still can't get it out of my head, constantly having nightmares of that day.

I force myself to forget, though. Forget the monster I had to live with. Forget what he took from me.

Right now isn't the time for that.

Tonight, I want to have fun and celebrate my birthday instead of being sucked into the past.

Once we arrive at the top floor, two guards with plain black masks let us through the doors, and the atmosphere changes the moment we enter. Flashing LED lights and hypnotic music surround us, creating an electric energy as bodies writhe together, lost in the music.

"This doesn't look so bad," Natalia whispers in my ear.

"That's because this is only the beginning." I scan the crowd, spotting a bar just to the right. "Let's grab drinks first."

No IDs are checked here, ensuring anonymity. Only those with permission, like us, are allowed entry. It's one of the perks of being family or tied into Konstantin's world. No one under twenty-one is allowed unless Konstantin says so, and that's rare.

We squeeze through the crowd toward the bar, Natalia already chatting about the night ahead.

"What can I get you ladies?" a bartender asks, her chest completely out in a red corset, nipples covered with two ruby-red stones.

"I'll have a cranberry vodka," Natalia tells her.

"Me too." Alisa nods.

"Make it three," I tell the bartender.

She scans each of our masks, processing the order. Konstantin's name is on our tab, but for others, everything gets charged to the card on file.

Minutes later, we're sipping our drinks, the warmth flowing through me, but a strange knot of unease settles in my stomach. Of course I'd be nervous at a place like this. I glance around, letting my mind wander.

"I heard girls sell their virginities here," Natalia says casually, swirling her drink.

"Marriage auctions too. Though I'm sure that's not even the worst of it."

A laugh dies in my throat when I catch sight of a man with a full-face demon mask dragging a woman through the crowd. That wouldn't be so bad, except she's on her hands and knees…and completely naked. Well, except for the black collar around her neck and a peacock mask. But other than that? Yep, butt-ass naked.

"Holy shit!" Alisa gasps, stepping back and bumping into me, which causes me to jolt backward.

And of course, my drink splashes right down my dress.

"Oh, come on," I groan, staring at the stain spreading across the fabric.

"I'm so sorry!" Alisa's face reddens as she grabs my empty glass.

"It's fine," I mutter. "Just grab some napkins, please."

She turns to head toward the bar, but stops, eyes wide. Natalia stills too.

"What are you guys doing? I know I'm a mess, but can someone get me some napkins so my nipples don't freeze to death?"

Better yet…

I start to turn.

Then I feel it. A hand, strong and firm, settling on my shoulder.

"You're not wrong," a low, masculine baritone husks in my ear, thick with confidence and something else. Something I can't quite name. "You're quite the little mess."

I pivot quickly, turning toward the voice, and my breath catches when I realize the hard object I had bumped into was actually this man, towering and built like a Greek god.

His eyes meet mine, the piercing pale green intensity sending a jolt through my chest. He's holding a stack of napkins, and his large hand—thick with veins—sends a rush of heat through me.

I take the napkins from him, avoiding his gaze at first, but it's impossible to ignore him.

His full lips curl into a playful, devilish smirk, and my stomach flutters in response. His eyes flicker over my body as I blot my dress, his gaze lingering there just a moment too long before he looks up again.

The fabric of his dress shirt stretches taut across his firm chest, two buttons undone, exposing just enough to make me want to see more. And the way his thick, sculpted biceps flex causes my breath to hitch.

It's a shame most of his face is hidden behind the sleek black mask resting on the bridge of his nose. But somehow, the glimpse of his sharp jawline beneath it only makes him more irresistible.

I lower my eyes, catching sight of a wet spot on his abdomen.

Crap. I made him spill his drink too.

"I'm sorry about that," I say, grimacing at the stain.

His deep chuckle vibrates through me. "It's okay, love." He dips closer until his mouth is against my ear. "I didn't like this shirt anyway."

His breath skims the side of my neck, sending a shiver down my spine.

You shouldn't be wearing one.

Just because I'm a virgin, it doesn't mean I'm not a dirty one.

"What's your name?"

I tense, suddenly aware of the intimacy of the question, the proximity of his body.

"I'm Cillian."

Should I tell him? Konstantin never said I wasn't allowed, only that everyone must keep their masks on. Not like I have to give him my full name.

Fuck it.

"Dinara."

"Pretty." His lips curve into a smile that makes my knees weak as his gaze runs over me again, taking in every curve, every movement.

"Are you new here?" His voice is like velvet, rough at the edges.

"Yes." I discreetly pull at my wet dress. "It's my birthday."

He glances down, his eyes narrowing briefly before he meets mine again.

"Then I'll have to buy you a drink," he says smoothly, his smile deepening. "Seeing as you've managed to spill yours all over your beautiful dress."

I swallow, suddenly aware of how much he's watching me. His

eyes don't leave mine, and a warmth spreads through me that has nothing to do with the alcohol.

"I'd love another drink. Vodka and cranberry, please."

He doesn't say a word, his gaze locking on my lips before he turns toward the bar, standing there like he owns the world.

There's something about him, though—something about tonight—that feels like it's just beginning.

"Holy fucking shit," Natalia whispers from right behind me. "The man looks like he could throw all three of us over his shoulder."

"And look at his hands," Alisa adds. "I once read that guys with thick fingers have big dicks."

I elbow her lightly, and she laughs.

"I'm just saying. You could use a big dick. Hell, you could use *any* dick at this point."

"Shut up before he hears you." My eyes widen at her in warning just as he spins toward me.

"Here you go." He hands me the drink with a slow, deliberate smirk, holding one for himself as well.

"Thanks."

As I take it from him, our fingers brush—just for a second, but it's enough. A rush of heat shoots through me, like a surge of electricity racing up my arm, leaving a trail of warmth in its wake.

His eyes lock on to mine, dark and intense, as if he can feel the exact moment the air between us shifts, crackling with tension so palpable I can almost hear it over the pounding music. I can't look away, trapped in the depth of this intensity, his presence pressing in on me, undeniable and magnetic.

Before I can even react, his arm slips around my waist, pulling me in close. His body, hard and solid, presses against mine—just enough to make my pulse spike. His lips graze along the curve of my ear, his breath hot against my skin.

"Careful," he whispers, his tone dark and laced with a teasing edge. "Wouldn't want you spilling that drink too. Don't think I could handle you making more of a mess of yourself than you already are."

His words sink under my skin, stirring something wild and untamed inside me, while his fingers press deeper into my hip—firm, possessive. It's like he's marking me, claiming me. Holding me here, right where he wants me.

And for a second, I wonder if he's just playing me. Toying with me. Trying to get under my skin. Under my dress. But my body doesn't care.

It wants this.

It wants *him*.

Maybe Alisa is right. Maybe all I need to make my birthday more memorable is a healthy dose of big dick.

I clear my throat, trying to mask the heat pooling low in my stomach, and take a long, burning gulp of my drink. The liquor slides down my throat in a fiery rush, the warmth lingering far longer than it should.

"So, do you come here often?" I ask, the question stained with a flicker of curiosity.

I want to know if he's a regular.

"Sometimes." His lips curl into a knowing smile, and my gaze instinctively drifts to his mouth.

It's a dangerous thing to do, because the way it tugs at my senses makes me suck on the straw slowly, like I'm savoring the taste of something I can't quite reach.

It's not that I haven't been around handsome men before. Half of the guards at Konstantin's, where I live, are nice to look at. But none of them have made me feel the way this stranger does. Like I wouldn't mind if he took me into a dark corner, pressed me up against a wall, and had his way with me. I don't know if he's gentle or rough, though a part of me desperately hopes he's the latter.

Cillian's eyes narrow, a flash of something dark flickering across his face.

Oh God. He didn't hear that, right?

A knot forms in my stomach, and I silently curse myself.

I need to stop imagining all the dirty things I want him to do to me before I actually say them out loud. That would be beyond humiliating.

"You seem a bit young to be here." His palm slides down to the small of my back, tightening against me, making it clear that I belong to him in this moment.

My heart skips, stuttering in my chest as the heat of his touch sets a fire in places I never thought I'd feel.

"How can you know when you haven't even seen my face?" I tease, my smile tugging at the edges.

"Am I wrong?" His lips turn into a wicked smirk, and I feel the pull of it deep inside me.

My body tenses, caught between the tension he creates and the hunger that starts to build.

"Try and find out," I say, lower than I intended.

But he doesn't smile. Instead, his hand tightens around my waist, pulling me closer, until I'm pressed against the hard length of him. Fingers slide up to my jaw, gripping it with a force that steals my breath.

"I'll take that bet." A low, gravelly growl rumbles from him.

His thumb brushes across my lips—once, then twice—as his gaze flickers to my mouth for a brief moment. When those eyes burn into mine, I inhale sharply, the air between us thick with awareness.

"Jesus," he mutters under his breath, chest rising sharply like he's fighting with himself. Fighting the urge to kiss me. To do more than that.

The energy between us crackles, undeniable and electric, and I know without a doubt I'd do anything to make him kiss me. But instead of leaning in, he holds back, his thumb still lingering against my lips, sending waves of heat through me.

He mutters something under his breath, something I can't catch, and lets out a deep, almost frustrated sigh. "I should go."

But instead of pulling away, his grip on my chin tightens and he draws me even closer, his breath hot against my skin.

"Why?" I can't hide the desperation.

I don't want him to leave. Not until I know who he is. Not until I've had more of him.

"I have somewhere else to be." His words make a knot of disappointment form in my chest.

"That's too bad." My mouth parts in protest, but before I can say another word, his thumb feathers across my bottom lip.

I can't help it. My tongue flicks out, tasting him.

"Fuck," he groans, his fingers tightening around my chin, and then he finally lets me go.

But he doesn't step back. Doesn't walk away. He stays right there, eyes never leaving mine.

"I'll see you around, a ghra." His words are a whisper, a promise.

And then he starts to pull away.

He's just a stranger. A man I'll never see again. So why does it feel like a piece of me is slipping away with him?

"Wait." I grab his bicep, and he jerks slightly, muscles shifting under my fingers.

"A ghra. What does it mean?" I ask, breathless, eager to hold on to whatever this is.

A roguish grin spreads across his face as he stalks closer. His lips brush the edge of my ear, sending a jolt of electricity straight down my limbs.

"Try and find out."

The need in my core intensifies, aching and raw, and I know I'm on the edge of something I can't pull back from.

"I'll take that bet," I breathe out, the words a challenge I never intended to make.

He chuckles darkly, low and rich, the sound vibrating through me. "Happy birthday, beautiful."

Then, before I can process what's happening, he presses a kiss to my cheek—so soft, so light, I almost don't believe it's real.

My hand moves of its own accord, wrapping around the back of his head, pulling him closer, wanting more.

His response is immediate. With a groan, he tugs at my hair, jerking my head back as his lips hover dangerously close to mine.

"The next time you touch me like that, I won't be able to resist."

"Who said I want you to?" The words spill out before I can stop them, breathless and reckless.

I don't know what I'm doing, but every inch of my body is screaming for him, my mind drowned in a haze of need.

He winds my hair around his wrist, pulling me in just a fraction closer, his breath hot against my ear. His teeth graze the sensitive skin, sending an electric shock straight to my core. Those eyes burn hot—dark, smoldering, possessive—and I feel the weight of them, like a secret promise I can't ignore.

"Delicate little thing… You have no idea what you're asking for."

His words hit me like a force of nature, making a tremor run through my body as the heat rises inside me.

I open my mouth to respond, but no sound comes out.

Before I can gather myself, he steps back, his fingers slipping from my hair, but his gaze never leaves mine.

"I'll see you around, Dinara. Don't get into too much trouble without me."

My body is still humming with the rush of him, the electricity of his touch.

I manage a shaky smile, trying to play it cool. "Are you worried about me already?"

He laughs—a low, dark sound that reverberates through my chest, like a melody meant just for me. Before I can say anything else, he's already turning away.

"What the hell was that?" Natalia brings me back as she appears at my side. "He was basically eye-fucking you the entire time."

"If you're not interested, I'll gladly take him off your hands," Alisa teases, watching him walk away with a hungry gleam in her eyes.

I throw her a pointed glare. "He's mine, girls. He just doesn't know it yet."

TWO

CILLIAN

I have no idea what possessed me, but the pull of that girl… it's like nothing I've ever felt. There's something about her, something that wraps itself around me, tightening every time I think of her.

The only reason I walked away is because she's too young for me. I didn't need to rip off that damn gold-and-black lace mask to see it.

She was a tempting, dangerous distraction…but I wasn't about to let myself fall for it.

"Who was that?" Fionn breaks through my thoughts, gesturing toward her.

She's still standing where I left her, her eyes locked on to mine with a slow, knowing smile.

"Someone I don't need to know," I mutter, but I can't tear my gaze away.

My brother's laugh is rough and mocking. "Then why the hell were you touching her like you had every right to?"

I growl low in my throat, finishing my drink in one long, deliberate swallow. She's still watching me, that oval diamond in the middle of her mask sparkling, a little flicker of mischief in her gaze. My pulse picks up, a hot, primal need stirring in my gut.

The urge to go back to her is damn near overwhelming. I know exactly what would happen if I did: words would turn into something else.

Maybe it would be only tonight. Just a single, intoxicating night. But I'd be lying to myself if I said I didn't feel a strange pull in my chest, telling me it could be more.

I continue to stare, unable to resist. Damn, those eyes—those rich, molten chestnut eyes. A man could drown in them.

"If you don't want her, I'll take my shot," Fionn says, his mouth curling.

I shoot him a death glare. "Don't fucking touch her."

Because she's mine.

The thought zaps through my head like it has always belonged there.

Before I can turn back to her, the sound of a low voice behind me sends a ripple of irritation through me.

"Gentlemen..." Konstantin's Russian accent cuts through the air like a blade.

I stiffen, trying to mask my contempt, but it's useless. I've never been able to shake the hate I feel for this man or his family, and I doubt I ever will. The memory of what his father did to our mother is burned into my bones, a scar I carry with me every single day.

Fionn gives him a curt nod. "Konstantin."

"How are you two enjoying the evening?" Konstantin's gaze flicks between us before narrowing, a sly grin pulling at the corner of his mouth. His eyes settle on me with a look that says he knows exactly what's going on in my head. "See anyone you like?"

"Not particularly," I mutter.

The only reason I even started coming here is because Fionn forced me to when Konstantin extended free memberships to us. It was his way of expressing that any feuds between our families from before are now over.

"Eventually, we'll be friends, Cillian Quinn." Konstantin slaps me on the shoulder, but I shove his hand off roughly. "Maybe even family."

I scoff. "I doubt that."

The bastard laughs. I want to punch him in that smug fucking face.

"Well, I'll leave you to it." He turns to go. "Please let me know if there's anything I can do for you. Anything at all."

My jaw clenches so tight it aches.

As soon as he's out of earshot, I mutter under my breath, "I really hate that son of a bitch."

Fionn chuckles. "No way. I had *no* idea."

Grinding my jaw, I turn toward the bar, needing another drink. As I wait for the bartender to pour it, I glance toward where Dinara was, but she's gone.

Panic claws at my chest. I scour the room, desperate to find her, but there's no sign of her. I know it's ridiculous. She's just a woman I bumped into, but there's something about her. Something unfinished.

What if she's already gone? What if I'll never see her again?

My teeth clench, and I feel Fionn's eyes on me.

"Where are you going?" he calls, but I ignore him.

The burning need to find her consumes me, and nothing, not even my brother, is going to stop me.

I should've gone back to her. Should've gotten her full name. Her number. Something.

Now, all I can do is hope it's not too late.

DINARA

I could've stayed right where we were watching that mysterious man all night, but the girls were eager to keep moving through the club.

The more we explored, the more we realized what really goes on here: anything and everything. Each room we entered seemed to offer a new kind of fantasy. A woman with multiple men. Another tied up from the ceiling with thick rope. A man being flogged by three women while on his hands and knees with a dog collar around his neck.

We move further into the club, passing an open space where women are on display while the crowd bids for their virginities.

My stomach tightens at the thought. There's no way I could ever do that. The idea of losing my virginity to a stranger, someone I didn't even choose, is terrifying.

I scan the seats, looking for Cillian. What if he's into this?

But I don't spot him. Thank goodness. That would be such a turn-off.

"Oh my God, there's no way in hell I'd ever do that!" Natalia exclaims, watching as a new contestant steps onto the stage in a sheer white gown.

"Never." I shake my head. "I want to have a choice in who I'm with for the first time."

Alisa giggles, nudging me. "I'm sure that hot guy from earlier would be very willing if you asked."

I roll my eyes. "He left, remember? Whatever he had to do was clearly more important."

"I'm sure we'll see him again."

"Whatever. Not like I'm about to go chasing after him."

Natalia bumps her shoulder into mine. "You guys had major chemistry. It's okay to be disappointed."

"I'm not disappointed."

Liar.

"Okay." She shrugs, but there's a knowing curve to her lips. "Maybe he wasn't the right guy. I'm sure you'll lose your V-card eventually…"

"Oh shut up!" I swat her playfully.

"I just can't believe you're still a virgin. I really would've thought you'd be the first of us to lose it."

"What the hell does that mean?" I glare at her.

"Nothing!" She raises her hands in mock surrender. "It's just, you've always been so open about stuff like that. I figured…"

"Well, I haven't found the right guy. That's all. Nothing wrong with waiting." I try to sound confident, but it's harder than I thought.

I didn't intentionally remain a virgin. It just never happened with anyone else. I either got bored or lost interest. I never felt that spark, that pull.

Until Cillian.

"Let me just say, the first time sucks anyway." Natalia grimaces. "You don't need the right guy for that."

"She's right." Alisa nods in agreement.

"I don't know, girls. But screwing a complete stranger probably wouldn't be the smartest choice here, especially with Konstantin lurking around."

"Come on, live a little." Natalia nudges me playfully. "These are the years we're allowed to do stupid stuff. Then we'll turn into our parents and get all responsible." She pretends to gag dramatically.

"I wouldn't exactly call my father responsible," I mutter.

And my mother...

The words fall flat, the air thickens, and my chest tightens. The ache, the hollow feeling, presses in on me.

I can't escape the memory. I want to, but I can't stop it.

Tears sting behind my eyes. I try to push them back, but it's too late. The moment floods me.

I wanted Mom to leave him so badly. But she never did. Well, couldn't is more like it. You don't just leave a man like him.

I pinch my eyes shut, my heart hammering in my chest. My hand reaches out, pressing against the wall beside me as I fight to keep it together.

The memory claws at me. That day two years ago. The same nightmare that always haunts me when I close my eyes. I'm unable to escape it even in my subconscious.

It's like it happened yesterday. And no matter how much I try to move forward, it still drags me back.

THREE

DINARA
TWO YEARS AGO

"**T**ake Gregory and go upstairs," I urge my little sister, Tatiana, my body tight with panic.

Tears streak down her face, and I can barely stand to see her so scared—so small, so fragile. She's only eleven. She should be playing with friends, not cowering from our father's rage.

From the other room, my father's voice erupts, sharp and violent. "You open your mouth to me, suka?"

His words are like a whip, followed by the sickening sound of a thud. My mother's muffled whimper breaks through the air, and my body stiffens with fear.

Tatiana clutches three-year-old Gregory to her chest, his face pale and streaked with tears.

"We need to get help," she whispers, barely audible. "He's hurting her so bad... It's worse than ever."

Her small hand shakes as it wraps around our brother, and I can't bear the anguish in his eyes. His fear is a mirror of my own.

"I'm going to try to help, okay?" I say, trying to keep my tone steady, though my heart is racing, each beat louder than the last. "Just take him upstairs and keep him safe."

She nods, barely holding it together. "Be careful."

I pull them both into a quick, desperate hug—one that feels like I'm giving them everything I have, even as I push them toward the stairs, my fingers trembling.

"Hvatit!" My mother's cry echoes through the house, raw and pleading. "Leo, pajalista!" Stop. Leo, please.

I don't wait another second. My feet move on their own as I rush toward the den, my hand gripping the cold doorknob like a lifeline. I close my eyes for a moment, inhaling deeply and trying to silence the terror crashing through me.

Be brave. Be strong. You can do this, Dinara.

When I push the door open, my father's anger cuts through the silence.

"You will learn your place in my house!" he bellows just as I step into the room, and he turns to me, his eyes dark with malice.

"Leave her alone, Papa!" My heart pounds in my chest, my blood roaring in my ears.

I want to move, to do something—anything—to stop him, but I can't. Fear has me rooted to the spot, though my body quivers with fury.

My mother tries to push herself off the ground, blood streaking down her face as she swipes at her mouth. But before she can get far, he shoves her back down with his bare foot, crushing her into the floor as if she's nothing more than an insect beneath his heel.

"Just like your mother." His lip curls with disgust. "Sticking your nose where it doesn't belong."

I step forward, adrenaline pumping through my veins. But then, with a cruel chuckle, he reaches for a small lion statue on the side table, lifting it in the air like it's a weapon.

His eyes lock on me, and I know what's coming. My body goes cold, but I stand my ground, refusing to back down.

"Let Mama go and stop it," I whisper. "Gregory is afraid."

This isn't the first time I've had to face him. It won't be the last. And I will never stop fighting. Ever.

"I teach Gregory how to be a man. Do not worry about my son." His words are slow, deliberate. Designed to make me flinch.

And it works. My stomach twists into a tight knot as he steps closer, intentionally cutting down the space between us to make me feel small.

"Dinara, just go. I'm fine." Mom's voice trembles, but I can hear the effort in it, like she's trying to convince herself as much as me.

But I can't leave her. Not now, not ever. The thought of turning away from her, leaving her alone to face him…it feels like a betrayal. I'd never do that. I'd never abandon my mother.

He moves again, closing the distance, and I step back, my pulse hammering in my ears and my breath shallow.

His footsteps are heavy, purposeful, and I feel them in my chest. "I will teach you lesson, Dinara. One you remember."

"Let her go!" Mom shouts out of nowhere, rushing out from behind him, a vase in her hands and a quiet, desperate defiance in her eyes.

The world tilts, everything slows down, and I scream.

"Mom! No!" But the words are barely out before it happens.

He's already grabbed the vase from her hands, tearing it away in one swift motion.

I don't think. I don't hesitate. I lunge at him, grabbing on to his back with all my strength, pushing with everything inside me as I try to get him away from her.

"Mom!" I shout.

The rest happens in a blur.

One second, she's screaming. The next, she's silent as he continues to bash her face in, over and over, while I punch his back, trying to stop him.

But it's too late,

"Mom!" I sob for her, but she can't hear me.

Not anymore

Blood is everywhere.

Her blood.

"Mom!" My small fists rain across his back.

But he doesn't even feel them. He just curses at her in Russian as he continues to bludgeon her until I can't even recognize her face.

If only I had seen her stand up. If only I had somehow warned her not to do what she did. Maybe she'd still be here.

Almost every night, I relive that day, as though I'm being punished for not doing enough. For failing her. I wake up gasping for air with tears choking me, or screaming so loud it echoes in the silence of my room. It's like I'm back there again, watching it all unfold right before my eyes.

God, it hurts. The pain of remembering her—of knowing I couldn't save her—is a suffocating knot in my chest that refuses to loosen. I can't get past the fact that she's gone. Gone forever. I'll never hear her laughter again. Never feel her warm, comforting arms around me.

She's dead. No matter how hard my mind tries to shut it out, the truth is undeniable: she's not coming back.

"Dinara?" Natalia's voice breaks through the haze of my thoughts, and it takes me a few seconds to pull myself out of the memory, to force my mind back to the present.

"Yeah, sorry. What did you say?"

"Are you okay?" Her hand rests gently on my shoulder before she hugs me tightly.

"I will be."

"That again?" she whispers.

I nod, unable to find the words to explain how much pain I still carry from her loss.

"Oh, babe, I'm so sorry."

Alisa's hand runs comfortingly down my back.

They both know what happened. Everyone in our inner circle does. But to the outside world, my mom had a nervous breakdown and killed herself.

I had to play along. There was no choice. But everything in me wants to scream the truth, to let the world know what that monster did to her.

"I'm fine now, guys." I force the biggest grin I can muster, even though pretending the way I am is choking me. "Let's go check out the rest of the place."

The last thing I want to do today is remember how badly I failed her. I do that enough already.

They loop their arms through mine, guiding me down another hallway until we stop in front of the last door on the right. A woman stands in front of a group of maybe twenty people, her confident stance commanding the room.

"What do you think's going to happen in here?" Alisa whispers behind me, the sound of her curiosity mixing with the beat of the music.

"I don't know," I answer just as the woman's voice cuts through the air.

"Welcome to the art of touch, where you will be paired at random and learn to explore each other's bodies."

Whoa.

A wave of nervous energy washes over me as I step forward, crossing the threshold into the room.

"You'll each be given items to use in whatever way you wish," she adds as she gestures toward a table filled with black string bags.

"This sounds intense," Natalia murmurs in my ear.

"Excuse me?" the woman calls out, her face hidden behind an intricate red-and-gold lace mask. "Will you be joining us before we close the doors?"

I freeze, unsure of what I'm stepping into.

"Do it!" Alisa urges. "We'll wait by the bar."

She pushes me forward, and as she does, my gaze lands on the man walking right toward me.

Not just any man.

Cillian.

He's here.

My stomach tightens, air catching in my throat. He locks eyes with me, that signature smirk tugging at his lips, and my heart skips a beat.

His approach is slow, deliberate, and with every step, every inch of me becomes more aware. It's like he's got a hold on me, pulling me toward him with every movement.

"She'll stay." His tone is deep and commanding, leaving no space for argument.

And in this moment, there's no place I'd rather be.

I can barely focus on anything else, the weight of his presence consuming me as he stops right in front of me. My body goes weak, like it recognizes him before I do.

"Glad you decided to join us. Please shut the door," the woman tells me, but I can't tear my gaze away from Cillian.

He shuts it for me before taking my hand, dragging me toward the corner of the room, guiding me behind a crowd of people. His arm slides around my hips, pressing me into his side.

Every inch of my skin feels alive with his touch, and I try to focus on anything else, but it's impossible. The way he looks at me, the heat of his body against mine…it's too much. Too intoxicating.

And I know deep down, I'm already lost.

"I was hoping I'd see you again." His words are a heated rasp against my ear, sending electric shocks down my spine that leave my skin tingling.

"Were you now?" I fight the smile that tugs at the corners of my lips. "Or maybe you were just stalking me."

A low, gravelly laugh rumbles from his chest, sending a shiver through me. "Unfortunately for you, I'm not in the habit of stalking women."

His breath dances over my nape, warm and irresistible.

"I'm sure there's a first time for everything." My smile curls just a little as I watch the darkening of his eyes. A deeper shade of green, like the depths of the ocean.

His arm tightens around my back, like he's making sure I can't escape even if I wanted to.

But I don't.

"You're right." His fingers slide through my hair, pushing a few strands behind my ear.

Shivers rush through me the moment his fingertips graze my skin. The electric connection between us sparks in every direction, making me feel alive in ways I never thought possible.

His lips are mere inches from me, the heat of his breath mingling with my own. His gaze locks on to mine, steady and intense, and I can barely breathe—can hardly think—as every part of me ignites under his stare.

"Am I?" My words are barely a whisper, the tension pulling tight between us.

"Mm-hmm." His thumb traces the line of my jaw, a low groan slipping from his lips.

The sensation of his touch on me is almost too much, too perfect. I'm swept up in a whirlwind of desire, unable to look away. Unable to think of anything but him.

He pushes me up against the wall, ignoring everyone else, crowding into my space until his entire body is flush with mine. And there's no mistaking the thick, unforgiving length digging into me. Alisa was definitely right about the whole thick-fingers-and-large-dicks thing, because his is definitely not just a few inches.

"I shouldn't be thinking the things I am right now." His breaths land hot on my lips.

But he doesn't kiss me, teasing me with his proximity until all I want is more. Until I'm craving it on a level I've never felt before.

How is that possible? How can I want such things with a man I don't even know?

But I *want* to know him. Want him to snap off that mask so I can see him, even if that's against the rules.

"What things are you thinking about?"

I want him to admit he feels what I do. That he wants to kiss me and touch me, have every inch of me.

He cages me with his large hands, his mouth stroking the corner of mine, and in a flash, he's got his hand wrapped around my throat. His eyes turn beastly and demonic, so raw I can practically feel him inside me, taking what I'd be willing to give.

"Like wanting to rip this pretty dress to shreds…" He traces the hem across my breasts. "…and have you begging me to fuck you while my tongue is inside your pretty cunt."

Holy. Shit.

A pulsing throb hits between my thighs. I would let him in an instant.

The thought is irrational and stupid, but maybe Natalia is right. Maybe losing my virginity to this man is the smartest idea I've ever had.

Okay, I'm probably pushing it. But like she said, this is the time I get to make all the mistakes in the world. Let's just hope he isn't one of them.

"You two back there seem to have gotten an early start." The woman laughs. "You'll be paired up."

Shit.

My stomach takes a nosedive. I completely forgot where I was for a moment.

Okay, maybe this was a terrible idea. Art of touch, did she say? What the hell does that even mean?

Will I have to remove my clothes? What exactly will we be doing? Oh my God, what if I'm supposed to get naked for him?

Hello! It's not like he's just gonna be touching your arms. Do you realize where you are, Dinara?

I should just walk away. *That* would be smart.

"Don't be nervous, love." His masculine and alluring voice zaps my attention back to him. "I wouldn't do anything you're not comfortable with."

The sincerity in his words makes me relax just a little.

"Is that so?" I tease, hoping to sound calm and collected instead of frazzled and nervous like a stupid virgin.

You are *a stupid virgin.*

Okay, maybe not stupid, but definitely a virgin.

Hopefully not for long.

"That's right." He caresses my jaw with his hard knuckles, and I just want to crawl into his big, strong arms and live there. "If all you want to do is talk, we can do that too. I'm not in a rush."

In a rush for what? I want to ask.

But instead, I let out a nervous laugh. "Are you sure you're in the right place?"

His thumb swipes across my bottom lip, his gaze following his movement. "I'm exactly where I want to be."

My pulse quickens, racing against the heat building between us. Every fiber of my being begs to rip off his mask, to see the man hiding behind that confident exterior, the one who speaks with such ease and charm. I want to know him—*really* know him.

"You may now go to the first empty room you find," the woman announces, and my stomach flips with anticipation.

His gaze lingers on me, the weight of his presence heavy and undeniable.

"You ready?" His voice slips under my skin.

I try to swallow the knot in my throat, but it sticks, thick and heavy.

Without missing a beat, I nod, forcing a smile. I tell myself it's fine, that I'm not scared. But the truth is, I'm not just nervous.

I'm petrified.

FOUR

DINARA

It's perfectly normal to go off into a room with a stranger, knowing he's supposed to touch you. Nothing to see here…

But I can't back out now. Showing weakness in my family will get you killed. Marinovs are bred to be strong, and I'm every bit a Marinov.

I can do this.

Cillian leads me to the front, taking a black bag from the woman's outstretched hand as a flutter of nerves and curiosity stirs inside me.

"Ever done this before?" I glance up at him as we make our way past her down the narrow corridor.

"This specifically? No," he responds, low and steady.

I nod, trying to push down the rush of anticipation. "What made you want to?"

We reach room number nine, and I nearly choke on my breath as the door clicks shut behind us. I might actually throw up.

He turns to face me, leaning back against the wall, arms crossed over his broad chest. The fabric of his shirt strains against every inch of hard muscle, and it takes everything in me not to let my eyes linger longer than they should.

"I was looking for you, actually. Then you showed up."

The shock must be written all over my face. "You were? Why?"

A half-smile plays on his lips, like he's holding something back. "I guess we'll find out."

With a swift movement, he steps past me, heading straight for a single sofa. He drops the bag at his feet and sinks down, his presence filling the room in a way I can't ignore.

"Sit." He pats the spot beside him, and I feel the air thicken with an undercurrent of something electric, making me shiver.

I glance around the spacious room: dimly lit, a four-poster bed in the far-right corner, the soft glow from a table lamp casting shadows over the sheets. My stomach turns to knots.

Was he serious? Can we just talk?

Clearing my throat, I make my way toward him, every step weighted with a mix of trepidation and excitement. As I settle beside him, he moves with a fluidity that makes my pulse spike. His arm wraps around my lower back, pulling me toward him until the side of his leg presses against mine, and my body reacts—every nerve alive, as though he's touching me everywhere.

I've never experienced anything like this. With anyone. But with him, everything is different. More intense. I don't know what he wants, but I can feel it: the pull, the magnetic force between us.

With him, I just want to feel more.

"How old are you, exactly?"

His question startles me, but the brush of his fingers creeping up my dress, grazing my knee, makes everything else fade away, leaving only the heat of his touch.

"Does it matter?" The words come out strained as his fingers slide higher, teasing me through the fabric.

His gaze locks with mine, and suddenly, every sensation sharpens, intensifying with a single glance.

"No, but I'm still curious."

He kneads my inner thigh, and a soft moan slips from me. As it does, his other hand tangles in my hair, pulling my head back as his eyes narrow.

"You can't sound that fucking good and expect me to behave myself, leannan. And trust me, I'm really trying."

"Never said I wanted you to."

"Fuck," he groans, his fingers sliding higher, almost to where I need him. "Who are you and what are you doing to me?" His voice is breathless, almost frantic, the question spilling from him like a desperate plea.

Before I can even process his next move, he grips my hips and lifts me with ease. In one fluid motion, he drops me onto his lap, a hand cradling my face while the other brushes lightly under my chin.

"You look much better on my lap." A teasing smirk plays on his lips, making my stomach tighten.

Beneath me, his hard and heavy erection presses right into my center. My hips circle of their own accord, wanting to feel him inside me.

The backs of my fingers feather over the rough stubble of his hard jawline, needing to touch him everywhere. He groans, picking up my hand, kissing my palm. My body grows so overwrought with sensations, I may explode.

Is this what lust feels like? Is this what makes people crazed for one another? Because I get it now. I want him to the point that it doesn't even make sense.

My thumb glides past his mouth, and he lets out a deep, throaty moan, kissing and nipping the pad.

"Tell me everything about yourself," his husky drawl demands while his palms drift down my arms.

My breasts ache, nipples pressing against the soft material of my dress.

"There's nothing to tell." I reach for his thick, full hair, messing it up as I work his scalp with my fingers.

We're supposed to be touching, right? Why should he have all the fun?

His smoldering green gaze fills with an intensity that's not easy to ignore, a curse slipping out like my touch pleases him just as much as his pleases me. "I find that hard to believe."

In a blink, I'm beneath him, pinned by the weight of his body, his thigh wedged between mine like a promise. His gaze drops to my lips and stays there, his own barely parted, breath mingling with mine.

What can I tell him that won't reveal who I truly am? Telling him I belong to one of the most dangerous Russian Mafia families in the world seems pretty stupid. I'd be killed if I told anyone outside our circle anything about our family. It's unheard of. So is marrying anyone outside the Mafia world we live in. It just doesn't happen.

Not that I'm planning on marrying this guy or anything, but the point is he can't know anything about me and we have no future.

This is a one-and-done situation, as much as it pains me to say that.

He rises to his feet, standing over me like a godlike statue, while I try to control my unsteady breathing. Fingers reaching for his cuffs, he undoes each one.

"Fine, don't tell me." His mouth tilts with a faint smirk. "I'll take my time finding out everything about you instead. Seems a lot more fun."

My throat goes dry. "What are you gonna do to me?"

"What do you want me to do?"

"Everything."

As soon as that word leaves me, his jaw grows visibly tight, his hand balling into a fist.

A finger rolls down my lips. "That is a very dangerous invitation, baby."

"I live on the dangerous side."

He has no idea how true that is.

His chuckle is sinful and full of promise, sending a shudder down my arms. "You have three seconds to change your mind, baby girl. After that, you're mine."

My brow arches as I let my fingers run between my breasts, and that's all it takes for his beastly side to make an appearance.

Hello, friend.

A small, deliberate smirk curls the corner of my lips. No matter what I thought before, I want this, and I want it with him.

Roughly, he flips me onto my stomach, practically ripping the zipper at my back. When the cool air hits my spine, I try to get up to take off my dress, but he stops me, planting a hand on the back of my head.

"You stay just like that. If I wanted you to move, princess, I'd tell you."

That forceful tone has me squeezing my thighs.

He leaves me this way while he heads to grab the bag, returning within seconds. "Let's see what we have in here."

The seductive way he says that makes me edgy with anticipation.

He removes a black braided leather whip, rolling it down my back while I arch into it. I squeeze my legs tighter to make the ache at my center ease, but unfortunately, it only gets worse.

He lets the whip fall beside my face, revealing a pair of handcuffs next. Slowly, he drags the cold metal down, his gaze never leaving me as I gasp from the chill.

On his third reach, he pulls out a black scarf.

What's that for?

His lips hover near my ear, the weight of his chest pressing against my back. "I'm gonna enjoy the sight of you blindfolded while I spread your thighs apart and taste your pink pussy."

Oh...wow.

I've never had a guy do that to me before, and I definitely want to know what it feels like.

"How does that sound, baby?" He nips my earlobe. "Because I've been wondering all night what you taste like and sound like when you come."

His hot mouth rains kisses down my nape.

"Are you loud?"

He fists my hair, dragging my head back as far as it'll go.

"Are you shy and quiet?"

His lips graze my shoulder, his exhales feathering down my sensitive skin.

"Do you like it when a man takes control?"

I don't know the answers to any of those questions—except maybe the last one, because I do like it when *he* takes control. The throbbing between my thighs becomes painful.

"Please. Touch me." I sound beyond desperate.

Maybe if I wasn't this turned on, I'd be embarrassed, but I don't care right now. I need this.

A hand snakes under my chest, and he grabs my throat in a tight grip. "So polite." His mouth lowers to my throat, and he kisses me there—once, twice—his lips brushing a line down to my collarbone. "Let's see how wet you are for me, love."

Oh God, he's gonna touch me. Finally.

He shoves the dress up, tracing my pussy over the thin lacy thong. With a finger, he shoves my panties to the side, delicately stroking my clit until I'm gasping and clutching the leather beneath me.

"Cillian!"

"You sound fucking good moaning my name like that, like you're desperate for my cock." He nips my earlobe. "Gonna feed every inch of it into your needy little pussy."

Those words make me crazed, wanting everything he just described.

Two fingers work my clit, and my eyes roll back, every muscle in my limbs coiling with untethered desire. He blows hot breaths across my neck while he presses a single finger inside me, my nails digging into the sofa.

The feeling isn't foreign. I've done it to myself enough times. But with him, knowing it's his thick fingers, it's even better.

"Fuck, you're tight," he husks, using his thumb on my clit while he forces another finger into me.

My walls clench from the slight burn, though the more he touches me, the more that pain begins to morph into pleasure.

"Oh God, yes!" My back bows, my ass pressing into his erection.

I need this man. I want to give him my virginity. He can have it all. This may be my one chance to have an amazing first time. I'll never see him again.

"Stand up," he demands, slipping his fingers out of me without warning, and I groan from disappointment.

He rises to full height as I try to find my equilibrium and get to my feet. Instead of waiting, he takes my hand, pulling me up before I have a chance to get my legs to move. As soon as I'm upright, I grab the front of my dress to stop it from falling, suddenly nervous for him to see me completely nude.

He steps back, eyes roaming down my body while I shudder internally from my anxiety. I'm sure a man like this has seen many women naked. What if I'm not what he likes?

"Lower your arms, Dinara. Now. Let me see you."

Shivers rush up my arms from his deep voice. The demand in it. And before I can chicken out, I let my arms drift down until the dress falls, pooling at my feet. He sucks in an audible breath, admiring me while tremors run down my flesh.

"Jesus." His need burns through his tone. As he nears me, his knuckles stroke over each breast before he tugs on one of my hard nipples, the sensation echoing in my clit. "You're so beautiful."

My heart flutters from the way he says that. From the way his eyes take me in, like he's worshipping me. There's no doubt that he likes what he sees, and that empowers me.

With the back of his hand, he tilts my chin up to meet his height, his mouth sinking closer and skimming past my lips. "I want to savor every inch of you and never come up for air."

I suck in a needy, desperate breath.

Yes, please.

I reach for his back and yank up his shirt, wanting him naked too. "Take it off."

He chuckles, all deep and raspy. "Take it off for me, love."

Eagerly, I start on his buttons, our eyes lost to one another as I let the fabric come undone. Then he's flinging it off, exposing his well-defined, hard flesh. When my gaze focuses on his abs, then lower, to the thick outline of his erection, he lets out a low growl.

"Touch me, leannan."

A gorgeous man like this asking me to touch him? How can I say no? The very thought of his big, strong body on top of me makes me slicker between my thighs. I need him to finish what he started.

My bottom lip disappears between my teeth, the desperation to touch him everywhere growing almost unbearable. My fingertips glide over each one of his hard abs, his skin velvety soft. I let my touch skim up to his chest, and his muscles there jerk in response. Feeling braver, I undo his belt, tugging it out as our gazes fuse, like we're about to enter a battle.

He wants this badly. I can feel his hunger as though it's real, as though it's latching on to my skin.

He doesn't have to know about my virginity. I don't know if that'll be a deal breaker, and I'm definitely not willing to find out.

"Tell me what leannan means." Popping the button of his trousers,

I let my hand fall over the thick outline of his cock, stroking him there.

He hisses, fisting my hair while dragging his mouth to mine. "Sweetheart. It means sweetheart."

He nips my bottom lip, growling when I whimper before his mouth captures mine. I gasp as he kisses me deeper, a kiss filled with fierce and unsatiated passion, sending butterflies to my gut.

My legs wrap around his hips as he lifts me up in the air. Swallowing my groans, he carries me to the bed and lowers me onto it, bringing his body down over mine. His eyes linger, the back of his hand stroking down my cheek, the other crawling down my body before he's roughly pulling down my panties to my ankles

"You're drenched, baby." His fingers feather over my slit.

My back bows, wanting more, while I slip my panties off with my feet.

"All mine." He enters me with a finger, kissing up a trail to my ear. "You need this, don't you?"

"Yes…please…" I grab the back of his head, loving the way his heavy body feels pressing into me.

He chuckles as he starts to rise, every note of his laugh charged with desire, simmering just below the surface.

What? No!

"Where are you going?"

I'm barely able to catch my breath, lying there as he gets to his feet, leaving me in momentary suspense before he goes to retrieve the whip and scarf.

Oh…

My skin prickles as he draws closer, running the leather between my breasts and down to my achy core, dragging it against my clit until I writhe in pleasure.

"Sit up for me."

I do as he asks, and when he ties the fabric over my eyes and everything turns pitch black, I start to get nervous again.

The whip licks over my beaded nipple, and my back arches. "Are you gonna hurt me with that?"

It lightly slaps across my skin, causing me to yelp.

"I only want to bring you pleasure. If you don't like something, you can use a safe word."

"Okay…" My stomach gnaws from within.

"What will it be?"

Ah! How am I supposed to come up with something on the spot? I play some words in my head until I pop out a random one.

"Sunrise."

His raspy laughter hits from somewhere on my left. "Sunrise it is."

Hearing his voice, but not seeing him, adds another layer of sensuality. The anticipation of what he'll do next makes this even more thrilling.

In an instant, he flips me onto my stomach, hands grabbing my thighs and forcing my knees up until I'm spread open for him. My face heats up knowing he sees all of me, but I fight the mortification and make myself enjoy it.

Soon, all those thoughts vanish as he strokes my clit, eager fingers entering me slowly, and I groan in pleasure.

"I'm gonna enjoy watching this tight pussy take every inch of my big cock."

My core throbs painfully. One thing I know for sure: I like dirty talk.

He wraps a hand around my throat, pulling my head back while he nudges another finger inside me. "You're gonna take every inch and beg for more. But first, I'm gonna make you come on my fingers. And if you're a good girl, I'll let you come on my tongue."

He pistons inside me, making my eyes roll back. That overpowering sensation begins taking over until I scream his name, coming so hard I can barely breathe.

Before I can come down from the high, his mouth is on me, lips sucking my throbbing clit.

"Oh God, I can't."

I'm too sensitive to go again. There's no way…

"One more. Be my good girl and give me one more."

His good girl. Why is that so hot?

The more he swirls his tongue around my achy flesh, the more I start to want it again, my body his to command.

And with his name on my lips, I let go, grasping the sheets. Giving him what I've never given any man before while enjoying the hell out of it.

FIVE

CILLIAN

My palms squeeze her ass as I force her deeper onto my face, needing to make her do that again. And again. Wonder what her record is, because I'm about to shatter it.

Dinara is breathtaking with her clothes on, but without them, she's simply stolen my breath away.

I don't deserve to even look at something so beautiful, let alone touch her or fuck her. And I am gonna fuck her—hard and deep until she's coming on my dick, begging me to stop because she can't come anymore.

I don't know what it is about her, what has drawn me in from the moment she spilled that drink on me. But there's something here, and I'm not leaving until I get her number so we can explore this beyond these walls without these damn masks that I wish we weren't wearing right now.

She whimpers as I slide my head out from under her, grabbing the whip and letting it slide over her perfectly round ass. Wanting to see it grow pink under my harsh punishment, I give her a single strike, my cock damn near painful from how badly I want her.

"Oh God!" She jolts, though remains on her hands and knees, her skin growing redder. "Do it again."

That surprises me. I expected her to use her safe word.

"Dirty girl." I grab a fistful of her ass, spanking her with my palm, then running my fingers over the skin to soothe it before I let the whip strike her, harder this time.

She gasps, her arms trembling, but she still remains upright.

"Good girl. I think you deserve a reward."

I sink my fingers inside her, and she greedily sucks me into her tight cunt, collapsing onto her chest when I thrust faster, coaxing another orgasm from her pretty lips.

"That's it, give me another. Let me hear you."

"Oh my God!" she cries as I curl my fingers, hitting her G-spot.

Then she gives me exactly what I wanted, shattering and screaming my name while her body thrashes in pleasure. Pleasure *I* gave her.

"That's it, a ghra. It's all mine."

I don't know why I'm calling her these things. I don't even know her, but it just feels right.

She cries out, grasping the sheets with her small hands. I want them on my back, nails clawing across my flesh while I fuck her.

Collapsing on the bed, she's unable to hold herself up anymore. I let out a small chuckle before grabbing her hips and throwing her onto her back.

Her breaths grow labored while I get to my feet, needing to free this painful erection so I can finally have what I've wanted from the moment I saw her at the bar, looking all cute with her dress soaking wet around her beautiful tits.

My gaze roves down her body as I wonder how many men she's been with, wanting to rip out their eyes and cut off their arms for looking at and touching what I have deemed to be mine already.

The thoughts make me insane. Images of her tangled in bed with them, crying out in pleasure for them.

Fuck. Seeing that play in my head makes me painfully hard, yet enraged all at the same time. I've lost my damn mind.

I rip off the scarf, wanting her to see me too, and when her gaze lands on me, her teeth tug on the corner of her bottom lip.

"So damn sexy," I tell her, and her face flushes at the compliment while I reach into my pocket, grabbing a condom before I strip off my pants and boxers.

Her wide eyes drop to my cock. "You're…huge."

A low laugh rumbles from my chest as I fist the thick length, slow and deliberate. "If you're worried, don't be. I promise we'll make it fit."

Her lips part with a slight tremble, her gaze flicking up to meet mine before shifting back down. "Are those…"

"Piercings?"

She swallows, eyes locked in fascination.

"Yes, they are."

I finger the four frenum piercings on the underside of my shaft. Moving in closer, I tear the condom wrapper open with my teeth and roll it on in one smooth motion.

"Did that hurt?" she asks, curiosity laced in her tone. "I bet it did."

I plant my knee beside her on the bed, grabbing her ankles and pulling her closer, desperate to see her face.

What's Konstantin gonna do if I break a rule? Try to kill me? That wouldn't end well for him.

"It hurt like hell." My lips trail down her abdomen, each kiss slower than the last, my eyes locked on hers. "Need you to make it better."

Her fingers weave into my hair, giving it a teasing tug. "And how do I do that?"

I throw one of her legs over my shoulder as I slide my body lower. "I think your pretty mouth wrapped around it would really make me feel better."

"Maybe I can help with that."

Letting out a growl, I pull her thighs apart. "Not yet." My tongue slides up her cunt, making her jerk. "I need to taste you one more time before I have you gagging on my dick."

I suck each lip into my mouth before taking her clit, pulling it with my lips. She sucks in a moan, whimpering and tugging on my hair. Two fingers slide inside her as my tongue rolls over her there, bringing another orgasm dangerously close.

I can't get over how tight she is. Need to feel all that wrapped around my cock.

"Cillian, yes!" Her hand sinks through my hair, pulling hard as her body bends in pleasure.

When I drive deeper this time, she comes all over my mouth. Tasting her is definitely my new favorite thing. Unable to wait another moment, I climb up her body, her legs hooking over my hips as she stares up at me.

"Hi there, baby." The back of my hand gently caresses her cheek, and when she smiles at me, I feel it everywhere.

Her thumb grazes over my mouth. "Hi yourself." She lets out a breathy laugh. "You're very talented."

"Is that right?" I work the length of my cock over her clit, and she cries out when my piercings rub over her.

Really wish I wasn't wearing this rubber.

"Women must love the things you can do with that tongue." Her brows furrow, and her mouth pops wide with a cry when I grind myself against her once again.

"The only woman who matters right now is you."

She laughs, but a second later when I rub into her again, she's groaning, desperate to come again.

My hand curls around my dick, lining it up with her entrance while I search her eyes. "I need to see you."

"You *are* seeing me." She places a soft palm across my nape.

Before she can stop me, I tear off my mask.

She gasps, eyes growing. "You…you can't do that."

"And who's gonna stop me?" I reach for the strap of her mask, needing to see her. Needing her completely bare.

"We'll get in trouble." Her fingertips trail over my forehead, my jaw, like she's memorizing me. Like she's been waiting for this moment as much as I have.

I drop my mouth to hers, my voice a rough whisper. "You're worth the trouble."

Slowly, deliberately, I slide her mask off, unwrapping her like a gift that belongs to me alone. And when I finally see her, I forget how to breathe.

I trace the delicate slope of her cheekbones, the curve of her narrow chin. "You're so damn beautiful."

Her hands slip behind my head, pulling me in until our lips barely touch. "You're very handsome too."

A smirk tugs at my lips. I've never cared for compliments, but from her? I could listen all night.

"I've wanted to know what you looked like since I saw you," she confesses, lifting up to kiss me again.

I groan, working the crown of my cock inside her, but barely making a dent. Shit, she really is tight.

When I try to push in further, her face tenses, a wince of pain flashing across it.

Suddenly, it hits me.

No. She can't be…

"Dinara…"

"Yes?" She grimaces, a slight wrinkle forming on her button nose.

There's absolutely no way she's a virgin. And there's absolutely no way I can do this if she is.

"Is this your first time?"

Fuck. Tell me it's not.

When she bites her bottom lip and doesn't say a word, I shut my eyes. "Ní féidir é seo a bheith ag tarlú." *This can't be happening.*

I need to get off of her. There's no way in hell I'm taking this girl's virginity. That wouldn't be goddamn right.

But I can't move. I can't tear my eyes away from her, even though every instinct tells me to stop. Because no matter what, I want this. I want *her*.

"Please," she begs, grabbing my wrist, her features tight. "I want you. Don't deny me."

"How the hell can I do this? I can't take your damn virginity, Dinara. Fuck!" I grab a chunk of my hair. "How old are you?"

She's definitely young, which makes it even worse.

"It was my eighteenth birthday a few days ago."

"Oh, Jesus, baby. You're too young for me. I can't do that to you." My teeth grind; I want to bury myself deep inside her and forget this damn conversation.

There's no way I'm gonna give this honor to some other man. Not when she feels like she's already mine.

She shakes her head. "No, I'm not too young! Please don't do this."

"Dinara, I'm thirty-five. I shouldn't be here with you."

Her body deflates, tension pooling between her brows. A hand reaches out to clasp my cheek.

"But you want to be here." Those eyes fill with emotion. "You want me, so stop fighting it and come back."

Her soft touch, that ache in her tone, has me wanting to forget why the hell this is all wrong in the first place.

She's an adult. She wants this. Who the hell am I to say no?

"Please… I need this, and I only want it with you."

Fucking hell.

Her words send me completely over the edge. I need her too, like my life depends on it.

I lower my forehead to hers, and her mouth strokes mine.

"Has any man tasted you before?"

"No." She kisses me softly while I groan. "Nothing before you."

"Fuck, Dinara." My cock jerks knowing I have that first too. "I want all your firsts."

My length rubs against her warm center, needing to find a home inside her.

"I want to give them to you."

"Fuuuck." My heart races. She's killing me.

"I've never felt anything like what I feel with you," she goes on. "And even though it may not make sense, I want you to be my first."

My muscles grow rigid as I gaze back down at her. "I'm gonna take care of you. Your first time should be special."

My heart and my mind are at war. I know I shouldn't do this, yet I refuse to let another man have what belongs to me. This sweet young thing is mine, and I've never been one to share.

She laughs, her eyes shimmering with emotion. "That's really sweet."

"You make me want to be sweet," I reply with a grin. "Just don't tell my brothers."

A soft giggle escapes her, followed by a sharp inhale as I ease in another inch, making sure not to hurt her.

"You're doing so good." Pushing deeper, I stroke her clit gently, keeping my eyes locked on hers, watching for any hint of discomfort.

She hides it well, her expression steady, though I can see the slightest tension in her jaw.

"That's it, baby. Let me in." I clasp her cheek, circling my hips as I sink a little more, her gaze morphing into pleasure. "You're such a good girl, letting me stretch this pussy."

"Oh God, Cillian." Her lashes flutter, those thighs spreading wider.

I force another inch, and her eyes tremble to a close.

"No, don't do that. Look at me. I want your pleasure and your pain. I want it all."

She grabs hold of my biceps while I lift her leg up over my shoulder, opening her up for me. Gazing down at her, I can't help this sense of possessiveness, this burning need to keep her that continues to overtake me, even more now that I've had something no man has before.

And I know right now, whoever she is, wherever the hell she came from, she's gonna be mine.

"I need more. Please." Those pleading eyes call to me, and if I could hold out, I'd make her beg some more, but I need her right now.

Inching deeper, I ease myself into her, moving slowly. When she winces, I still.

"Don't stop." She grabs my shoulder. "Just fuck me."

I smirk. "You sure you're a virgin, babe?"

"Not anymore." A teasing smile dances across her face. "Please, Cillian, don't hold back. I want you. I want this. Don't treat me like I'm made of glass."

My teeth grind, my cock throbbing from my ravenous need to fuck her until she can't walk tomorrow. Before I can stop myself, I drive deeper, only getting halfway in before she cries out in pain, her nails digging into my skin, her face contorting with strain.

"You okay?"

"I will be."

My mouth forms a hard line. "I don't wanna hurt you."

"I know, but it's inevitable."

She's right, but it doesn't make it any easier.

Working my hand between us, I finger her clit while I sink another inch, and she whimpers in pleasure. "This is gonna hurt, love."

She nods, and this time when I thrust inside her, an inhale dies in her throat.

"Breathe, baby. Just breathe."

Tears shimmer in her gaze, and I hate myself right now.

"I'm sorry, leannan." My lips trace over her jaw.

"It's okay. Just keep going."

I continue to stroke her clit, rising onto my knees so I can watch myself go in and out of her. "You're so damn sexy, letting me use your virgin pussy like this."

"Yes, keep talking." Her eyes roll back. "Those piercings feel so good even through the condom."

A growl slips out, my hand wrapping around her throat while I slide out, then drive all the way in with a hard thrust.

"Oh shit," she winces, her brows pinched.

"You alright, baby?"

She nods.

My fingers squeeze around her delicate throat as I begin to move, increasing the rhythm, her mouth trembling with each shift.

"Yes, that feels good," she moans, her voice sweet and innocent, which only makes me take her harder.

"Such a dirty little thing, letting me do whatever I want to this gorgeous body." My thumb continues to roll over her clit as her back bows, her walls clinging tighter around my dick.

"Oh God, I'm close."

Looking into her eyes, I slam my hips faster, her pussy wet and tight around me. She's like a damn high I can't escape from. I'd rather die than walk away from whatever this is.

Flipping her over, I take her from the back, her knees up, face pressed to the mattress, my palm slapping her hard across her ass.

"Oh fuck, fuck, yes!" she cries, all traces of her pain now gone.

Grabbing a fistful of her hair, I use my other hand to touch between her thighs, teasing her while she begs me to come.

"You take my cock so good. Gonna force you to come over and

over until you're begging me to stop."

She glances at me over her shoulder, and the need to taste that mouth consumes me. I give in, tilting her face up and pressing my lips to hers, losing myself in the way she melts against me.

SIX

DINARA

Who knew my first time could feel like this?

Sure, it hurt at first, but the moment he took control, that was when everything shifted. The pain faded as he gave it to me without hesitation, without fear. And I didn't want him to stop.

I can't wait to tell the girls all about it. Oh God, I wonder if they're okay. But I know Konstantin will look after them if anything goes wrong.

Does he know I'm here with Cillian?

My chest tightens. I hope not! That would be mortifying.

Letting out a sigh, I nestle into Cillian's chest, a smile slowly spreading across my face. His fingers drift lazily up and down my spine, the sensation sending shivers through me. This feels so right, to be tangled up in him like this after what we just did. My muscles are weak like jelly, and the thought of standing up makes my head spin. If I even tried, I'm pretty sure I'd just collapse.

"We should probably get dressed now," I murmur, the words heavy with reluctance.

"Why? Got somewhere better to be?" His voice is low, teasing, as he lifts my chin with two fingers, pulling me in for a kiss—soft, lingering.

I sigh against his lips, the kind of sigh you see in those old romantic movies Mom always loved. The kind that makes you feel everything all at once.

At the thought, the memory of her crashes down on me, sharp and sudden.

A hollow ache spreads through my chest. She wouldn't approve of what I've done. She always told me to wait until marriage. She was old-fashioned like that. It was how she grew up.

I can only hope she'd understand why I did what I did, and I can't help but wonder if she ever experienced the same level of passion. If, before my father, there was someone who made her feel this fire too. I hope she had that. Because if he was the only one, I can't even imagine the loneliness she must have lived with.

I blink away the sudden mist in my eyes, trying to push the thoughts aside.

"It's just that my friends are here," I tell him. "And we all came in my limo, so I should probably get them home."

His knuckles graze my cheek, and I feel the weight of his gaze, heavy and unhurried. "That's too bad."

The heat of his hand leaves a warm trail on my skin, spreading through me, making everything feel hazy and…dangerous.

"The more you touch me, the harder it is to leave." My words are barely above a whisper, filled with something I can't name. "But I really should get up."

I prop my chin on my palm, looking down at him. He's sprawled out, so impossibly relaxed, and I don't wanna leave.

This is just sex. Don't get any ideas.

"Thanks for the…well, you know."

"The fucking?" He grins, his smirk devilish and confident, and my stomach flips.

He's infuriatingly charming, and the way he watches me, like he's already unraveled every part of me, knocks the breath from my lungs. Add in that rugged, rough-edged sex appeal, and it's ridiculous how easily he checks every one of my boxes.

But it doesn't matter. This was great, but that's all it was.

My heart betrays me, thudding against my ribs at the thought of never seeing him again.

You knew this would end before it even began, so stop pretending there's a happily ever after in here somewhere.

I start to move, but his arm tightens around my back, pulling me closer again. "I'm not done with you yet."

The warmth of his body is too much, and the world outside suddenly feels a little colder.

As he flips me beneath him, his mouth lowers to mine, so close I can almost feel his lips. A growl escapes from deep in his chest when I grind my hips into his.

"What do you plan to do to me now?" I nip his bottom lip, and he grunts, making me want to stay right here for the rest of my life.

"So many things…" His fingers slither between us until they land over my core, still throbbing with an ache from how roughly he took me.

"Oh God, I can't… It's too much."

"You can take it." He thrusts harder while his thumb plays with my clit, lips skimming over mine. "Just one more. Come on my hand one more time. Let me feel this tight cunt squeeze my fingers again before I let you go."

He doesn't give me a choice, plunging deep with a wild intensity, his gaze locked on me until I shatter beneath him.

"Cillian!" The strongest orgasm rolls over me, and I don't know what's happening.

"Shit, look at you squirting for me, love." His piercing gaze burns with radiating heat before his mouth crashes over my lips, consuming my cries of pleasure. Consuming everything I give.

He kisses me like it's the last time. Like he'll never have the chance to touch me, taste me, feel me again. And as the rush fades, a wave of sadness crashes over me, settling deep in my chest.

What the hell is happening? Why should I care if I ever see him again? He's just a random guy.

Who gave you the best orgasms you'll probably have in your life.

"Fucking hell," he mutters, grabbing the back of my head and pinning his forehead to mine. "I can't get you out of my system. If I was a bastard, I'd fuck you again, but I'll save that for next time."

Next time? He thinks there will be a next time? Then what? We ride off into the sunset together? The thought is laughable.

His semi-hard cock rubs against my center, and my need for him builds, like a fire crackling with that first spark.

No, this is ridiculous. There's no reason for me to get attached to some random guy I met at a club. He may even know Konstantin.

Shit, what if he does? What if Konstantin doesn't approve and decides to kill Cillian for it?

Then again, he allowed me to come here. It's not like he expected me to just watch and take notes.

Doesn't matter, though. I can't see Cillian again. How would that work? Have him over for family dinners?

Hey, let me introduce you to my family. Surprise, we're in the Russian Mob! We like loud parties, alcohol, and good food. We're also fiercely loyal and will kill you if you're not. I can really see this relationship going somewhere, can't you?

Yeah, right. Whoever I end up with will be in the Mafia. Konstantin could even decide to arrange a marriage for me, and I'd have no choice in the matter.

"What are you thinking about?" He presses a kiss to the corner of my mouth, and instead of pushing him away, I hold on tighter.

I can't seem to get you out of my system either.

He's like a tasty snack you can't stop eating.

"You'll have to," I whisper, stroking his back.

"What?" He looks down at me.

"You'll have to get me out of your system. This was a one-time thing."

He chuckles, low and gravelly, and it only makes it harder to escape this bed.

"So you give a man your virtue, then leave him with a broken heart?" A showstopping grin makes a slight dimple appear on his right cheek. "That seems unfair, a ghra."

Really? He has to have a dimple? Those are my kryptonite. A dirty-talking, dimple-wearing gorgeous man takes my virginity and I can't see him again? How is that even fair?

"I wasn't that attached to my virtue." I pop a brow. "And I'm sure a woman or three will heal your poor little heart right up."

"Unless you're that woman, that's not possible."

My heart skips a beat. Naïve, stupid heart. I'm sure he says that to all the girls he screws.

"Such a smooth talker. You almost have me convinced."

His jaw clenches. "I want to see you again."

"What?" There's no way I can do that. "When?"

Oh my God, shut up! Stop talking before you get this dude killed.

"I don't know. We can figure it out after you give me your number."

"We don't even have our phones."

His wry laughter fills the room. He cups my cheek, his eyes sinking into mine like they're trying to find something they've lost. "We have napkins, and I have a pen in my pocket."

Crap! Don't do it.

"Okay."

You definitely can't be trusted around men, because then you do dumb shit like this.

"Where do you live?" I wonder.

Maybe he's too far and this won't ever work out. I'm absolutely not doing a long-distance anything.

"I'm in Jersey," I elaborate.

"Not too far. I'm in Massachusetts."

I scoff. "That's far. How do you plan on seeing one another?"

"Why does it sound like you don't want to see me again?" His thumb sweeps over my lips.

"I didn't say that. I just don't do long-distance. It never works."

"It will the way I do it." He hits me with a crooked grin, and my body grows languid.

This man is dangerous.

"And how is that?"

"I have a jet." His knuckles roll across my chin. "I can come to you, or I can take you anywhere you wanna go. A penthouse in New York City. A villa in France. Literally anywhere. Would you like that?" His tone grows all husky.

I nod, my pulse hiking up the more he talks, the more he touches me.

"Good." His eyes dance over my features, like he's committing them to memory. "I told you we'd work it out. I'm gonna pick you up next weekend and take you to dinner."

Oh yeah, that's not happening. Then again, I can have him pick me up at a random place. I'll just say I don't want him to know where I live for safety reasons.

Shit, what the hell am I going to do when my bodyguard follows us? Maybe I can say my family comes from money and they take my safety seriously. He sounds rich. He'd understand.

That makes me wonder who he really is. Maybe I can ask Konstantin. Or maybe not. I don't want him knowing my business, though I'm sure he'll find out about Cillian eventually. But he doesn't have to know right away.

"Okay, we'll figure it out. But I really need to go now." I start to get up, and this time he lets me, sitting up himself to grab his pants.

He gets dressed while I do the same, his gaze never leaving me, as if he can't get enough.

When I slide into my dress and place the mask over my face, he finishes the last few buttons on his shirt, then moves toward me. His arm wraps around me, pulling me tightly against him, his lips grazing mine before he deepens the kiss, claiming me completely. It's slow, intimate. Like we're rediscovering each other all over again, each kiss a silent promise.

His tongue sweeps over mine, a growl—animalistic and raw—vibrating in his chest until I feel it rattling in my bones. And when we come up for air, a wild, untamed gleam burns in his eyes, as if he's struggling to rein in the fire raging inside him.

"I may not be able to wait a week to see you."

"You'll have to manage." I press my lips together, holding back a smile at the longing in his voice.

"No, I won't. I'll see you in two days. Just tell me where to get you."

"You're gonna come to Jersey?"

No, no, no! This is too soon!

"Yeah. Is that a problem?" A furrow builds between his brows.

Yes! A huge problem!

"No. Not at all."

Now I really need a plan. Maybe poison my bodyguard? Give him severe diarrhea? Beg him not to tell Konstantin who I'm meeting?

Fuck! What do I do?

Okay, worst-case scenario, Konstantin finds out, doesn't approve, and makes me end it. I'll survive. Right?

Ugh.

"Let me write down your number, then I'll give you mine." He pulls away from me and moves toward the small bar across the room, picking up a napkin and retrieving his pen.

Looking toward me, he waits for my number, and once I give it to him, he returns with a napkin for me.

"Keep it safe." He smirks.

"I will."

Maybe Konstantin will force me to end it before we see each other again. Maybe this is it.

The thought is like a punch to my gut.

Before I can change my mind, I grab the back of his neck and kiss him. His palms clutch my behind as he groans into my mouth. Teeth nipping, tongue sliding with mine, he sucks my bottom lip, making it harder for me to go.

"I can't control myself around you." He exhales roughly, touching his forehead to mine, palms clasping my hips.

Neither can I.

"You should go." He holds me closer, while my arms circle his back.

"I know." I let out a sigh. "Alright, well, I guess this is goodbye."

"It's goodbye for now, love." His gaze turns molten, and goose bumps spread down my arms from the hungered way he takes me in. "I'll be seeing you real soon."

His lips skim up my throat, causing me to groan while my fingers slide into his hair. He takes my hand in his, kissing my knuckles as he gazes down at me, and I don't think my heart can take much more.

"I'll walk you out." He pulls me toward the door, and the woman who led the group nods her goodbye.

When we slip out of the room, the music from the club surrounds us again.

"Are you gonna let me go now?" I hit him with a playful grin.

He laughs, squeezing my fingers. "Not until you've found your friends and are safe."

And they say chivalry is dead.

Maybe he'd approve of my unconventional family. I'm not even giving him a chance. I'm sure I can convince Konstantin too. We can all be one happy family. I can see it now.

Yeah, good luck with that.

As we make it closer to the bar, I find both Natalia and Alisa there, chatting up two men.

"Hey, guys," I call out, and that has them both turning in our direction.

"Oh my God, there you are!" Natalia peers between Cillian and me, her mouth curling. "Had fun?"

"Maybe." I quirk a brow.

The two men they were talking to order drinks, standing behind them.

"Aren't you going to introduce us?" Alisa asks, glancing at sexy dimple man.

"Alisa, Natalia, this is Cillian."

"Hello there. Got any brothers?" Natalia smiles flirtatiously.

He chuckles, extending a hand to each of them. "Two, actually."

"This is perfect!" Natalia flips her hands in the air. "One for me and one for Alisa."

"She's just kidding." I expand my eyes at him.

"I'm totally not." She snickers.

"Anyway, we should go." I separate from Cillian. "It was nice to meet you."

He eyes the napkin in my hand. "Let me know when you get home."

My heartbeats flutter so loud, I can almost hear them. "I will. Promise."

His fingertips reach for mine, and this time when he lets go, he starts to turn. But at the very last moment, he pivots back around, grabs my face with both palms, and kisses me. All the air evaporates, and everyone ceases to exist. Right now, I don't care if Konstantin finds out—if the whole world does—because it's worth it.

"Damn." Natalia's voice seems almost distant while the kiss lasts forever, though not long enough at the same time.

"Now I can go." His thumbs gently trace my cheeks while those eyes stare deeply into mine.

Then, just like that, he steps back, his warmth disappearing as he turns.

As I watch this stranger slip away, melting into the crowd, I can hardly believe any of this just happened.

"So, did you fuck him?" Natalia stares at me in the limo, while Alisa narrows her eyes, like this is an inquisition.

"Fine." I raise my hands in the air. "I did, okay? I know you both have been dying for me to say it."

"I knew it!" Natalia spins toward Alisa, her eyes wide with excitement. "Didn't I tell you?"

"She did. I had my doubts, but Natalia was certain you let the hot man pop your cherry. Was he good? Please tell me he was good."

A smile crawls on my face. "He was amazing. Even better than that."

"That's what I'm talking about!" Natalia slaps me on my forearm, donning a huge grin.

"Too bad you won't see him again." Alisa sighs. "What a shame."

"Actually..." I hesitate, watching as both of them stare at the napkin I just pulled from my handbag.

Of course, I've already saved his number in my phone, but I couldn't bring myself to throw away the scrap of paper he gave me.

Natalia's eyes expand. "You got his number! That's my girl. Are you going to call him?"

"I'll wait for him to call me first."

I'm not about to seem desperate. If he wants me, he knows where to find me.

"Maybe he's future-husband material. Imagine telling people how you met." Alisa laughs.

"Okay, relax, Cupid. No one is marrying anyone. This is just a fling. Nothing more. You know very well I can never have a relationship with some random guy."

"Never know…" Natalia wags her brows. "He may be from our world, and you just don't know it yet."

"Yeah, right." I roll my eyes, but in the back of my head, I wonder if she's right.

The rest of the conversation turns to the guys they were talking to and how Natalia made out with one, but neither of them did anything else. Soon enough, Pavel drops them both off, and I make it home to Konstantin's in about thirty minutes. The moment I arrive, I grab my phone, ready to send Cillian a message to let him know I made it, just like I promised.

But as I unlock my screen, I find a text from him already waiting.

CILLIAN

I can't get you out of my mind.

A huge smile spreads across my face as I step out of the car, waving goodbye to Pavel. I nearly trip on my heels as I make my way up the steps to the door.

DINARA

Sounds serious. Maybe they have medication for that.

He starts to type, then stops, and my heart seems to freeze in my chest. Did I say something wrong?

I stand by the door, anxiously waiting for his reply. Just as I'm about to lose hope, my phone lights up with his message.

CILLIAN

I'd rather live with the pain.

I fight back a laugh, shaking my head, but every part of me feels lighter, giddy with excitement.

DINARA

Doesn't sound healthy. Maybe a therapist?

CILLIAN

My infatuation with you is quite unhealthy, but I don't plan on getting rid of it.

DINARA

That's a shame. I barely even thought about you on the way home.

CILLIAN

Bet you'll be thinking about me the next time you're fingering your pussy.

Holy shit. My cheeks heat up.

DINARA

You're full of yourself.

CILLIAN

I liked it better when you were full of me.

I shiver, a throb pulsating between my thighs.

DINARA

Bye now.

CILLIAN

Made you blush, didn't I?

DINARA

Of course not.

CILLIAN

☺ Bye, love. I'll talk to you tomorrow so
we can plan our dinner date.

DINARA

Yeah, I'll think about it.

CILLIAN

It's cute that you think you have a choice
in the matter. Sleep well, leannan.

Biting the inside of my bottom lip, I fight a smile as I stuff the phone in my bag and head inside, two guards opening the door for me as I do.

Slipping off my shoes, I rush up the stairs, needing to get to bed so I can read his texts all over again.

SEVEN

CILLIAN

I have no idea what the hell I'm doing with this girl, but I can't get her out of my mind. The next day, the need to see her again hits me harder than anything else.

Every logical part of me says I should walk away, but I can't seem to stop myself from getting my phone out and sending her a text.

CILLIAN

Good morning, leannan.

Seriously, what the fuck is wrong with me? Why did I just do that? I stare at the screen, waiting for her to reply, but nothing comes.

I shouldn't have sent it. She probably thinks I'm some desperate idiot.

Shit. I wish I could take it back.

"Where did you disappear to last night?" Fionn's voice causes me to stuff my cell back in my pocket. He assesses me curiously. "What the hell was that about?"

"What? Nothing." I march over to the coffee machine in my father's kitchen, pouring myself a cup and pretending I wasn't just staring at my cell, hoping a girl texts me back like I'm in high school all over again.

I really should get back to my place now that the meeting with my family is over. The last thing I want is for them to start questioning me. I don't need them to know about Dinara. Not until it's something to tell them about.

"Are you hiding something on your phone?" He narrows his eyes.

"I'm not hiding shit. Get off my back."

"That definitely sounded like a whole load of bull."

Great, here comes Iseult.

My sister pushes her crimson hair behind her shoulder, lowering into the chair in front of the island while staring at me with a smirk. "So, is it a woman? Or a man? We're a judgment-free zone. Right, Fionn?"

"Right, sis." He grins, throwing a palm on her shoulder while standing beside her.

"You're both fucking crazy." I take a sip of coffee, almost burning my tongue off.

"Oh, look, our bro met someone and he's being all shy about it." She casts me a coy, teasing glance.

Iseult may be second to youngest of the five of us, but you would never know it. She lives to give us hell. But we let her get away with it. We all feel for what she's gone through. Not only did that prick Sergey Marinov burn our mother alive, but he kidnapped Iseult when she was younger and tortured her until she got away.

The only silver lining is that she killed him. My only regret? I didn't get to do it first.

"I didn't meet anyone. What the hell, guys? And don't *you* have a husband to get back to?" I ask her, knowing she has to fly back home to New York.

"Distance is good. It'll make his heart grow fonder." She grins. "Now tell me about her. Will you be bringing her to family dinners? Can I scare the fuck out of her?" Her grin widens.

"That wouldn't be nice, Iseult." Fionn shakes his head. "You wouldn't want to scare off his future wife."

"Shit, man. You two are annoying together."

He throws an arm around her. "We work well as a team."

I mutter a low curse. "It's no one. Now lay off." Finishing my coffee, I drop the mug in the sink. "I'm going to Caellach to work out. Don't bother me." I hit them with an irritated glare.

"You won't even give us her name?" Iseult throws a hand in the air, laughing with Fionn as I start to head out.

"Fuck no."

"See, I knew it was a girl." She laughs while I shake my head, fighting a smile.

Pain in the ass or not, I'd kill for each one of them.

I step outside the house and make my way toward the towering mansion that houses Caellach, the school my father established years ago to train the next generation. Once inside, I take the elevator down, retrieve my keys, and scan one of them over the doorknob. Each key holds a chip inside.

The moment I enter, I head straight for the workout room, where recruits and trainers are already busy. Just as I'm about to grab a bar to add more weight, my phone pings from the floor.

Shit, maybe it's her.

Anticipation shoots through me, and I hate it because I've never been this damn juvenile over a girl.

DINARA

Hey, morning. How's your day? Sorry I didn't see your text before.

See, she didn't see your text. She wasn't purposely ignoring you, psycho.

CILLIAN

Spent it thinking about you.

DINARA

I may have done the same. Thinking
about you, I mean. Not myself. That
would be weird.

CILLIAN

Did you just admit you were thinking
about me?

My grin widens, and the young seventeen-somethings glance at me like I've grown an extra arm. I'm never what one would call cheery. When I zero them in with a laser-focused glare, they dart their stares away, shuffling to return to their workouts.

DINARA

I did, but I won't tell you in what capacity
because all you'd do is gloat.

My mind fills with dirty thoughts, and blood rushes to my dick.

CILLIAN

It isn't fair to make a man think about you
like that when you're not close enough to
touch or taste. And shit, do I still taste you
on my tongue.

DINARA

Are you always this vulgar at nine in the
morning?

CILLIAN

I am now, love.

DINARA

So, what's your full name? I think I should
know that, since you wanna take me out
and all that. What if you're a serial killer?

CILLIAN

And how will knowing my full name help
exactly?

DINARA

It won't. But I think I should know the
name of the man who may or may not
end up killing me.

CILLIAN

I promise, if I wanted to kill you, I would've
done it by now. There are so many other,
far better things I'd rather do to you.

DINARA

I bet that's what all serial killers say.

CILLIAN

I guess you'll find out soon.

DINARA

I'll make sure to bring my gun.

CILLIAN

I don't think you're supposed to warn
serial killers about weapons you might
have.

DINARA

I'm sorry. This is my first encounter with one.

CILLIAN

That's okay, baby. We all make mistakes.

DINARA

I don't make mistakes. I'm perfect.

Damn, I can't stop grinning like an idiot.

CILLIAN

You ARE perfect.

She doesn't say anything for almost a minute.
Damn, did I scare her off?
Too bad. It doesn't matter either way. I'm gonna get to know everything about her. It already feels like I've known her forever.

CILLIAN

Any particular place you'd like to go tomorrow? And make it good. Wouldn't want to embarrass myself when our grandkids ask where our first date was.

DINARA

You're being quite presumptuous.

CILLIAN

There's a difference between being presumptuous and being right.

DINARA

I can't figure out if you're crazy or charming.

CILLIAN

Whatever helps you agree to our date.

DINARA

I thought I didn't have a choice.

CILLIAN

You don't. I was just trying to be a gentleman. But I think you like it better when I tell you what to do. Isn't that right, baby girl?

I know I'm right. I saw how her body reacted when I took control. It takes her a few seconds to answer.

DINARA

Surprise me. Now tell me your name.

CILLIAN

Cillian Quinn. And yours?

There's no chance in hell she'll find anything about me online, so giving her my name doesn't worry me at all.

DINARA

Dinara Matrovskaya.

That sounds Russian. Though as long as she's not a Marinov, I don't care. She could be just about anyone…except one of them.

CILLIAN

Pretty. Where should I pick you up?

DINARA

Landon Park, right by the entrance at 6.
Don't be late.

CILLIAN

Wouldn't dream of it. See you then, a ghra.

DINARA

You ARE perfect.

Those words swim in my head, playing on repeat. I've never quite felt perfect, always finding fault somewhere. I've never been the smartest or the prettiest in the room. Sometimes I don't know when to keep my mouth shut, like when my father…

Those thoughts send an ache to my chest. I should've done something else. I should've called Konstantin and asked for help instead of going into the room and trying to help her myself. What did that even accomplish? Nothing.

I shake my head, frustrated with myself for thinking about him again. It's why I gave Cillian my mother's last name, something I've always done. The thought of being tied to my father makes me sick. Konstantin gets it and hasn't pushed me on it. He knows how broken I was after my mother's death—though, of course, we never spoke of it.

In this family, we just accept things. Everything…except betrayal. That, of course, can't be tolerated. But murder? Perfectly fine. Makes sense, right?

As I pick up my coffee at the breakfast table, my mind drifts back to the conversation with Cillian, my fingers itching to pick up that phone again and read over our exchange.

"What's got you smiling this morning?" Konstantin pulls me from my thoughts, taking a bite of his blin.

Tatiana glances at me with a curious look. Was I really smiling that much?

"Nothing. Just thinking about something funny Natalia said."

Every time I lie, I worry Konstantin will see right through me, but he doesn't press the issue and goes back to his breakfast.

I still don't know how I'll make things work with Cillian. If the date goes well and we continue to see one another, I'll have to be honest with Konstantin. Maybe I should just tell him. I have no idea what the right answer is.

"And you, Tatiana?" He shifts his attention to my sister, while Gregory stuffs half of a blin into his mouth. "Any plans today?"

"My friends invited me to see a movie later today. Can I go?" Tatiana cuts into a piece of her toast, the table filled with all the food we could ever want.

"Of course you can. The driver will take you where you want to go, and Anatoly will go with you."

"Awesome! Thanks." Her grin grows.

She's completely used to having a bodyguard, like we all are. Our protection is of utmost priority to Konstantin, especially with our father around.

We continue our breakfast while my mind returns to Cillian, thinking of last night and the fact that I'm no longer a virgin. I still can't believe I did that. But I have no regrets. In fact, I can't wait to see him soon so we can do that all over again.

As my cousin glances at me every now and then, I start to wonder if he knows something. Then again, he seems to know everything, so keeping secrets from him isn't exactly the smartest move.

I push aside the uneasy feeling in my gut, and once we're finished, Tatiana and Gregory are the first to excuse themselves, leaving the grand sitting room.

"Dinara." That commanding baritone stops me dead in my tracks just as I rise to my feet.

Shit. He knows.

Of course he does, you dumbass!

He's gonna tell me to stop talking to Cillian.

"Yes?" I clear my throat and offer a small smile, trying to mask the unease brewing inside me.

"Are you alright?" His dark brows draw together, and a tight knot forms in my stomach as I settle back down.

"Yes, of course."

Coffee. I need more coffee. Or alcohol. Yes, definitely alcohol.

"I never got to ask you how the party was last night. Any problems I need to concern myself with?"

My stomach tightens. "Nope. I had a nice time."

I definitely didn't let a hot stranger fuck my virginity out of me. Absolutely not.

"Good, good." He takes a long sip of his black coffee, his eyes narrowing, and it's like he's slicing my insides, carving out each organ to see what he can find. "You know you can tell me anything, right? Anything at all."

"Of course!" My voice cracks, higher than I intended.

"Very good." He nods, a faint smile briefly flickering across his face. "I may be older, but I remember what it was like to be your age."

Just tell him, Dinara! If he finds out you're lying, he won't forgive you.

Once you betray him, there's no coming back. I've seen him kill men for less. Not that I think he'd kill me for this, but he may not trust me afterward.

Huffing out a breath, I close my eyes momentarily before staring right at him. "I met someone there. I wasn't gonna say anything because honestly, I don't even know if it'll go anywhere or if I can even date him, considering who we are, so I—"

"Dinara." He raises a palm to stop me, his expression deadly serious, and a lump forms in my throat.

This is it. He's gonna tell me to end it, and I'll have no choice.

"You're free to date anyone you want. I'm not your father."

I exhale sharply, and he scoffs.

"You don't have to be nervous around me, dorogaya. I'm not going to kill him." His smile fades, his features hardening. "Unless he gives me a good reason. Understand?"

I nod.

"I just ask that you're careful and that Boris accompanies you anywhere you go. That's all."

I'm so beyond relieved. "He asked to take me to dinner tomorrow. He's gonna pick me up at Landon Park."

He leans back, eyes narrowing. "Who is this man? What is his name?"

He's definitely going to start doing his 411 on him, which is fine. I'd rather know if I should stay away from him now before I start to like him more.

"His name is Cillian Quinn."

"Hmm." That's all he says, his expression unreadable.

Was that a good *hmm*? A bad one? Does he know him?

"Yeah, he seemed nice and respectful."

"Ochen horosho." *Very good.* He nods thoughtfully. "Do tell me if anything changes, and I will personally take care of it."

"Of course."

Let's hope it never comes to that. The last thing I need is for my new…whatever he is…to be murdered by my family.

"I did want to show you something if you're up for a drive," he adds.

"Oh?"

"It's your birthday gift."

"You didn't have to get me anything else. The shopping spree and new gun were plenty."

Yes, he did get me a gun. A Glock forty-five, much lighter than the last one I had. In this family, if you don't know how to protect yourself, you'll get killed. I learned how to shoot when I turned ten.

His elbows drop to the edge of the table as he leans in, his tone growing darker. "You took my side against your father. That will always mean a lot to me. You understand?"

I shrug a single shoulder. "It wasn't a difficult decision. You're giving me too much credit. I've always hated him, and you know it."

He flips his hands in the air. "We don't get to choose our parents, unfortunately. We make do with what we have. But I promise I will always protect you three with my life."

"I know that."

I curl my fingers on my lap, not wanting to think about him gone. I love him like a brother. Imagining a world without him is painful.

"Now enough of this talk, yes?" The small smile returns to his face. "How about we go so I can show you the surprise? I think you're going to like it."

He pushes the chair back, getting to his feet just as Ludmilla, the head housekeeper, walks in to clean up after us, the sides of her eyes crinkling as she smiles.

I follow him, not able to venture a guess as to what he got me.

"We're going to go for a little drive. Not far, maybe twenty minutes."

"Okay…"

Completely puzzled, I follow him out to the foyer, exiting through the heavy door, where a car is already waiting for us. One of his drivers opens the SUV door, and we slip inside. Silence lingers between us until he finally breaks it.

"Has Roman reached out recently?"

The question sends my mind spiraling. I don't want to think about my older brother or the cruel messages he sends just to wound me. I read them, let them cut deep, then delete them. Yet for some reason, I can't bring myself to block him. Maybe some part of me feels like I deserve the punishment for betraying my own family.

But my father never deserved my loyalty. He doesn't deserve Roman's either. My brother has always been tangled in his web, swallowing his lies like oxygen and playing the obedient puppet.

Like believing it was my father, not Konstantin, who was the rightful heir to the Bratva.

After Sergey—Konstantin's father—died, Dad convinced himself that leadership should have passed to him, ignoring the fact that Konstantin, as the eldest, was always meant to take the throne. When Natalia's father, Nikolai, sided with Konstantin, my father's resentment only deepened, twisting into something ugly.

I told Konstantin everything. Every poisonous word my father spread, every delusion he clung to. And when Konstantin offered us a place in his home shortly after Mom died, I didn't hesitate. I chose our freedom. We were finally out of that hellhole.

If Roman still wants to stand by a man like our father, that's on him.

Mom deserved better. We all did.

Roman's last message flashes through my mind, sending an involuntary chill through me.

You think you're safe with him? You're not, Dinara. You never will be. When you least expect it, I'm gonna make you pay for betraying Papa, and that asshole won't be able to do anything to stop me.

I shake off the cold fear creeping up my spine. He'd do it if he could. I wonder why he hasn't tried yet. What their plan is. They definitely have a plan, and I know Konstantin knows more than he's telling me.

"Dinara? Did you hear my question?"

"Oh, sorry." I fling a loose strand of hair away from my face. "Uh, no, he hasn't contacted me for a while."

I realize I just lied, and if he doesn't forgive me for that, then I'll have to live with it. But I don't want him to know. There's already too much conflict between him and my father. I don't want to add more fuel to the fire.

"If he does, make sure you let me know, yes?"

I nod. "Of course."

"Very good." He stares straight at me, a sharp and intense scrutiny, as if he can see straight into my soul. "I will never let anyone hurt you."

The intention of his words makes me feel even safer.

We drive in silence for the rest of the way, reaching a set of black iron gates with a security booth to the left.

"Ah, we're here."

"Where is *here*, exactly?"

A half-smile tugs at the corner of his mouth as we drive through a private residential area, passing mansion after mansion. What is this place?

When we stop in front of a light gray house—smaller than his, but still enormous—he turns to me. "This is your new home, Dinara. I hope you like it."

"Uh, what?" I let out a laugh. "I live with you."

Clearly, he's joking.

"You will always have a home with me, but I thought since you are a woman now, you should have a place of your own."

My eyes nearly pop out of my head. "You're serious?" My gaze darts between his amused expression and the towering house in front of me. "This is too much."

"Nonsense." He waves it off. "Come on, let's take a look inside."

"I don't even know what to say."

Emotions tighten in my throat. He didn't have to do this for me.

"A thank-you would suffice." He smirks.

"Spaseba." *Thank you.*

We approach a pair of security guards at the entrance, who greet us as they open the door.

Inside, a few housekeepers move about the foyer, one polishing the small glass table at the center with fresh orchids resting inside a vase, while the other dusts off the mirror and the sketched fashion art pieces already adorning the walls. Everything is sleek, contemporary, and somehow…so me.

A glistening chandelier hangs from the cathedral ceiling, drawing the eye upward. I can't help but wonder what I'm supposed to do with such a giant home all to myself.

"Mr. Marinov, Ms. Marinova." One of the housekeepers comes over, wiping her hands on her apron as she approaches.

"This is Sonya, your head housekeeper. She's Ludmilla's friend."

"Yes. Hello." She nods, her blue eyes glistening as she smiles, a few gray and black hairs sticking out from her almost perfect bun. "Anything you need, you tell me. I'm here to help. So is everyone else."

"Thank you."

"Let's go see the rest of the house," Konstantin says, leading me toward the staircase and turning into a pristine gray-and-white kitchen.

A man stands at the stove in a white jacket, and when he turns, the tips of his mustache curl upward.

"This is Lenny, your cook."

"Ms. Marinova, it's a great pleasure to meet you." His heavy Russian accent matches Konstantin's.

"I chose him just for you," Konstantin adds. "He's one of the best chefs in Russia."

Lenny's face pales for a moment before he recovers and smiles at me. "Yes, when Mr. Marinov told me he would bring me to America to cook for his family, I was honored. Truly honored."

"Only the best for my family." Konstantin's jaw tightens, and Lenny nearly trembles.

What's going on here?

"It's nice to meet you." I extend my hand, and he shakes it with a slight shudder.

"You as well, Ms. Marinova. I will get back to making lunch for you both."

As he turns back to the stove, we head for the doorway. When I glance back at him, something unspoken passes between us.

Konstantin is already several steps ahead, so I quickly catch up, pushing any lingering curiosity about the chef to the back of my mind.

"Do you like the house so far?" Konstantin asks. "If not, I can always get something more suited for you."

"Are you kidding?" My eyes grow wide. "This place is amazing."

He tilts up his chin. "I'm glad you like it. I'll have all your belongings moved in shortly. Ludmilla and the other girls are already gathering them as we speak."

All alone in this big house? I've never lived without my siblings before. I'll admit it's a little scary, but I'm sort of looking forward to the freedom.

"Are you okay, Moya milaya?"

"Yes, sorry. I'm just a bit nervous, I guess."

"Of course. But don't worry. You can come by whenever you want, and Gregory and Tatiana can come here anytime they please."

"Thanks."

His mouth twitches. "You're a woman now, and you should learn how to be on your own. That's important, you understand?"

"Mm-hmm."

"Maladets. Let's go see the rest of the house."

"Okay."

Maybe Konstantin has a point. And now that I have my own place, I can do whatever I want. And the first thing I want to do is invite Cillian over just so he can fuck me in every single room.

EIGHT

CILLIAN

I arrive a little before six, making sure she won't have to wait for me.

I'm not offended that she didn't want me picking her up from her place. Coming from the life I do, I understand the need for caution.

When an SUV pulls up exactly at six, I stay where I am, wondering if it's her. At first, all I see is a man, clearly armed, getting out of the driver's side and heading toward the back.

Then she steps out. When his hand lands on her shoulder, a surge of possessiveness hits me, and I'm ready to tear his arm off for touching her.

I don't know what the hell is wrong with me. I barely know her, but I don't want any other man's hands on her. I know she's not mine. But damn, I'd like her to be.

He shuts the door and scans the perimeter, his gaze landing on me. That's her bodyguard, if I had to put my money on it.

But why does she need one? Who is she, really?

Of course, I've looked her up and found nothing. But I've got someone in IT at Caellach running a deep dive, just to make sure she's not a threat. In our world, you can never be too careful.

The moment she spots me stepping out of my blue Royce, parked a few yards away, her dark eyes lift, sparkling with a smile. And that alone just about stops my heart.

I'm completely done for.

"Hey there, stranger," she says, her grin spreading.

"Hey, baby. You look beautiful."

"Thanks." A soft blush blooms across her pale skin, making my chest tighten.

I reach over and pull her in for a quick kiss on her cheek before drawing back. My gaze trails down her figure. The skintight black dress hugs her curves, stopping just above her knees, with the beige sandals adding a few extra inches to her height, though she's still so small compared to me. Her hair blows in the wind, and a desperate urge to push it from her face washes over me, just so I can touch her again.

My pulse races, as if she holds the key to my heart.

The man behind her steps forward, his gaze locking with mine. He's about my height, maybe a little older, and the way he sizes me up isn't lost on me.

I nod in greeting, noting the way his hand rests on something concealed. He's definitely armed. But that's okay. So am I.

"That's Boris. He's my…bodyguard. We're kind of a package deal." She crunches her nose in the most adorable grimace.

My arm instinctively slides around the small of her back, tugging her close, and the tiny hairs on her bare forearm prickle against my skin. I like the power I already have over her body.

"You ready?"

"Mm-hmm." She turns to Boris. "You can go back and follow us."

"As soon as you're in the car, Ms. Ma—"

Her eyes flare at him for a split second. "Dinara is fine."

"Yes, miss."

Her bodyguard is Russian too. Does her family know Konstantin's?

"So, where are you taking me?" she asks as we head toward my car.

I lower my mouth to her ear, feeling the heat of her breath against my skin. "I thought you wanted to be surprised."

"I do," she whispers back.

Her head drops against me, sending a surge of warmth through my bloodstream. It feels like she already fits perfectly beside me.

I press the button for my Royce as I pull out my keys, and when Boris moves to open the door for her, I reach for the handle instead.

"Territorial, huh?" she breathes with a little smirk.

Before she can get in, I stop her, pushing her against the car. My front presses against her back, her palms bracing across the roof.

I drop my mouth to her ear, inhaling the faint scent of her rosy perfume. "If you think that's bad, wait 'til you see what happens when you're really mine."

She swallows, a flicker of uncertainty flashing in her eyes as she glances back.

What's going on in her head? Does she not want this? Or is she just nervous?

My fingers slide to her front, trailing up her thigh, sweeping over the fabric of her dress.

"I like this dress." I shift the conversation, giving her the escape she's clearly craving.

"Do you now?" Her voice is barely a whisper.

"I do. But I'd much prefer to see you out of it." My fingers slide up higher, one pressing into her core, right through her panties.

She sucks in a breath. "You know he's still watching, right?"

I let out a low dry laugh. "If he's going to be following us, might as well make it worth his while."

"You're so bad."

She grabs my wrist and forces me deeper into her core while footsteps pummel away from us, like Boris finally realized he should get the fuck away when I'm touching my woman.

"Look who's being the bad one now."

"I can be good or bad. Which side do you prefer?"

I shove her panties to the side so I can feel her bare. "Why choose? I can play with both and see which one begs for more."

"Oh God," she cries out while my finger sweeps through her cunt.

"Fuck, you're so wet."

Her moan is a hoarse breath, like she's unable to hold it in as I tease her clit, wanting to suck it into my mouth and watch her fall apart.

"Get in the damn car before I fuck you right up against it."

Inhaling sharply, she shivers against me and looks over her shoulder, the same desire coursing through me reflected in her gaze. I need to stop this before I do exactly what I just said.

Grinding my jaw, I back off of her, and she spins toward me, her hand reaching for my face and cupping my stubbled cheek in her soft grasp. Closing my eyes, I lean into it, enjoying the feeling of her hands on me. My body moves into her space, pinning her to the car, my mouth drifting lower until it brushes hers.

"Mmm," she groans, snaking her long, slender fingers through my hair.

Without hesitation, I close the distance and take her lips, the kiss deep and urgent. The sounds of her pleasure send blood shooting to my already rock-hard erection. Pulling on my hair, she swirls her tongue against mine, dragging my mouth deeper to hers like she can't get enough either.

What is she doing to me?

Her other hand slides down my back, and every muscle in my body tightens at the sensation.

"Fuck," I grunt, pinning my forehead to hers. "You should warn a man before you kiss him like that."

"Thanks for the advice. I promise to remember that the next time I kiss someone else."

My jaw snaps, and instantly, my hand is wrapped around her throat. "Say that again." I nip her bottom lip with a growl, and she smirks playfully. "You kiss someone else, and you might as well be sending him to an early grave."

Her brows shoot up, but that smirk never disappears. "Are you usually this psychotic?"

"No. This is me on a good day."

As she laughs, my hand slips into her silky hair, and then I'm kissing her again—harder and rougher, like I'm claiming her for the world to see. I'm not sure if it's the fact that I took her virginity or because I just like her, but whatever the reason is, I know this woman is gonna be mine, and there's nothing anyone can do about it.

I don't know how long we stay like this, but I'm positive we'll be late for our reservation.

When we finally come up for air, that glimmer in her dark eyes has me wanting to kiss her all over again.

"Get in." I guide her into the car before sliding into the driver's seat and pulling onto the road, with Boris trailing behind us.

My hand rests on her thigh, the touch instinctive, and I can feel her shift in her seat, clutching her small purse tighter against her lap. I watch my hand on her leg for a moment, noticing she's staring at it too, and I can't help but wonder if she's feeling what I am. That this feels…right.

"So, have you always had a bodyguard?"

She clears her throat, her gaze flicking to the side for a moment before meeting mine again. "Yeah, for a while. My family owns some banks, and they're pretty obsessive about my safety, so wherever I go, he's with me." She rolls her eyes, a frustrated laugh escaping. "Trust me, if it was up to me, he wouldn't be here."

"Safety's important. I can't fault your family for that."

"Right." She twirls a lock of hair around her finger, a faint smile tugging at her lips, but I sense something behind it. Frustration, maybe, or something deeper.

"So how did you end up at the club?" I continue.

"Oh, my family has connections."

"And they didn't care that you were there?"

"No. Why would they? I'm eighteen." She shrugs like it's no big deal, but it's a big deal to me.

My jaw tightens. "I don't want you going back there without me."

"So possessive…" She laughs—a low, sultry sound that stirs something primal inside me.

The tips of her fingers trail up my forearm, sending a jolt of heat through me, and I feel the touch all the way down to my bones.

"I have a feeling you like it." My palm tightens on her thigh, holding her close, as if marking her in some way I can't explain.

Her smirk widens, and it's almost like she's daring me to push further.

"What are you doing this weekend?" I ask.

I need to see her again. I need more of this.

"Why?" She eyes me curiously, a glimmer in her gaze.

"I want to take you away for the weekend."

Her giggle catches me off guard, and I can't help but grin. Damn, I don't think I've ever smiled like this before. Like it's coming from somewhere deep inside me.

"We haven't even gone on our date. What if you don't like me?"

"That's not possible."

Her cheeks flush a deeper pink, and I can tell it's not just from the makeup she doesn't need. She's beautiful, effortlessly, in a way that has me thinking she doesn't even know how breathtaking she truly is.

"What if I won't like *you*?" Her brow curves, chin tipping up.

"You'll learn to." My hand slides up, squeezing her inner thigh.

Her head falls back as my fingers drift higher.

"Sounds like torture," she whispers, mouth parted, breaths growing tight as I stroke her pussy through her thin lacy panties.

Dragging them to the side while keeping my eyes on the road, I work her clit while she grips the seat with small, tight fists, twisting in pleasure.

"Ready for me already." I drive a finger inside her.

"Don't stop."

When I glance over, her eyes are fastened shut, teeth tugging on her bottom lip.

"Wider. Spread your legs wider for me." She does as she's told, brows furrowed, gasping and moaning. "That's it. That's my good girl. Show me that pussy."

She bucks against the invasion as I feed another finger inside her, those walls clenching around me. I pummel deeper, faster, her moans sounding more desperate and less in control. Teasing her, I decrease and increase my tempo, driving her wild.

As soon as we arrive at the restaurant, my movements freeze and I slide her panties in place.

"What the hell? You're gonna just leave me like that?" She gasps in protest, her chest rising and falling as her shock-filled expression captures my smug one.

"That's right." I roll the car into an available spot, turning to her, sucking the fingers that were just inside her into my mouth. "So fucking good."

Her lips part as she watches me, those thighs squeezing tight.

"If you behave all night, I'll let you come on my tongue." I grab her jaw and pull her close. "If you're really good, I'll even let you come on my cock. I remember how much you liked it."

Her eyes narrow. "You're gonna regret this."

"Promise?" My tongue flicks out to trace the curve of her lips.

A cunning grin stretches across her face as she pushes the door open, stepping out. I follow, tugging her hand in mine, the tension between us crackling.

She tries to slip from my grasp, but I pull her closer. "Best behavior. Remember?"

"I hope you make it worth my while," she murmurs, her voice low and playful.

I let out a laugh. "You're just gonna have to wait and see."

Boris follows closely behind as we make our way inside. A maître d' greets us with a practiced smile, and we walk past her into the restaurant.

"I love this place, by the way. Thank you." She casts a grin in my direction.

I raise her hand to my lips, pressing a soft kiss to her knuckles. "No need to thank me. I just want to make you happy."

Her cheeks flush and she glances down, clearly trying to hide the effect I'm having on her as we move toward the private room I've arranged.

"You can wait out here," she tells Boris, and he nods, stepping aside to stand just outside the door.

The maître d' leads us further inside, where a single round table sits in the center of a dimly lit room, three flickering votive candles casting soft shadows around us.

Just us. Exactly how I wanted it.

She sits gracefully in the chair I pull out, and I take mine across from her, the space between us feeling charged. For the first time ever, as I watch her settle into her seat, a thought crosses my mind—one that feels almost foreign.

Would my mother have liked her, had they ever met?

NINE

DINARA

"**S**o, about this weekend in New York City you mentioned. Where exactly would we go?" I ask, taking a sip of the iced tea I ordered, my eyes lingering on the attractive, enigmatic man across from me.

I can't believe he's already planning another date before we've even finished this one, but honestly, I wouldn't say no. The more we talk, the more I find myself wanting to spend every single second with him, wishing we weren't so far apart.

"We'd catch a show, then I'd take you on a shopping spree and spoil you a little before I fucked you in every room of my penthouse."

I shiver at his words, the heat in his gaze searing into me and sending a storm through my pulse.

"I think I'd like that," I manage to say, my tone barely steady.

He chuckles, that smirk curling at the corner of his mouth, sinking deep into my gut. My core throbs in response.

"I thought you were afraid I was a serial killer," he adds. "Doesn't it scare you to be alone with me all weekend?"

If he only knew how many killers I've crossed paths with…

I shrug, trying to play it cool, twirling my straw between my fingers. "Well, my mother always said those who don't take risks don't drink champagne."

His expression shifts, the teasing fading as he takes a quiet breath. "Your mother…she passed away?"

"Yeah. About two years ago." My throat tightens, and I quickly glance away, swallowing hard.

"I'm sorry." His voice softens, and I feel the sincerity in his words. "My mother passed away too, when I was a few years older than you."

"I'm sorry too."

He pauses, then gently asks, "So, who do you live with? Your father?"

I shake my head, trying to push past the sting of memories. "My siblings and I moved in with my older cousin. I never really got along with my dad."

My eyes drop as I'm haunted by the last time I saw my father— furious when he found out I was leaving with Konstantin.

"Are you okay?" His hand finds mine, holding it with a tenderness that makes my chest tighten.

"Yeah…" I force a smile.

When his brow furrows, I'm not sure if he believes me. But he doesn't press further. Instead, he shifts the conversation.

"So, what does that saying mean? The one your mother used to say?"

I fight the urge to laugh at the confusion that flashes across his face. "It's a Russian proverb. Like the American saying 'nothing ventured, nothing gained.'"

"Ah," he muses, his grin widening as his eyes darken, the room's soft lighting casting shadows across his features. "I like it. And…am I that risk?"

I meet his gaze. "You are. And if I don't take it…I'll never know if there's a reward waiting for me."

He chuckles. "I promise there is."

"I don't mean the one in your pants, even though that isn't so bad."

"I didn't mean the one in my pants either, love." He leans in, his elbows resting on the table, the veins in his large hands straining against his skin. "And not so bad, huh?"

"Mm-hmm. Plenty of fish in the sea to try out. You know, for comparison," I add, a mischievous tone to my words. "Wouldn't want to settle."

The muscle in his neck jerks. I don't know why I like making him jealous. Maybe because I can. Maybe because I enjoy knowing that he hates imagining me with other men already. Maybe I have daddy issues and am starving for love. Whatever the reason, it doesn't matter, because I really like torturing him.

"Say that again and see what I do to you, Dinara."

"I'd say I mind, but I really don't think I would."

In an instant, he's up on his feet, striding over to my side. There's a steely look in his eyes, and the way his chest rises and falls just before he grabs my hips sends a jolt through me.

He lifts me into his arms.

"What the hell are you doing?" I fight a laugh as he carries me over to his side of the table and drops me onto his lap.

My legs straddle him, dress hiked up to my upper thighs as he grabs my jaw, staring so deep into my eyes, I feel it in every cell of my body.

"I thought you needed reminding whose pussy this is."

"You've fucked me once. My pussy is not yours, Cillian Quinn," I whisper, his lips pulling closer to mine.

"Once, twice, a hundred times. It doesn't matter, Dinara. You're gonna be mine. Because I've already decided."

"Decided what?"

His cock presses into my pulsing core. "I'm your first, and I plan to be your last."

My heart skips a beat, completely overtaken by his words even when I know logically that all these feelings I'm experiencing, the things he's saying… It's all too soon.

What is it about him that draws me in? Is it his self-confidence? His masculinity? The commanding aura? The way he just claimed me as his when we barely even know each other?

This truly could go one of two ways. He's either insane or I've just hit the jackpot.

"My last, huh? Well, that doesn't seem fair." I nip his bottom lip, and he groans, threading his fingers through my hair and pulling until it stings.

"What doesn't?"

"You got to fuck God knows how many women and I only ever get to fuck you?"

Even though I'm one hundred percent certain there's no one better out there.

His jaw tightens. "None of them ever meant anything. And if I could go back, I'd change it all. But it doesn't matter now, baby, because you're stuck with me."

His smirk makes the ache between my thighs grow until I find myself grinding on his lap, his cock thick and hard against my core.

"Is there a way to get unstuck?"

His hand brushes gently under my chin, his eyes dark and burning with raw intensity. "No matter how hard you try, leannan, I'm always going to be there, reminding you how right we've been from the moment we met."

A rush of need floods through me as his free hand fists my hair, dragging my face down until his mouth crashes into mine. "Cillian," I groan in between kisses.

His growl is deep and demanding as he takes me roughly, teeth nipping, his tongue invading me and sucking mine into his mouth. I've never in my life been kissed this way. Like this man is trying to devour me or remind me that I am his in every sense.

Maybe both.

For a moment, I wonder if my mother would've liked him.

And then the reality hits: she'll never be there to see me get married or be there when I have a baby. She'll never share in those moments, never laugh or cry, because she's gone. A tightness grips my chest, the sadness creeping in just as he pulls away, his hand gently resting on my nape.

I sigh deeply, letting my face fall into the curve of his neck, my arms wrapping around him and holding him close. His palm moves in slow, comforting strokes along my back, and even though he doesn't know it, his touch eases the ache.

"You alright, babe?" His voice is soft, laced with genuine concern, and it twists something inside me.

I swallow hard, fighting the lump in my throat, and force a smile as I pull away from his touch. "Yeah, sorry. I'm good."

He doesn't buy it. His eyes stay locked on mine, his brows knitting as he studies my face for any crack in my mask.

Before he can respond, our waitress arrives with the food, rolling a cart toward us, but Cillian doesn't even look at her. His focus never leaves me, concern still written across his face.

"That looks good," I say, trying to redirect him, hoping the distraction works.

When the waitress stops right in front of our table, I can't help but notice how unfazed she is by the sight of me practically humping Cillian. Then again, I'm sure he's paying a lot for this private room.

We both thank her, and once she sets the plates down, I try to stand, but Cillian tightens his arm around me.

"Where do you think you're going?" His warm breath grazes my neck, igniting a rush of sensation that ripples through me, heat pooling low and urgent.

"My seat, so I can eat?" I raise a brow, but there's a smile tugging at the corners of my lips.

His gaze darkens, desire flickering in his eyes. "You'll stay right here on my lap like a good girl, where I can feed you."

My stomach clenches, heat sparking in the space between us. The tips of my fingers trace his jaw, grazing his rough stubble. A surge of heat pulses through me as I lower my lips to his, the kiss soft and tentative.

He groans, his fingers threading into my hair, but he doesn't rush it, letting me lead instead.

"I can be a good girl." My lips drop to his throat, kissing up that beating pulse, that rough skin. "A very good girl."

"I don't know about that." His head falls backward, and I love watching him turned on.

I suck on his skin, circling my hips against his hardness while he grunts and arches into me until a moan slips out from my throat. I slide a hand between us, stroking his hard erection through his trousers.

"Fuck, you need to stop."

"Don't think so." I stroke him faster, my lips feathering over his while my hand slides up and down to a quicker tempo.

His teeth grind, the need rattling his bones until he grabs my wrist and roughly drags my hand away.

"What the hell are you doing?" he growls.

The corner of my mouth angles up. "Paying you back for earlier."

His chuckle is low and raspy, still drowning in his obvious need. "That's not gonna work well for you, baby."

In an instant, he grips my hips, flipping me so I'm still on his lap, but facing the table. He drags the chair closer, positioning me on one of his powerful thighs as he calmly starts cutting the steak into small bites. He does the same with the lobster tail, his focus unwavering as I wait, curious to see what he'll do next.

"Open your mouth." He brings the fork with a piece of the steak close to my lips.

As I hungrily take a bite, he widens my thighs and slides the lace of my thong to the side, completely exposing me.

"What are you doing?" My tone grows hoarse, my face heating up from the possibility that the waitress will catch us.

"Playing with my food before I eat it." He nips my earlobe as I try to chew, his fingers taking a leisurely swipe through my soaked center. "If you don't finish your meal, I won't let you come."

He flicks my clit just as the steak glides down my throat, stars forming in my eyes from the intense sensation.

"Think you can do that?" He slowly slides one finger inside me, then another, until I'm stretched to what feels like the max, but I know that's nothing compared to his cock.

"Yes." I nod frantically, needing the release so badly, though I'm sure he won't have pity on me.

"We'll see." He pops another piece into my mouth, his thumb barely grazing over my clit while his fingers curl as he fucks me with them.

"Oh God," I groan, unable to swallow, the need clawing at my skin.

"Eat," he demands, his rough tone making my body tremble with anticipation.

He works me faster, his thumb rubbing me in hurried circles. I attempt to keep it down, fingernails digging into the top of his thighs as I fight not to moan as loud as I want to, the feeling permeating every pore in my body.

"Look how soaked you are, messing up my pants with that perfect pussy." He slips his fingers out, running them over my lips. "Suck."

I obey, instantly tasting myself, while his lips drop back to my ear.

"So submissive. I like that."

My walls clench, enjoying his praise.

His touch returns between my thighs, adding a third finger until it burns, but when he flicks my clit, all I feel is pleasure. The need climbs and claws until I'm barely able to take another bite of the food, but he pushes the fork into my mouth, reminding me of the rules.

Eat and keep quiet.

I can behave. I can do whatever he wants. I'm a good girl.

He pistons his fingers faster, and my eyes roll back, my breath stilling in my chest.

Fuck, I don't wanna be a good girl right now. I wanna be bad. I want to release his dick from his pants and fuck him right here, not giving a shit who sees us.

"Cillian!" Pleasure permeates through my tone.

"Every bite, love," he reminds me, increasing and then decreasing his tempo as he feeds me another bite, then another.

I don't taste the food anymore, completely overtaken by the sensations he's brought out in me.

"I'm close," I cry out, arching my back toward him, needing to come so badly.

The fork makes it past my lips, and I think it's lobster this time. I don't even care what he gives me; I'll eat it all because all I'm hungry for is this orgasm.

"Come on now. You're almost done." He drives deeper and faster, and my breathing turns labored.

Oh God, I'm almost there. Just a little—

The door creaks, the waitress approaching.

Nonono!

"Better keep quiet."

Thrust.

"Or you're gonna put on quite the show."

He circles my clit, penetrating me harder as he uses the tablecloth to cover my hips.

Fuck. This can't be happening.

"How is everything?" The waitress smiles just as he tips the fork to my mouth once again.

"It's quite delicious. Right, baby?" He peers at me while I try to formulate a response that doesn't sound like a dying cat.

"Mm-hmm. Perrrr-fect." I clear my throat.

Oh my God, I'm gonna come.

"That's great to hear." She refills our waters.

Just fucking leave, lady!

"If there's anything you two need, just let me know."

"We will."

Thrust.

"In about twenty, please bring out a piece of your chocolate mousse cake."

"Certainly." She bows her head, turning toward the door while he continues to torture me.

"Good girl," he tells me. "I don't think she had any idea that you were being finger-fucked under the table like a dirty slut."

"Please, Cillian, please." I bite on the edge of my lower lip, begging and pleading for this to end.

His other hand grips my throat, his mouth across my ear. "Look how you beg for it."

A growl escapes him in a sharp, breathless rush. And that only makes me that much hungrier for the release he keeps denying me.

"Please. Please let me come."

He thrusts his fingers deeper, faster. My clit's tender, pulsing with need.

He squeezes tighter around my throat. "Not yet. You haven't finished all your food."

"I-I'm not hungry."

Except for you.

In a flash, he flips me around over his thighs, roughly dragging up my dress until my ass is exposed. "Cillian, what are—"

He slaps me hard across my behind, soothing my skin with his palm. His hand slides into my hair until he's fisting it tight.

"You didn't follow the rules, love. So you don't get to come."

"No, no, please. I'll beg. Please. *Please* let me come."

The throaty rasp of his chuckle makes me shiver. He spanks me again and again, until the pain is nothing but a throbbing burn he soothes away before it returns with a vengeance.

"Good girls follow rules, while bad girls get punished." He shoves my panties to the side, cool air hitting my core.

I'm a little afraid someone is gonna walk back in and see me like this.

My God, the mortification, especially with Boris right outside the room. But I need this so badly that I don't care.

"Please. I'll be good, I promise."

His gaze turns molten, teeth clenched as he slaps me again. "I know you will."

Another heavy strike has me gasping with a cry, whimpering and writhing, as he touches me there, teasing me before another slap comes. The pleasure and pain morphs into one, tears forming in the corners of my eyes from the sheer need, the throbbing of my skin. I've never understood what orgasm denial felt like until now. It's torture.

He rams two fingers into me, teasing me to the brink before slowing his rhythm. Beneath, his rock-hard dick pushes into me, making me crave it.

But being like this—over his knee, completely exposed and at his mercy—it's hot. I'm enjoying every bit of this sweet torture.

His fingers slide through my core, playing with my opening, teasing me with my own slickness as he drags his fingertips to my puckered hole. "Going to have this too."

He pushes into it, and I moan from the sensation, knowing I'd let this man do anything he wants to me.

"Please, please…"

"I love hearing you beg me for pleasure."

His touch returns to my center, thrusting deeper, working my clit at the same time while my hair is still trapped in his curled fist.

"Hear that?" He takes me harder, the sound of my wetness filling the space around us. "Your pussy is soaked, baby. All for me."

"Yes, it's all yours." My voice drops, crying out for more.

When he touches my clit this time, I fall apart, completely overtaken by the most intense orgasm of my entire life.

"Oh fuck, that's it, baby. Squirt all over me."

I can't believe he made me do that again. I've read about this, but never believed it was real.

He continues to drive his fingers deeper until I'm completely spent, breathing out heavily as I collapse against him. He tugs my head back by my hair, his gaze locking on to mine as he searches my eyes. Then, without warning, he captures my lips in a kiss that's both deep and intoxicating. Every part of me is completely captivated by him.

His growl is thick and strained, a raw and savage sound that resonates through my core as his tongue twists around mine. The man is pure animal, and I'll gladly volunteer to be his prey every single time.

He pulls back, his stare intensifying as he fixes my panties and lowers my dress before placing me back on his lap. When I glance down, I find a wet stain on one of his pant legs.

"Oh my God." My hand cups my mouth, but he only laughs.

"I'll wear it like a badge of honor."

"You're truly a madman."

The back of his hand strokes across my jaw. "I'll be anything you want me to be."

My head falls against his shoulder, and he winds his arm around me, holding me so tight, I feel like I somehow belong with this man. This crazy man who makes me feel things. Scary things. Not just sexually, but emotionally.

I'd really like to keep him, but the universe has never cared about what I want. It takes without warning, just like it took my mother.

My heart pounds, but I force those thoughts back into the dark corner of my mind, where I'd rather not go.

I glance up at the door just as it opens, our waitress stepping in with an enormous slice of the most decadent double chocolate cake. She clears out the table, then places two empty plates and the cake before us.

"Thank you." He pulls a stack of bills from his wallet and hands them to her.

She looks down at it, her eyes wide. I'm pretty sure it's close to a thousand, if I counted the hundreds right.

"Do you need change?"

He shakes his head. "We'll leave when we're ready."

"Not a problem. Thank you." She glances back at him as she walks away.

I raise an eyebrow. "Do you always leave such a generous tip?"

He chuckles. "Depends on my mood."

His hips shift against me, his gaze darkening with desire.

"And you're in a good mood now?"

"I'll be in a better one once I have you bent over this table with my cock deep inside your cunt."

Shit.

His words send a zap to my core.

"Is that right?"

He leans in, his lips ghosting over mine. "Why do you think I gave her so much money and told her to fuck off?"

His smirk does sinful things to me.

"You're so polite." I nip his lip, and he groans, winding my long hair around his wrist.

"Always."

His mouth takes me hard as he stands, effortlessly lifting me with him. In one swift motion, he bends me over the table, shoving the plates aside, clearing space for what's to come.

His body molds to mine from behind, one hand tangled in my hair while the other glides up my dress, bunching it past my hips with a slow, deliberate touch.

"Stay just like that," he warns as he reaches into his pocket.

I don't see what he's holding at first until he's ripping a condom wrapper with his teeth.

"You have no idea how badly I want inside you, a ghra."

That word, his desperation for me…it all makes me want him even more.

"Show me."

His eyes ignite like a fiery flame, fingers lowering the condom over his thick erection. Those piercings are insanely sexy and I want to experience the feeling of them again.

"There are so many things I can show you." He lines the crown of his cock against my entrance, and I welcome the instant sting, needing more, pushing my ass into him.

"Fuck me, Cillian. Don't hold back."

"I don't plan to."

My center throbs; I love what those words do to me. His fingers land on the zipper at my back, slowly lowering it. The sound fills the room, adding to the erotic current we're both trapped in.

"Is that what you want?" His caress trails slowly along my bare skin, and my back bows from the sensation.

"Yes."

"Be careful what you wish for." His mouth drops to my shoulder, leaving a kiss behind.

The more he touches me, the more aroused I become. The more desperate. He knows exactly what he's doing. I have to remind myself that he's a grown man. Not like the little boys I've kissed before.

His crown pushes into me just as his teeth sink into my nape before he licks the pain away. "All I want to do right now is take you hard and deep, but I don't wanna hurt you, baby."

Turning backward, I stare into his eyes, finding kindness within them. He's definitely not from my world, that's for sure. The last thing those men care about is whether they're hurting the girl they're fucking.

"Do it. I told you, don't hold back." I grab his forearm.

His mouth twitches with a half-smile, and before I can utter my next breath, he slams his hips into me, sheathing his thickness inside me. I wince from the pain. I should've reconsidered what I told him, but it's definitely too late now.

"Shit, I'm hurting you." He turns my head gently, his palm resting on my cheek, brows creased with concern.

"No, I'm fine." My mouth trembles slightly, betraying me.

"You're a terrible liar."

"This is new for me. It's okay if it hurts."

"It's not okay." He leans down and kisses me, his touch soft and reassuring, making my heart flutter at his tenderness.

"Look, someone had to do it. Might as well be you." I crack a smile, hoping to ease the tension in his face.

Instead, his expression tightens, like he's just learned someone's ruined his favorite car.

"That's right—it'll be me." His hips begin to move, slow but deliberate. "It'll always be me."

All restraint leaves him as his thrusts grow harder, driving deeper with each one, until all the pain is completely replaced with the pleasure he allows me to have. His fingers curl around my throat just tight enough to steal my breath, leaving me with only enough air to savor this intoxicating moment.

"Oh God, yes!"

"Stay quiet, love," he hums, his voice rich and smooth, like velvet against my skin. "Unless you want an audience. Because I promise, I won't stop for anyone."

I sink my teeth into the inside of my cheek, desperate to muffle my moans, but it's useless. The more he pumps into me, the more I'm spiraling.

"You're the hottest thing I've ever fucked." His hand climbs up from my throat, grabbing my jaw hard as he whispers against my ear. "And I'm never gonna let you go."

Please don't.

With every deep, commanding thrust, he consumes me, and I surrender to him completely. His fingers trail down my hip, gliding to my core before teasing me with a flick that sends my eyes rolling back.

"Yes, don't stop!"

"Never. Gonna give my greedy girl exactly what she needs."

When he pinches my clit, white-hot pleasure bursts behind my eyes, my fingers gripping the tablecloth in a frantic attempt to ground myself. But he doesn't stop. He pulls out only to hoist me onto the table, the plate of cake crashing to the floor as his mouth devours every last tremor of my release.

"Best pussy I've ever tasted." His moans vibrate against my skin, his tongue gliding over me, teasing and tormenting until I'm powerless to contain the desperate cries spilling from my lips.

I don't know how long he fucks me or how many times I actually come because I've lost all ability to count.

Or think.

Or do much of anything except feel everything with him.

But I do know one thing: this man is mine just as much as I am his, and nothing and no one will change that.

TEN

CILLIAN

would've kept her bent over that table for hours, but I knew we had to go. Wouldn't be fair for her to get fucked with management walking in on us. Then I'd have to kill them, and the whole thing would be messy.

She glances at me from the passenger side as I stop right in front of the park, not ready for her to go. Her face flushes, the warmth spreading like a gentle burn across her skin, probably from the memory of what we just did.

Wish I didn't have to wear a condom every time.

Wouldn't have to if you married her. Could fuck her raw every single day.

Or maybe she can get on the pill.

I do like the first option a lot better...

When I chuckle, she stares at me curiously. "What are you laughing about?"

"Just wondering what I have to do to make you get on the pill so I can feel your pretty pink cunt when I'm inside you."

She swallows, clearing her throat. "I can speak to my doctor about that. I never had a reason to be on it before."

"You do now." I smirk, and her smile expands before she huffs out a breath.

"This is crazy, right?" She shifts toward me. "We barely know each other, and it feels like I've known you forever. Does it feel like that for you? And be honest." She throws a hand in the air. "It's okay if you don't feel that way."

She shakes her head when I stare at her without a word, finding her nervousness quite cute.

"Crap. Maybe I should've kept all that psycho mumbo-jumbo to myself. Sometimes I say things I shouldn't."

I clasp her thigh. "I'd listen to you all day, Dinara. Even if you were reading the damn dictionary." My hand glides higher, slipping between her legs. "And you're right. This *is* crazy because all I want is to be around you, and the fact that you're miles away kills me. Maybe I can convince you to move in."

She laughs. "Be serious."

"I *am* serious."

"Now *you're* being crazy." Her face twists playfully.

I slide my palm up and cup her pussy. "I thought you liked it when I'm crazy."

"This is *too* crazy." She bites her lip, suppressing a moan as I work my palm into her.

"You know, back in our great-great-grandparents' age, couples used to know each other for like two days before they got married."

"Whoa. Now you're asking me to marry you?" Her laugh is rich and throaty, vibrating through the air with an alluring warmth.

"Trust me, sweetheart." I grab her jaw and lean in. "When I ask you, you'll know."

Her cheeks flush.

"So you don't wanna move in, huh?"

"Don't sound so wounded." She runs a single finger up my forearm. "I promise to make it up to you in other ways."

"What ways, baby?" My cock jerks because it definitely just sounded like she meant her mouth sucking me dry.

Her brows arch, and from her facial expression, I bet the same thought just hit her.

"Um…I…"

Grabbing her hand, I squeeze it. "You don't owe me anything. Ever."

"But I didn't…you know…"

"Suck my dick?" I grin.

"Mm-hmm." The way her cheeks get all red is damn adorable.

"That's okay, love. There's always next time." I bring her knuckles to my lips. "I was very happy to eat that pretty cunt of yours instead."

She clears her throat, a jerky hand pushing hair away from her face. "You can do that anytime."

"I plan to do that every chance I get. I just don't know how I'm going to survive not seeing you until Friday."

"That's only four days away." She pops a brow. "I'm sure you can survive it."

"Doubt it."

Her laugh rings out, and it's the sweetest cure for everything rotten inside me.

In the rearview mirror, I catch sight of Boris's SUV.

"It's not too late to come home with me."

"Very tempting." Her giggle sends a jolt through me, igniting every inch of my body with a hunger I've never known with anyone else.

Our eyes align, and with every breath she takes, it grows heavier. My lips find her forehead, pressing a soft kiss as my hands gently cradle her face, pulling her closer.

"Make sure you text me when you get home," I tell her.

"Okay."

"Good girl." I lower my mouth to hers, kissing her slowly, inhaling the floral scent of her perfume. Think I need a bottle of my own so I can carry her scent with me when she's not around.

Damn, you've seriously lost it. What has gotten into you with this girl?

Fuck if I know.

"Thank you for tonight," she whispers. "I had a really nice time."

"Me too."

Her fingers tangle in my hair, her breath coming in quick, shallow gasps that fill the car. In a single motion, I drag her onto my lap, my hands threading through her silky hair as I lose myself in the depth of her gaze.

In this moment, it feels as if everything has aligned—like the universe itself conspired to bring her to me.

"Cillian…" Her fingers graze my cheek, and the sensation pierces me to the core.

My jaw clenches, fingers curling into fists as I fight the overwhelming urge to take control, to own her in ways I know I shouldn't.

Not yet.

She's so fragile—so soft under my hands—but there's a darker hunger rising in me, a need to devour her, to make her mine in every sense. To possess her so completely, she won't remember a time when it was anything but me.

When her tongue slides into my mouth, my control snaps. Before I can stop myself, a growl escapes, and suddenly, I'm the one kissing her—hard and unrestrained, as if one kiss can make her mine. My hands roam freely while hers grip my back and neck, drawing me closer, as if we're trying to become one. Completely consumed by one another.

No hesitation. No boundaries.

The way I crave her, the way I feel her hunger reflected in me, it's unlike anything I've ever known. I can't let go of this. Of her. I can't walk away.

If I was a better man, I would. She's too young, too innocent, to be thrown into my world. But I can't bring myself to care. I want her. And when I want something, nothing and no one will stop me from having it.

Her hips grind over me, my cock throbbing for her. She can make me hard with a single stare. That's how much power she has.

My fingers slither between us, finding her pussy still soaked. My God, I want her. Need her again before she's gone for days.

I should fuck her right here. It's dark enough outside. The windows are tinted. No one here but us. Pushing her back a little, I reach for my belt, my eyes glued to hers as I undo it, lowering my zipper down slow.

"What are you doing?" Her tone is urgent and aroused as she catches my movements.

"Lift up," I demand, sliding my pants down just enough to get my dick out.

Her eyes widen when I stroke myself, her exhales growing raspier. "Like that?"

She nods, her tongue snaking out.

"Can't wait to have this pussy raw so I can feel you stretch around me."

Her chest falls in quick succession while I reach for a condom in my pocket and rip off the wrapper before slipping it on.

"Slide those panties to the side."

She does as she's told, exposing her glistening cunt, and all I want is to taste it and fuck it until she can't move her legs.

Before she can protest, I push my seat all the way back and toss her onto the wheel, her startled yelp filling the air. Her legs are over my shoulders, my hands on her hips as I maneuver her closer until my tongue slides up her pussy.

I let out a deep growl, pulling her clit into my eager mouth, nibbling softly as she moves against me, desperate for everything I give, while the horn blares beneath her.

"Shit," she chokes on the word, positioning her arms so she doesn't hit it again.

She jolts with a moan when I work her faster, my tongue plunging in deep before I'm sucking and flicking her again. Nothing beats the taste of her: raw, intoxicating, mine.

"Yes that's it…" She stares right at me, making me insane as she grinds into me.

And when I swirl my tongue over her flesh this time, she grabs fistfuls of my hair and cries out while I continue to taste her, to feed my own crazed depravity. Her walls spasm, giving me every drop, but I want more. I'd fuck her for hours and not let her leave if I could.

When her body starts to ease, I know she's through, but I'm not.

I lower her back down on my lap, positioning the crown of my cock at her entrance. Slowly, I push her down onto it, sinking inch after inch into her perfect wet cunt, watching the way her face twists up in both pleasure and pain.

"That's it, baby. You can take it."

She circles her hips around me, her hands clinging to my shoulders, and with a single thrust, she's filled completely.

"Oh God, Cillian!" Her core shudders.

"Ride me, baby." I wrap my hand around her throat and squeeze. "I want you to use me and make yourself come while I play with your clit."

She nods and starts to move, my eyes on hers while she takes everything from me.

Body. Soul. My beating heart.

And in this moment, I realize she has me completely, and there's no turning back now.

ELEVEN

DINARA

"**B**oris said your date was a success, yes?" Konstantin asks casually as he steps into the foyer, features laced with an unreadable expression.

He's here at my place to drop off Gregory and Tatiana, and the air feels heavier as soon as he speaks.

Gregory hurries over to me, his small arms wrapping around me in a tight hug. I return it, my heart swelling with affection, before pulling Tatiana into my embrace.

"Yes, it was nice." I keep my tone light, though inside, my feelings for Cillian are anything but casual. "I kind of like him."

"Good." Konstantin nods, his lips pulling into a thin line—a ghost of a smile that doesn't quite reach his eyes. "I look forward to meeting him."

My stomach lurches. Meeting him? Oh God, I'm definitely not ready for that. Not yet.

Tatiana's attention darts between us, her gaze sharp with curiosity.

She knows I've met someone, but I haven't told her much. I'm sure she'll want every detail once Konstantin leaves.

"From what Boris has said," Konstantin continues, "it seems he likes you as well."

A blush rises to my cheeks. What exactly did Boris tell him? I really hope he didn't mention *everything*.

Like my fucking session in the car…

"I think he does." I quickly brush a lock of hair behind my ear. "He's planning to take me to New York City for the weekend. That's okay, right?"

Konstantin waves a hand dismissively. "You're an adult. You do as you please. But of course, Boris will come with you."

"Right." I nod, the word falling flat. "Boris will stay in a hotel, though, right? Cillian has a penthouse."

He chuckles, the sound almost cold. "Don't worry. I'll cover his stay."

My face heats up as the embarrassment creeps in. Obviously, he knows we're not planning on knitting together.

"I'm hungry," Gregory pipes up, his big brown eyes watching me expectantly.

"Sonya has perogies waiting for us." I attempt to regain my composure. "And she made a chocolate cake for dessert."

Gregory's face lights up with the kind of pure joy only a child can feel. I'm grateful for that innocence. He doesn't have the cloud of Mom's death still looming over him the way I do.

The scent of Sonya's cooking in the kitchen only makes me miss her more. She'd always make those perogies for us when we were younger.

"Tatiana, take him to get something to eat," Konstantin suddenly adds.

His eyes lock on to mine, intense and full of something unspoken. He doesn't want to discuss whatever's next in front of the children.

"Sure." Tatiana takes Gregory's hand. "Come on, buddy."

They step out of sight, and as soon as they do, Konstantin's posture stiffens, his expression turning darker.

"I don't want you to worry, but…" His hand lands firmly on my forearm, and for a moment, I freeze. His gaze pins me in place, and the weight of his next words hits like a physical blow. "I hear rumblings. Your father and brother…they're out for blood. *Your* blood, dorogaya."

A cold shock sends a tremor through my body, panic shooting through my veins. My brother's last text makes sense now, and I'm suddenly not sure if I want to hear any more.

Why can't they just leave me alone?

I glance at Konstantin, the tension thick between us. If he could find my father, he'd be dead by now. Roman too. But they're still out there, and they're coming for me. They're afraid of Konstantin, and they should be. But it doesn't make it any easier to breathe.

"It will be okay. Don't worry." His voice is softer now, though the concern doesn't leave his eyes. He squeezes my arm. "I've increased the security at your house, and I'll have a second bodyguard assigned to you."

My mind spins, trying to make sense of it all. "What about Gregory and Tatiana? Will they get more protection too?"

"Of course. No one will get to them. I'll make sure of it."

The tightness in my chest loosens slightly at the thought. My father wouldn't hesitate to take them back just to punish me. He knows how much I love them, how far I'd go to protect them.

"Come," Konstantin says. "Let's eat."

I stride beside him, my mind racing. If my father could, he'd kill me without hesitation. He's never been subtle about how much he wants me gone. He'd do it with his bare hands if given the chance.

But I can't let that happen. If he wants to get to me, he'll have to get through Konstantin to do it.

After Konstantin leaves, Tatiana, Gregory, and I settle in to watch a movie. I sit between them, handing out popcorn while we try to distract ourselves.

My sister leans in, her voice barely a whisper. "I don't understand why you live alone. You're not married or anything."

I shrug. "It's what he wants."

She sighs and rests her head on my shoulder. "I miss you. You should be with us."

"I know." I kiss the top of her head. "But I'm close, so you can come over whenever you want."

She pulls back, her eyes wide and distant, and for a moment, I see a flicker of something. Fear, maybe?

"What's wrong?" I ask softly.

She bites her lip, and I realize how much she's been holding in. She may be younger, but I sometimes forget how quickly she had to grow up, just like I did. We saw too much. The abuse, the fear…it scarred us all. After Mom died, I knew I had to get us out.

"I'm scared," she whispers.

"Of what?" I glance at Gregory, who's intently watching the movie, his little body pressed against mine.

"Of Dad." She swallows hard. "I heard what Konstantin said. About him wanting to…you know…" She breaks off, tears filling her eyes. "Please be careful. I don't want you to die like Mama."

My heart shatters. I draw her in, pressing a palm to her shoulder, trying to soothe her. "I promise I'll be okay. Konstantin will protect us. That's why I wanted us to live with him."

"I know, but I'm still scared, Din." She sniffles, her body trembling. "When I sleep, I see his face. The way he'd get angry, the way he hit you. Mama. Me."

I hug her tighter, closing my eyes against the memory of it all.

When Tatiana got older, he turned on her, too. Gregory was lucky; he was too young to remember any of it. At least that bastard didn't touch him.

"Daddy is not scary," Gregory says suddenly, looking up at me with wide, innocent eyes. He's eating popcorn, oblivious to the conversation we've been having.

I gently ruffle his hair. "Of course not, buddy. Watch the movie."

He nods and snuggles into my side. He was so young when we left. I don't think he remembers what we went through, and I'm thankful for that. If not for the photos of Mom around Konstantin's house, he wouldn't even know what she looked like. I don't ever want him to forget her. She loved him more than he'll ever know.

We continue watching the TV in silence, but my phone buzzes in my lap, and I can't help the smile that tugs at my lips when I see Cillian's name.

Tatiana leans over with a knowing grin. "It's him, isn't it? Your boyfriend?"

"Shh!" I giggle, trying to hide my phone while she playfully tries to grab it.

"When can I meet him? He sounds nice."

"Soon, hopefully," I reply, forcing my smile to stay hidden. "Now hush and watch the movie."

She shakes her head, stuffing more popcorn in her mouth, while my pulse quickens, a grin threatening to break free.

CILLIAN

3 days until you're mine for 48 hours.

DINARA

I'm packing tonight. Can't wait.

We've already made plans. Boris will drive me to a small airport, where Cillian will be waiting with his private jet.

CILLIAN

Don't pack much. Plan to have you naked
most of the time. Maybe fuck you in my
hot tub.

Heat floods my body at the thought.

DINARA

Behave. I'm with my younger siblings,
and you're making it hard to pretend
I'm watching a movie.

CILLIAN

How old are they?

DINARA

My sister is 13 and my brother is 5. We're
close.

CILLIAN

That's good. I'm close with my 4 siblings
too. Family is important.

DINARA

Absolutely.

Except when part of your family is toxic as hell.

A chill runs through me. What if my father or Roman find out
about Cillian? What if they try to use him against me?

The anxiety twists in my gut, but I shove the thought down. I don't
want to focus on the what-ifs. Right now, I'm talking to a guy who's
making me feel good. A guy who's proving that maybe, just maybe,
I deserve this.

CILLIAN

Enjoy your day, baby. I'll talk to you later.

DINARA

You too. XO

I put my phone down and try to push away the unease in my chest. For the first time in a long while, it feels like it's okay to want something good.

CILLIAN

Hours later, I'm still staring at her text, that XO she sent making me grin like a damn fool.

I'm already counting down the minutes until I see her again. The whole weekend is mapped out, and I wasn't entirely joking about having her naked most of the time. But I do want to get to know her better. Take her out, show her the city. We'll hit all the cheesy tourist traps first, then I'll take her to my favorite spots. The hidden waterfall in Central Park, Belvedere Castle just as the sun dips below the skyline, and Little Italy, where the food's as authentic as it gets.

But most of all, I just want to spend as much time as I can with her.

"You're doing that thing again," Fionn says from beside me, and I swear I forgot where I was for a moment.

"Doing what?" My eyes narrow as I shift in the seat at Tynan's office, waiting for the Russians to arrive.

"Smiling." He laughs. "It's her, isn't it? The girl from the club? What's her name?"

"Fuck off."

His grin widens. "Why are you keeping her a secret?"

"Because. I like it that way."

He chuckles again just as Tynan passes a stern look between us. "I hope you both are being careful. Women are nothing but trouble."

"Well, if you keep talking like that, you're gonna die alone,"

Fionn retorts.

Tynan definitely has no interest in relationships. In fact, he prefers solitude. Maybe it's the loss of Mom and realizing that not everything lasts forever, or maybe he can't bring himself to trust anyone. Whatever the reason, his world revolves around Brody, our cousin's son, whom he adopted after both of Brody's parents died. Tynan constantly worries about him. The poor kid stopped talking after the tragedy. He was only six, just a baby. We all wish we could help, anything to make him talk again.

"I have Brody. I don't need anyone else."

"One day, you'll eat your words, brother." Fionn folds his arms over his chest.

"Never gonna happen."

A sharp knock on the door cuts through the tension, and we all rise in sync as the four Russian brothers walk in.

"Konstantin," Tynan greets, shaking hands with the biggest of them all—a hulking presence, towering over everyone by a good few inches.

Konstantin moves with a calm, predatory air, his gaze never leaving us. He sits first, flanked by his brothers as they all settle on the sofa across from Fionn and me.

Tynan gestures toward the bar. "May I offer you all a drink?"

Konstantin's smile doesn't quite reach his gaze. "Vodka, please."

Tynan's attention flicks to the others. "And for you?"

"Same," Kirill replies, his jaw clenched tight, the skull tattoo on his neck shifting as his muscles tense.

"Me too." Aleksei nods, his expression as cold as his voice.

"Same for me," Anton adds, leaning back into the sofa.

"And where is your drink?" Konstantin asks us.

Without waiting, he pours a shot for each of us and brings them over. I take mine reluctantly, but keep my face neutral.

"Nu davayti! Na zdorovie! To health, as we say in my country."

We all raise our glasses, the burn of the liquor biting down my throat.

Tynan leans forward. "So, to what do we owe this pleasure?"

Konstantin settles back down.

"We need a favor." His tone is smooth and deadly.

"What kind of favor?"

"Councilman Elias Rhodes. We want him dead," Aleksei interrupts, his voice flat.

Elias isn't a friend—more of a friend with benefits. We scratch his back, he scratches ours, so killing him is out of the question.

"Why?" I cut in, unable to hold back. "We still need him. Taking him out would hurt us more than you."

Konstantin glances at his brother. "My brother's a bit hasty."

"No, not hasty." He folds his arms over his chest. "Correct."

Konstantin scoffs. "No one needs to die—not yet. Just talk to him. Make him understand we're all friends. A big, happy family."

Family? I'd rather watch the whole Marinov clan burn.

Tynan's voice stays even. "What's he done?"

Konstantin throws up his hands. "He's blocking a land deal. We need permits. He's refusing money and asking for more than we can give. You know how these corrupt politicians are."

I'm the one to ask, "What's in it for us?"

Konstantin chuckles, but it's dry. "My gratitude isn't enough?"

"No." I hit him with a glare.

His grin widens. "You're funny, Cillian. I like you."

"It's too bad the feeling's not mutual."

Kirill growls low, squeezing his shot glass until his knuckles turn white. I meet his gaze, unflinching.

Konstantin gives a thin smile, slapping his brother's chest. "One day, we'll all be good friends."

"I doubt that." My teeth grind.

Konstantin's smile doesn't waver. "We have a proverb in my

country: *Chto bylo, to proshló.* It means 'what's done is done.' Perhaps one day, you'll see it that way. I'm a patient man."

Tynan cuts in, trying to steer the conversation back. "We'll talk to Elias. Tell him to accept your terms, or he loses us."

Konstantin's grin deepens. "Now this is what family is. I appreciate that. If you settle this, I'll double your next order."

He means weapons. The Bratva is unfortunately our gun supplier.

Tynan nods, his agreement clear.

Konstantin rises, his brothers following. "Let me know how the meeting goes."

"We will."

As they turn to leave, Konstantin pauses, his eyes locking with mine. "Ah, and the woman from my club? How is she?"

My pulse spikes.

Shit. He knows.

"It's new. I don't know yet."

"I heard she's Russian." He smirks.

Aleksei chuckles low.

"I told you I could set you up with someone from my family. We could make this alliance official."

"I don't care that she's Russian," I bite out. "I just care that she's not a Marinov."

Anton's nostrils flare. The others look like they want to rip me apart. Let them try.

"On suma saydot kakda on uznayit," Kirill mutters, but it sounds more like a cryptic threat.

I definitely need to learn the language.

Konstantin chuckles dryly, eyes still on me. "We'll see ourselves out. Have a good evening."

Once they're gone, I slam the door behind them. "We need a new supplier."

"We're not switching. The Russians are the best."

I shake my head in disgust. "How the fuck can you work with them after what they did to our family?"

Tynan's face hardens. "He's not Sergey. He didn't do it."

"They're all the damn same!" I dig my fist into the desk.

Without waiting for his response, I storm out, ignoring my brothers' calls.

The Marinovs are pure evil. And I'd rather gouge my own eyes out than ever get involved with one of them, let alone marry one.

TWELVE

DINARA

Boris and my new bodyguard, Artem, drive me to the private airport Cillian arranged for me. The moment we pull up, I see him.

He's standing at the bottom of the steps leading down from the plane, and as soon as our eyes meet, he starts strolling toward me. His grin spreads wider the closer he gets, and damn, does he look good. Expensive gray suit, black dress shirt with a button casually popped open, every muscle on display even through the fabric. The sunlight catches his large silver watch, making it glisten as he reaches for my hip and leans in to kiss me on the cheek.

"Goddamn, you smell good," he murmurs, his hot breath grazing my nape. "And you look sexy as hell too." His voice is low and seductive, making my skin heat in an instant. "Can't wait to get you to my place and take you right up against the window."

His words hit me like a bolt, zapping straight to my core. As he backs away, his gaze slides down my body as if he can't help but admire my short black strappy dress and nude stilettos. And even with the heels on, he's still way taller.

His attention shifts momentarily, and I notice it flicking to the two men behind me.

"Oh, this is another one of my bodyguards. Cillian, Artem. Artem, Cillian."

Artem gives a nod of acknowledgment, and Cillian returns the gesture. Friendly bunch.

Cillian grabs my rolling luggage from them and looks at me, his lips twitching in that confident, teasing way. "Babe, did you pack for two weeks or two days?"

I shrug a shoulder, strutting beside him and offering him a mischievous glance. "A girl never knows what she needs until she needs it."

He laughs, and I love the sound of it. With a playful smile, he helps me up the steps.

I follow him onto the plane and settle into the soft cream leather seats. He stows my luggage in the overhead bin and takes the seat beside me, buckling in. Boris and Artem head to the back, giving us some space. This day's looking better and better.

Cillian reaches over, and before I know it, his fingers brush mine as he straps my seat belt around me. A jolt of electricity shoots through my limbs.

He stills, gaze locking with mine, and for one fleeting moment, the rest of the world disappears. His hand gently cups my cheek, and it's as though time stands still again with me and Cillian at the center of it—a big, brewing storm.

And in this moment, I know we're both ready to drown in it. Together.

CILLIAN

When we arrive at my penthouse near Central Park, I drop her luggage in the living room, watching as she walks ahead of me toward the floor-to-ceiling bulletproof windows. The city sprawls out before us, but my focus is entirely on her.

She has no idea how she affects me. How she ignites something deep inside me—something primal, something protective. Every instinct I've tried to ignore for years comes rushing to the surface. It's as if she awakens parts of me I didn't know were there, and she doesn't even see it.

I've been with many women, but none of them have ever felt like this. None of them have ever made me feel like I'm home just by standing in the same room. It's like I've been searching for her my entire life without even knowing what I was looking for.

"The view is incredible…" Her voice drifts as she stares at the cityscape, while all I see is her.

I step behind her, wrapping an arm around her waist and pulling her close. "It is."

My lips drop to her throat, fingers inching down toward the hem of her dress. I slowly drag it up just enough to touch between her thighs, sliding her panties to the side. Her palms press against the glass as I tease her with my fingertips, the sounds of her pleasure filling the air around us.

With every touch, she cries out for me, deepening my desire for her.

Fisting her hair, I pull her head back, locking eyes with her as I slide my fingers inside her. Her brows furrow, her mouth parting in a silent gasp.

When I add a third finger, she grabs my wrist, shaking her head. "That's too much."

I thrust inside her all the way, jaw tightening, my cock fucking hard for this woman. "You're gonna take everything I give you."

Sliding a hand down from her hair, I clasp it around her slender throat, working her faster. Her cunt is so wet, we both hear it as I ram deeper.

"Yes! Oh God!" Her hands slip down the glass, body quivering.

"I'm your God now, baby. Pray to me." I tighten my hand around her throat.

And with another thrust, she falls apart, her core clutching me tight as wave after wave washes over her.

"I need inside you."

I pitch back, my movements hurried and desperate as I unbuckle my belt, pop the button, and drag the zipper down, all while she watches me over her shoulder. Her face is flushed, her body begging for more. Roughly, I yank the straps of her dress down, exposing her perfect tits, until the material is pooled around her feet.

My heavy-lidded eyes rake her curves, naked in just a thong and heels. "So damn perfect."

Her shy smile just makes this even more perfect.

"What if someone sees us?" She glances outside before looking back at me.

"Sees you begging for my cock before you're filled with it?"

She nods, her cheeks flushed.

I spin her around and grab her chin, caging her between the glass and me. "Unfortunately, no one can see us this high up. But I wish they could, 'cause I want the entire world to watch what I do to you so every goddamn man knows who you belong to."

My mouth skims her lips, her ragged pants making my dick harder.

"Of course, after they do see you, I'll have to kill them." I laugh under my breath.

"Why?" She lets out a husky moan as my fingers play with her clit, slowly teasing her.

"Because no one gets to see you like this and live to talk about it."

"You're crazy." She nips at my bottom lip, and I growl, my hand threading into her soft, luscious hair.

"We've established my insanity already."

"Did we?" She kisses me slowly, her hands gliding around my back and pulling me closer. "I think we underestimated it."

"I guess that's something you're gonna have to figure out for yourself."

"Sounds like a challenge." Her thumb lightly grazes my lips.

"I hope you're up for it, baby."

"I always am."

She slams her lips against mine, and I groan as her tongue sweeps over my own, my hand quickly reaching into my pocket for a condom.

When she notices, she pulls away breathlessly, shaking her head.

I freeze, completely confused by what she's asking for, until she begins to drop to the floor. The condom slips from my grasp and my pulse races, pounding faster than ever.

"Fuck, baby. You sure?"

She nods, our eyes locked as she drags my pants and boxers down until my cock is in her silky grasp. As she tries to wrap her hand around my shaft, she falls short, and the realization that I'm too big for her to handle completely does something to me.

Her thumb rubs over my piercings, and once her mouth drops to the crown of my erection, swallowing it into her warmth, need zaps through my body.

"Tell me if I do it wrong, okay?" She comes back up, gaze filled with nerves.

I grasp her chin between my fingers. "Nothing you do could ever be wrong."

Her face flushes, and her damn sweet smile will be the death of

me.

My words seem to give her confidence, and she takes me back in her mouth, sucking the tip before moving deeper, her head bobbing with each pull. I grit my teeth, my hand at the back of her head, struggling not to push her down completely.

"That's a good girl. Take it all."

The sounds of her moans pulse through my body, her hand gripping tighter around the base as she takes me even deeper.

"Shit, how have you never done this before?" Inadvertently, I push the back of her head down, and when she groans in response, I do it again, harder this time until my cock hits the back of her throat.

She stares at me with glistening eyes while I have her trapped around my dick, gagging on it just the way I imagined—except the reality is so much better.

"You look so good. On your knees. Pleasing me with that perfect mouth. You like pleasing me, don't you, love?"

She nods.

"Such a good girl." I stroke her hair. "Now suck me."

She obeys, dragging her mouth up and down, glancing up at me as though for approval.

"You're doing so good, baby." I wrap her hair around my wrist, controlling her pace.

The feeling of her tight, warm mouth has me throbbing, needing that release. When she only takes half of me into her mouth, I push her down until she chokes on it.

"Yeah, that's it. Gag on it." I force her up and down, the need climbing until it takes over.

My head falls behind me, my muscles tensing, more blood rushing into my cock.

"Fuuuck!" I let out a guttural growl as I release down her throat, my hand gripping the back of her head. "Take every drop and swallow."

She whimpers, and that sound only makes this more intense.

Jerking my hips, I give her all of me. When I'm done, I slowly loosen my grip, pulling her head back.

"You're incredible. I'm not worthy."

She smiles, and in this moment, the overwhelming need to own her, kiss her, make her mine in every way consumes me.

"Come here." My voice is low and ragged as I draw her to her feet, fingers tangled in the back of her hair, pulling her in until my lips graze hers.

"Cillian..." Her breaths are jagged, each one igniting every nerve in my body, as if her very presence is sending shockwaves through me.

The air hums with an undeniable energy, an electric pulse crackling between us.

"Right here, baby," I groan, crushing my mouth with hers, kissing her with every damn fiber of my being.

My tongue sinks deep into her mouth as I wrap my arms around her hips, lifting her effortlessly. Her legs curl around my waist, pulling me closer. Kneeling with her still clinging to me, I grab the condom from the floor, tearing the wrapper apart with my teeth. With a swift motion, I lift her up my chest, pressing her up against the window as I roll the rubber down my length. She stares at me, her gaze burning with the same desire that courses through my veins.

"I'm gonna take care of you, baby." Gradually, I sink the tip into her entrance until it stretches around me.

"Oh God." Her brows knit, her nails clinging to my shoulders, unable to look away as I thrust another inch, my fingers wrapping around her throat.

"Mine. All mine."

She nods with a moan, and in that moment, I drive all the way inside, a raw, animalistic growl escaping from deep in my chest. Her mouth falls open, a desperate cry caught in her throat.

"You okay?" I manage to ask, even though every part of me aches to fuck her like an animal.

I gently stroke her cheek as she nods.

"Don't stop." She circles her hips, her hand reaching for mine to kiss my fingers.

"Fuck." My teeth grit, and when she kisses me again, I lose control.

My body takes over with raging lust, my hips driving relentlessly, the sound of skin against skin echoing in the air. Our eyes never let go as I take her deeper, this passionate thirst radiating between us until it overflows. Fisting her hair, I kiss her hard, taking her deeper with each stroke until her walls ripple around me.

"That's it, baby. Let me feel you come."

Her mouth trembles, her body quaking, her cries of pleasure intensifying until she screams my name as she falls apart. With a rough growl, my hips pounding, I release inside her.

And in this moment, it hits me: she's all I'll ever want, this woman who appeared from out of nowhere and turned my world upside-down.

THIRTEEN

DINARA

"Where are we going now?" I ask, the curiosity practically eating me alive as I walk beside Cillian, still reeling from our spontaneous lunch date in Little Italy.

"You'll see." A tiny, dangerous smirk pulls at the corner of his lips.

His smile is infectious, like a secret only he and I share, and it makes my pulse race in a way I'm trying to ignore. I squeeze his hand a little tighter as we continue down the street.

The throbbing between my thighs reminds me of what we did earlier and how fun it was to be taken like that—roughly and possessively.

"So, where are we *actually* going, though?" I ask again, my tone teasing, but I can't help it. The man has a way of keeping me on my toes.

"Patience, love," he teases, his thumb brushing over the back of my hand as he looks at me with that same playful gleam in his eyes.

"I'm not giving it away just yet."

When we stop in front of a jewelry store, I arch a brow, instantly suspicious.

"Uh, what's this about?"

"Don't worry, I'm not proposing. Yet…" He gives me a look that's half smirk.

I blink, trying to hide the way a rush of heat floods my chest at the thought.

Wait…

Did he just say *yet*? He's messing with me, right? We've known each other for about five minutes.

"I wasn't thinking that." I roll my eyes, amusement playing on my features even with the little flutter in my chest.

"Mm-hmm." That smirk grows wider as he tugs me toward the door. "Come on, love."

My bodyguards wait outside as we step in, and a little bell rings, drawing the attention of an older man from behind a glass counter.

"Mr. Quinn, welcome. Your piece is ready."

"Thank you," Cillian says smoothly, but then adds with a little squeeze of my hand, "This is my girlfriend, Dinara."

Girlfriend. He called me his girlfriend.

My stomach does a flip. He didn't just say my name; he declared me as his.

The man gives a polite nod. "It's a pleasure."

He turns, disappearing behind the counter, and when he returns, he's holding a long blue box. A surge of excitement rushes through me.

What the hell is that?

Leaning in closer, I try to get a glimpse.

Cillian catches my eye, his gaze filled with affection. He opens the box slowly, and I suck in a breath. A delicate tennis bracelet glints up at me, sparkling under the dim lights of the shop.

"This is for you." His voice is low and warm as he lifts the bracelet, holding it with care like it's something precious.

My heart skips. It's not the bracelet itself that's the most overwhelming thing—it's the fact that *he* got it for me.

"It's beautiful," I breathe.

"I'm glad you like it." Warmth shines in his eyes. "I added something to the back."

I glance at him, and then at the little lens he hands me to inspect the inscription. The words are simple, but they hit me like a freight train: *Those who don't take risks don't drink champagne.*

I laugh, the sound a little shaky, but genuine. I can't help it.

I beam up at him as the man steps back to give us space. "This is so sweet. Thank you."

"Of course." He slides the bracelet onto my wrist, his fingers brushing my skin, and I feel a tug in my chest.

"My mom would've liked you," he says softly, his words almost too quiet for anyone else to hear.

I swallow hard, the lump in my throat thickening. "My mother would've liked you too."

He drags me closer, his arms enveloping me like I'm the most important thing in the world. Our bodies press together, and I find myself rising on my toes to kiss him. It's gentle at first, before it grows more urgent, full of everything unspoken between us.

And in this instant, I know with every fiber of my being that we're destined for something. Something real.

We're not just two people playing pretend. We're exactly where we're meant to be.

I can't believe I'm back home after the best weekend ever. Cillian took me to a Broadway show like he promised, and we did all the classic touristy things: sights, sounds, even the cheesy souvenirs. I don't think I've laughed that much in forever.

And the best part? He got gifts for Gregory and Tatiana. Didn't even need to, but he did.

As I pull into Konstantin's driveway and make my way up the steps, the door swings open before I even have a chance to knock.

Ludmilla stands there, a warm smile already in place. "Moya milaya, I missed you!" She wraps me in a hug, squeezing me like she's trying to put all of her affection into one greeting. Then she jerks back, her eyes scanning me. "Are you eating? You look too skinny."

I can't help but laugh at her. "I'm fine, Ludmilla."

"What you mean, fine? You're young woman. One day you have kids! You need strong hips." She smacks her own, giving me a proud grin. "I have six kids with these hips. I know what I say. Come, I made borscht for lunch. You have some."

"I'm not really that hungry."

"What you mean, not hungry?" She hits me with an agitated glower.

Letting out a full laugh, I throw my arm around her. "Okay, okay, you win. I'll eat your borscht."

"Good." She leads me toward the kitchen, where the smell of her cooking is already in the air.

Even though Konstantin has a full-time chef, Ludmilla still insists on making her special meals. It's how she takes care of all of us.

"Din!" Tatiana rushes in, with Gregory right behind her. She wraps me in a tight squeeze, then pulls back with wide eyes. "How was New York?"

"It was great." I hold up a bag, which immediately grabs both their attention.

"What's inside?" Gregory asks, trying to sneak a peek.

Ludmilla slaps his hand away with a laugh. "Let your sister eat! You see she's turning into skeleton. You come live here again so I can feed you."

Tatiana's face lights up, but she knows it's not happening. Konstantin's decisions are final. And besides, I've grown to love having a place of my own. It's the kind of independence I've never had, even with Konstantin's men on guard.

I turn to Ludmilla, hoping to distract her. "Can you warm the borscht for me, please?" I give my sister a knowing wink, then quickly open the bag. "Cillian got you both gifts."

"Ooh!" Tatiana eagerly waits as I pull out a small jewelry box and a remote-control car.

I give the car to Gregory, who's already jumping with excitement.

"Can you open it?" he asks eagerly.

"Of course." I kiss the top of his head. "And this is for you." I extend the small box to Tatiana.

Her eyes widen as she opens it, revealing a delicate white gold tennis bracelet.

"Oh my gosh, I love it. Tell him thank you!" She can't stop staring at it.

"I will." I slip the bracelet onto her wrist, tightening it a little. "It's perfect on you. Stand next to Gregory and I'll take a picture."

They both grin as I snap a photo, sending it off to Cillian. A minute later, my phone buzzes with his reply.

CILLIAN

I'm glad they like the gifts. Can't wait to spend another weekend with you.

DINARA

Me too. How about you come to my place this time?

I'd mentioned that I had my own place, so why not have him over?

CILLIAN

This weekend?

DINARA

Sure. Thanks again for everything.

CILLIAN

Anytime, baby.

I smile as I stare at the screen, but before I can reply, Tatiana's voice pulls me in.

"My God, do you hear anyone when you talk to lover boy?"

"Shut up!" I shove her playfully, and she giggles, throwing an arm around me.

Meanwhile, Gregory has already zoomed off to play with his new toy.

"Okay, davay, eat," Ludmilla calls. "It's probably cold now."

I glance at Tatiana with a playful grimace as I start for the chair. She bites her lip, fighting a laugh.

"Where's Konstantin?" I settle onto one of the stools, while my sister takes the seat next to me.

"He's in his office with Aleksei. I don't know what they're doing," she explains.

I nod, taking a deep breath. I haven't spoken to him since I returned from New York, but I'm sure Boris has already given him the full rundown. Hopefully, he continues to accept my relationship with Cillian.

Maybe it'll be that easy. Maybe I can be with this guy even though he's not part of our world. The biggest hurdle will be him accepting me. It's one thing to know the Mafia exists and another thing to date someone who's a part of it. But I can't change who I am. I hope Cillian likes me enough to appreciate that.

I'm almost finished with my borscht when I register footsteps approaching. When Konstantin walks in, his small grin greets me like a punch of familiarity.

"There she is. Privet, dorogaya." He pulls me into a hug as I get up. "When you're done, I'd like to have a talk with you."

A knot forms in my stomach. "Uh, sure. I'm done."

What could this be about? Is it about my father? Or maybe something to do with Cillian? My mind races with the possibilities.

"Come to my office. We talk there, yes?" Konstantin gestures.

I nod, trying to mask my nerves. As we walk across the house, I glance back at Tatiana, but she's already lost in her own thoughts.

Glancing at me, he furrows his brows before he laughs. "Are you scared? Because you look scared."

"Uh, no, of course not." My voice trembles, giving me away.

"I promise there is no dead body in my office. Okay? I already gave it to the pigs." His laughter grows, but I'm not laughing.

Because he does have pigs. Big, black Calabrian pigs—and if the rumors I've heard are true, he does feed human body parts to them.

A shiver runs down my arms at the imagery.

When we reach Konstantin's office, Aleksei's already there, holding a crystal glass filled with clear liquid. He nods in greeting, his usual stoic expression in place.

"Oh, you're here too?" I say, trying to ignore the tension that suddenly fills the air.

"Sit. We must talk." Konstantin shuts the door behind him with a loud bang.

I settle beside Aleksei, my foot bouncing nervously.

Aleksei lets out a small snicker. "I promise no dead bodies hiding in the closet."

"I already told her that." Konstantin chuckles as he makes his way to the bar.

"Want a drink?" he asks.

I shake my head quickly. "No, thank you."

He pours himself one and lowers down into his chair with a sigh. I can feel my stomach turn.

"So, how is everything with you and Cillian Quinn?" His tone is casual, but his eyes are sharp. "You had a good weekend?"

My heart skips. "Yes, I did." I force a smile, glancing between them both. "He's a great guy."

Aleksei gives Konstantin a look—a silent conversation between them. The tension in the air thickens.

"Did he tell you about his mother?" Konstantin asks. "Or about his family at all?"

I frown, confused. "Uh, no… Only that she died." I pause. "Why? Is something wrong?"

"It's how she died that's the problem." Konstantin drains his glass, setting it down with a loud clink.

"What does that mean?" I gulp down the lump in my throat.

His jaw tightens, his gaze locking with mine. My stomach twists.

"I wasn't forthcoming when I found out about you and him."

"What are you talking about?" I ask, barely able to breathe, the chill of his words settling deep within me.

Aleksei cuts in, his voice icy. "Our father killed her."

A bone-deep shiver races through me, as though hitting me from every side.

"What?" I can barely whisper, my head spinning. "I don't understand. What are you saying?"

Konstantin throws his hands up. "Nu ti dalbayop." *You're a dumbass.* "I was going to ease her into this."

"You take too long," Aleksei mutters, arms crossed.

I'm struggling to take in enough air. "What the hell is going on?"

Konstantin leans in. "Let me explain. You see, Cillian is Irish Mob and—"

"WHAT?! Oh my God, and you didn't say anything? Especially after I told you about him! What the hell?"

"I know, I know. You're pissed." He dismisses my anger with a wave of his hand. "But I had reasons, and now you know them." He offers me a half-smile. "I'll tell you everything. Just don't interrupt me this time, understand?"

I nod, my anger rising. While I was questioning whether Cillian even had ties to our world, Konstantin knew exactly who he was and kept it from me. And then there's the part about his mother. What the hell do I even do with that?

"Cillian's mother…" Konstantin continues. "She wasn't just killed. She was burned alive, and he sent them a video of it, just to make it hurt more."

I slap my hand over my mouth, trying to steady myself as the shock hits.

"His father and mine were at war. A detente was reached, but Cillian…he's not a fan of ours still. And if he finds out you're a Marinov, it's going to be a problem."

Tears sting at the back of my eyes. "But I…I didn't kill his mother."

"I don't think that will matter to him." He shrugs nonchalantly. "But you need to tell him. Before he finds out on his own."

"He hates us. He'll never stay with you if he knows you're a Marinov." Aleksei's harsh words slice through the tension.

A tight knot forms in my throat. "No, he likes me. He wouldn't just dump me because of that."

Would he?

I stare at them both, but no comfort comes.

Konstantin leans back in his chair. "You must tell him, Dinara, or it will be worse."

The air is thick with dread. I don't know what to do, but I can't let him go. Cillian's perfect. He'll have to understand.

"I'll tell him," I whisper. "This weekend. I'll make him understand."

"Good," Konstantin says. "Now go. Have fun with your brother and sister. We have business to discuss."

I stand, trying to hold it together as I walk out of the office.

As soon as I'm out, emotions hit me all at once.

Every memory.

Every laugh.

Every second I've spent with Cillian in this short time rushes through my mind like a movie.

And as the weight of this new information presses down on me, I know one thing for sure: nothing will be the same once Cillian finds out.

FOURTEEN

CILLIAN

I've been counting down the days until I see her, and each one feels like an eternity.

The fact that I can't just jump on the jet and be with her whenever I want drives me insane. But between my work and her college schedule, it hasn't exactly been practical.

She's been quiet the last week, playing it off as stress from exams. I get it; I've been in her shoes. But the more I think about it, the more I wonder if something else is going on. Maybe something at home, something she isn't telling me. I figure I'll get a read on her once we're face-to-face.

Rolling up to the entrance, I hand my ID to the guard. He checks it against his tablet and then, with a click, the gate opens.

I take the left turn like she told me, heading toward house number six. A red sports coupe sits in the wide driveway, flanked by two SUVs—one of which I know is Boris's from the plates.

Stepping out of the car, my shoes hit the pavement as I make my way up the stairs. Before I can reach for the bell, the door swings open…and there she is.

Fucking perfect.

She's in a short, flared black dress that hugs her in all the right places, her hair falling in thick waves over her shoulders. Those long, tanned legs, the thin heels that make me think of her wrapped around my waist. And that bracelet—the one I got her—glistening against her wrist like she's wearing it for me.

God, I can't wait to get my hands on her.

I've never come in my pants just by looking at a woman, but I may start now.

"Are you gonna keep staring, or are you going to come here and give me a kiss hello?" Her pink lips tip up at the corners, and I remember to breathe.

"Damn, baby." I drag my gaze over her, taking in every inch. "You got all dressed up for me?" I close the last bit of distance between us, my hands aching to touch her.

She shrugs, her hungry gaze sweeping down my body, and I like it—like knowing she enjoys what she sees too.

"Looks like you did the same."

"Oh yeah?" I grab her jaw and bring her mouth dangerously close to mine. "Are you saying I look pretty?" My lips curl, mouth stroking hers.

"So pretty," she groans.

My hands cup her ass as I bring her flush against me and kiss her deeper, my cock instantly hard.

"Damn tease in this tiny dress." I drop a kiss to her throat, my fingers inching up her inner thigh, finding her…

What the fuck?

"Where are your panties?" I back my head away just enough to look at her smug expression.

"Oh, no." Her brow arches, a devious glint in those eyes. "I must've forgotten to put them on. Silly me."

"Jesus Christ, Dinara," I grunt, adjusting my hard-on.

When she notices it, she appears proud of herself.

"Yeah, you just keep looking at it like that and I'm gonna bend you over right here and fuck you."

Her face blooms with heat. "You make it sound like that's a bad thing."

"Damn, baby." I grab her ass and pull her back to me. "What the hell am I gonna do with you?" My mouth feathers over her pretty lips, inhaling her like oxygen.

"Hopefully have dinner with me and maybe enjoy a dip in the indoor jacuzzi after?"

"Mm, you wet and naked. It's like you're trying to top our last weekend."

"Never said I'd be naked."

I chuckle, rolling my knuckles down her cheek. "Oh, baby, you will be."

She throws her arms over my shoulders and smiles, giving me a quick peck on the mouth. "You're cute."

"Pretty. Cute. You're giving me a complex."

"Would you prefer devilishly handsome and endowed as a motherfucker?" Her full lips quirk up.

I fist her hair. "That's much better."

As I'm about to kiss her, a throat clears behind her, and I glance back, a little annoyed to be interrupted. A short woman with dark hair stands there, not much younger than my father.

When Dinara turns around, her face flushes. "Sonya, hi. Do you need something?"

"I'm sorry," the woman says. "The cook said dinner will be ten minutes."

"Right, of course." Dinara takes my hand, and I like how she doesn't hesitate, like she's taking charge. "This is Cillian. And this is Sonya."

"Ma'am." I nod in her direction.

"Nice to meet you. I'll go now," Sonya adds, giving a small, knowing smile before she heads out.

Once she's out of view, Dinara looks back at me. "She's the head housekeeper. I'm not really used to managing everyone on my own. My family did all that before."

"Must be a big change." I follow her through the house, past a sitting room and into the dining area.

In the center is a grand ten-person table, already set with a white tablecloth and two place settings, a blue floral arrangement in the middle.

She shrugs a little, blowing out a breath. "My family thought I needed to grow up and try living on my own. I miss having my siblings around, but…it's been okay. Kinda starting to like the independence. Plus…" She smirks, and I catch a hint of something mischievous in her expression. "I get to have you here without interruptions."

I raise a brow. "Is that so? And what would we be doing?"

Her grin widens, and it's all the invitation I need. My fingers slide up her back, twining in her hair as I back her up against the wall, needing my fix.

"I didn't mean right now." She exhales a cry when my fingers stroke her pussy, drenched and pulsing for me already.

"That's too bad, because I did."

I thrust a finger inside her, and she groans against my chest. When I tilt up her chin, our eyes lock as her arousal grows the more I touch her, rubbing her clit at the same time.

"What if someone walks in?" She can barely speak, fighting her feminine gasps.

"Then you'd better hurry up and give me what I need."

"Oh shit." Her head falls back, eyes shut, face twisting with desire when I add a second finger, working her faster and deeper.

"So you walk around with this perfect pussy out with your bodyguards here?" My free hand slides to her back, lifting up her dress before I spank her hard, the sound resonating through the space.

"Yes. Is that a problem?" She sucks her lower lip into her mouth.

I clasp her throat, working her faster while her eyes roll back and her body trembles.

"This is mine, Dinara."

Thrust.

"I don't share."

Thrust.

"So if anyone so much as looks at you the way I do, they're already dead." I drive into her again while her nails dig into my flesh.

"Is that a promise?"

"I never say anything I don't mean."

She drenches my fingers, her tightness snug around me, and I only wish it were my dick.

Footfalls from somewhere in the house draw nearer, and her eyes widen for a second before they're lost to the pleasure once again.

"Whoever is walking over is about to hear you come, baby."

"Cillian, oh God! Please…" she whispers, breathing labored, lips quivering.

Those footsteps grow closer, her pussy clasping me tighter, convulsing with waves while I continue to tease her clit at the same time.

"Come for me, baby. Show me how much you've missed me."

"Cillian!" she groans just as her release shakes through her.

My mouth slams to hers, swallowing her desperate cries, wringing every drop of her orgasm. Her cunt squeezes me like a vise as I draw back to watch this beautiful thing give in to me.

"You're so damn tight. If my cock was inside you right now, you'd suck all the cum right out of it."

"Oh God, yes, don't stop."

Her body continues to writhe and twist in pleasure, and I wouldn't stop even if God himself asked me to. When she relaxes, I slip out of her, running my fingers over my mouth before sucking them dry.

"Damn, you always taste so good." I grab her nape and run my lips over hers, my tongue sinking into her mouth so she can taste herself too.

Her kisses turn savage, biting and hungry, her tongue tangling with mine. She's a wild little thing, and I can't wait to teach her everything there is to learn.

"That was so hot." Her lips skim mine.

"Which part?" I laugh under my breath.

"All of it."

"Forget food…" My mouth drops to her neck as she bends her head back, giving me space to explore every inch of skin. "I want you upstairs so I can have my fill of you."

My fingers return to her drenched core, and I don't even register the footsteps. Don't notice the presence lingering in the doorway or the throat-clearing meant to get our attention. Not until—

"Ms. Marinova, the food is ready. Should we serve it?"

My body goes rigid. A deafening pulse pounds in my ears.

What *did he just call her?*

I heard it. Clear as day.

Marinova.

The name slams into me like a sledgehammer, splitting through my chest, ripping something vital apart.

Why the *hell* did he call her that?

FIFTEEN

CILLIAN

Ms. Marinova.

Why? Why would he call her that fucking name?!

A wave of cold dread slams into my chest, choking the breath out of me.

I pull away from her instinctively. Confusion plays in my features as my gaze snaps between her and a man dressed in a white chef's coat.

Dinara's face pales, her chest heaving as though she's suffocating, and the terror in her eyes is unmistakable.

Fear.

"What did you just call her?" My voice cracks like broken glass, raw, jagged.

Before I even realize it, I'm on him, my hand tight around his throat as I lift him off the ground and slam him against the wall.

"Cillian! What the hell are you doing?" Dinara's words are shaky, frantic, as she tries to pry me off the guy whose face is rapidly turning purple.

His chest spasms, his lips parting as he struggles for air, his hands clawing weakly at mine. But I don't care.

"What. Did. You. Call. Her?" My teeth grind, my words laced with a fury I can't contain.

"I-I don't understand. What did I do?" The chef's voice shakes, gasping for air.

"Answer me, you son of a bitch! What did you call her?"

"Cillian!" she cries my name, her hands grabbing at me, the pain of her touch searing through me. "Please let me explain!"

"No!" I peer over at her from behind my shoulder. "You keep quiet." My attention returns to the chef. "I asked you a question. What did you call her?"

He's barely able to breathe, stuttering out his answer. "Ms....Ms. Marinova?"

"Why?"

A ferocity builds inside me, an anger so deep it threatens to consume everything.

"WHY?!" I shout when he doesn't answer right away.

He jerks, complete panic on every inch of his face. "Th-that is her name. Dinara Marinova."

No. Nonono!

"FUCK!"

Every muscle in my body locks. My mind goes blank, and then— everything crashes down.

"Is she related to Konstantin Marinov?" My tone comes out barely a whisper, but the words feel like venom on my tongue.

He nods, shaking with terror.

"How?!"

"She-she's his cousin. Her father, Leo, and his father, Sergey, were brothers."

And in that moment, the world tilts. I stagger back a step, the room spinning.

She can't be a part of that family. She just can't be.

No. Not her.

My hand falls, my body buzzing with adrenaline and fucking hatred.

"Get the hell out of here!" I bark, shoving the chef away.

He stumbles before jolting upright. Without a second glance, he bolts from the room. The space falls silent, but it only lasts a second.

"Cillian, please, look at me."

Her hand rests on my back, but instead of warmth, it burns. I search for something to say, anything that won't make this worse, but every word feels wrong.

And I know: once we have this conversation, whatever we are will be over.

"I didn't know," she pleads. "Not at first. I just—"

"So you did know!" I flip around, curling my hands to control the rage running through my veins. "You knew about what happened to my mother and my feelings about your family, and you said nothing?"

"No, it's not like that! I—"

"You told me your name was Dinara Matrovskaya." The rage courses through me like wildfire. "You're a fucking liar, aren't you?"

"No!" Her eyes well with tears, and the sharp sting of guilt pierces me. "That's my mother's maiden name! I don't use Marinova because I…because I hate my father." Her voice cracks. "I hate him."

But I can't hear it. I can't seem to stop my anger from taking over, reliving those moments of watching my mother screaming as she burned alive. I see it, hear it, feel it, and it rips something inside of me open, leaving only pain and emptiness.

"Fuuuck!"

My fist slams into a nearby wall, the impact echoing in my bones. My knuckles crack, blood spilling across my hand as I pull it back.

"Oh my God!" She rushes to the table and takes a napkin, picking up my hand to stop the bleeding.

Her touch is nothing but poison.

But even as the venom fills me, I want it. She's a craving. A need.

One that I can't let myself have. Not now. Not ever.

I'll never fall in love with the woman whose family broke mine.

She glances up as she presses the napkin on my wound, and my jaw clenches. I want her to continue touching me even while I hate myself for needing her so damn bad.

"Dinara…why?" I don't even know what the hell I'm asking.

Why didn't you tell me?

Why the fuck do you have to be a damn Marinov?

Tears spill down her cheeks, and with each drop, my heart breaks more.

"I found out a few days ago." Her hands tremble as she wipes away her tears. "Konstantin told me everything. Who you are. What his father did. And I…I planned to tell you after dinner." She pinches the bridge of her nose. "I'm so sorry, Cillian. I can't—" She chokes on a sob, her words faltering. "I can't imagine, but I can because my father… My father killed my mother. Right in front of me. And I couldn't stop it. I still hear it. Every night."

Her words break me in ways I didn't think were possible. She knows. She understands. But that doesn't make this any easier. It doesn't make her family's betrayal any less real.

"I'm so sorry, baby." My hand cups her face, forcing her eyes to meet mine, the weight of her sadness dragging me deeper into despair. "I'm so damn sorry."

I tug my hand away, and I see it: her soul shattering right in front of me. And it's all my fault. The agony in her face twists the knife even deeper.

She presses her hand to my chest, a desperate plea in her eyes. "I never meant to hurt you, Cillian. I swear."

She doesn't get it, does she?

"It doesn't matter." Every syllable is a tortured rasp. "Your uncle…

He's the reason my mother is dead. Don't you get it? I can't be with you. I can't love you, not when your family destroyed mine."

I can't believe this is fucking happening.

Her face crumples, her lips trembling.

"Please don't walk away from me," she whispers, breaking into pieces. "We can figure it out. Together."

"You think I want to?!" I roar, pushing her up against the wall.

My hand circles around her throat, but not enough to hurt her. It's to keep me from falling apart. I don't even know what I'm doing anymore.

"You think I *want* to leave you? The thought of never seeing you again, of losing you for good… It's killing me, Dinara. But you know what kills me the most?" The pain's so thick I can barely speak.

Her breath catches, and I know she feels it too—the pull between us.

But it's not enough.

"Knowing that I could fall in love with the woman who killed my mother."

"I…I didn't." She shakes her head.

"You might as well have." I draw in closer, my lips stroking hers, wanting her so damn much. "Every time I look at you, I'll remember her screams. The way she begged. The way she died so brutally while I couldn't save her."

The words are like a knife. Silently, she cries, and every part of me continues to break.

"Tell me," I choke, my throat closing. "How would you feel if my family killed your mother? Could you ever be with me? Could you lie beside me every night knowing *that*?"

She doesn't answer.

"I'm sorry, Dinara. But I just…I can't." As I step back, the words rip me apart. "I'm sorry."

Her eyes flutter shut as more tears spill down her cheeks. She doesn't say anything, but I see it in her face: the anguish, the plea.

But I can't stay.

Before I can change my mind, I turn away, every step harder to take.

"Cillian..." Her pained sob cuts through me, and my chest rips in two.

And when she does it for a second time, that's all it takes. I'm rushing back before I can stop myself, my lips crashing to hers in a desperate, savage kiss—a flickering flame consuming us both until it fades and dies. My hands are everywhere, gripping, pulling her closer, even as my heart screams for me to stop.

But I can't. I can't stop touching her. I can't stop wanting her.

Because the moment I let go, this will all be over. I know it. And so does she.

I grip her hip, clasping her nape with my other hand, her pulse pounding against my touch. And for a moment, I forget who she is and why this is wrong, and I let myself remember why she's felt right from the moment I first kissed her.

I don't know where to go from here. How to forget I ever met her. How to live knowing I can't have her anymore. That someone else will.

My chest tightens, my fist clenched at the small of her back, but I don't let go, kissing her with a savagery I've never felt before. If I don't stop, then I don't have to walk away.

Not right now. Not until it's over.

I don't know how long I stay there, how long I let myself have what I'm no longer allowed, but soon, it comes to an end. My palms cup her face, her lips skimming mine like she doesn't want this to end either.

But then the image of my mother, her body scorched, comes crashing back, and I know there's nothing left for us.

I don't look back as I walk away, even though her sobs cut through

me.

Slipping into my car, I grip the steering wheel like a lifeline. When I glance in the rearview mirror, I see her standing there watching me drive off, her face streaked with tears.

But I can't stop. I have to keep driving.

Because I'm already gone.

SIXTEEN

DINARA

I've lost track of time, sitting here with my knees drawn to my chest, quietly sobbing in my bed.

The sound of his footsteps as he walked away still lingers in my ears like an unbearable echo, a reminder that he's gone. Now he's nothing but a shadow I can't reach, a dream slipping through my fingers, while all I can do is sit here, broken, feeling the pieces of my heart scatter with every passing second.

I called him, desperate for him to pick up. To say something. To tell me this isn't really over.

But he didn't answer. He's done.

And that realization slices through me, sharp and unforgiving.

Sonya was the one who found me. It felt like hours before she helped me up and guided me to my room. I wanted to fight it, to stay curled on the floor where the pain felt easier to bear, but her presence was like a raft pulling me back to something, anything that wasn't just the crushing pounding of loss.

She helped me into bed, but the tears never stopped. Not even after my eyelids swelled, after my body shook with the kind of sobs I didn't know I could make.

It shouldn't hurt this much. But it does.

And the more I replay those final moments in my head—the way he looked at me, the hesitation in his voice, the cold finality of his words—the more I cry, like I can somehow undo it all. Like maybe if I just cry long enough, he'll come back. But I know he won't. He's already made his choice.

"Din, you've gotta eat something," Natalia says softly, rubbing my back.

I completely forgot she was here. Her touch, warm and soothing, tries to pull me out of my misery. I shake my head, wiping my eyes roughly, but it doesn't stop the tears from coming.

"I don't want to eat," I manage to say.

I can't even remember how to breathe right now. My body is so heavy with grief that I'm barely aware of anything else.

She sighs beside me and then, without saying a word, she shifts, lying next to me in a protective curl. She pulls me into her, her arms surrounding me like a shield, her warmth seeping into my frozen soul.

"He doesn't deserve you. Fuck that guy, okay? None of this is your fault."

I bury my face in her shoulder and cry harder. She holds me tighter, but nothing changes the fact that he just shattered everything we could've had into pieces.

"Crap." She laughs weakly. "I thought I was making you feel better."

"No, it's not you," I sniffle. "I just miss him. I miss him so much, and I don't understand why this is happening." I clench my comforter, clutching at it like it's the only thing holding me together. "Why the hell did the universe mess with us this way?"

Natalia doesn't answer immediately. She doesn't need to. She just holds me, her fingers gently stroking my hair, steadying me.

"I don't know, but I swear you'll be okay. You'll meet someone who deserves you. Someone who sees you for everything you are, everything you *deserve.* If he can't see past what happened when it wasn't even your fault, then he sucks. And I mean that."

I shake my head, the ache in my chest only intensifying. "But he didn't suck. That's the problem. He was…good. He was everything I wanted, and I thought we could make it through. I really thought…" I falter, a hollow laugh escaping me. "I really thought he was the one. That maybe I was enough."

Her body sags beside me, her worry palpable as she tries to find the right words. "You've gotta just forget him."

I nod, squeezing my arms tighter around her. "I know. But how do you just...forget someone like that? Someone you thought you had a future with. How am I just supposed to erase him from my life?"

"You're right," she says gently. "But you can't let it eat you alive either. Don't let him take more from you than he already has."

Before I can respond, my phone vibrates on the bed beside me and a rush of hope floods my chest. I sit up quickly—hoping, praying it's him. Maybe he changed his mind. Maybe he's realized what he's done.

My fingers tremble as I reach for the phone, but Natalia snatches it from my hands before I can even check.

"Let me see," she says, low but sharp.

She glances down at the screen and shakes her head. "Not him."

Disappointment hits me but I hide it.

"Too bad, because I was looking forward to telling him to go fuck himself." She glares at the screen like she hopes he calls.

With my eyes still raw, I manage a weak smile. "As much as I'd love for you to do that, I'm capable of telling him myself."

She raises a brow, her expression skeptical. "Right now, you look like you'd jump right back in if he asked you to."

I swallow hard, the lump in my throat almost choking me. "Well, why not?" I whisper. "It's not like he cheated or anything. His mom was murdered, for God's sake. Doesn't he get a pass for not being sure about things?"

"No." Her grip on my arm tightens. "He doesn't get a pass. Not from me, and not from you. If he can just leave you like this, without even trying to fight for you, then he's not the guy you thought he was, and you need to let him go."

Despite the tears still streaming down my face, I manage a small smile. "Fine. We won't give him a pass, then."

"That's my girl." She smiles softly at me, but it's tinged with sadness. "Now, how about you get cleaned up and we hit the sauna? Sonya said she can make us drinks too, if you'd rather drown in liquor instead."

The thought of the sauna sounds like a kind of sweet release— letting the heat wrap around me, suffocating the sorrow until it's just a distant memory.

"Okay." I let out a heavy sigh. "I want to be obliterated. Just… don't let me drown, okay?"

"I promise." Her hand's warm on my back, steady and sure.

And for the first time since he walked out that door, I feel like maybe, just maybe, I'll survive this.

CILLIAN

There's nothing worse than sitting in a board meeting when your mind's elsewhere.

Like on her. The woman I can't stop thinking about, even after I left her heartbroken.

I tried texting her all night, but I couldn't bring myself to do it. What's the point? I can't be with her. It'd only drag it out, and we'd both end up worse for it.

But still, I can't forget her. The way she smelled. The way she felt in my arms. Her taste still haunts me. I was pissed at myself after jerking off to thoughts of her and realizing she wasn't there.

I was alone again.

For the longest time, that didn't bother me. Until she came along.

I grip the edge of the table, pretending to care about some proposal to expand our hotels. I'd rather be anywhere else. When the meeting finally ends, I'm the first one out the door.

"What the hell's wrong with you today?" Tynan asks as he catches up with me, Fionn right behind him.

"Nothing. I need to get home."

"Nah, something's off." He grabs my arm. "Come on, let's go to my office. You can tell us what's got you so wound up."

Great. Just what I need.

"You seriously look like shit." Fionn gives me a quick once-over. "What the hell did you do last night?"

Stayed up all night trying to figure out how to be with her. Got nowhere.

I bite back a response, and he assesses me even more curiously.

We head into Tynan's office, and I slump onto the leather sofa, Fionn plopping next to me.

"Talk." Tynan crosses his arms. "What happened?"

I let out a heavy sigh and rub my face. "Where do I even begin?"

"At the beginning," Tynan insists.

"Fine." I take a deep breath. "I met someone."

"That girl from the club?" Fionn smirks. "Is that why you've been smiling more than usual?"

"Probably." I shrug

"So, what happened?" Tynan gestures for me to continue.

"I found out she's a Marinov."

"No way." Fionn leans forward, his eyebrows shooting up in

surprise.

"Yeah. Found out yesterday, so I ended it."

Fionn snickers. "Why the hell did you do that? You need to let it go. She's not—"

"Don't you fucking dare." My voice hardens.

Fionn holds his hands up in surrender. "Fine. But just hear me out. Messing up your future over something *she* didn't do...that's damn stupid. Mom wouldn't want this for you."

My chest tightens, anger bubbling up. "What do you know about what Mom would've wanted? Not like we can ask her. We didn't even get a body. Konstantin's *fucking* father took that from us." My hand clenches, trembling with rage.

Fionn stays silent. I know it hits him.

"If I'd kept going, it would've been bad for both of us. I can't marry a Marinov. I can't have kids with her. The thought of our blood mixing...it makes me want to burn everything down."

Tynan exhales. "Look, I'm not gonna tell you what to do. You're a grown man. But don't let this consume you. And get some sleep. You look like shit." He smirks.

"Yeah, yeah. Fuck off." I shake my head. "Are we done here?"

"Yeah, go. But get your head in the game. The board doesn't need to see you like this." He waves me off.

"Right."

I head for the elevator, almost bumping into a woman. My pulse falters, because for a second, I swear it's her.

"Dinara?"

She turns, a look of confusion crossing her face, and my stomach clenches.

It's not her. Of course it's not her.

"Sorry," I mutter, stepping aside as the woman enters the elevator. I wait for the next one, my stomach sinking.

This is crazy. She isn't here. I'll never see her again. And it's all my fault.

SEVENTEEN

DINARA
TWO WEEKS LATER

It's been two weeks since I've heard from him. Since I've felt his touch, smelled his cologne, felt his skin on mine.

Every day should be easier, but it's not. It just keeps getting harder.

I see him everywhere I go. Every man, for a second, feels like him—until I look closer and realize it's just my mind playing tricks on me.

He's never coming back. He doesn't even want to talk to me.

It's over. Cillian is really gone.

Alisa and Natalia are speaking, but I can barely hear them. I'm staring at my phone, hoping for some sign, some reply, but he hasn't answered. He probably never will.

DINARA

Hi.

That's all I wrote. It was stupid. I know that. But last night, the memories hit me like a wave—us ice-skating in New York City at Rockefeller Center. It was so real. I could almost feel his hands on my hips, his breath in my ear.

"Steady, baby," he whispered, tightening his grip. "You're doing great."

I laughed, not even afraid of falling because he was always there to catch me.

"Dinara, are you even listening?" Natalia's voice breaks through my thoughts.

I jerk toward her. "Huh? What?"

She tilts her head. "I won't ask what you were daydreaming about. I already know."

I pick up my glass of water, pushing the untouched salad around. Why did I even bother coming out? I'm terrible company.

"I was asking if you're going to the club this weekend. Rzvrt is hosting an event on Saturday. We're going."

"No, I'm not going. But have fun."

The idea of being there makes me want to crawl out of my skin. I can't bear seeing him, feeling the sting of him ignoring me again.

"What do you mean, no? You need to come!" Alisa says. "You've been holed up for way too long, Din. This isn't healthy. You look like a damn ghost."

"Wow, thanks," I mutter, rolling my eyes.

"What she means is…" Natalia shoots Alisa a look, almost like she's scolding her. "We love you, okay? We just want to help you move on. And even if you were a ghost, you'd still be hot as hell." She grins. "Please say yes. We don't want to go without you."

"I can't. I'm done with that place. It'll only remind me of him."

"Stop it!" Natalia's brows knit. "All you've done for weeks is mope around."

"I haven't been moping."

"You definitely have," Alisa chimes in, a sympathetic look on her face. "Hey, he might even be there."

My gut twists, a sharp, ugly knot of jealousy coiling inside me.

What if she's right? What if he's already moved on?

The thought slams into me like a blade, cutting deep and leaving behind a burn I can't ignore.

He wouldn't. He couldn't.

But what if he did?

If Cillian thinks he can just show up there with some new woman at his side like I never fucking mattered, like I was replaceable, then he'd better be ready for what's coming.

Screw this. Now I have to go and see it for myself.

"What the hell are you doing?" Natalia's voice shakes me from my spiraling thoughts. "She doesn't need to hear that!"

"No, it's fine," I quickly say, waving it off. "I'll think about it and let you guys know."

They both nod, but I know the truth.

There's no way in hell I'll be staying home now. And when he sees me, I'm gonna make him eat his heart out.

"How are you doing, Moya dorogaya?" Konstantin asks, sitting across from me at the table, eyes studying me like he's trying to read every piece of me that's falling apart inside.

Are you really okay? I know that's what he's asking, even if the words sound casual.

Everyone is here—my siblings, his brothers—but I feel more alone than I ever have. We're all gathered around his large, gleaming dining table, but I just want to be alone.

They all know what happened. Knew it would end this way. And even though they warned me—even though deep down, I knew there was a chance they were right—I still hoped.

I wanted so badly for Cillian to pick me. To choose *us*. I wanted him to be the one to fight for what we had. But I didn't matter enough.

The back of my throat burns as I swallow the sting of my own pain. I grab the club soda in front of me, forcing it down in large, shaky gulps, trying to drown out the ache.

"I'm fine." The words come out too loud, too eager. I don't mean for it to sound fake, but it does.

Tatiana, sitting beside me, squeezes my hand under the table. Her fingers wrap around mine with a silent understanding that cuts deeper than anything anyone could say.

Konstantin watches me for a moment longer before nodding, his expression softening. "Good. I'm glad. I'm sorry it turned out this way. I had hopes that maybe you two would get married someday and help bring the families together. But he's stubborn." He shrugs. "What can you do?"

Married to Cillian? I could laugh…if the thought didn't feel like a knife twisting in my gut.

Now we'll never know.

"Yeah, what can you do?" I mutter, the words cold in my mouth.

Nothing. I can do nothing.

"Want me to…" Kirill drags a finger across his throat, and I know exactly what he means.

His gaze flickers to his five-year-old son, Lev, who sits beside him, carefully lining up his broccoli before taking a bite—hopefully too focused to catch any of this conversation. He looks just like his dad, and thank goodness for that. The last thing Kirill needs is a constant reminder of the woman who walked out on them.

I don't know what it means to be a mother, but I'd like to believe I'd never abandon my child—especially not because they were on the spectrum.

Kirill leans in, his near-black eyes glinting with a chilling promise. "I'll make it look like an accident." A slow, calculating grin tugs at his mouth. "You just tell me how much pain you want him to be in, and it's done."

A brittle, hollow laugh escapes me. "No, Kirill. I don't want him dead." I exhale, shaking my head. "But thank you for having my back."

He doesn't flinch. "Of course, sister. We are family."

I should feel better, but all I feel is emptiness. It's thick, palpable, like something pressing down on my chest.

Aleksei's voice cuts through, sharp and bitter. "You love him or something?"

His words are blunt, no softness at all. He takes another shot of vodka, his eyes not leaving mine.

My heart skips. The pain is a physical thing now, heavy in my chest, but I don't say anything.

Do I love him? I don't even know. But that doesn't stop the ache from ripping at me every time his face flashes in my mind.

Aleksei's eyes narrow as I stay silent. He slams the shot glass down with a scowl. "He's an idiot, Dinara. You can do better."

Better? I've heard that before. Especially from Natalia. But it doesn't make it easier. It doesn't change the fact that Cillian was the one I wanted. Not some *better* version of him.

I could have the world, but I want him.

"Literally anyone would be better." Anton joins the mix, his mouth pulling into a thin smirk.

"Boys, boys," Konstantin joins in, his tone shifting, softer now. "The heart wants what the heart wants." He meets my gaze. "Don't be ashamed of that. We're only human. Once you let someone in, it's hard to get them out. It's why it's better not to find yourself in that kind of predicament in the first place."

The silence after his words feels like it could break me. He's right; I know it. He knows it too. It's why he keeps everyone at arm's length. Why he never lets anyone get close enough to hurt him. Because *this*—what I'm feeling now—is the only inevitable end to love.

Anton chuckles. "Is that why you plan to be alone forever? Like a hermit?"

Konstantin's lips twist in something close to a smile, but it's grim. "That's right. Better to avoid the unnecessary entanglements that only end one way."

He lifts his glass and finishes his drink off in one motion, as if it's nothing more than another empty habit.

"End how? In heartbreak?" The words slip out before I can stop them.

His gaze slices into mine. "Net, dorogaya. In death."

EIGHTEEN

CILLIAN

> Hey. I miss you. I haven't stopped thinking about you since I left. But I can't do this. I'm sorry.

I finish typing it, staring at the screen for a moment before I save it to my drafts, like all the others. Over twenty messages, all waiting for her to read, but none of them ever sent.

I only write them to get it out. To say what I can't. What I shouldn't.

But the noise in my head is too loud, the memory of my mother haunting me. Her screams echo in my ears. The sound of her burning alive. It's all there, like it never left.

Leaning my head back on my sofa, I try to block it out, but it's still fresh in my mind. And I relive every moment of that day, like it's happening all over again.

"I'm sorry, Pat. But she's gone," Fred, one of the detectives, tells my father.

"No! Don't fucking tell me that!" My father fills with rage. "She's fine! She's fucking fine."

When I glance at Tynan, his face is tight, breaths even and controlled, but I know he's upset too. We all are.

"We got the video he recorded. It's her. I'm so sorry," Roy, the other cop, says.

"Play it!" Dad's on the brink of losing it, his voice simmering. I don't think I've ever seen him this scared, this angry. "Play the fucking video!"

"It's not a good idea." Roy shakes his head.

"Don't feckin' tell me what's good for me. Play it. Now!" He bangs a fist on the kitchen counter.

"Pat…" Fred tries to calm him down. "You don't want to see this. Trust me, you don't want to."

If what he said was true—if Sergey Marinov burned my mother alive—I'll never forgive him. Any of them.

"She was my fucking wife! You play it, or I swear I will rip out your bloody throat!"

"Maybe tell the boys to go, then. No child should see their mother this way, no matter how old they are."

My father snaps the collar of Fred's shirt, ready to kill him.

"My boys are no boys. They're men. Play the damn thing," he spits out.

"Just do it," Roy tells him.

"Jesus Christ, Pat." Fred shakes his head, picking up a laptop and pressing a few keys before I hear it.

My mother.

Fuck!

My heart races.

"No! Please!" she screams, while Sergey holds a red canister in his hand, walking around her in circles.

She can't move. Her hands are zip-tied behind her on the chair in some warehouse.

Sergey laughs. "Kak zhal', chto ya dolzhen ubit' takuyu krasivuyu zhenshchinu."

"Please," she sobs. "Please, I'll do anything. Just name your price. My husband will pay whatever you want. Just call him."

"Your husband..." He laughs. "...is the reason you're here."

"What?" Her body trembles.

Does she know he's recording her? Does she think we're gonna save her? How the hell could we have missed this? How the fuck did we not know he took her?

"Nu da, moya dorogaya. He didn't give me something I wanted, so I take something that belongs to him. I say that's fair, yes?"

Popping open the canister, he spills the kerosine all over her body as she chokes on it. When he lights a match, my pulse quickens.

God damn it. I can't watch this. I can't...

"Oh m-my God, I beg you, please. No! I have children. Don't do this..."

His laughter...I'll never forget it. And when he tosses the flame at her, I close my eyes, her screams piercing through the air before dying with her.

And when I look back, she's not there anymore.

Nothing but charred-up flesh.

I'll kill him for this. I'll kill them all for this, and I won't rest until every one of them pays.

I never got what I wanted. Aside from Sergey, the rest of the Marinovs are still alive.

And Dinara? She's out of reach. For good. I meant what I said: she and I will never happen.

I throw my arm over my face, and when I close my eyes, she's there. My angel and my curse.

Why can't I get over her? What's so different about this woman?

My phone buzzes. I grab it, hoping it's her—maybe a message, her voice that I miss. Even if it's her cursing me out, I'll take it. I deserve it.

Wish it was easy to forget everything from the past and just be with her, but I can't let it go. I can't be a part of that family, making a life with her like Mom's death meant nothing at all. She wouldn't want that. *I* don't want that.

Fionn's name flashes on the screen. When I ignore it, he calls again.

Fuck me.

"What?"

"We're going to Rzvrt this weekend."

"Maybe you are, but I'm good. There's nothing there for me."

"Are you sure about that?"

I blow an annoyed breath. "What the hell does that mean?"

"What if she shows up? Wouldn't you wanna know if she's fucking someone else?"

That's never gonna happen. If she shows up, I'm bringing her back home. And if she's with someone else, he's gonna end up leaving in a body bag.

"I left her. Can't tell her what to do." I don't even sound believable.

Fionn laughs. "You're full of shit. You'd kill him. We both know it."

Of course I would.

"So, you coming or not?" he continues.

Well, of course I have to go now. His words will haunt me. If she's not there, I'll leave. Simple. But if she's with someone else...

Good luck to him.

She belongs to me. No one else.

"Fine. I'll go. Just to make sure she's not there."

"And if she is?"

"Don't worry about it."

He chuckles with a flicker of amusement. "You can't keep her single forever."

"Watch me."

His laughter grows. "I used to think Tynan was the stubborn one, but you're worse."

"Whatever."

"You're an idiot." He snickers.

"Tell me something I don't know."

NINETEEN

DINARA

"**G**lad you came with us tonight," Natalia says, tucking her phone away and crossing her legs.

Alisa gives a slow clap, eyeing my long trench coat. "And can we talk about this outfit?"

She knows exactly what I'm hiding under it. If Cillian's here, I'm going to make him regret ever walking away.

"It's so risqué," Natalia adds. "I love it! You're really stepping out of your comfort zone just to spite him, huh?"

I shrug, half smiling. "What's the point of being here if I can't torture him?"

"Hell yeah!" Natalia high-fives me. "And we're finding you a hot guy to make him jealous."

The idea of being with someone else doesn't interest me.

But seeing Cillian jealous? That, I can work with.

The limo stops in front of a random building in the middle of nowhere, a sea of cars filling the parking lot. Pavel opens the door for us.

"See you later, Ms. Marinova," he says with a tip of his hat.

I wave as we head for the entrance, passing through security and stepping into the elevator.

Nerves flood me. Will he be here? Or am I just wasting my time?

When the doors open, I rush out, the girls hot on my heels. I head straight for the coat check, sliding off my coat to reveal the outfit underneath. Cillian's going to lose it when he sees me.

Once through, we make our way into the main room. The smell of liquor and sex hangs in the air, the pulse of sensual music vibrating through the floor.

"Where do you want to go first?" Natalia asks, glancing around the room.

"Let's grab drinks." I nod toward the bar.

We head that way, but my eyes scan the crowd. Disappointment hits when I don't see him, but I push it down, ordering drinks for all of us.

"He'll be here," Alisa murmurs in my ear. "I'm sure of it."

"I don't care," I reply, but it's a lie.

The more time passes, the more I feel like I'm dying inside. I shouldn't care. I know that. But I do. It's a sickness, wanting someone who doesn't want you back.

We wander through the club, slipping in and out of rooms, some filled with people screwing, others tied in more extreme situations.

He's not here. I can't find him anywhere.

"I think I'm done." A sigh escapes me. "We've been here for an hour, and nothing."

"Okay." Natalia throws an arm over my shoulder.

Just as we turn toward the main room, two men approach.

Neither of them is Cillian. They don't walk like him, don't have his size or presence. But they're coming straight for us.

As we try to walk past, one of them places his hand on my hip.

"Hey, gorgeous," he says, his dark eyes probing me up and down. "I've been watching you all night. Just wanted to tell you how—" He stops mid-sentence, his gaze flicking to something behind me.

"I'd get your hand off her if you want to keep it."

A chill shoots up my spine. Every inch of my skin prickles.

It's him.

Cillian.

The guy and his friend back away. "Whoa, didn't realize she was taken."

"I'm not." I turn to glare at Cillian. "He must be confused."

My hand drops to my hip, an eyebrow arched as I take him in.

His eyes? Icy cold. His jaw? Tight with restraint. And his mouth? God, it's so firm, so damn kissable. I want to slap him just for making me want to taste him.

He grabs my hips and pulls my body to his.

"What the hell are you doing here, especially dressed like that?" His tone simmers, and a smile coils my lips.

"Oh, this?" I roll my fingers down the bare center of my chest, only wearing a tight black corset around my stomach with my breasts completely out, nipples covered by two black jewels.

His palm rolls down my back and he grabs a fistful of my ass, barely covered in a pair of tiny black shorts.

"You're going home." His tone is maddening and possessive, and I ache for it. For everything.

Every inch of me burns from his touch, wanting more, but I fight it. He doesn't deserve it after what he did.

"I'm not going anywhere, and if you know what's good for you…" I attempt to pry his hands off me, but they won't budge. "I suggest you get your filthy palms off of me."

His fingers slide up my back, slipping into my hair until he grasps it tight and whispers against my ear, "I thought you liked it when I'm filthy."

My body prickles, my core throbbing, but I try not to show the effect he has on me. "We're done, remember? Or should I remind you?"

He growls, squeezing my ass tighter. "I don't need a reminder. I'm quite aware of who you are and why we can't be together."

His mouth feathers down my throat and my head falls backward, craving everything he gives. I'm weak, and I hate it.

When I look around, I realize it's just us now. I didn't even see the girls leave.

"Then what are you doing here?" I tug at his hair, drawing a deep, primal growl from him as his lips trail down my neck, sending shivers through me.

"I have no idea." His sultry tone hums across my flesh, my skin burning and aching.

"That's great. Let me go, damn it. I have things to do." My continued attempts at escaping him are futile.

His eyes flash to mine, radiating with heat. He grabs my jaw, pinning me to his body. "Like what?"

"Well, you know what they say, right? The best way to get over someone is to get under—"

"Don't fucking finish that sentence, Dinara. I swear to God."

I let out a laugh. "What will you do, hmm? Are you gonna spank me? Dump me? Oh, wait. You did that already."

With both palms, I push at his rock-hard chest.

Is he even human? Clearly not, because he lacks a heart.

"Now let me go and enjoy my evening."

"You can enjoy it with me."

I snicker. "No, thanks. Find someone else to use for sex, because it won't be me."

"That's not what this is." His jaw stiffens.

"Then what is it? Tell me." Anger traces every syllable. "We're done, right? It's over. So leave me the hell alone and let me move on with my life."

"I wish I could…" he whispers, and I almost don't catch it.

But I won't let him do this to me. Make me fall back into this magic we created. I need to face the facts that he doesn't want me anymore.

"I'll make it easy on you, Cillian. We're done. And if you think stopping me from talking to some guy will stop me from talking to the next one, you're crazy. Because guess what?" I lean in close, staring up. "I've already fucked someone else, and he was so much better than you."

In an instant, I'm up against the wall, his hand around my throat, his nostrils flaring.

"What?" His chest flies up and down with deep, growly breaths.

"That's right, baby." My mouth thins into a cocky smile.

"It hasn't even been that long and you just…"

"Guess it didn't take much to get over you."

He grits his teeth, and I swear steam is coming out of his ears. This is too easy.

But a part of me hates hurting him. The part that still cares so much about him.

"Dinara, don't fuck with me."

"What? You suddenly care?" I narrow my gaze. "Because you can't have it both ways. You can't break up with me and then tell me I can't be with anyone else."

"Is that what you think?" He lets out a dry chuckle, inhaling deeply, as if steadying himself.

"You're not being rational."

"Never said I was, leannan."

When he calls me that, when one of his hands gently cups my cheek, something inside me twists. The anger, the pain…it all melts together in a way I can't fight.

Tears threaten, but I refuse to let them fall. The tenderness in his touch reminds me of everything I lost—and everything I can't seem to let go of.

"You expect me to be a spinster for the rest of my life?" My breath hitches as his lips linger just a whisper away from mine, sending a jolt of electricity through me.

"That doesn't sound so bad." The warmth of his breath brushes against me, and a wave of goosebumps blooms across my skin.

"Is that what you're gonna do?" My hands tighten around his biceps, my fingers trembling against the heat of his skin. "You're just going to be alone forever?"

"Nothing will ever come close to what we had, Dinara."

His words hit me like a punch to the gut, freezing the air in my chest. As though he's realized what he said, his eyes lock with mine, a hint of vulnerability there.

"This isn't fair." I shake my head, the tightness in my stomach knotting even more as I try to push him away, as though distance can somehow protect me from this pull.

All I want is for him to tell me he wants to try again, that he wants to fight for us, because no one else can ever make me feel the way he does.

"Fair has nothing to do with it." He slips a hand into my shorts and panties, and I know what he'll find.

"Always so wet for me." He rubs circles around my clit, his husky baritone across my throat setting me ablaze. "Did *he* make you this wet?"

Those talented fingers slide inside me with a deep thrust.

"Did he make you scream like I did?" Another one sends me over the edge. "Did he make you squirt all over his mouth? His cock?"

Oh my God, what is he doing to me? I shouldn't be letting this happen, but I can't stop it either.

"Did you kiss him?" He backs away to stare at me, rage set deep in his irises. "Did you suck his dick?" The fingers around my throat tighten while he finger-fucks me until my eyes roll back. "Answer me."

Pinching my clit, he waits for my reply while a cry dies off in my throat, the sensations he brings out overtaking my entire body.

"Yes." My chin hikes up defiantly as I revel in his jealous state of fury. "I did it all."

He drags my head back until the ache is painfully delicious. "What's his name, Dinara?"

I laugh in a mocking tone. "Fuck off."

A possessed growl escapes from his chest. "I'll find out, baby, and I'm gonna kill him."

Heat coils low in my belly. I'm enjoying his insanity.

"You're mine. You'll always be mine. You won't touch anyone again. Do you understand me?"

My fingers curl around his throat, barely even making it across. "I was never yours, Cillian Quinn, and I never will be."

"Wish that were true."

He drives into me so hard, stars explode before my eyes, the world growing dimmer until all I feel is him. His voice. His touch. Just him.

"I can't get you out of my damn head." His lips near mine, so close I can feel them.

"Maybe that's because you don't want to."

"I fucking want to. I just can't." He grips my hair. "What have you done to me?"

Same thing you did to me.

But I don't tell him that. Let him think I've gotten over him. That this is nothing but sex.

He flips me against the wall, his mouth latching to my throat as he fumbles behind me, like he's undoing his pants until I feel the nudge of his erection against my back.

His fingers return to my center, rubbing me in slow tantalizing circles. "Look how needy you still are for me. I own you."

My hand slides behind me until my fingers are curled around his thick, hard cock. "Look who's talking."

"Fuck, baby. You're the only woman I can ever get hard for now."

The rough timbre of his voice, the heat rolling off him, the unyielding desire in his gaze…it's intoxicating. I want him so badly—not just in this way, but in every way that matters.

I tighten my grip, stroking him faster, desperate to taste him, to unravel him until he's the one begging.

"Dinara…" My name leaves his lips in a rough, guttural sound as his hand wraps around my throat, his other trailing down to rip away my shorts.

I don't care that he's about to fuck me in front of people. It doesn't even cross my mind that we're not alone when I feel him guiding the tip of his erection where I need him most.

My head falls back, a sharp cry escaping as he stretches me, the cool bite of his piercings only amplifying the pleasure.

"You're not wearing a condom."

"Good." He nips at my ear before thrusting into me in one powerful stroke, forcing a gasp from my lips as my trembling hand presses against the wall for support.

"You're not worried?" I wrap the other arm around the back of his neck, desperate to pull him closer, until there's nothing left between us.

"About what?" His teeth sink into my shoulder as his hips slam into me, fingers expertly working my clit while I struggle to find my words.

"That I slept with someone else. That maybe he didn't use a condom either." A moan slips from my lips as he drives into me.

His response is a rough, knowing laugh. "I don't believe you." His lips brush my ear, his pace quickening, relentless, until the pleasure builds to a breaking point, threatening to consume me whole. "I don't think you've fucked anyone. I think this pussy has only ever felt my cock, and that's how it's going to stay."

"Oh God!"

The more he touches me, the harder it is to resist. To keep from giving him exactly what he wants. But I won't. I can't. He needs to believe he means nothing—because, clearly, I never meant enough to him.

"Admit it," he demands, forcing me closer to the edge with expert precision…only to stop, leaving me teetering on the brink of madness.

"Just because you don't wanna hear it…" I breathe. "…doesn't mean it isn't true. I have needs."

"When you have needs, you call me. I'll take care of them."

"I don't want you."

"That's not what your pussy says, soaking my cock like a good, obedient slut."

"Shut up."

Why does he have to say those things? Every word only tightens the grip he already has on me, pulling me deeper into a desire I can't escape.

He chuckles, rubbing me in hurried circles, pounding into me until I lose all ability to speak. "You hate hearing the truth. But just because I've sworn to myself that I'll never love you doesn't mean we can't have *this*."

He thrusts roughly for emphasis, while his words land like a blow and I fight the sharp sting they leave behind.

I want to say something back, but all that comes out is a moan. And when he rams into me this time, a scream dies in my throat. My heart and my mind race, hating this. Hating that I allowed him to have me.

With a growl, he releases inside me, and I feel the warmth spread, marking me, taking me.

But as the euphoria fades and my body begins to relax, I realize what we've done.

He withdraws slowly, his breath hot against my skin, trailing down my neck. As I turn to watch him fasten his pants, a quiet sadness creeps in.

"This is the last time," I whisper as he adjusts his mask.

"Last time, huh?" His knuckles graze my cheek, the warmth of his touch seeping deep into my skin, sending a shiver that should be illegal.

"That's right," I manage, but my tone wavers, betraying me. My lashes flutter, helpless to the power he holds over me.

He draws closer, his breath warm against my lips. "If this is the last time…" His voice is thick with a longing that makes my pulse surge. "May I have a kiss goodbye?"

Every fiber of my being screams for him. His lips hover so close I can feel the heat between us, but I fight to stay still, to hold back, clinging to the fragile distance that remains.

"I don't think you deserve it." My mouth curls defiantly, even as my heart pounds violently, betraying the desperate longing I can't escape.

"Maybe not." His hand grasps my nape, sending an electric jolt through me. "But I'm asking anyway."

The heat in his eyes sears through me and a nervous flutter stirs deep in my gut, leaving me momentarily speechless, caught in the intensity of his gaze.

"Beg." The challenge leaves my lips before I can stop it. "Beg for a kiss."

His laugh, low and rich, rumbles through me, sending shivers down my body. It's like a magnet—impossible to resist and hard to walk away from.

Without warning, he grabs my throat, his thumb pressing against my pulse, and my lungs seize. Every time he touches me like this, it's as if I'm sinking, drowning in him, unable to escape the flood of sensation.

"Please," he breathes. "Let me kiss you just one more time before I let you go."

The rawness in his tone, the way his eyes are locked on mine, makes it hard to say no.

But the truth is, I could never say it. Not to him. Not ever.

"I'll do anything." His words hit like a vow, and I almost want to crumble under the weight of it.

"Anything?" I scoff, though it's hollow. "That's not true, is it?"

You won't be with me. Not like I need.

He exhales a rough sound. "You don't get it, do you?" His voice cracks, raw and desperate. "I would if I could. I just can't."

His pain presses into me, and though anger and sadness churn inside me, I can't shut him out. I can't. Instead, I lean in, brushing my lips against his, just barely a touch—enough to feel the world crack open around us.

"Kiss me," I whisper, though it comes out more like a plea, even as I try to hold on to what little remains of my resolve.

His hands cradle my face, his gaze so intense it feels like he's searching through every corner of my soul, and just like that, everything else fades.

He leans in, slamming his mouth against mine, and the world explodes into flames. His kiss is everything—yearning, wild, desperate. It's the last of us, and we're both starving for it, hands roaming, trying to fill the space between us.

I want it to last forever. I wish it didn't have to be this way. I wish we didn't have to be this: two halves that can't fit anymore, no matter how much we want it. And as tears threaten behind my eyes for what could've been, I let go, losing myself in him one last time.

For one moment, in this kiss, we are us again. Dinara and Cillian, before everything shattered. Before the world tore us apart.

I wish it could be enough. But it isn't.

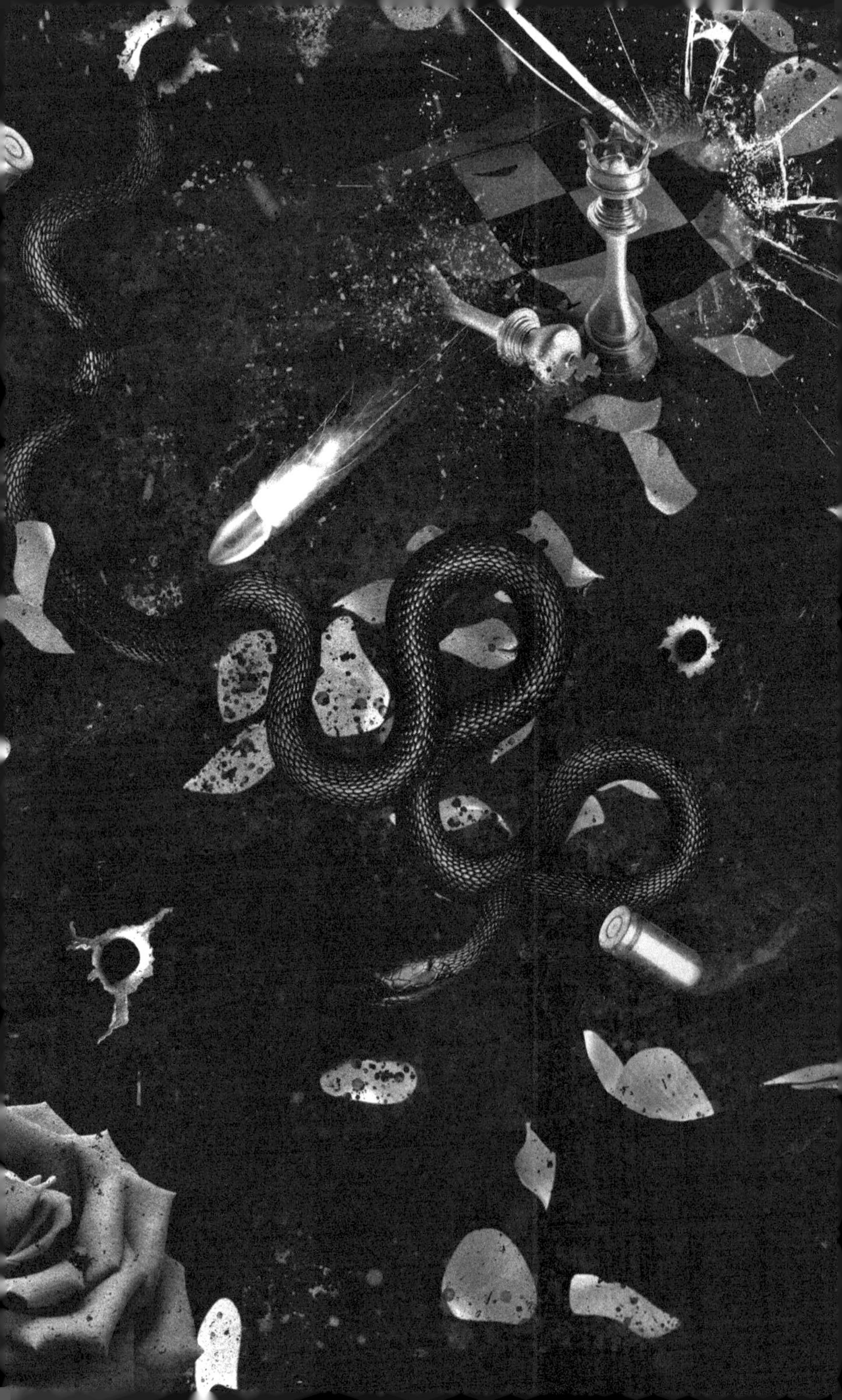

TWENTY

CILLIAN
ONE WEEK LATER

"**W**here are you?" Tynan's voice slices through the phone as I step out of my car, tugging my black hoodie tighter around my face.

"What do you want?" I snap, already on edge.

I don't have time for his shit right now. My focus is on what I came here to do, and I need to finish it fast, without anyone seeing me.

"The meeting starts in ten. Where the fuck are you?" His irritation simmers.

Shit. I forgot about leading the damn investor meeting today. The frustration builds in my chest as I clench my fist at my side.

"It slipped my mind."

"A lot is slipping your mind lately." He exhales sharply like he's losing patience with me. "What the hell is going on? If it's that girl, you need to figure it out, or I'll have the board vote you out."

My jaw tightens; I've heard enough. "Fuck off."

"I'm telling you, don't screw this up again." His words hang in the air, thick with warning.

"Anything else?" I'm barely holding on to my temper.

"Yeah. I need you to go see that councilman, Elias, and have a word with him."

Fucking great. That's all I need right now.

"Why me?"

I can't back out now. After blowing the meeting, I can't afford to say no.

"Because I said so." Tynan's words hold a note of finality. "I'll send you the details."

God damn it.

He may not be the official head of the family, but it's just a technicality. My father made it difficult for him, of course—forcing him to find a wife before he can have the title. But Tynan wants nothing to do with marriage.

The phone buzzes with a text, and I glance down at it, my lips twitching into a grim smile. The councilman's at a restaurant not far from here. It's almost like fate.

"I'll get it done." Heat rises in my veins as I slip the phone back into my pocket.

He doesn't understand the chaos inside my head since I saw her at that club. The way I can't stop thinking about her, can't stop wondering if she's with someone else. The mere thought of it tears at me. The jealousy burns hot, and I let it consume me.

Fixing my sunglasses, I march up the driveway of the house I'm buying, my attention zeroing in on the woman standing by the entrance.

"Mr. Quinn!" She flips her short blonde hair with a wide grin. "You made it."

I barely acknowledge her greeting, tone flat. "Mm-hmm. Let's get this over with. I have places to be."

She falters, but quickly recovers, leading me inside.

"Well, let me show you around first," she insists, though I couldn't care less about any of this. "This beauty has ten bedrooms, twelve bathrooms, a greenhouse, and a tennis court."

She's trying to sound cheerful, but I'm not listening. None of this matters. None of it.

She takes me outside, gesturing to the manicured lawn. "The pool is absolutely gorgeous. And with only six homes in this gated community, it's very quiet and secure, so you'll never have—"

"I'll take it."

She stops in her tracks, blinking in surprise. "But, sir, don't you want to look around some more to be sure?"

"No. I already told you on the phone. I'll take it. Thirty million, right?"

She nods, still stunned.

"Done."

"Uh, okay," she stammers, a nervous laugh escaping. "I've never had such an easy sale before."

"Then you've never met a man desperate enough," I mutter under my breath.

Desperate enough to be near the one woman I can't have. Desperate enough to make sure no one else touches her.

I close my eyes briefly, cursing myself. If it wasn't for her family, things would be different. And I sure as hell wouldn't be spending thirty million on a house I'll barely use just to be near her. But that's the price I have to pay for a past I can't change. And sometimes, that past fucks with your future in ways you never expected.

"Did you say something, sir?" She glances over her shoulder, her eyes flicking to mine.

"I want the keys. Today."

Her unease echoes in the otherwise silent air. "I'm afraid that's not possible. There are still things I have to finalize before I can—"

I step forward, crowding her personal space, my voice low and lethal. "Ms. Rivers, right?"

She tips her chin up defiantly. "That's right."

"Well, Ms. Rivers, you're going to make it happen. I'm not leaving here without those keys. Do we understand each other?"

Fear flashes in her eyes for the briefest moment, but she quickly hides it behind a forced smile.

She pulls at her bright pink suit jacket, fidgeting as she clears her through. "I'll see what I can do. It'll only take a moment to call the owners. I'm sure they'll understand, given the nature of the transaction."

The *nature* she's talking about is cash. Cold, hard cash. I already have the money in the car. I need this done—fast. I can't wait weeks to keep an eye on Dinara, especially after what she said. That she might've been with someone else.

A growl escapes my throat before I can stop it, and her eyes widen in surprise.

"Something in my throat," I mutter, trying to sound casual.

"Oh…okay," she stammers, backing away with a shaky grin. "I'll be right back."

I watch her scurry off, my gaze distant.

The thought of Dinara being next door fills me with a dark sense of satisfaction. There are acres of land between us, but that won't stop me. It actually makes it easier. I can watch her without ever being noticed. I can track her every move, whether she's alone or with someone else.

I didn't hesitate when this property became available. I offered above asking just to secure it. It's perfect. There's nothing she'll do that I won't see. Nothing she can hide from me.

She won't even know I'm here.

If I can't have her, no one can. And that's all there is to it.

A few minutes later, the woman returns, looking pleased.

"Good news, Mr. Quinn. The seller agreed to your stipulation. Once I have the funds and the papers are signed, I can hand you the keys. The rest will be finalized on my end."

"Good." A cold smile tugs at my lips.

Now the real fun begins.

I'm parked a safe distance away, the binoculars steady in my hands as Dinara steps out of her house. Two men flank her, but I don't need to see their faces to know they're her bodyguards. I pull out my phone, my fingers tight as I call Grant.

"Cillian, what's up?"

"I need a favor," I mutter.

He laughs dryly. "Let me guess. Trouble again?"

"This is important." My eyes track her as she climbs into her car, the bodyguards getting into the SUV behind her.

"Yeah, yeah. It's always important. What do you need?"

"I need you to disable an alarm just in case it's on. One of yours."

"Oh, that's it?" He snickers. "I swear I need to start screening all your calls."

"Can you do it or not?"

My patience is thinner than paper. She's leaving soon, and I need to move fast. If I know Konstantin, he'll have her turn on the alarm even with the staff in the house. Can never be too careful.

"Whose place is it?"

"It doesn't matter. I also need access to her phone. One of yours too."

Grant mutters something under his breath—probably regretting ever becoming friends with us. It's no one's fault but his that he's a tech genius, running Westfield Enterprises, which creates AI tech and all kinds of other shit.

I can almost hear the click of his keyboard as he starts working. "Alright. Give me the address, and I'll take care of it."

I send it to him, and fifteen minutes later, I'm in her house, slipping in through a back entrance, keeping my movements quiet. Grant gives me a code to bypass the alarm and tells me what app to download to track her cellphone activity, another one of his creations.

"Better not hurt her," he warns.

I let out a heavy sigh. "The last thing I want is to hurt her. If I wanted her dead, it'd be easier."

"Lucky girl." He scoffs. "Call if you need help."

I hang up, my phone heavy in my pocket as I adjust my sunglasses and force myself to blend in. I can't afford a mistake.

Making my way upstairs, I try to figure out where her room is. I open the first door, finding a generic bedroom with blue walls and white bedding. Not hers. I check the next two rooms: a bathroom, another guest bedroom.

Fuck!

But I can't give up. I keep moving, until I finally find it. Her room. The bed is large: cream upholstery with lacy white curtains and pink-and-yellow floral bedding. But it's not the décor that gives it away. It's the scent. That sweet floral perfume.

Walking over to her vanity, I pick up the bottle, bringing it up to my nose and inhaling. I close my eyes, trying to feel her presence, to pretend she's right here with me. But when I stare back, all I find is the emptiness around me.

My anger festers.

What the hell am I doing? Breaking into her house, stalking her. What the fuck is wrong with me? When did I become this guy?

But I can't seem to stop myself either.

Moving toward her hamper, I find her clothes, a pair of black panties lying right on top. I let myself feel the thin scrap of fabric, my cock throbbing at the mere thought of her wearing a strappy thong and nothing else.

My pulse jerks as I grab them and bring them to my nose, the smell of her pretty cunt invading my nostrils.

I miss her smell. I miss the way her eyes sparkled like stars when she looked at me. I miss everything about her.

God, Dinara, I wish this was easy. I wish I could say fuck it all and have you.

As I run a hand down my face, frustration sets in. I hate myself for not being able to just forget what happened to Mom.

But I won't betray her. I can't. As long as I live, Dinara and I will be nothing.

Except you're in her house, smelling her panties like a psycho. So what does that make you, asshole?

Stuffing the panties in my pocket, I walk over to her bed and settle on top of it.

Grabbing one of her pillows, I inhale the scent that still lingers. Jasmine, maybe? If I could, I'd drown in it. In her.

But I can't stay here forever.

Blowing a breath, I get to my feet, returning the pillow where it was before running my hand over the comforter so it's as neat as it was when I came here.

When I return to the vanity, I grab the perfume bottle, promising myself I'll replace it. I can't leave without it. I need something that smells like her. I need something to hold on to.

I don't care if she realizes I was here. That I took something of hers. Let her know I'll never let her go, no matter how sick and depraved that makes me.

Removing a small listening device, I set it up with my phone. But when I try to get it to work, I realize it's useless. Konstantin must have a block installed around her perimeter.

Damn it. This will make spying on her a little complicated. At least I'll still be able to track her cell activity thanks to Grant.

I stuff the device back in my pocket, ready to leave, but footsteps on the other side of the door stop me.

Shit!

I slip into the walk-in closet, shutting the door softly behind me. Heavy footfalls stop right outside her room before the door opens and someone walks inside. With my hand on the Glock at my waistband, I ready for a fight if it comes to it.

"Net!" a voice calls. It's the chef—the one I almost killed. "I'm not doing it. Stop calling, okay? I need to go."

What the hell is that about?

I stay quiet, listening as his footsteps fade away and the door shuts behind him.

Once I'm sure he's gone, I slip out, heading back down the stairs. I nearly bump into a cleaning lady, but she just nods and keeps moving, oblivious to my presence.

I can't believe how easy this is. I'd love to rub it in Konstantin's face, but I can't let him find out what I'm doing.

Leaving the way I came, I return to my car parked down the block. Once I'm back at my own place, I set up the app on my phone, finding her browser open. No texts yet. But I'll be ready. When she starts sending them, I'll have it all.

There won't be a single thing she does without me knowing about it. I'll make sure of that.

TWENTY-ONE

CILLIAN

Standing outside the restaurant, knowing Elias is still inside, I wait for him to exit so we can have a nice chat. Shouldn't take too long to scare the shit out of him into giving the permits to the Russians. Helping them is the last thing I want to do, but doubling our order like Konstantin said he would isn't a bad deal in exchange for setting some idiot straight.

When he gets out, heading toward the parking lot, I'm instantly behind him.

"Elias."

He gasps, turning my way, a nervous grin on his face. "Cillian, hey. Shit, you scared me. What…uh…are you doing here?"

"We need to talk. Now."

"Can it wait? I have to get home." He laughs. "You know how the wife is if I'm late."

"No, it can't. We have business to discuss."

He fixes his red tie. "Do you want to go back to the restaurant so we can—"

"My car. Let's go." I shove at his back without drawing attention. When we make it to my vehicle, I open the passenger side. "Get in."

As soon as he's settled, I round toward the driver's side and slide in, locking the doors.

"So, what's this about?" he asks, keeping his voice steady, though I wonder if he's shitting his pants yet. He knows what we're capable of.

I put the car in drive and head back to my house, needing more privacy.

"I'll let you know once we're back at my place. I don't discuss business openly."

"Yeah, I get it. I just want to make sure we're okay. I have a lot of respect for your family and our relationship has benefited both of us."

"It has. Let's hope it stays that way."

We make it to my house in silence, and as soon as I get out, he follows.

"This is a nice place you've got here." He looks around the ivory brick home.

"It's new. Just got it today."

"Congratulations."

"Mm-hmm." I let him inside and the door bangs shut.

Stuffing his hands in his pants pockets, he shuffles a step just as I point him in the direction I want him in.

"Take a seat." I gesture toward one of the stools around the kitchen island, choosing to stand over him instead. "I'll cut to the chase. We need you to stop standing in the way of the permits the Russians need."

He chuckles smugly. "Look, I said the same thing to Konstantin. What he's asking for will take a lot of finesse, and for that, I require something more for my efforts." He shrugs. "It's not my fault he didn't like the deal I proposed."

"What deal?"

"It was simple. Three million, and a night with that girl. That's all I wanted. When I even suggested it, one of his brothers almost killed me."

He keeps talking but all I hear is *girl*.

"What girl? What the hell are you talking about?"

His forehead creases with thick lines, showing his age, a good twenty years older than me. "Dinara, I think her name was. Pretty thing. You should—"

But he never gets to finish that sentence. My hand's around his throat, a gun pointed between his brows.

"You wanted to fuck Dinara?" I'm barely able to get the words out, heart racing, blood pumping in my brain, breathing like a madman.

He thinks he can touch her?

"I-I…uh, it was just a suggestion. I'm sorry. I didn't know you knew her." Fear pierces through his tone, his eyes filled with pure dread.

"A suggestion?!" I howl. "Did you fucking *touch* her?" I dig the muzzle in deeper. "Answer me!"

The grip of the butt strikes him in the jaw, and he groans in pain, blood spilling from his bottom lip.

"No, no!" He raises his hands in the air, while my other hand tightens around his throat. "I just saw her once a-and I liked her. I'm sorry! I'll tell him I'll accept the money. We're good, okay? We're good."

"You're a sick fuck, you know that?" I aim the gun back to his head. "You'll never touch her. And after today, you won't even have the pleasure of thinking about her. Do you understand what I'm saying, Elias?"

"Oh, fuck! Nonono! Please, please, please. Don't do this, okay?" He clasps his hands in prayer. "I'm sick. I-I know. I shouldn't have asked for that. It's wrong. I'll never—"

Pop.

He falls to the floor instantly, blood pooling around his head, eyes staring at the ceiling.

The rage still floods my system. To think he thought he could have her… I spit at him, curling a fist, regretting that I didn't torture him before I ended him. But I just couldn't listen to him anymore.

Why the fuck didn't Konstantin mention what Elias wanted in exchange? I would've killed him on the spot.

Removing my cell, I call him, the phone ringing a few times before his voice comes through.

"Cillian, what a pleasure it is to hear from you. How can I help you, my brother?"

I ignore the brother part and cut right to the chase. "Why the fuck didn't you tell me what he wanted in exchange for the permit?"

"Ah, so you spoke to him." There's a hint of amusement laced in his tone.

"I did. Tell me why you didn't say shit."

"Because…I wanted to see what you would do once you found out on the spot." He pauses. "What *did* you do?"

"What do you think I did?"

He chuckles. "Oh, Cillian, Cillian. You know, it's a shame we won't get to be a family. Of all the men I could choose, I would choose you for her. Every time."

Pressing two fingers into my temple, I take a deep breath. What the hell do I even say to that? I can't admit what she means to me, though I'm sure he already knows.

"Next time, you'd better tell me."

He sighs. "Look, if you don't want her, then she's not your responsibility. You leave her protection to me, and you? Well, you find someone else to make you happy. You let her go once and for all."

Does he know what happened at the club? Is that why he's saying this shit?

Unfortunately for me, there's no one else. Never will be. I'm royally fucked.

"Yeah, thanks for the advice. Why don't you take your own?"

His laugh is low and contemplative. "That isn't in my future. The last thing I want is a woman to complicate my already complicated life. Do you know what I mean?" He snickers. "Of course you do. Well, good day, my friend, and please accept my sincere gratitude in getting rid of the problem."

He drops the call, and I shake my head at the mess in my kitchen.

Nothing like christening the new place with a little blood. Or a lot, in my case.

TWENTY-TWO

DINARA

Getting out of my car, I glance over my shoulder, an eerie sensation crawling up my spine. It feels as though someone's watching me, and I can't shake the unease settling in my chest.

My footsteps falter as I climb the stairs, heading toward the safety of my front door. I tell myself it's fine. No one can get to me here. Konstantin makes sure of that. He has eyes everywhere. If anyone tries anything, he will make them pay.

But at what cost? Who else would have to die just to protect me?

Am I even worth it? I couldn't protect my own mother. Why do I deserve protection?

With a sigh, I step inside, shedding my shoes and coat before heading straight up to my room. It was nice to see Natalia and Alisa earlier, but all I really want right now is to curl up in bed, surrounded by memories of Cillian. The photos from that weekend we spent in New York are all I have left, and looking at them breaks me every time. We were so happy then. But that feels like a lifetime ago.

The moment I collapse onto the mattress, I bury my face in the pillow, but then…something hits me. The unmistakable scent of *him*.

For a moment, I think I'm imagining it. My mind is playing tricks on me, conjuring his presence when he's not here. I even thought I saw him earlier—some guy in a hoodie and sunglasses, staring at me across the street—but when I looked back, he was gone.

Great. I've officially lost my mind.

But as I inhale deeply, the unmistakable scent fills my senses, and I know it's real. I'm not crazy.

Or maybe I am…

But how can this be? Cillian wouldn't have come here. He couldn't have gotten in.

I laugh to myself and grab the pillow, walking into the hallway to find someone from the cleaning staff.

When I spot one, I call out to her. "Lena, can you help me with something?"

She looks up, her blonde hair pulled tightly into a neat ponytail.

"Of course, Ms. Marinova. What do you need?" Her Russian accent isn't as thick as the others.

"Can you smell this pillow and tell me what it smells like?"

Her eyes widen, concern flashing across her face. "Is something wrong with it?"

"Oh, no, no. It's not that," I reassure her quickly. "I know this sounds strange, but I broke up with this guy, and I swear I smell his cologne on my pillow. I just need to know if I'm losing my mind, or if you can smell it too."

She hesitates, then leans in, inhaling softly. Her eyes widen even more.

"You smell it, don't you?" I ask, a mix of disbelief and relief flooding me.

She nods, her lips parting in surprise. "Yes."

"I knew it!" I exhale, my heart racing.

"Do you want me to tell Mr. Marinov?" she asks, her tone a little hesitant.

"No!" I raise a hand quickly. "This stays between us. Please."

"As you wish," she responds before backing away and disappearing down the hall.

I return to my room, my mind spinning with questions. If he was here, what does it mean? Why would he come? Does he miss me? Or is he just playing games?

Then my eyes land on my vanity, and I freeze.

My perfume. It's gone.

"What the hell?"

I walk closer, checking the drawers to see if I misplaced it. But no. It's gone.

Cillian took my perfume? What for?

A rush of anxiety floods me as I pull out my phone and start typing a message to Natalia and Alisa, desperate to share what I just discovered.

DINARA

Okay, are you guys sitting down? Because I swear Cillian was in my room. My perfume is missing, and I smell his cologne on my pillow.

NATALIA

WHAT?! No fucking way!

ALISA

That's crazy! Can you look at the security cameras?

DINARA

I can, but I don't want Konstantin to find out.

I'm going to install a nanny cam in my room, though, just to see if I can catch him here again.

NATALIA

Then what? Are you going to confront him?

DINARA

Maybe?

ALISA

He's clearly still obsessed with you.

DINARA

So much good that does. He can be as obsessed as he wants, but since he won't be with me, it doesn't matter.

A throbbing hits my chest. I miss him so much it physically hurts.

ALISA

I hope he comes to his senses soon.

NATALIA

No, screw him! Stop pining over him and get back out there. I'm sure he isn't wasting any time.

The thought of going out with some other guy doesn't sound appealing.

DINARA

Yeah, yeah. Gotta go.

NATALIA

You know I'm right. You can't waste your
hot years on some guy who dumped you
like you meant nothing.

Ouch.

DINARA

I know, but I'm not ready to move on.

ALISA

I understand.

NATALIA

I guess I do too. I just hate seeing you
sad. That's all.

DINARA

I'm not sad. I'm bitter. I think there's a
difference in there somewhere.

NATALIA

Don't think so.

DINARA

Yeah, whatever.

ALISA

Let us know if he comes back!

DINARA

I will.

NATALIA

Love you.

DINARA
Back at ya both.

I rise from the bed, grabbing the pillow again, and press my face into it, inhaling deeply.

His scent still lingers, and for a moment, I almost convince myself that he's here, lying beside me. But I know he's never coming back.

Natalia's words echo in my mind. She's right. Eventually, I'll have to move on. The thought of moving on feels impossible right now, but maybe she's right. It doesn't have to happen today.

I pull myself together, grab my phone, and head downstairs, hoping a snack will distract me. I didn't eat much earlier while I was out with the girls, my appetite lost in the swirl of emotions that have been consuming me.

As I enter the kitchen, Lenny is busy mixing a bowl of Olivier salad. He looks up and gives me a quick nod.

"Ms. Marinova," he greets me. "Can I get you something to eat?"

"Please."

"Salad okay? I also made shashliki." He glances at me briefly before quickly averting his eyes, his usual way of avoiding direct contact.

I suspect it's out of respect—or fear of Konstantin. I've never asked about their history, but I know there's one there.

"Salad's fine, thank you."

Lenny turns his back to me, taking a bowl from the cabinet and serving me a generous portion. He hands it to me along with a fork, his gaze still not meeting mine.

"Thank you."

He nods before retreating out of view.

I head to the fridge for a bottle of water, hoping it'll help clear my mind. But before I can reach it, Sonya's voice rings out behind me.

"Ms. Marinova, what are you doing? I can get that for you."

Laughing lightly, I turn to face her, already holding the bottle in my hand. "Sonya, I can get my own water."

"I know." She shrugs, a small, almost uncomfortable smile flickering across her face. As I sit down, she glances at my plate, her eyes narrowing. "That doesn't look like enough food. You need meat. Let me get you some."

I shake my head, pulling the bowl closer to me. "No, I just wanted the salad."

Her smile falters for a brief moment, something unreadable passing through her expression. It's so quick, I almost miss it.

She recovers almost immediately, though, and waves it off. "No, no. Salad's no good. I'll get you something else."

She grabs my bowl and moves toward the fridge with purpose, her back to me for a few seconds.

"Sonya, really, I'm fine with the salad," I insist.

Her laugh is quick and hollow, as if she's trying to fill the awkward space between us. "Sorry, I don't know what came over me."

She starts toward me again, but just as she lowers the bowl back down, it slips from her hands. The ceramic shatters against the counter, pieces flying everywhere.

"Oh God!" I jump back as shards scatter across the kitchen.

"I'm so sorry! I'm an idiot," Sonya exclaims. "Let me clean this up quickly, and I'll make you another bowl, okay?"

"Yeah, sure," I mutter, still shaken.

She calls in help, and within ten minutes, the mess is cleaned up and a fresh bowl is placed in front of me. But even as I begin to eat, I can't shake the strange feeling gnawing at me.

Something feels off, and I have no idea what to do with that.

CILLIAN

I didn't expect her to install a camera in her room, but it doesn't change my plans. I don't need to go into her bedroom. I've already got what I came for: the perfume bottle that's always beside my bed, her panties right next to it.

I take a drag of the cranberry vodka, letting the cool liquid burn its way down my throat, then close my eyes. My mind drifts back to the night we met, when she drank the same drink. The way she lit up the room. How perfect she was.

How perfect she still is.

Leaning back into the sofa in the sitting room at Tynan's, I register the sound of the door opening in the distance.

My family's starting to trickle in for dinner, and if I didn't have to be here, I wouldn't be. But we all show up for these dinners, no matter what. No escaping it.

I take my time finishing my drink, not in the mood for the small talk that's inevitably coming. They're going to start asking about Dinara, and I can't deal with that right now.

Then I hear the familiar click of high heels and look up to find Iseult striding in.

"What are you doing here all alone?" she asks, dropping onto the love seat across from me and crossing one leg over the other.

"Hiding," I mutter, the bitterness in my laugh matching the tightness in my chest.

"I get it. Our family can be a lot sometimes." She watches me for a few long seconds. "Are you okay? Fionn told me."

I just shrug.

She exhales, dragging out the breath like she's measuring her words. "I'm not great with advice, and I know Mom's death messed us all up in different ways, but I don't want to see you sabotage your happiness."

I rub my face, the feeling of disgust creeping in. Disgust at myself for letting it get this far, for letting Dinara get under my skin this much.

"I can't be with her, but I can't be without her either."

"I can see where you have a problem," she says with a light chuckle.

"What the hell am I supposed to do, Iseult?" My voice cracks, the frustration thick in my chest.

She leans back, studying me like I'm some puzzle she's trying to figure out. "I don't know. But you'll have to decide, because this whole mopey, brooding thing?" She gestures at me with a flick of her hand. "Not working for you."

"Yeah, thanks for the insight," I grumble dryly.

"I'm only half kidding," she says, letting out a short laugh.

I exhale sharply. "What would you do? Could you just get over it if Gio's father or uncle killed our mother?"

Her face tightens, her mouth forming a thin line as she thinks. "Honestly? I don't know. And that's the truth. But you have to decide. Either move on or find a way to be with her. Because if you don't figure it out, it's going to eat you alive."

"Feels like it already is."

She snickers. "Looks like it too." Standing up, she stretches, as though ready to move on from this conversation. "Come on, let's go. Being alone isn't going to help you."

I shake my head. "Neither is the inquisition I'm about to face out there."

"Don't worry." She drapes an arm around me as we head toward our family. "I'll scare them into silence."

I can't help but laugh. "Yeah, I believe you."

TWENTY-THREE

DINARA

The next day, Sonya approaches me as I grab my handbag from the foyer, ready to head out to see a movie with Tatiana and Gregory, who are already waiting for me in the car.

"There's a package for you, Ms. Marinova." She holds out a small brown box.

"I'll open it," Boris says, taking it from her. He removes a flip knife from his keychain and slices the tape.

As he pulls the contents free, my breaths falter.

A perfume box—the same scent I wear. The one Cillian stole from me.

He got me another one.

A throb spreads through my chest, heavy and bittersweet. I hate that he had to steal the first bottle. I hate that we can't be normal. That we can't just be us.

My fingers draw over the sleek packaging, wanting to smash the perfume across the floor.

I picture his face, the way he would've looked as he gave this to me. Like a normal boyfriend. I would've sprayed a little and he'd have leaned in, dragging his nose up my throat as he inhaled it off my skin.

But no. He stays in the shadows, and I stay behind this invisible line he's drawn between us.

I clutch the box tighter, swallowing the lump in my throat. I'm surprised he didn't just break in again and leave it on my pillow. Would've been nice to catch him on camera this time. Would've been nice to see him at all.

"Could you bring it to my room?" I ask Sonya, needing it away from me before I really do smash it to pieces.

"Of course. I hope you all have fun!"

She waves goodbye as I head out with Boris, opening the back of his SUV, with Artem waiting in the passenger seat. As soon as I'm inside, we set off. Gregory, absorbed in a show on his tablet, barely notices as Tatiana shifts closer, her eyes flicking to mine.

"I need to tell you something." Her voice is thick with tension.

Instantly, I sit up straighter.

"What's wrong?" I whisper, not wanting Gregory to hear.

"I got a text this morning."

My brows furrow. "From who?"

She leans in and whispers, "Papa."

All the blood drains from my face.

"What?" I attempt to control the panic. "What did he say?"

She hands me her phone, and I open the message, reading it over and over as a wave of dread crashes over me.

DAD

I miss you, Moya Tanushka. Your brother too. I will have you home very soon. I promise.

We will be a real family again. You will see.

He'll have them home soon? What the hell does that mean? Is he planning to take them?

My pulse hammers in my temples. I need to tell Konstantin about this as soon as we're done here. This is not something I can keep from him, especially if my father's plans against Konstantin may be escalating.

"I don't want to go with him." Tatiana's words tremble out, and I notice the tears threatening to spill. "I want to stay with Konstantin."

"I know." I pull her into a tight hug. "I won't let him take either one of you. Don't worry."

As I hold her, Gregory's voice pulls me back to reality.

"Is Papa bad?" he asks, his innocent eyes searching mine.

I freeze. What do I even say to him?

I try to answer the best way I can. "He's done bad things, buddy. That's why we don't live with him."

Gregory nods seriously. "Was Mama bad too?"

My face contorts in disbelief, and I take his small hand in mine, squeezing it gently. "No, of course not. Mama was the best."

"I don't remember her." His face cracks with sadness, and it shatters me.

"I'm sorry, bud." I pull him close. "But I want you to know she loved you so much. Every second of every day."

He wraps his arms around me. "I don't want to go with Papa either."

The words break my heart. He shouldn't have to be burdened with any of this. He's just too little.

"I'll never let that happen. You and Tatiana will always be with me, even if I'm not always right there with you." I tilt his chin up. "Understand?"

He nods, his dark eyes softening.

"Good. Now, who's ready for the movie?" I try to lighten the mood.

"Me!" Gregory exclaims, his excitement returning as we pull into the theater parking lot.

As we step out of the SUV, I glance around, my eyes scanning the lot. I can't shake the feeling that my father and brother might be lurking somewhere, waiting for their chance to strike.

After dropping Tatiana and Gregory off, I make my way to Konstantin's study, where Ludmilla said he'd be.

I knock, and his invitation comes through, sharp and clear.

"Come in."

Taking a steadying breath, I turn the doorknob and walk inside. Konstantin isn't alone; he's there with his three brothers.

"How are you, Din?" Kirill asks, his face taut, his fists cracking in a way that only hints at his anger. He hasn't been thrilled about how much Cillian hurt me.

"I'm fine." I flash a smile, hoping it masks the unease inside me.

I know him well enough to know he's looking for any excuse to go after Cillian for ending things with me.

Before I can say more, Konstantin interrupts, his voice calm, though there's an edge beneath it. "Ludmilla said you needed to talk to me."

"Yes." My throat tightens as I step closer, my nerves pressing down on me.

"Sit." Konstantin gestures to the empty chair in front of his desk, while his brothers lounge on the black leather sofas flanking the room.

I take the seat, my heart racing despite the familiarity of the surroundings. But I can't shake the anxiety, especially as they all stare at me.

"So, what's going on?" The intensity in his tone is palpable.

I take a deep breath and lean forward, trying to steady myself. "Tatiana told me that our father texted her this morning."

The muscles in Konstantin's face strain as he leans back in his leather chair. "Did he now? And what exactly did he say?"

I swallow hard. "He said he missed her and that he'll take Gregory and her back very soon so they can be a family again."

Aleksei lets out a low, dark chuckle. "We need to find that rat and kill him. I'm tired of this cat-and-mouse game they're playing."

Konstantin's icy smile flickers. "We'll deal with them. Slowly. Painfully. But in the meantime…" His lips curl into something like a grin, but it's more dangerous than reassuring. "We send a message. A very effective one."

"What kind of message?" I ask, the words barely a whisper.

"We destroy everyone who works for them. We strip away their power until all that's left is those two svolichy." His fingers curl into fists, knuckles turning white. "They won't be able to hide for long."

A chill runs down my flesh.

"You don't need to worry about this," Konstantin attempts to reassure me. "Leave everything to me."

I nod, though fear pushes down on me.

"You can go now. But if anything else comes up, let me know."

I stand and say my goodbyes, the coldness in the room lingering long after I leave.

The SUV is waiting for me outside, but I don't feel any relief. The thought of leaving Tatiana and Gregory behind twists in my stomach.

As Artem helps me into the backseat, the weight of what's coming crushes down on me. The war between my father and Konstantin is unavoidable—and it's the aftermath that fills me with a paralyzing dread.

TWENTY-FOUR

DINARA

The past couple of weeks have been unnervingly quiet. No updates on my father or any hints of what Konstantin might be doing with his men—not that he'd ever share that with me.

But the hardest part has been the absence of Cillian.

No cologne lingering in the air after a surprise visit. No trace of him at all. I want that again. Something, anything, to hold on to. But it's just emptiness now, a gnawing ache that never seems to fade. It sits in my chest, invisible but constant, a reminder of everything I once had and lost.

I tried texting him after he bought me the perfume, but he never responded. It stung to be ignored like that, even knowing he's been inside my house—either because he cares or because he misses me. Or maybe he's just insane. Whatever the reason, it doesn't change how much I wish he was here.

Letting out a deep sigh, I glance at the time on my phone as the

SUV rolls over a few pebbles with Boris's turn. He and Artem are taking me to the coffee shop to meet Natalia and Alisa.

Given everything that's happening, I'd rather have them driving me around than trailing behind me. It's not just paranoia; it's reality. I know all too well what my father is capable of.

We walk inside, and they head for an empty table while I head for the girls, who wave as soon as they see me.

"Hey, guys."

"Hey, you." Natalia's eyes scan me with a mix of amusement and judgment. "Why didn't you dress up? Leggings and a sweatshirt? Come on, Dinara. You're not even *trying* to attract the opposite sex."

I roll my eyes. "Exactly. What I'm trying to attract is caffeine."

I grab the menu, searching for a latte option, but I catch a look between the girls. A look that doesn't sit right with me.

"What was that?" I narrow my eyes at Natalia, already knowing that if there's trouble, she's at the center of it.

Before she can answer, the waitress arrives. I order a vanilla latte and a chocolate croissant, my eyes still fixed on the girls, sensing something's up. When she leaves, I lean in closer.

"So, what's really going on here?"

Alisa bites her lip, while Natalia's smile turns devious.

"Remember, I only do things because I love you," Natalia says.

"What the hell does that mean—"

Before I can finish, a guy's voice cuts through. "Nat!"

Two others follow behind, pulling up chairs and sitting with us.

My blood freezes.

"What the hell is this, Nat?" I whisper, my voice sharp with disbelief.

She meets my glare with a tight one of her own. "Boys, this is my hot cousin, Dinara. The one I told you about. Just got out of a breakup, so be gentle with her." Her gaze locks on to the guy who's about to sit next to me.

I can't believe she did this. The last thing I want right now is small talk with someone I'll never see again. What a waste of time.

"I'm Ace. Nice to meet you." He smirks, a little too confidently.

He's tall, lean—attractive, I guess—but there's no spark. Not the way Cillian has always made my heart beat faster.

And there it is. That rush of thoughts about him.

Where is he? What's he doing? Who's he with?

A pang of jealousy stabs at me, sharp and bitter. I don't want to think about him moving on, falling in love with someone else. Not that he ever loved me.

"I'm not dating," I say quickly.

"She's not dating *yet*," Natalia adds, grinning.

Ace laughs, but it's too cocky. "That's fine. We don't have to date. We can get to know each other in other ways."

His hand brushes my knee, making the hairs on the back of my neck stand on end. I shove his hand away, glaring.

"Don't touch me."

He raises both palms in mock surrender. "Sorry. You're just so pretty."

"That doesn't give you permission to touch me."

His eyes slide over me, and I feel exposed. It's like his gaze strips me bare, and I want to crawl out of my skin.

"I need to use the restroom."

"Do you want us to come with?" Natalia calls after me.

"Nope. You've done enough." I narrow my eyes as I start walking toward the restroom.

But as soon as I turn the corner toward the ladies' room, the hairs on the back of my neck stand straight. A sharp inhale stutters through me, and I feel it settle deep.

He's right behind me.

"Tell him to leave, Dinara." His voice is rough, his arm curling around my front and pulling me into his chest.

His presence washes over me like a wave, disorienting and warm all at once. I should be angry at him, but the truth is, there's nothing more comforting than the way he touches me.

"Why should I do that?" My fingers trail up his forearm as I let myself feel him again. Feel his heat, his presence.

"Because if you don't, I won't be able to control what I do to him."

A sardonic laugh escapes my lips. "I thought I told you at the club, you can't tell me what to do. Did you forget?"

A growl vibrates against my neck as his lips hover right up against my pulse. "Get rid of him, Dinara. I won't ask again."

"I don't take orders from you," I whisper, fighting the need to melt into his touch.

The way he feels against me…every part of me aches for more.

"We'll see about that." His fingers trail up my thigh, teasing me in places where I ache for him.

"I'm glad you got my gift." His words are a low rumble across my skin, his lips ghosting over the sensitive spot behind my ear.

A shiver betrays me before I can stop it.

"Thanks for ignoring my text." I exhale sharply, but it almost sounds like a moan.

"It's better that way." But he doesn't even sound sure.

"Really?" I turn my head just enough to catch the flicker of something dark in his eyes. "Is this better too? You stalking me like some desperate little puppy?"

Cillian doesn't answer. He just watches me, jaw clenched, pulling me in, pressing my back flush against his firm chest.

The heat of him, the hard lines of his muscles against mine… It's maddening. It's exactly what I don't want to feel.

"Can't seem to get over me, huh?" I taunt, my voice steady even when I don't feel grounded or whole.

My hand slides behind me, fingers grazing down his stomach, lower…finding him hard and wanting. I squeeze him, reveling in the way he groans in response, his grip on me tightening.

"I wish it was that easy," he growls, thick with frustration. "All I want is to get over you."

The words cut deep. Deeper than I expect. I force myself to swallow down the sting, to keep my face cold, unaffected.

I tilt my head slightly, my lips almost brushing his jaw. "Then do it."

He stills. I can feel the war inside him. The way his fingers twitch against my skin. The way his inhales turn ragged. For a moment, it feels like we're teetering on the edge of something dangerous. Something inevitable.

But I can't let this happen.

"Leave me alone, Cillian." I flip around to face him all the way. "Whatever this is, I'm done with it."

When I try to walk away, he catches my wrist, curling an arm around my back.

His lips draw nearer, breaths hot against my lips, and for one traitorous second, every part of me wants to melt into him.

I wish forgetting you was easy too.

When he wrenches away, I grind my jaw, and he groans.

"Dinara. I'm sorry. I just—"

"You just what?" I laugh, but there's no humor in it, only sharp edges and exhaustion. "Want to have your cake and eat it too? This isn't fair. To either of us."

Agony flashes across his face before it turns into something darker. "What's fair has never been part of the equation, leannan. If it was, you'd be mine."

Every piece of my soul tears wide open.

"I could be." My fingers slip into his, trembling, desperate. "But you won't let me."

His breath is shallow, uneven, every exhale burning against my skin.

"This has been the hardest thing I've ever done," he whispers in a raw and broken way. "Walking away from you. Pretending I don't want you every second of the damn day. I swear, Dinara, I feel like I'm bleeding out."

He presses a kiss to my forehead for just a moment—just long enough for me to feel the wreckage in him, the same one tearing through me. When he pulls away, the loss is immediate, like something inside me has been ripped out.

I turn my back to him, inhaling shakily and fighting to stay upright, to keep the flood of emotions inside where they belong. I refuse to fall apart in front of him.

But when I finally gather the courage to look at him again, he's gone. Like he was never there at all.

That's when the tears come. I rush into the bathroom, staring at the broken girl in the mirror, the one I no longer even recognize.

No more. I can't go on like this. He doesn't get to control me. Doesn't get to own my emotions anymore.

Except...my heart.

That's been his since the moment he came into my life.

Grabbing a napkin, I clean up the last of the pain, and a few minutes later, I return to the table, finding the guy I'd been forced to talk to gone.

"There you are. Are you okay?" Concern threads through Natalia's features.

"Fine. Where'd what's-his-name go?"

His friends laugh, and one of them responds, "Someone slashed his car tires. He went to call his dad."

A faint smile tugs at the corner of my mouth.

Cillian.

TWENTY-FIVE

THREE MONTHS LATER

Every time her friends try to set her up with someone new, I'm there. Lurking in the shadows. Ruining any chance she has to move on.

I know it's messed up. Twisted, even. But then again, I never claimed to be sane.

She's mine. Every inch of her. Every breath. Every thought. It's all mine. Even when I can't have her. Even when I shouldn't.

It's a kind of hunger that gnaws at me relentlessly. A desperation so deep, I can taste it on the back of my tongue. And if that makes me a bastard, so be it.

The days blur together. I go through the motions, but every moment is consumed by thoughts of her. Every woman I pass, every voice I hear, every whisper of a scent in the air…it's all her.

She's everywhere, yet she's nowhere.

Not with me.

Even when I watch her, close enough to touch, I can't get close enough to feel her skin against mine.

I can't stop. It's an obsession. A sickness. She's embedded in my marrow, a disease I can't shake off.

I'm back in Massachusetts, sitting in the dark, crushing my phone in my hand while I stare at the screen, my breath shallow.

I watch her respond to messages from men on some dating site. It's like she's trying to force herself to forget me, to let someone else take my place. But she can't. And neither can I.

My blood boils with rage, so thick I can almost taste the venom. I intercept every message, every conversation, before it has a chance to go anywhere. I reach out to them and I make it clear: they stop talking to her, or they won't live to see another day.

They block her. One by one. While she probably thinks something's wrong with her.

But it's me. It's always been me.

I should feel bad. I should feel guilty. But I don't.

I recall the text she sent her cousin a few weeks ago, telling her she wanted to move on. She's trying. I know she is.

But it's too bad. Because I won't let her go. Not now. Not ever.

DINARA

What the hell am I doing wrong? Every guy I try to talk to ends up blocking me after a few messages. It's like I have a curse on me, like I'm unworthy of anyone else's attention.

But deep down, I know the truth: I don't even care. None of them are him. The one man I can't seem to stop wanting, no matter how hard I try.

I should be over him by now. He's gone. He left me behind. But instead of moving on, I find myself clinging to the broken pieces of us, obsessed with the thought of him, like a phantom who won't leave my mind.

Snatching my phone from my nightstand, I force myself out of bed and head downstairs for lunch before visiting my siblings.

Lenny's in the kitchen when I walk in, his back rigid as he stirs something in the pot. But the moment I step closer, he freezes. His gaze darts to me briefly, then quickly shifts to the counter.

"Ms. Marinova, may I get you something to eat?" His tone is tentative, unsure, like he's measuring every word.

"That would be great." I force a smile, but his gaze flickers to the floor, as if the act of making eye contact is too much to bear.

"I have dolma and plov, if that is acceptable, or I can make something else." He adds the last part quickly—almost too quickly, like he's afraid I won't like what he's made.

"No, that's perfect. I love that." I can't help but smile a little more sincerely. Azeri cuisine is one of my favorites.

He plates the food with careful precision, then sets the plate in front of me. Heading for the fridge, he pours water into a glass with a soft clink before returning and placing it before me, gaze never fully meeting mine.

I take the first bite, the rich flavor instantly making me close my eyes in pleasure. Heaven. As I continue to eat, Sonya walks in, carrying a large rectangular box.

"This was just delivered for you." She places it on the island. "Would you like me to open it?"

"No, I'll do it." My stomach churns.

Every package makes my nerves spike, because it could always be from my father. I'm not sure if he knows where I live now, but I have no doubt he could find out.

I can't tear my eyes away from the box, a growing sense of dread crawling under my skin like a slow poison.

Sonya leaves the room, but my gaze lingers on it—that damn box taunting me. The fear gnaws at my insides, but I refuse to let it win. I won't let it control me.

I march toward the drawer, grabbing a box cutter with steady hands. The blade slices through the packaging with a clean cut, revealing a simple white box inside. No company name. No return address.

A chill skates down my arms, my heart hammering in my chest with a frantic warning, an instinct telling me to stop. But I can't.

I pull the box out, my fingers shaking. With a deep breath, I open it.

Six black roses lie on white tissue paper, their dark petals unnaturally perfect, like a morbid bouquet meant only for me. A cold sweat prickles at the back of my neck, my hands turning clammy. I know exactly what black roses mean.

Death.

A quiet panic settles deep in my bones, cold and suffocating, as though the walls are closing in.

They found me.

My fingers hover over the envelope, the weight of it like a countdown. A sense of inevitability presses down on me. When I finally pick it up, my pulse surges so loudly in my ears that everything else fades away.

With unsteady hands, I rip open the note. The words blur before my eyes, as if they're waiting to drag me under.

Moya lubimaya sistra, I like your new house. I think I'll live in it once you're gone. Until I see you again. It's been too long, wouldn't you say?

The world tilts beneath me, the room spinning as I stumble back a step. They know where I am. They've been watching. They're coming for me.

I can't breathe.

My hands tremble as I force the box back into its packaging. I don't even realize I've moved until my feet are already carrying me toward the door, every step a frantic blur.

"Are you leaving?" Boris breaks through the fog of distress in my head.

"Uh, yes. We…we need to go to Konstantin's. Now."

He nods without hesitation, guiding me toward the car. I climb into the backseat, my body stiff with terror. Every nerve feels on edge.

What will they do to me? Drown me? Shoot me?

The thoughts spiral, every scenario more gruesome than the last. I squeeze my eyes shut, the images searing through my mind like a nightmare that won't end.

The drive feels endless before we pull up to Konstantin's place. Before Boris can open the door, it's already swinging open as my legs move on their own. The box remains clutched tightly in my hands as I race toward the entrance, heart pounding with every step.

"Is Konstantin here?" I ask the men stationed outside.

"He's in the back at the farm." One of them grins, and I don't miss the dark edge in his smile.

I return to Boris, who's still waiting in the car. "Take me to the farm."

"Are you sure? If Konstantin's there, you don't want to go—"

"I don't care. I need to see him now." The words are harsh, cutting through the anxiety that's rising within me.

Boris shrugs before I get in, and he starts the car. The few minutes of the drive feel like an eternity, but eventually, I spot Konstantin in the distance, standing by a fence that holds over thirty pigs.

When the car stops, I jump out and rush toward Konstantin, catching his attention as he wipes his hands on a towel.

"Dinara?" he calls, his stare narrowing with concern. "Is everything okay?"

"No…" The word is barely a whisper, caught in my throat.

My gaze flickers down to the crate next to him.

"Are those…?" The words stick in my mouth.

"The remains of your father's men." His voice is cold, almost clinical. "They were a problem. Pigs like meat. It's better than letting them go to waste."

I can't take it. My stomach turns violently, the bile rising in my throat. I choke it down, forcing myself to look away, to breathe through it.

"Can we talk somewhere else?" I ask in barely a whisper, trying not to look down at the severed body parts.

Konstantin nods, leading me away from the gruesome sight. The air feels colder, heavier as we move further from the chaos.

"So, what's in the box?" He glances at it casually.

I swallow hard, pushing down the panic that threatens to rise in my throat. "Black roses. From Roman."

Konstantin chuckles darkly. "Your brother doesn't learn, does he? Always daddy's little bulldog. But he's nothing more than a yapping chihuahua. Woof, woof."

"I'm scared, Konstantin." The words barely escape my lips. "They know where I live now. They'll come for me."

He halts in his tracks, his expression softening just enough for me to see a flicker of concern.

"I understand your fear." He steps closer, his tone calm and reassuring. "But my men will protect you. They know what happens to them and their families if they don't. They've seen it. No one will set foot on this property. I won't let anything happen to you."

Even with his words, the storm inside me won't settle. The terror still claws at my chest, suffocating and relentless.

"If you want to stay with me for now, you can. Whatever you need."

I hesitate. It's tempting—so tempting. But I don't want to run. I don't want them to know how afraid I truly am.

"May I think about it?"

"Of course." Konstantin reaches for the box, taking it from me. "I'll keep this for now."

I nod, happy to be rid of it.

"I'm going to see Gregory and Tatiana," I tell him.

"Good. But you're always welcome here. I still have your room, just like you left it."

A small grin tugs at my lips. "Thank you."

"I'll see you in a few hours. I still have the pigs to feed."

I nod and turn away from him, my heart heavy with dread. I don't know how to forget the note, the black roses, or the sickening threat they carry.

They haven't stopped thinking about me, and now I can't stop thinking about them.

And I know for certain, this is just the beginning.

TWENTY-SIX

DINARA
FOUR MONTHS LATER

I thought I saw Cillian today. Or at least I felt him. The familiar scent of his cologne hit me as a man brushed past, then disappeared as quickly as it came—like a shadow, slipping through my fingers.

I'm losing it. I must be. My mind's spiraling into this maddening obsession. Seeing him everywhere, even when he's not there. I'm sure I'm just imagining things.

He hasn't reached out. Hasn't even bothered to text. He's moved on, yet I can't.

With a heavy sigh, I step outside dressed for the night, instinctively glancing over my shoulder, just as I always do. My father and brother are still out there, and every day they remain free only feeds my fear.

Alisa and Natalia wait in the limo, their quiet presence grounding me. The moment I slide in, Pavel shuts the door behind me.

"Hey, guys."

"Hey yourself," Natalia greets, eyeing me up and down. "You look fire in that dress."

"Thanks," I mutter, glancing down at my semi-see-through gown. It hugs my curves just the way I know he used to like.

"I'm surprised you actually agreed to come tonight." Alisa raises a brow. "You've turned us down the last few times. What changed?"

"Maybe I'm finally ready to move on." I attempt to sound convincing.

It's a half-truth. Maybe part of me wants to move on, but most of me still aches with the memory of him.

"Right," Alisa giggles. "You say that, and then you're staring at his photos when we're out to dinner."

"That was *once*," I protest.

"Twice, actually." Natalia smirks.

I shrug, forcing a nonchalant smile.

"What can I say? The heart wants what it wants," I repeat the words Konstantin once said to me.

"Tell your heart to stop," Natalia fires. "He doesn't want you back."

Her words hit like a punch to the gut, but there's no denying the truth in them. He doesn't. And I wish to God I could just forget him. But it's proven impossible.

"Leave her alone," Alisa says softly, glancing at me sympathetically.

Alisa's been through it herself, dating someone recently who turned out to be a liar and a cheater. I don't know if she's ever truly moved on from that.

As for Natalia, she's made of something stronger. She doesn't crumble like the rest of us peasants. Sometimes I wish I could be more like her.

If she knew the real reason I was going to Rzvrt tonight, the real reason I put on this dress and stepped into this limo, she'd throw a fit.

I'm not going to have fun. I'm just hoping to see him again, even if it's just one last time.

He's probably with someone else by now. Someone classy and elegant. Someone who hasn't wrecked his life the way my family destroyed his. But I have to know if he's still going to the club. If he's with someone else.

The thought is like a knife to my chest.

As the limo rolls up to a secluded mansion in the woods, an unsettling awareness washes over me. It's like the air itself shifts—thicker, charged, electric.

I feel him. He's here. I just know it.

The question now is, what am I going to do about it?

CILLIAN

Reading her texts has its advantages, the biggest being knowing her every move.

I haven't stepped foot in this club since the last time I saw her here, but after seeing the messages with her cousin and knowing she'll be here tonight, I couldn't stay away.

Fionn knows why I agreed to come. He knows the game.

And do I care that she'll see me here? No.

I want to know if she'll do something with someone else. Because I'll always be there to fuck it right up. I'm just a savage in a suit who can't let go of the one woman who mattered.

"Are you just going to watch her all night, or are you going to say something?" Fionn smirks, taking a swig of his whiskey.

"That'd be a bad idea," I mutter, my eyes never leaving her while she's talking to Natalia and Alisa.

"Why? Afraid you're gonna fuck her?"

"Probably."

His laughter grows; he finds amusement in my misery.

It's been months since I've been with her. And yeah, the sex was good. Really good. But that's not the only thing I miss. I miss the way she looked at me with those soulful eyes. The way it felt to just be with her, holding her.

I rub my face, frustration building, and order another drink. The burn of alcohol does nothing to cool the fire inside me.

Turning back to watch her, I let my eyes roam that figure, barely covered in a white lace see-through dress that hits her knees. My instincts scream to wrap my jacket around her and hide that damn body so no one looks at it. I can make out her damn tits from here.

I need to take her home.

As I drag a step forward, our eyes meet and everything fades. The crowd, the music, the noise…it all vanishes. It's just her. Always her.

This is damn overwhelming. Wanting her. Needing her. Knowing she's the one.

But there's no future for us.

My blood pounds in my ears as I move toward her, not even sure what I plan to do. Talk? Kiss her? Tell her I can't stop thinking about her?

I have no idea. All I know is I can't stay away.

When I approach, she grabs some guy's arm and starts talking to him, her eyes growing as I start to get closer.

Does she think I'm just gonna wait here while she has her damn hands on someone else? Does my girl not know me by now?

My girl.

Fuck. I shouldn't think of her like that. Shouldn't even let myself feel it. But it's there, clawing at me.

"Dinara." Her name bursts from me like a dam breaking, the hunger too raw, too possessive.

Her eyes snap on me, darkened with something sharp and knowing. She sees the madness in me. I can't hide it. Not even if I tried.

The guy turns. His face is hidden behind a mask, same as mine.

"Hey," she says, sounding too damn cheery, pissing me off even more.

Her fingers trace his arm, and it makes my skin burn.

I don't think. I move, grabbing her wrist and pulling her away from him like I have every right to. Her touch, her warmth, the feeling of her skin beneath mine…it's everything I've missed.

She doesn't fight me. Instead, her eyes widen—a flicker of recognition, how right her body feels next to mine.

My lips brush against her knuckles. I kiss them, softly, desperately, like I've been starved of this for too long. I close my eyes for a moment, holding on to this touch.

God, I've missed everything about you.

Her friends watch, silent and still, while I touch her like she still belongs to me.

"Should I go?" the guy mutters, stepping back.

"No—" she starts, but I cut her off.

"That's a good idea."

My eyes never leave hers. Lust, anger, desperation, fear…all of them create a storm inside me. Fear that I'll lose her for good. That I've already lost her. And yet here I am, holding her hand like I own it.

I pull her closer, lips against her ear. The scent of her perfume wraps around me, and for a second, it's like we're back—back when things were simpler, before the chaos.

"We need to talk."

"Yeah." Her voice is tight, like she's holding back the words she wants to scream. Her jaw clenches. "We do." She turns to her friends. "Excuse us for a minute."

Natalia watches me, her glare lethal.

"She doesn't like me, does she?" I laugh, looking back at Dinara as we move through the crowd.

"My cousin?" She scoffs. "No, she hates you. In fact, I think she pictures your face when we go ax throwing."

My chuckle deepens. "I deserve that."

"At least you're self-aware."

I offer a half-smile. "I have some redeeming qualities."

"Not many," she snickers, her eyes lighting up with that spark that used to make everything feel like it was possible.

"Funny." I pull her through the maze of bodies, past the chaos, until we find a more secluded corner.

I turn her toward me, my hands caging her against the wall as though holding on to her is the only thing keeping me from shattering completely.

"What do you want from me, Cillian?" A soft ache bleeds through her words. It's an ache I put there, and it breaks me every time I hear it. "When are you going to stop this?"

"Stop what?" My muscles tense, despising the irritation in her tone.

"Hurting me." She looks at me like I'm a stranger. A monster.

I don't want to hurt you. I never did.

"That's not what I'm trying to do," I whisper, the truth breaking through.

Her laugh is empty, a sound that cuts deep. "Then why the hell are you here? Why are you following me like this?" She pulls her hand from mine, her fingers trembling with anger. "Are you stalking me? Because that's what it looks like."

If she only knew I live next door to her, she'd have me committed.

"I'm not gonna deny it." My lips curl into something bitter. "It seems you were right. There *is* a first time for everything."

"What?" Her features twist in confusion.

"You don't remember, do you?" My knuckles trace the curve of her jaw.

"Remember what?"

"What you said to me the night we met."

She shakes her head.

I reach for her cheek, softly caressing the skin that once made me feel complete. "You told me I was stalking you. And I said I wasn't in the habit of stalking women. You laughed and said, 'I'm sure there's a first time for everything.' You were right, a ghra."

Her eyes widen, like she's surprised I remember at all. I lean in, close enough to feel the heat radiating off her. My lips brush hers tenderly, like I'm afraid this will all slip away if I press too hard. Her breaths stutter as her hands slide toward my back, fingers hesitating like she's fighting herself. It takes everything in me not to lose control right here and now.

"You need to stop," she whispers—breathless, needy, like she hates how much she still wants me.

"That's what I keep telling myself." I pin her closer to my body, needing to touch every part of her, to remind her that she's mine.

Her brows furrow, her hand trembling as it cups my cheek. "I hate this." She sighs, the sound raw and heavy with emotion. "It feels like you've forgotten everything."

Everything. The way we fit. The way we burned for each other. The way it was perfect before the truth ripped us apart.

She has no idea how wrong she is.

My hand wraps around her throat, tilting her chin up, forcing her to look at me. "I didn't forget a damn thing." My lips brush against hers. "You don't understand what you represent, Dinara. You're everything that's wrong, and I can't look past it."

Her grip tightens on my bicep, every part of her breaking. "Then leave me alone. Turn around and never look back."

"If only it was that simple." I lean in, my lips grazing her ear. "I lost myself the moment I first saw you, and there's no antidote for that."

Her breath shudders, a frustrated, helpless sound.

"That's not my problem," she groans as I press against her. Her nails rake up my back, and I crave for them to dig in deeper, to mark me with a brand only she can leave. "You can't keep chasing me away from every guy I talk to."

She has no idea just how deep my sabotage runs.

"Watch me." My fingers trail up her inner thigh—slow, deliberate, testing the boundaries of her resistance.

She should push me away. I need her to. But we both know she won't. A quivering sigh slips past her lips as I brush aside the last barrier between us, my fingers finding her warm, slick, and aching.

"Oh God," she breathes, sounding like something between surrender and despair. "This isn't fair."

Nothing about this is fair. Not this moment. Not the past. Not the way my body still begs for her like an addiction I'll never break.

I roll her clit between my fingers, and she trembles. Every muscle in my body tightens, wanting her to lose herself in this, to give in, to remind me she still feels this torment too.

"I'm a bastard," I murmur against her throat, feeling the frantic pulse beneath her skin. "But you like it, don't you?" My thrusts deepen, my thumb working her into desperation, forcing her to feel what she does to me. "You like knowing I can't forget you. That I still need you."

A sharp inhale quakes through her, but then her eyes flash with rage, and before I can stop her, she grabs my wrist and yanks me away.

"How does that help me?" Her voice breaks, raw with anger, with grief. "The best thing you can do is forget me."

I know that. God, I fucking know that.

She shoves at my chest, shaking her head like she hates what we are, what we've become. "*You're* the one who ended this, remember?"

The words land like a punch to the ribs. The knot in my throat tightens, but I force myself to let her go.

"For good fucking reason."

"Then stop this madness!" She throws her hands in the air. "Stop it once and for all."

I want to. Fuck, I want to. But I don't know how.

Her bitter laugh slashes through me, but it's the pain in her eyes that guts me. I open my mouth, but nothing comes out. There's nothing I can say that won't make this worse.

"God damn it!" I grip the back of my head, trying to shake off the chaos inside me.

She's not yours. You did this.

"I'm leaving now," she says, smoothing down her dress with shaking hands, each motion so heartbreakingly final. "Don't follow me."

Everything in me screams to stop her. To pull her back. But I just stand there as she turns to go.

Then she peers over her shoulder. Just once. And it's that look—that quiet, devastating look—that destroys me.

Before I can think, I'm on her, crushing the space between us, my fingers tilting her chin up as I kiss her. Desperate. Unforgiving. A war between everything I can't have and everything I still need.

I'm so damn sorry.

I miss you.

I could've loved you.

She's the first to pull away, and I know: this is too much. Too much for her. Too much for me. I rest my forehead against hers right before I press a kiss there, a silent goodbye neither of us wants to say.

"Go," I whisper. "Please…just go. And don't look back. Because if you do, I won't be able to stop myself."

Her fingers brush mine—hesitant, lingering.

"I…" she falters.

I hold my breath. Waiting. Dreading.

But she doesn't finish. Whatever she wants to say, whatever confession is on the tip of her tongue, she swallows it down and lets

me go. And just like that, she turns and walks away.
The silence she leaves behind is unbearable.
And I know I will never be whole again.

TWENTY-SEVEN

DINARA

I toss and turn in bed, the memories of the night pressing down on me. Hours ago, I could still hear the ache in his voice, the desire he couldn't hide, but it all dissolved into the bitterness of his hatred for my family.

There's nothing I can do to change his mind. But I can't do this either. I can't let him turn me back into that heartbroken girl I was when he first left me. I won't go through that again.

Time slips by, each minute dragging me deeper into a restless pit. The clock ticks to three in the morning, and I still haven't slept a single second.

Footsteps in the hall thud in the distance. Slow, measured. Maybe just the bodyguards on their rounds. But then they stop outside my door, and my heart races.

The door creaks, and I freeze, my eyes shut tight, pretending to be asleep, even as every nerve in my body awakens.

Is it him? Could he have broken in again?

I can't shake this feeling that I'm right.

And if that's true, I can't let him know I'm awake. I want to know what he'll do.

I hear him inch closer, each step a whisper against the silence. The room is drowned in darkness, only the faintest light sneaking through the curtains. I'm almost holding my breath, every second stretching into eternity.

Then I smell him. His cologne. That familiar, intoxicating scent that's been burned into my memory.

My body trembles, a shudder running through me as I feel his finger brush my temple, as if pushing away a stray lock of hair. I squeeze my eyes shut tighter, trying to stop the ache that's tearing me apart.

I can't do this. I can't let myself fall to pieces again. But I can't stop wanting him either. He's a part of me now, whether I like it or not.

"God, I miss you," he whispers.

My breath falters, caught in my chest.

"Dinara?" His hand pulls away, and it feels like the distance between us has grown unbearable.

My lashes flutter open, and he's there, towering over me, his presence filling the room, gaze shadowed by regret. He stands there like he doesn't know what to say or how to fix this.

"What are you doing here?" The words are out before I can stop them.

He pinches the bridge of his nose, like he's holding himself together by a thread.

"I don't know. I just missed you," he admits roughly. "I hated the way we left things."

The heaviness of his words settles in my chest.

I miss you too.

"I should go." He turns as if to leave, and I can't let him. Not like this.

I reach out and grab his wrist, and he stops as though I alone control him. I wish that was true.

"Stay. Please, just stay the night." The words spill out, even though I know I shouldn't say them.

I know I should push him away. Keep him at arm's length. But right now, none of that matters. All I want is to be near him, even if it's only for a few hours.

He shakes his head. "I don't think that's a good idea."

But when he finally looks at me, I see the conflict there, and for a moment, it feels like he's really considering it.

"Please." My hand slides down to his, gripping it like it's my last chance. "Don't go."

I can't bear another goodbye, even if it changes nothing between us.

He hesitates, his fingers curling around mine, and then his other hand gently cups my cheek, tilting my head up.

"You know what will happen if I stay." His thumb brushes over my lips.

I nod, the truth between us too heavy to ignore.

His jaw tightens, and in that split second, all of the space between us vanishes. He leans down, his lips brushing over mine before he captures them with an urgency that takes my breath away. And for just a moment, nothing else matters but the two of us.

The rest happens in a blur. One second, he's standing; the next, he's shirtless and in my bed, grinding his body on top of mine and kissing me with a frenzy.

He drags up my nightshirt, circling his hips into my center, his cock hard, causing my pent-up need to drown out the voice that tells me I shouldn't do this. That I'll only get hurt in the end.

But what if tonight changes everything? What if he sees how perfectly we fit together? How right this is? Maybe then he'll want to make it work. Maybe it's worth the risk.

My hands grip his back as he kisses me, both of us clinging to one another with raging passion, while he works his sweats down until I feel his bare cock rocking against me.

"Do I need a condom?" he asks out of respect, even when we've done this without one before.

And that just makes me fall for him even more.

"No." I shake my head. "I'm on the pill."

He growls, rolling his hips into me, making me cry out in pleasure.

When the crown of his erection enters me, my teeth sink into my bottom lip, his eyes watching me take every inch in one brutal thrust.

In this moment, I feel alive, as if everything else—the pain, the loneliness—fades into nothing. He cups my cheek, his movements slow yet deep, and for a fleeting moment, it's as though we're one. Connected in a way that feels stronger than anything we've shared before.

I don't want this to end. I don't want to close my eyes and wake up to the brokenness that will be left behind. The shattered pieces of us that we'll never be able to put back together.

"Dinara…" His gravelly voice stirs something deep within me as his lips lightly brush mine.

"Don't," I whisper, shaking my head. "Just don't say anything."

The last thing I want is for him to tell me this is wrong or we should stop. Right now, there's nothing I want more than to be with him, just like this.

He groans, like he knows I'm right. Gripping my thigh, he throws my leg over his shoulder, his pace quickening, driving deeper, harder, until I'm nothing but a mess of gasps and frantic grasping.

His body moves over mine with effortless precision, like we've fallen back into something familiar. Like we've rewound time.

But it's a lie. A fleeting illusion. And soon, I'll wake up.

His mouth crashes against mine, his fingers curling around my throat as a desperate, punishing kiss steals my breath. He growls my name, thrusting deeper, taking everything.

My heart pounds, threatening to shatter under the weight of emotions I can't contain.

It's too much. And yet not nearly enough.

When he thrusts into me again, I come apart, calling his name, clinging to him even more, needing him to remember. Fingers tighten around my throat as he stares into my eyes, pounding roughly like he can't get enough. With a guttural cry, he releases inside me, claiming every last bit of my soul.

His breaths are ragged as he collapses onto his back, kissing the corner of my mouth. "I've missed this."

"Me too."

Though I don't know what he means. Did he miss the sex, or me? Or both? I'm scared of the answer.

As he holds me over his chest, his eyes flickering closed, I peer over at him, and I can't help but wonder.

Will he still be here in the morning?

I wake to the sound of something hitting the floor. Groggy and disoriented, I open my eyes and immediately feel the absence beside me, his side of the bed empty.

"What are you doing?" I ask when I catch him pulling on his shoes and shrugging his hoodie back on like it's just another morning.

"Leaving."

I blink, trying to clear the fog in my mind, my heart pounding so loud I swear it could drown out the world. My gaze darts to the clock.

"Why? It's only six in the—"

He cuts me off. "I'm sorry, Dinara. This was a mistake."

A bitter taste rises in my throat, sharp like acid. I swallow it down and fight to keep my emotions steady.

"What? No." The words are barely a whisper, and I sit up, the sheets tangling around me like they're trying to hold me back. "Why are you doing this? I know you feel it too. Don't you want us to be like we were?"

He steps closer, reaching for my face, but pulls back in the last moment like I'm made of poison.

"Every damn second," he strains, his brow furrowed in something that looks like regret but feels so much like defeat. "But we can't go back. It's just…what it is."

I can't even breathe for a moment as the heaviness of what he said sinks in, suffocating me. "That's bullshit. Your mother wouldn't want this. She wouldn't want you to throw everything away. She'd want you to be happy. To be with me."

His eyes snap to mine, fury flaring in them. "How the hell would you know what my mother would've wanted? If it wasn't for your family, I could've asked her. But I can't, can I?"

The harshness in his tone slices through me—clean, merciless. My eyes squeeze shut, the sting of tears threatening to spill.

He sighs, heavy and defeated, and when I look at him again, I see nothing but coldness. "I'll never love you, Dinara. Ever. This is over."

His words are a final blow. The dam breaks and tears spill down my face, uncontrolled and hot against my skin.

His jaw tightens, a fist curling at his side, but he doesn't move. "This will never happen again. Just forget I ever existed."

Each word is like a fresh wound, deeper than the last. "You're being cruel. You don't mean it." I choke on every syllable, another sob wracking my chest. "Tell me how you really feel. Forget our families. Forget everything. Just tell me, how do you *feel*?"

For a brief second, his gaze softens, like he's going to say something. Something that will pull me back from the edge. But instead, he turns away.

I can't stop the flood of tears, my chest heaving with the weight of everything he won't say.

"I hate you!" I scream, my voice breaking.

Scrambling to my feet, I push him toward the door, hands pressing against his chest, but he doesn't budge. Not even an inch.

"Get out!" My hands tremble as I shove him again. "Get out. Now!"

Finally, he starts to walk away, but his fingers catch my wrist before I can slip out of reach. His stare lingers, emotions that I can't even begin to understand passing between us.

"For what it's worth, I'm sorry."

I yank my arm out of his grasp, my chin trembling with rage and heartbreak. "For what it's worth, go fuck yourself."

A flicker of something—maybe guilt, maybe bitterness—crosses his face.

He opens his mouth, but all that escapes is a quiet, nearly pitying, "Goodbye, Dinara."

The words are barely more than a whisper, yet they crash through me like a scream. With one final glance, he turns and walks out of the room.

Out of my life.

And in the silence that follows, as the door clicks shut behind him, all I can do is stand here, frozen, lost.

The weight of his absence presses down on me, suffocating every breath. I don't know how long I stand here, but time doesn't matter anymore. The only thing that does is the hollow ache in my chest—the kind that feels so deep, so relentless, that I can't help but wonder…

How much can a heart break before it stops beating altogether?

TWENTY-EIGHT

DINARA

"How far away are you?" Natalia's voice crackles through the phone the next day, her concern cutting through the fog of my thoughts.

My grip on the steering wheel is so tight my knuckles are white, and the tears still streak down my face, falling unchecked onto my lap. I don't even care at this point.

"About ten minutes," I whisper, the words thick and heavy, as if they've been torn from the very depths of me.

I'm trying so hard not to let it all unravel, not to collapse in on myself. Because I can't. I won't.

The rain taps against my windshield, the sound like a hundred tiny hammers hitting metal. I reach up to wipe my eyes again, but they keep filling faster than I can clear them.

"God, if I could, I swear I'd go kill him," Natalia mutters.

I know her too well to think she's entirely joking. But I know she'd never really do it.

I choke back a sob and try to force some strength into my voice. "I don't hate him enough to want him dead. Not yet, anyway."

I can barely breathe through the pain in my chest as I press my foot onto the gas, feeling the car jerk slightly as it speeds up. The road's slick with rain, and the world outside is a blur of gray and black—the kind of day where everything feels suffocating.

"I don't know, Din." I hear her frustration and love for me in the sharpness of her words. "You need to get rid of him. He's a fucking liability. And if you see him again, tell Konstantin. He'll take care of it, and if he does kill him…I mean, oh well."

"I know," I cut in with a deep sigh. "I know. But it's not that simple. I still care too much."

An ache rips through me before I can stop it.

God, why is this still so hard? Why does it still hurt like the day he walked away? Why do I let him do this to me?

I swallow back the lump in my throat, then try again. "I knew this could happen. I just…I wanted to believe he'd come to his senses after…"

"After he fucked your brains out?" She sounds almost too casual, but I can hear the protective edge in her voice.

"Yeah." I laugh, but it's hollow. "Obviously that didn't happen."

There's a beat of silence on the other end of the phone.

"From now on, Din, if he contacts you, don't respond. Don't even look his way. For your sake, he doesn't exist."

The words hit me harder than I expected. It's what I've been telling myself ever since he broke up with me.

He's gone. I have to let go. He's not worth it.

But how? How do I pretend that the man who tore my heart apart doesn't exist when I can still feel the echo of his touch, the taste of his kiss, the sound of his presence lingering in my mind?

I blink back tears as the rain picks up even more, the pitter-patter now a roar against the roof of the car.

"Shit," she says. "How far are you? It's getting bad out there."

"Only a couple of miles." I fight the tightness in my chest, trying to hold myself together.

"Okay, good," she replies. "Because I've got—"

And then everything shatters.

One moment, I'm gripping the wheel. The next—

Headlights explode in my vision. Tires shriek. Metal crumples.

The impact slams into me like a freight train. My body whips forward, the seat belt biting into my skin as the car spins out of control. The world tilts and twists, and I'm weightless for a terrifying second before gravity yanks me down.

A crash. A crunch. A sickening jolt. My phone flies from the cup holder while Natalia's voice crackles through the speaker, distant and frantic.

"Din, are you there? Answer me! Din!"

I try to breathe. Try to move. But the world is already slipping away.

Darkness swallows everything.

CILLIAN

My foot bounces relentlessly against the floor of the jet as I sit here with my hands clenched tight around my phone, trying—desperately trying—to convince myself that I did the right thing. I keep staring at her name on the screen, my thumb hovering over the keys, wondering if I should send her a text. Apologize again.

Maybe this time it'll make sense to her. Maybe I can undo the damage I've done.

I was harsh, I know I was, but it was for the both of us. I couldn't let her cling to something that was never meant to be.

But what if she's still crying? What if she's lying there in bed, her heart breaking the same way mine is?

I can't stop the guilt from clawing and tearing at me.

My body grows rigid with indecision. Every fiber of me is screaming to go back, to hold her, to make her see things from my perspective. That we can never have this. That no matter how much I care for her, I can't let myself have her.

The jet starts to roll down the runway, and I'm out of my seat in a heartbeat.

"Fuck! Stop the plane."

The stewardess blinks in confusion. "Sir? Is there a problem?"

"I need to handle something," I grit out. "Tell the pilot to stop the plane."

She hesitates, but a second later, her voice crackles over the intercom. The pilot responds. The engines cut. The plane slows.

I'm already moving, jacket in hand, heart hammering.

This is a mistake. I know it. But I can't walk away, not after leaving her like that.

As the plane comes to a full stop, my mind's running wild with thoughts of her, of the last few hours, of how I could have handled things better.

I was an asshole. She deserves better than this. She deserves more than I can give her.

As soon as the door opens, I'm rushing down the stairs and ordering my rental car to return.

An hour later, I'm standing in front of her house, the rain falling in sheets. I'm fucking soaked to the bone, but I don't care. The guards let me through without question as soon as they hear my name, and I stand at the door, the gravity of the moment sinking in.

I could leave. I could turn around and walk away right now. But I know if I do, I'll never forgive myself.

A woman from the cleaning staff opens the door as soon as I ring the bell, her eyes flicking over me with no recognition. "Hello. Can

I help you?"

"I need to speak with Dinara." I force myself to sound calm, controlled, like I'm not going insane. "Tell her it's Cillian."

Her expression shifts, the smallest twitch of her lips, and then she sighs.

"I'm sorry. But she left," she explains in a thick Russian accent. "I can tell her you come."

My heart drops into my stomach.

"She's here," I demand, my voice barely in control now. "She's just hiding from me, right? She doesn't want to see me?"

The woman shakes her head, her lips thin and tight. "No, sir. She left."

When I glance at the driveway, I realize her car is gone.

She's not here.

One of the guards standing to my left steps forward, a smug look in his eyes. "You heard her. She left. Now go."

I whip around to face him, fury flashing through me like a bolt of lightning. My hand instinctively moves toward the grip of my gun.

"I don't know who the fuck you think you're talking to," I growl, the words scraping out of me. "But I suggest you shut your mouth and stay out of my way."

The woman's eyes go wide and she starts to close the door in my face, but not before I see the flash of fear. The guard laughs, clearly thinking I'm bluffing, but I'm not. I take a step closer, the adrenaline pumping through my veins.

"Hvatit," the other one snaps at him in Russian like he's scolding him. "Ti nekhochesh problemy s bossom."

I nod sharply, my temper dropping to a dangerous edge. "Yeah. Listen to your friend."

The guard finally steps aside and I head back into my car, my hands gripping the steering wheel with white-knuckled intensity. I send her a text, just to check on her, but deep down, I know she won't answer.

Even hours later, nothing.

It's probably for the best. Maybe this is exactly what we both needed.

But I can't shake the hollow feeling. The emptiness. The raw hole in my chest where her smiles used to be. Because no matter how many miles I put between us, no matter how many mistakes I make, she'll always be the one.

And I'll never stop wanting her.

TWENTY-NINE

DINARA

My eyes flutter open, but they feel heavy, like I've been asleep for far too long.

Everything's blurry at first, the harsh white light above me too bright, making my head pulse. My body aches in places I can't quite name, a deep, throbbing pain in my limbs and chest. I try to move, but my muscles won't obey, as if they've forgotten what it's like to work.

Panic rises in my chest.

Where am I? What happened?

I blink a few more times, focusing on the sterile walls around me, the beeping sound of a machine beside me, and the faint smell of antiseptic.

Slowly, it comes back to me. The accident.

My heart skips a beat, and I try to sit up, but the effort sends a wave of dizziness crashing over me.

I'm in a hospital.

What happened?

How did I get here?

Boris and Artem… They must've brought me.

Letting out a groan, I attempt to sit up.

"Don't do that, dorogaya." Konstantin's voice gets closer. "You scared us."

He looks visibly worried. I've never seen him this way: bags under his eyes, as though he hasn't slept in days.

"What happened?" My throat's dry and the words sound hoarse.

"Boris called me. Said someone hit you, but they got away." His entire face visibly shudders with rage. "Did you see anything?"

I shake my head, lying back down. "I just remember the car spinning and me screaming."

"Blyat. I'm gonna find who did this, and he or she will pay."

"How long have I been here?"

"Three days."

"What?" My heart races. "Why? How hurt am I?"

He pulls up a chair beside me, and anxiety sets in, gnawing in my gut.

"You had an internal injury and a concussion, but they fixed you." He holds my hand. "They put you to sleep to help with the brain swelling. You got knocked around a lot before the car stopped."

"But they say I'm okay now? Can I go home? I don't want to be here."

Hospitals remind me of death. It's where my grandpa died, where one of my cousins died. I hate it here.

"Soon. But not now. You need to rest. Then we talk, okay?" He starts to rise.

"Talk about what?"

"Cillian." He drags in a long breath. "You're done with him."

"The accident wasn't his fault." I find it necessary to come to his defense, because I don't want Konstantin doing something to him or starting a fight with his family.

"It's not? Natalia told me how upset you were. Maybe you weren't paying attention because you were crying, and *that* is his fault."

I shake my head. "No. That car came out of nowhere."

"Either way, you and Cillian—that is over. He bothers you, you come to me."

"Okay."

But no matter what I tell him, I know I'm not strong enough to resist the pull between us. It's like a magnet, drawing me in, and I can't break free.

And I'm so tired of it. Tired of him. Tired of me. Of the endless cycle we've spun ourselves into.

"Maybe I need to leave." The words are raw, but barely above a whisper, as if saying them out loud might make them real.

Konstantin's eyes narrow, a flicker of concern flashing within them.

"Leave where?" he asks casually, but I can sense the tension in his shoulders.

"Out of the country. Somewhere far away. I need real space. I can't keep doing this to myself. I can't keep pretending I'm fine when everything I feel, everything I want, is still tied to him."

I can't believe I'm actually saying this, but the truth is finally spilling out of my mouth like it's been waiting to escape.

"I need to go, Konstantin," I continue, barely holding back the tremor. "I need to get away from him. From this…obsession."

His gaze softens, and I know he understands.

I take a shaky breath. The thought of leaving is so final, so forever, making me feel both terrified and relieved. But I know it's the only way to break free. To truly heal.

"If that is what you want, I will arrange it." His tone's low and steady, like he's already planning every detail in his head. "But you can't tell anyone where you'll be, not even Tatiana. We don't want your father or Roman knowing where you are. I want you safe."

He's right. I'll have to keep that a secret. My heart twinges.

"Tatiana and Gregory," I murmur, barely able to get the words out. "I hate to leave them."

He reaches out, his hand gentle on mine for the briefest moment. "You're not leaving them forever, Dinara. But you need to get away from him, as you said. You can return whenever you wish. Whenever you're ready."

"Right. You're right. Please don't tell Tatiana yet. I want to tell her myself."

"Of course not. That isn't my place. She's right out there, if you want to see her. I know she's been upset ever since she found out."

"Yes, let me see her. Is Gregory here too?"

"No. This is no place for a child. You will see him when you get home. I will move your things to my house until you're recovered, and then I will arrange for your trip." His expression hardens. "I'll get you a new phone and number. Your old phone is broken. You can't contact Cillian anymore. Understand?"

The finality of his words hits me like a punch to the gut, but I nod, swallowing down the knot of panic rising in my chest.

"Okay." The word tastes like surrender. "Will I know where I'm going?"

His mouth tips up. "Not until you get your plane ticket."

Well, that's not at all terrifying.

As Konstantin strides away, I close my eyes and whisper a goodbye to Cillian, even though he's not here to hear it. It's a goodbye I never wanted to say, but somehow I know it's the only way forward.

PART II

THIRTY

CILLIAN
TWO YEARS LATER

Two years. Two fucking years, she's been gone.

At first, I spent them trying to forget her—trying to bury her name in the back of my mind—but it was like trying to drown a fire with gasoline. Every time I thought I was done, that I could forget her, it burned brighter, hotter. The obsession, the pain… it never left. It only grew stronger.

I tried everything. Every method, every distraction, every damn trick in the book. But nothing worked, and soon I gave up on the idea of ever forgetting her. Instead, I embraced the fire and let it burn me whole.

I searched for her relentlessly, but nothing ever led me to wherever she was. And here I am: still stuck, still lost, with nothing to show for it but the ashes.

Her phone's GPS is wiped clean. I've traced every number, every connection. Her friends, her family, even her damn bodyguards. But it's all dead ends. It's as if she's completely vanished, erased from the world.

I know she's out there, though. I can feel it in my gut. But the woman who used to be my everything is now nothing more than a shadow, fading from me no matter how tightly I hold on.

I sit in the dark, the low hum of New York City outside my penthouse window doing nothing to soothe the fire raging inside me. If anything, it only intensifies it, reminding me of the days we spent here, when everything felt possible. When we were still alive in a world that was ours.

My hands are clenched tight around my phone, wondering where the hell she is and when I'll finally see her again.

Konstantin? He's been a dead end too. Not that I would ever ask him about her. But I've tried following him, and he hasn't led me to her either.

Where are you, leannan? Where the hell have you disappeared to?

I don't need to know where she's hiding; I just need to know that she's alive. That's all.

Fuck, who am I kidding? I just want to see her again. To touch her and hold her. But she's slipped through my damn fingers.

And here I am, staring at her picture on my phone, cursing the day I let her walk out of my life, even while knowing I couldn't have her. It's a sick game my mind plays with me: toying with me until I break.

I should be relieved. I should be happy. But there's nothing but emptiness.

I feel like a fucking liar. A coward too. I was the one who pushed her away, who told her that it couldn't work, that it would never work. I told her I couldn't be the man she needed. But it's been two years, and the only thing I feel is regret.

I want to know what she's doing. I want to know if she's moved on. If she's found someone else. If she's happy.

Without me.

But I don't want her to be damn happy, because all I've ever wanted is to be the one to give her that.

As I swipe through the old photos of us, it's almost like a different life. The way she used to laugh at my dumb jokes. The way she'd look at me, like I was the only thing that mattered in the world.

But I've burned that bridge. I know that.

The storm outside picks up, rain slapping against the glass, and I can't sit still anymore. I stand up, running my hand through my hair, pacing the length of the den like a caged animal, desperate to escape the thoughts that have been eating away at me.

What the hell am I doing?

I should've let her go completely. I should've erased her from my mind, just like I told myself I would.

But I couldn't. No matter what I told her, no matter how many times I convinced her that it was for the best, I still want her.

She's still the one. The only one.

I slam my fist into the wall, the pain sharp, but it does nothing to dull the ache that's been there for these years. Nothing can make this go away. Not all the money in the world. Not all the women who've tried to get my attention, only to be disappointed.

Because no matter how hard I try to forget, no matter how many distractions I throw myself into, her memory is always there. *She's* always there, haunting me, like a ghost that won't let go.

And maybe this is exactly what I need. This pain. This brutal realization that no matter how hard I fought it, how many times I tried to move on, she's the one. Always has been. Always will be.

I can keep fighting it, keep denying it, or I can finally admit what I couldn't say before: that I'm ready to go all in. Ready to love her.

Because I wanna try. I have to.

Grabbing my jacket, I head out, calling Grant again to see if he has any new leads.

Right now, finding her is the only thing that matters. And this time, I won't let her slip away.

SIX MONTHS LATER

I shouldn't be here.

The thought drums in my head as I step out of the car, but I don't let it stop me. Konstantin's estate looms ahead, its iron gates swinging open before I pull into the driveway and step out. The doors open, and his guards don't even try to stop me, though their eyes track me like they're waiting for the moment they'll have to step in.

"I need to see him."

"Come," one says as he leads me to a sitting room.

Konstantin is already there, swirling a glass of something dark and expensive. He barely spares me a glance as I stop a few feet away, tension hanging thick between us.

"Cillian," he says, drawing out the syllables like he's savoring them. "To what do I owe the pleasure?"

I promised myself I wouldn't ask. Told myself I wouldn't give him the satisfaction of seeing me beg. But the words burn on my tongue, and before I can swallow them down, they escape.

"Where is she?"

Konstantin exhales slowly, the sound almost amused. "Dinara doesn't want you to know."

The sentence slams into my chest, knocking the air out of me. I clench my fists, nails digging into my palms to keep myself grounded.

"You're lying."

He takes a deliberate sip of his drink, watching me over the rim. "Am I?"

I move before I can think, my body acting on pure instinct. My fist is halfway to his jaw when something in his expression stops me cold.

He doesn't flinch. Doesn't tense. Just watches me. A slow smirk pulls at his lips as he sets his drink down.

"I understand you're angry," he says, his voice measured, calm. "But try that again, and you'll be the next one I feed to my pigs."

The words are quiet, but they land with the weight of a death sentence. I force myself to take a step back, my pulse hammering against my ribs. I let out a sharp breath, hands still clenched at my sides.

I should never have come here. I knew it the second I walked through the door, but now it's too late. Konstantin has seen my desperation. Worse, he's confirmed my worst fear.

She doesn't want me to find her.

I turn and leave without another word. By the time I'm back in my car, my body tenses with frustration and anger.

Not at Konstantin. Not at Dinara. At myself. I had her, and I ruined it.

Now she's gone, and I don't know if I'll ever get her back.

THIRTY-ONE

DINARA
TWO YEARS LATER

I've spent four and a half years in this villa deep in the heart of Italy, surrounded by vineyards, sun-dappled hills, and new friends. But I haven't spent them all basking in the sunshine. Some of that time I've spent sharpening my aim, firing at targets and pretending they were Cillian's face.

I figured I'd need to be ready if my father ever found me.

When I left, I told myself it was for the best. That I could find peace in this isolation.

Konstantin arranged everything, and I fell into this quiet life, trying to forget. I buried myself in books. In the rhythm of mornings spent walking the grounds. In the feeling of the Italian sun on my skin. It was enough, or at least I convinced myself it was.

But today? Today, everything changed. I could feel it the moment his name slipped through Konstantin's mouth. He had been talking—

something about business with the Quinns—and then, just like that, it was there.

"Cillian," he said so casually, like it didn't shatter the fragile peace I've worked so hard to build.

His name in the air between us was like a weight, like a chain pulling me under. And I was drowning in it all over again.

I hadn't expected to feel this way. Years. It's been *years*.

Yet when I close my eyes, I can still hear his voice. That rough edge when he said my name for the last time. I can still see the way he looked at me, like I was something he wanted but couldn't keep.

And now that part of me I buried so deep is clawing its way back to the surface.

I'm so damn tired of pretending. Pretending I'm fine. Pretending I don't still ache when I remember the way he touched me, the way he looked at me when the world was collapsing around us.

He broke me. And I let him.

But no matter how hard I try to move on, he's still there—lingering, inescapable, woven into the fabric of my past.

I finger the tennis bracelet he gave me, the one I never take off, and my heart twists. Some ghosts never really leave.

The phone buzzes in my hand, and I glance down to see my younger sister's name flash across the screen, calling me like she does every night.

I don't know what I expected from this call—some casual chat about her classes and the boys she likes, maybe—but when I swipe the screen and her face fills the display, it's not what I imagined at all.

She looks…off. Her usual easy smile is absent, replaced with a nervous tension I can feel through the phone. I lean forward instinctively, trying to pick up on whatever's going on in her world. But before I can speak, her eyes flicker to the side, like she's checking to make sure no one's listening.

"Hey," I say softly. "You okay?"

She hesitates, her lips pressing together like she's searching for the right words. That's when I know something's wrong.

I lean back on the sofa, the peaceful quiet of this villa pressing in on me, making everything feel that much more foreign. My sister's in New Jersey. My brother. My family. And I've been so far away from it all—hiding from my own past, hiding from him—that I've let everything fall into pieces without even realizing it.

"I saw them." The words come out in a rush, her voice trembling just enough for me to hear the fear beneath it.

I frown, sitting up straighter.

"Dad's men. They were at my school today."

My stomach drops. The air in the room goes thick, pressing down on me.

"What do you mean, Dad's men?" I whisper, even though I know exactly what she means.

Even after all this time, my father isn't done. He was just beginning.

"They've been watching me, Din. I know it. They were outside by the gates the other day. I'm so afraid."

My pulse is a hammer in my temple. "Where were your bodyguards? Have you told Konstantin?"

"They didn't notice them, and no, I haven't. I just…" She sighs. "I didn't know what to do. I've wanted to tell you for a few days now, but I didn't want to make you worry."

My throat is tight, filled with the panic I've tried to keep buried all this time. I thought it was over. I thought my father had given up. But I was wrong.

My little brother too. God, where is he? Is he safe?

"I'm scared," she goes on. "I don't know what to do."

And that's when it hits me like a crashing wave.

I can't stay away any longer. I can't hide in this villa, pretending I'm not still part of that world.

"I'm coming home," I tell her before I can stop myself.

The words sound final, even to my own ears. I can feel the heaviness of it settle into my bones.

"Are you sure?" But there's relief in her eyes. I know she wants me there. She has for a long time.

"I am."

I'm sure I'm making the right choice, but I also know it's going to be harder than anything I've ever done before. Facing Dad. Facing my brother. Facing Cillian—the one man who has the power to break me all over again.

But it's time. It's time to stop running.

"I'll call Konstantin and tell him," I add, pulling in a breath.

"Thank you. I can't wait to see you."

"Me too. Until then, stay safe and watch out for Gregory."

"Always."

"I love you." And I mean it with all my heart.

"I love you too."

The line goes silent, and I'm relieved that I'm finally going home, though I know the hardest part is yet to come.

I landed in New Jersey over an hour ago, and the familiar smell of home is a comfort I've missed. Italy was breathtaking—so much beauty, so much peace. The food, the people, the landscape… It was everything I thought I needed. But none of it ever felt like home.

Home is here. Home is family.

As much as I tried to escape, as much as I convinced myself that running away was the best thing for me, I always knew I'd come back. The thought of seeing Cillian again sends a nervous shiver through me, but I'm done. I have to be. There are bigger things to focus on now. Things with my family.

I'm not looking back. I won't let him keep me chained to the past. I'm moving on. For good.

Letting out a long breath, I climb the steps to Konstantin's house. The guards at the door nod in greeting, and I feel their silent protection surrounding me.

"There she is!" Ludmilla breaks the tension, and before I can respond, she's enveloping me in a tight hug. Her arms are warm, and I can feel the familiar pressure of her comfort around me. "I missed you. Never leave us again!"

More footsteps follow, and Gregory is there first, followed by Tatiana. Their faces are like pieces of a puzzle I've missed. My baby brother's grinning up at me, his eyes bright and his features older—too old. He's not the little kid I left behind.

My heart twinges with regret as I run my hand through his hair, feeling the length of it, the way he's grown in my absence.

"Are you leaving again?" he asks, face scrunched with concern.

"No." I smile through the lump in my throat. "I'm here to stay." I step back to look at him. "My God, you're almost as tall as me now."

He laughs.

Tatiana steps forward next. Her smile is soft, but there's an edge to it—a quiet strength that mirrors the woman she's becoming.

"I can't believe you're really here," she says, thick with emotion.

"Welcome home." Konstantin's voice cuts through the moment, deep and commanding.

He stands in the doorway to the foyer, impossible to miss. Konstantin is the kind of man whose mere presence fills up a room, demanding attention and respect. But there's something in his eyes that makes me pause.

"Come with me, Moya dorogaya. We have things to discuss."

I follow him, my heart a little heavier with each step.

Konstantin's house is like a fortress—secure, but with an air of cold efficiency. He's always been the protector, the one who keeps things in balance, no matter what. But as we walk down the hallway toward his office, I feel the tension building in my chest.

What's really going on?

He opens the door for me, and I step inside with the feeling of his eyes on me as he closes it behind us. His office is dark, lined with bookshelves and leather furniture, everything designed for business and comfort.

"Sit," he commands, gesturing to the sofa.

I lower myself onto the leather cushions, my body tense.

He takes a seat opposite me, his large frame folding into the love seat with ease. "So, Tatiana told you about the men at her school. That's why you came back."

I nod slowly. "Yes, she did. But why didn't you tell me?"

Konstantin leans forward as his gaze sharpens. "I don't owe you an explanation. I do what I do to protect this family, and you're a young woman. There's nothing you can do to help your sister. So, why did you really return?"

"I can't keep running." I let out a sigh. "I need to be here, with all of you. I won't let them keep me away anymore. I won't let *him* keep me away either."

"Cillian?" From his tone, he already knows the answer.

But as soon as he says the name, my chest tightens. No matter how much I tell myself that I'm over him, the ache never fully fades.

"Yes, him." I run a hand through my hair, swallowing thickly. "But he doesn't matter anymore."

Konstantin chuckles, his eyes glinting with something like amusement. "Are you sure about that?"

I nod, even though the flip in my stomach tells me I'm lying to myself. "Positive."

"Well, good." He leans back. "Because we're throwing a party to celebrate your return, and the Quinns will be invited."

The words hit me like ice water. "The Quinns?" I repeat, my tone rising higher than I intend. "I don't want a party. That's the last thing I need."

Konstantin gives me a look, like I'm being dramatic. "Nonsense. You've been gone too long. We must celebrate."

"But with my father out there—"

"He's insignificant. A cockroach," he spits, his face coiling with an undercurrent of pure anger. "I'm glad he and his little lapdog are back from Russia. After I killed all their men, I did not think they would have the balls to return, but I'm relieved. It will be my pleasure to kill them and the new army they have raised."

Nerves skitter up my arms.

"I'm not scared," I say, the statement coming out firmer than I expected.

Konstantin smiles, his pride palpable. "That's my girl." He stands. "Go get settled. We're all happy you're here."

But as I turn to leave, a strange feeling settles in my gut. Being home isn't as simple as I thought it would be. Too much has changed.

And too much is about to change.

CILLIAN

Finishing up the meeting at the company, I make my way toward the elevator, my mind already drifting, consumed by thoughts of Dinara. I wonder where she is right now. What she's doing. If she's thought about me at all. It's like a curse—the way she haunts me, never really leaving, even though she's been gone for years.

Even after all this time, the memories of her remain as vivid as ever. The way she laughed, the way her eyes softened whenever she looked at me, as if I was her entire world. I can still feel it all, even though it feels like a lifetime ago.

A life I destroyed.

I could've loved her. I *should've* loved her. I should've fought for her when I had the chance.

But now it's too late. I've spent all this time searching for something I lost, and in the end, I know I'm the one to blame.

"We're invited to a party at Konstantin's in a few days." Tynan steps in front of me, blocking my path.

I barely slow down.

"That's great. Have fun," I mutter, already thinking about how much I don't want to be there.

After Konstantin told me she didn't want me to know where she was, it broke me.

She was really gone. I threw away the best thing that ever happened to me. I wish I could undo it, but there is no second chance.

"We're all going." Tynan's voice cuts through the fog of my thoughts, irritating me even more.

I stop in place, tension running through my shoulders. The last place I want to be is in a room full of Marinovs. There's only one Marinov I ever want to see, and she's not here anymore. The thought hits me like a gut punch, sharp and relentless. Fuck knows if she'll ever come back, or if she even wants to. The slicing pain settles deep in my chest, familiar and unforgiving.

"The hell I am."

His hand lands firmly on my shoulder, preventing me from leaving. I exhale sharply, frustration coiling in my chest like a vise.

"This is business, Cillian. We go because we have to. No one said you have to like it, but you're going, and you're going with a date."

I let out a dry, humorless chuckle. "That was almost funny."

His expression doesn't waver, not a single crack in his steely demeanor. "Who said I was joking?"

A mix of irritation and disbelief spreads through me. "What the hell are you talking about?"

"The Italian families. They'll be there too. Adriano Scutari has a sister, Lucia. She likes you. He wants you to marry her."

I burst out laughing at first, but it dies quickly, my mouth flattening into a thin line. "Tell him I'm not interested."

Adriano runs the Grazia family. Well-liked and respected. But I don't want his sister. Or any woman for that matter.

All I want is her. There's been no one since Dinara, and I'd like to keep it that way.

"You can tell him yourself at the party." Tynan doesn't flinch.

Between the Russians pushing for a marriage alliance, the last thing I need is pressure from the Italians, too.

I don't say anything else as I make my way toward the exit instead, desperate to clear my head, desperate to stop thinking about Dinara. About everything I've lost.

Tynan calls after me, just loud enough to catch my attention. "You're forty, Cillian. It's time to start thinking about having a family."

I freeze, my back still turned to him, and let out a bitter laugh. "Just because you fell in love with Elara doesn't mean we all want that."

"You did back then."

I don't respond. There's nothing to say.

The truth is, I don't want a family. Not with Lucia Scutari or anyone else. What I want—what I've always wanted—is something I can never have.

I push the thought aside, the throbbing in my chest spreading, but there's no escaping it. Not ever.

Not when her name is still in my head and her face, her smile, is still in my heart.

THIRTY-TWO

DINARA

Two days pass in the blink of an eye, and the day of the party arrives. I tell myself I'm ready, but the second I step onto the grounds of Konstantin's estate, something tightens in my chest.

The gold strapless dress I bought just for this occasion hugs my body, metallic and shiny with rhinestones cascading down the front. As soon as I put it on at the store, I felt untouchable, and I knew that if I were to run into him tonight, it would be in this dress.

The sprawling property hums with life: acrobats twirling high above, stilt-walkers weaving through the crowd, and floral canopies glowing under the night sky. But none of that matters. Not when I'm scanning the crowd.

But he's not here. Not yet, at least.

I remind myself that I'm fine, that I'm stronger now. But even so, my eyes can't stop searching for him.

"I see you looking for him," Tatiana whispers, sliding into my side with a teasing smile. "I thought you wanted to forget he ever existed."

"I do," I answer quickly. "But that doesn't mean I don't want him to see what he's missed."

Her laughter dances around us.

Every inch of me is on edge, fighting against the ache inside that I can't shake.

A man suddenly approaches out of nowhere—dark hair, sharp eyes, polished smile. He takes both of our hands and presses a kiss to the top of each.

"Adriano Scutari. Pleasure."

I recognize the name immediately. Boss of the Grazia family. Mob ties everywhere. Just what I need.

Tatiana smiles, a flush in her cheeks. She's already charmed. I'm about to say something to her when a chill races up my spine.

Cillian.

I know he's here before I even turn in his direction.

I don't even have time to think. Everything I've tried to bury for these last several years surges to the surface. The warmth when he held me, the weight of his touch, the ache I've fought so damn hard to forget…all of it comes rushing back.

I shift toward him, my vision tunneling as he walks closer, a woman by his side. My body locks in place, and for a split second, I'm too stunned to breathe.

That familiar knife to my gut twists. It doesn't matter that I told myself I was over him. Seeing him with someone else cuts deeper than I ever could have imagined.

He's moved on. He's completely forgotten me.

I bite down hard on the inside of my cheek, fighting to keep my face neutral, to hide how much this hurts.

"Are you okay?" Adriano asks, but I barely hear him.

My entire world has narrowed to Cillian and the woman at his side.

I can't stand it. I can't stand *her*.

Who is she? How long have they been together? How do I get rid of her?

"Pretend to be my boyfriend." The words are out of my mouth before I even think them.

My voice sounds foreign to me—desperate, even. I don't care. I just need him to hurt like I do. If he even cares, that is.

Adriano chuckles, clearly amused, but my focus stays locked on Cillian as he approaches, his gaze slicing through me, dark and unreadable.

"Please." I turn to Adriano, my eyes searching his. "Just do it."

His gaze flickers between me and Cillian, the shift in his expression telling me he understands. A slow, knowing grin spreads across his face, mischief dancing in his eyes.

"Ah, I see." He tilts his head toward Cillian. "That your ex?"

"Yeah. Real jerk." The words come out too easily. "Now help me make him jealous."

"How can I refuse such a request?" Adriano's arm slides around my waist, pulling me close. His mouth drops to my ear, his tone low and dark. "How jealous do you want him to be?"

"As jealous as possible." The words are sweet poison on my lips.

And when I look at Cillian again, the rage in his eyes is almost enough to satisfy me.

Almost.

The woman at Cillian's side flashes a smile when they're only a few feet away, but I barely see her. I don't see anyone but him. I'm a woman possessed, driven by something I can't name. I pull Adriano closer, pressing my body against his as though it's the only thing that can shield me from the storm of emotion threatening to swallow me whole.

Then Cillian's voice cuts through everything. Deep and familiar and crushing.

"Dinara."

The way he says my name—sharp, laced with longing and something far more dangerous—makes my chest tighten. I feel the shift in my body. The cold heat of recognition. The way everything inside me freezes at the sound of his voice.

It's all I can do not to fall apart right here, but I won't. Not for him. Not ever again.

"Cillian." My voice is steady, betraying none of the trembling I feel deep inside. "It's been a while."

"I'll say." His nostrils flare, his eyes locked on mine like I'm the only thing in the room. His chest rises and falls faster. "Can we talk?" He glances at Adriano with rage-filled eyes.

"Not right now." I shake my head, holding on to Adriano's arm even tighter. "I'm busy with my date."

"I think I can spare you for a few minutes, darling," Adriano says.

My hand rests on his chest, and I swear Cillian growls.

"You sure, babe?" The sugary sweetness of my words is the only thing that keeps me from cracking under the intensity of Cillian's gaze—like he can't breathe without me.

"Absolutely." Adriano's grin deepens. "I need to catch up with my sister anyway." He flips his gaze to the woman next to Cillian.

Sister?

My eyes widen.

"You're related?" I say, more of a statement than a question.

"That's right," she answers with a smile, and in this moment, I want to claw her eyes out.

"Excuse us." Adriano pulls her aside and starts walking away, leaving me and Cillian alone in a space full of people.

Yet I don't see anyone but him. I never have.

"So, what did you want to talk to me about?" My heart hammers, like it's tearing out of my chest.

"Let's go inside."

I open my mouth to refuse, but before I can, his hand is in mine. His touch is electric, sending a shock through my veins, filling every hollow part of me with a fire I haven't felt in so long. The burn, the heat, the ache…it's there, all of it.

How can I still feel like this after everything? After all this time? No matter the distance. No matter the time we've been apart. He's always been embedded in my marrow, rotting me from the inside.

And maybe that's the worst part of it. Because somehow I've always belonged to him, even when I wasn't his anymore. But clearly he's moved on, and maybe it's time I do the same.

From the corner of my eye, I spot Konstantin watching us, a knowing glint in his eyes, his mouth tipping up just slightly.

I don't have time to digest what that look means as Cillian leads me into the house, past busy staff and the hum of the party, but none of that registers. Only him. Only the feeling of his hand in mine, the heat between us that won't ever die.

"Where's the closest bathroom?" His words are rough, demanding, and it makes my pulse race even faster.

"Down the hall."

He practically drags me down the corridor.

"Which one?" His tone is gruff, impatient, and it causes my pulse to hike up.

I point to the last door on the left, and he's quick to open it, ushering us inside. The moment the door slams shut behind us, the small room feels suffocating with the heaviness of everything unsaid between us. His eyes roam my body—hungry, desperate—and I feel it on every inch of my skin.

A fist curls at his side.

"Where the *hell* have you been?" His voice is tight, and there's something almost painful in it.

"Oh, you know…" I cross my arms, but I don't miss the way his gaze lingers on my chest. "Basking in the Italian sun, under a hot

Italian or three."

In an instant, he's on me, pinning me to the wall, his fingers around my throat, and it feels like a brand. His jaw grinds, and I swallow hard, fighting the dizzying mix of anger and desire.

"That's not funny, Dinara," he growls.

"Right, because I've spent all this time pining over you like the sad little girl you left."

His breath escapes in harsh, frustrated bursts.

"Guess what, baby?" My mouth curves. "In all this time, I didn't think about you at all."

His smirk is predatory. "Really? Not even once?"

His body presses into mine, and I let out a groan, aching for him already.

"Nope."

"Then why the hell did you run? Why didn't you come back sooner?"

"Because I was having too much fun. Obviously." I snicker.

His husky laugh shivers across my curves. "Don't you know by now, a ghra? I know when you lie."

I hate the way my skin prickles when he calls me that.

His full lips skim across mine, and I feel it everywhere, warmth cascading down my limbs. I shut my eyes, hating that I still want him after everything. He still looks just as good as I remember.

"You know nothing about me." I hike up my chin. "We weren't together long enough for you to know anything."

When he pulls back, there's a fury trapped in his eyes.

"That's bullshit, and you know it." His hand squeezes my throat, his cock hard against me. "You want to hate me, but you can't. Can you, baby?"

"You wish." I huff out a laugh. "I don't know what you're doing, but I'm leaving."

Pushing at his chest does nothing at all. He's a brick, hard in all the right places.

"No, you're not." His jaw clenches, and the possessive undertone makes me feel things I hate to admit.

"Shouldn't you go back to your date? Or is she your wife?" My mouth curls, while the pain is almost unbearable.

"I should be asking you the same thing." His gaze burns through me.

"So ask." My lips tip up.

He pushes up my chin, forcing my head higher, his eyes boring deeper. "Does he fuck you like I did?" His mouth brushes mine, and I let out a gasp. "Does he make you tremble when you come?"

His fingers stroke up my inner thigh, grazing my core through my panties.

"You should stop."

He flips the lace to the side. "Is that what you really want, Dinara?" He rolls a finger over my clit. "Or do you still ache for me the way I ache for you?"

No. No, I don't. Please don't stop.

But I can't say that out loud. I won't give him the satisfaction.

"Does he touch you like this?" He pushes a tip into my entrance. "Does he make you this needy? This wet for him?"

"He's better." I grit the words out, barely able to speak.

"Don't do that," he husks, tightly clasping my throat. "Don't you fucking lie to me."

"You really think you're the only man who can fuck me like that? You're not."

His features twist with one part lust, the other rage. It's so hot, I almost come just from looking at him.

He bites my bottom lip, his voice rough with frustration. "I hate that I still want you this much."

His fingers slowly press inside me, stretching me as I gasp, unable to stop the moans slipping from my lips.

"Don't worry, the feeling's mutual."

His chuckle is dripping with arrogance. "Look at you." His hand slides from my throat to twist my hair around his wrist. "You're still mine."

"Never." I narrow my eyes as he sinks deeper. "All you are, and all you'll ever be, is a good fuck. Nothing more."

"Is that right?"

Thrust.

"Mm-hmm."

Thrust.

"We'll see about that."

And in a split second, he flips me around, pushing my head down until I'm bent over for him, my ass completely on display.

"Fuck," he hisses, giving it a slap. "So damn perfect."

Practically ripping my panties down, he slides his fingers even deeper until I'm clawing the wall, crying out in sheer pleasure. He doesn't stop, not until I'm dripping. I barely register the sound of his belt buckle as it comes undone, the zipper next, until his pants are pooled against his ankles.

His fingers return to my throat, clasping it tight. "I'm gonna remind you what a good fuck is, baby, and I'm gonna erase every bastard who took my place."

There's no one who could ever take his place, and that's the most heartbreaking truth of all.

With one ruthless thrust, he's inside me, and I let out a cry, my core throbbing and burning and aching for him. But he doesn't move while my body stretches around his, his thumb rolling over my clit while I let out a series of needy cries.

The feeling of him bare after all this time, it's something else entirely. It's primal. Raw. Like he's claiming me all over again.

"Tell me to fuck you." His hot breath crawls down my neck, lips grazing my earlobe. "Beg for it, leannan. Tell Daddy what you want."

My pussy clenches at those words, and I have no idea why. I never imagined liking something like this.

His husky laughter makes it harder to breathe. "Beg. I wanna hear you begging and pleading for it like the slut I remember."

"I won't beg you for a thing. In fact…" I turn my head and stare at him over my shoulder. "*You* should beg *me*."

He fists my hair. "Please…" His whispered breath rolls down the shell of my ear. "Please let me kiss you. I'll die if I don't."

"Then die." My mouth curves.

Roughly, he arches his hips into me with a beastly growl, spanking my ass harder. "Goddamn, baby, only you can make me this hard."

When he starts to move, grabbing my hips, I fall into the sensations, letting them consume me. Forgetting how wrong this is and how right it is all at the same time.

He doesn't want you. He's with someone else. You shouldn't be doing this.

But everything about this feels familiar and right. The way he moves, the way he calls out my name, the way his hands glide across my skin. It's all I know. It's all I remember. And it's all I want.

There are so many things I want to ask.

Do you regret it?

Did you think about me?

Did you fall in love with her?

But I can't seem to ask any of them because I have to pretend he means nothing.

"Is that all you've got?" I say instead, wanting that fire in his eyes to burn brighter.

He fists my hair, pulling my head back to meet his harsh stare while his mouth drops to my ear, his pace intensifying. "You're gonna regret that."

He takes me harder and deeper. My body is on the brink of collapse, my mind forgetting everything else I was just thinking about. Everything but him and the things he makes me feel.

This intensity, it's unexplainable. Earth-shattering in every way.

I lose control, moaning shamelessly, while the man who let me go somehow finds me again, bringing me back to that girl I was when he left.

He roars with his own orgasm, body rigid as he rams into me until he's fed me every drop. Instead of sliding out of me, he holds me tighter, breathing heavily across my ear.

"I've missed you." His confession makes my heart flinch.

But I won't let him have any more of it. He's taken enough.

"No. Don't do that." My eyes pinch shut. "This was just sex. That's all."

"With you, it was never just sex." He drops a kiss to my shoulder, and tears threaten behind my eyes. "You may not be mine, but I'll always be yours, Dinara."

I swallow down the ache carving up my throat.

Don't you dare show weakness. He's not worth it. Remember how much he broke you. You won't become her again.

I pry his hand off me and straighten, lifting up my panties and dragging my dress down with a half-smile. "This was fun."

He stares at me intensely as he pulls up his boxers and pants.

"Thanks for the orgasm, Quinn." My hand wraps around the cold doorknob. "I'll see you around." The words fall from my lips like an echo of someone I used to be.

I start to move, my steps steady, but then I hear him.

"Dinara." It's a whisper of my name, the sound of a ghost.

The girl I was—vulnerable, full of hope—would've stopped. Would've turned. Would've let him pull me back in with just that one word. She would've crumbled, just like before.

But not me. I don't hesitate. I don't falter. I walk away, keeping my eyes forward. I don't look back. Not even when the twinge in my chest feels like it could tear me open.

Because I've grown. Because I've learned. And this time, I'm the one who chooses.

THIRTY-THREE

CILLIAN

My fist crashes into the punching bag, the sharp impact rattling through my bones like a jolt of electricity. I don't feel it. The pain in my knuckles is nothing compared to the fire in my chest. The memory of seeing Dinara with Adriano replays in my head over and over again.

Each punch I throw is a desperate attempt to obliterate the image of them together. Him with his arm around her, his face too close to hers, as if he has any fucking right to touch her.

I shouldn't be surprised. I'm the one who left her. Of course she chose to move on, while I sat here all these years wishing I had the chance to make things right, to tell her I'm sorry.

But now, she's too hurt to ever give me that chance.

She's gone. Completely gone. And it's all my damn fault.

But the way she felt in my arms after all this time… It was better than I imagined, until that moment she walked out the door like I meant nothing at all.

Muttering a curse, I hit the bag harder, my fists throbbing with the force of my rage. The burn in my arms doesn't matter. I can't focus on anything but that scene: her in his arms, like she belonged there. It's all I can see when I close my eyes.

Dinara is mine. She's all mine.

I tell myself to calm down. Killing Adriano wouldn't be smart. It would start a war with the Italians, and with Gio married to Iseult, it would fuck everything up. The Marinos are family now, and they'd be stuck in the middle.

My mind knows that. But the part of me that's consumed with rage—the part of me that still cares for Dinara—doesn't give a damn about family.

I should call Adriano and talk to him, man to man. Tell him she's mine. But if he's been with her all this time, if he's had her in his life the way I used to, he won't just let her go. I know that. If I was in his shoes, I wouldn't.

My punches get faster, harder, until the bag seems to blur in front of me.

I've never felt this fucking shattered. I'm falling apart. I waited all this time to find her, but all I did was lose her all over again.

"Looking to break your hand?" Fionn's voice cuts through the noise in my head.

I don't turn around. I just punch the bag again, my teeth gritted.

"Fuck off."

"That was some party, huh?"

Why is he still talking?

I don't answer him, just keep swinging.

But he doesn't stop. "You two disappeared for a while. How did that go?"

I stop mid-punch and whip around to face him, my temper flaring. "How the *hell* do you think it went?"

Fionn leans against the wall, watching me like he's studying some kind of animal in a cage. "Based on how miserable you were afterward, I'd say pretty damn bad."

I let out a curse, so done with this conversation already.

"Why not just ask her to marry you? Maybe she'll actually say yes." He smirks.

The words hit me like a hammer.

Marriage? Jesus.

There was a time when I couldn't even stand the idea. I couldn't let myself get trapped in that kind of life, tied to a family who had already taken so much from me. From us.

But now? The thought of her saying yes doesn't feel so sickening anymore. Not after I've felt the agony of her being gone.

But it's pointless. She'll never say yes. I fucked up. She hates me.

"Not interested," I mutter.

Denial is easier.

Fionn shakes his head like I'm some kind of idiot. "You haven't learned shit, have you?"

I clench my fists and snap, "Mind your business, Fionn. Just let me work out."

"You look like you're trying to beat the hell out of someone, not work out." His eyes glint with amusement.

"Maybe I'm imagining it's your face," I scoff, unable to hide the flicker of a challenge in my tone.

Fionn raises an eyebrow, his smirk turning into something more intense. "Remember what happened the last time you wanted to fight me? You ended up with a shiner."

"That won't happen again."

He shrugs, his grin unfading. "Guess we'll never know. See ya tonight at dinner."

Dinner. Fuck. I forgot.

Tynan's hosting family dinner. That damn tradition my father started. Now I'll have to sit there and pretend I'm not a goddamn mess.

And worse, everyone's going to ask questions. They'll know something's off. They always do.

I shake my head, the frustration clawing at me, but Fionn's right. I'm not here for a workout. I'm here because if I don't hit something, I'll snap.

I need this. I need *her*.

Dinara can't be with Adriano. I won't let it happen.

And today? He'll learn how far I'm willing to go to make sure he knows that.

She's mine. Always was. And I'll tear apart anyone who tries to take her from me.

Hours later, I find myself staring at the phone in my hand, the weight of it almost suffocating.

I've been pacing for God knows how long, fighting the urge to throw it across the room, but I need answers. I need to know. My fingers slide over the screen as I hit dial, and the phone rings three times before he picks up.

"Cillian Quinn. To what do I owe this pleasure?" Adriano's voice is smooth, too calm, like he's been waiting for this call.

The bastard knows exactly why I'm calling.

"Adriano." My tone is steady, but it doesn't hide the edge, the simmering anger beneath. "I need to know. How long have you been with her?"

I run a hand over my jaw, trying to keep myself from losing it. A silence stretches, thick and heavy, before he answers, and I can almost hear him smirking.

"I'm not with Dinara. We just met at the party. But she's lovely, that's for sure."

Lovely.

That word ignites something inside me: a rush of heat, a surge of pure fucking possessiveness. He's talking about *my* woman, even if she doesn't know she's mine anymore.

My fist clenches. He needs to shut the hell up.

"She's mine," I growl before I can stop myself.

He laughs, low and amused, like this whole thing is some damn game. "Really? According to her, you're an ex. An asshole, as she called you. What the hell did you do?"

The bastard is enjoying this. The question hangs in the air, sharp and biting, and I fight the instinct to tear him apart with my words. Instead, I force myself to stay calm and in control.

"That's none of your business." The words are sharper than I intend, but I can't help it.

Adriano chuckles again, colder this time. "Perhaps not. But I'm disappointed it won't work out with you and Lucia."

"She's great," I mutter through clenched teeth, my pulse spiking. "She's just not *her*."

"I understand. But you don't need to worry about Dinara and me. I have no interest in her."

I can't help the small laugh that escapes me, bitter and hollow. "I wasn't worried."

"Of course not," he responds, like the whole conversation is beneath him now. "Have a good day."

The line goes dead while my hand clenches around the phone. I drop the cell onto the kitchen counter like it's a hot stone, the cool surface offering some kind of relief, but it doesn't last.

I should feel relieved. She wasn't with him. She lied. She was just trying to make me jealous.

And shit, it worked. I was burning with it.

But so was she. And that just means she still cares.

She can pretend all she wants, but the way she looked at me when she saw me with Lucia…I know the truth: she's not done with me.

And neither am I. I haven't let go. I never will.

If it takes all my damn willpower, I'll make her remember exactly what we were. And what we can be.

THIRTY-FOUR

CILLIAN

I walk into Tynan's house right on time, greeted by the whole family.

Gio and Iseult; my youngest sister, Eriu, with her husband, Devlin; Tynan and his family—they're all gathered around the living room. The noise and movement are familiar, but tonight, everything feels heavier.

Brody, Tynan's oldest, pulls me into a quick hug before his four-year-old sister, Adora, charges toward me. Her tiny arms stretch out, eager for attention.

I scoop her up, pressing a kiss to the top of her head. "Hi, sweetheart."

"Hi!" She grins, her hazel eyes sparkling. Then, without a moment's hesitation, she asks, "Uncle Cillian, do you have a girlfriend?"

I freeze. And just like that, the interrogation begins.

"I don't," I say, keeping it simple, hoping that'll be the end of it.

"Why?" Her brows knit. "You're so old. You need a girlfriend. Or a wife," she adds thoughtfully.

Well, that doesn't make me feel ancient at all…

"Adora!" Brody scolds just as Fionn walks in with a grin plastered across his face.

"He sort of has a girlfriend. He's in love with someone, but refuses to admit it. Isn't that right?"

I shoot him a death glare. "Don't listen to Uncle Fionn."

"I always listen to him." She lifts her chin proudly. "He's smart."

"See? Smart." Fionn taps his temple, looking far too pleased with himself.

"You're lucky the kid's here." I elbow him, and she giggles when he fakes a dramatic collapse.

It's all lighthearted, but beneath it, tension coils tight in my chest, wrapping around the truth I've never said aloud.

Love. I never admitted it, never dared to name it. But what I feel for her…it's more than that. Like the word itself isn't enough to contain the depth of what she means to me.

And I wonder if it's too late to tell her.

Dinner is served, conversation flowing easily, laughter filling the space. For a while, it feels normal. Until my father's voice slices through the noise, shattering the illusion.

"So, son…" His eyes fix on me from across the table. "When are you going to settle down like the rest of your brothers and sisters?"

Here it comes. The question that's been asked a thousand times before.

"Now that the love of his life is back, I'm sure it'll be any day now," Iseult throws in, a teasing smile curling on her lips.

Of course. Fionn told her.

Gio's head snaps between the two of us, curiosity flickering in his eyes. "Wait, who are we talking about?"

"You know, that Marinov girl. Dinara," Iseult says with a knowing look.

"Oh…" Gio nods, then takes a long sip of his drink.

My father's face contorts, a flicker of hatred darkening his features.

"A Marinov?" he mutters, almost choking on the words.

Fernanda, his wife and Gio's mother, rests a soothing hand on his shoulder.

"You can't marry a Marinov." His words are thick with the heaviness of the past.

"I'm not marrying anyone, Dad. Let it go." I try to keep my tone neutral. "Dinara and I are in the past."

Or more like she wants nothing to do with me anymore while I'm still obsessed.

"Then why the hell did I see you with your tongue down her throat?" Fionn laughs, a low, teasing sound.

"Children are present!" Tynan's wife, Elara, scolds, covering their daughter's ears.

"Uncle Cillian, how do you put your tongue into someone's throat? Do you have a very long tongue?"

The entire table erupts in laughter, and I slam a hand over my face. This is *not* happening.

Adora's voice slices through the laughter. "I wanna meet her. I bet she's pretty." Her eyes widen. "Can we do a tea party together?"

Great. Now a kid is planning my future too.

"Probably not, sweetheart," I tell her gently. "She's not gonna wanna have a tea party with me."

She pouts, clearly disappointed. "But how do you know if you don't ask her?"

"Oh, don't go breaking her heart," Elara says lightly.

I release a sigh. "Seems like that's what I'm good at with the whole female population."

She laughs. "Well, we're a forgiving bunch, if you play your cards right."

"Speak for yourself," Iseult intercepts, arching a brow. "I hold a grudge."

"You'll like Dinara, then," I grumble, half to myself.

"I think I would." Her grin widens. "I should introduce myself next time I see her. Maybe teach her a few ways to really get under your skin."

"Don't worry, she already knows just how to do that," I tell her, the sting of it all still fresh in my chest.

My father interrupts before I can think of anything else to say. "You don't need some Marinov. I'll find you a fine woman, someone who isn't tied to that family." His Irish brogue grows with irritation and his jaw tightens.

"You have to let it go, Dad," Iseult says, calm but firm. "You both do." She looks between my father and me. "Nothing will bring Mom back. Being angry at a woman who didn't do anything to us isn't going to help anyone. Yes, Sergey was a son of a…but he's gone. I made sure of that," she adds, her jaw setting. "We have to let this go or it will eat us alive."

I know she's right. Back then, I wouldn't have listened. But now, with a clearer mind and all the years I've spent without the one woman I've desperately wanted, I'm able to.

"Fine." My father throws his hands in the air. "Maybe you're right." He sucks in a deep breath, his shoulders sagging with resignation as he returns his attention to me. "As long as she makes you happy, son, you do what you want with this girl. Marry her, don't marry her. But just give me some grandkids, will ya?" He looks at Eriu and Iseult. "All of you."

Tynan is the only one with kids so far, and Dad's taken well to the role of grandpa.

Iseult smiles at him, her expression softening.

The rest of the dinner is mercifully uneventful, the tension easing into small talk and laughter. But I can't shake the weight of the questions that linger.

I wonder, for the hundredth time, if it's even possible to move forward with Dinara. To build a future together, the one I've wanted since the moment we first met. To take all this—our families, our past, the ghosts that haunt us—and somehow make it our own.

But I know the truth: it's not just about what I want. It's about whether she's willing to take the chance and forgive me.

DINARA

Two days.

Two days since I saw him with her. Since jealousy clawed its way through me, sharp and relentless.

Seeing him again was hard. Seeing him with someone else? Unbearable.

Because no matter how much time passes, he still has this hold on me. This power to drag me back in, to make me forget everything except how it feels to be his.

But none of it matters. Him with someone else is irrelevant. It doesn't change the truth: we can never go back. I can't trust him. Not after everything.

What happened in that bathroom? That was a mistake. Nothing more. One I won't make again.

My heels hit the floor with a sigh of relief as I kick them off, the exhaustion of the day pulling at me.

Today, I asked Konstantin to teach me more about how he runs his legitimate businesses, and he was more than happy to oblige. He owns an investment firm, along with many other businesses, including a portfolio of high-end hotels and casinos across the globe. He's sharp, calculated, and he knows exactly what he's doing. I wanted to learn from him, to understand how a mind like his operates. Maybe even build something of my own one day.

Thankfully, he didn't mention Cillian. Nor did I. I'm sure he realizes just as I do that Cillian and I have no future.

Rushing upstairs, I'm already thinking of the relief a hot shower will bring. But when I push open my door, I freeze. My hand tightens around the doorframe, legs unsteady, breath catching in my throat.

"What the *hell* are you doing here?"

There, in my room, standing like he owns the place, is Cillian. His presence fills the space—tall, broad, imposing. It's like he's carved from stone, the same fire in his eyes. The fire that's never gone out.

"You live at Konstantin's again?" His voice holds that cocky edge, like he's suddenly entitled to know everything.

The shock of seeing him here hits harder than I expected, but I force myself not to show it.

"For now. Not that I owe you an explanation. Now get out."

"Not until we talk."

I roll my eyes, the frustration bubbling up. "I've got nothing to say to you. Go back to your girlfriend, or whatever she is."

"Lucia?" He laughs like I've just told a joke. "We're not together. I just met her that night. We only walked in together."

My eyes widen for a quick second, and the smirk he's wearing is cocky as hell.

He takes a step forward. "But I told her there was only ever one woman for me."

Before I can even process what he said, he's marching closer, forcing me back against the door. His body presses against mine, and I can't escape the intensity of it. Of him. The air between us crackles with that same tension—the kind that's always been there, threatening to break everything apart again.

"Adriano told me you're not with him either," he murmurs, his heat seeping into my skin. "Were you trying to make me jealous?"

"It doesn't matter." I hike up my chin. "I don't care if you're with her or not."

His laugh—that damn husky laugh—shakes me to the core.

"Yes you do, baby." His mouth grazes my ear, and I shiver from the warmth of it. "It drives you crazy, doesn't it?" he whispers. "To know you still want me?" His hand slides over my hip, then lower until his fingers caress up my inner thigh. "Because it drove me insane with jealousy thinking that you were with Adriano in Italy all those years."

My body betrays me. I try to laugh, to distance myself, but it's impossible when he's this near. His hand is on my throat, his grip tightening as he stares at me, eyes dark with something deeper than anger.

"None of this changes anything," I force out with enough edge to sound like I mean it. "We're done. You mean nothing to me anymore."

The words feel hollow.

His grip tightens. "I called you." His tone comes out strained and raw, desperation cutting through each sound. "When you disappeared. I called, searched for you everywhere…but I couldn't find you. Fuck, Dinara, I wanted to find you."

Why?

His confession makes my pulse flutter.

"I had a new number." My mouth tips up.

His jaw tightens, his eyes narrowing as if he's piecing together something that will never fit anymore.

"Why did you look for me?"

"Because I wanted…" His gaze locks on to mine, fierce and vulnerable all at once. "I wanted to try."

His words hit me like a slap, cold and disorienting. I laugh—a sharp, empty sound—and shake my head.

"You wanted to try?" My hands push him back, forcing him to step away, every ounce of hurt flooding back. "You broke my heart— not once, but twice—and now you think you can waltz back in and tell me you want to try?" The anger surges, sharp and unforgiving.

"It's too late for that, Cillian."

I swallow, fighting the lump in my throat that threatens to choke me. I can never trust him. He could turn around at any moment, change his mind, and let what my family did crush him all over again. And when that happens, I'll be left picking up the pieces of a heart that's already been shattered beyond repair.

Straightening my skirt, I meet his gaze one last time. "You wanna fuck, we'll fuck. You're good at it." My lips twitch. "But that's all you're ever gonna get from me."

The fire in his eyes flares and the tension thickens again, swirling around us like a storm on the verge of breaking.

But it doesn't matter. *He* doesn't matter.

I can't look at him anymore. Can't let myself believe in his promises. All we have is the wreckage of what we were, and I can't keep picking up the pieces. Not anymore.

My palm clasps his cheek, his jaw clenching beneath my touch. "I'm done with you, Cillian. Whatever we had, it's over."

The hardness in his eyes shifts to something that resembles pain.

I should stay. I should say something, anything, to make him hurt less.

But I don't. I've already learned how to live without him.

THIRTY-FIVE

CILLIAN

Days later, and her words keep echoing in my head, haunting me. The look she gave me, full of hurt and anger…it hit harder than anything else. That was the moment I realized the depth of the damage I've done and how much I'll have to work to fix it.

The hum of the engine dies down as I pull up to the industrial building, slipping the black mask over my face. I didn't plan on returning to the club, but it's the anniversary party, and there's a gut feeling she might be here. Can't let her show up without me keeping watch.

Fionn slides his mask on next to me. He invited himself when he caught wind of my plans. Said he didn't want me doing something reckless and ending up dead. Fair enough. But if he gets in my way tonight, he won't be able to stop me. No one will.

We move into the elevator, and Fionn chuckles. "You look like you could use a drink."

I throw him a cold glare, the doors sliding open as he continues to laugh behind me. The moment we step into the party, my eyes are scanning, darting from room to room.

She's here somewhere; I know it. If she's with another man, it's not going to end well for anyone.

The place is packed, more so than usual and it's harder to find her. My patience is close to thinning.

Then I see her. That mask she always wears on her beautiful face.

My chest tightens. She's stunning, as always. A sheer white gown that clings to her curves, hair pulled high into a ponytail with a few strands loose, framing her face. She's the kind of beauty that makes everything else fade in comparison.

Time's changed a lot of things, but not much has changed for me. I'm still crazy about her. Always will be.

She doesn't notice my presence at first as she talks to some women. A few men stand around her, listening. If they don't walk away, they're gonna end up dead.

I slip behind her, tension coiling tighter in my chest. But then one of them reaches out, fingers brushing her back. The next moment is a blur. One second, he's laughing; the next, he's howling in pain as I twist his fingers backward.

"Keep your damn hands to yourself," I growl, my face inches from his.

Dinara's voice rises in the chaos, shouting my name. But there's no stopping this.

"You don't touch her. You don't even look at her. Understand?"

"Yes, yes!" He's nodding frantically, wincing through the pain.

When I shove him off, he staggers back, then rushes off. The others quickly retreat as well, leaving only Natalia and Alisa behind.

But my focus is locked on *her*.

Dinara stands there, gaze icy, contempt dripping off of her in waves. The sharp edge of her silence cuts through the air between us.

"Can we talk alone?" I ask her.

Her chest rises and falls heavily before she nods, her gaze flicking toward the girls.

"Are you sure you're okay with him alone?" Natalia's voice slices through.

"I'll be fine," Dinara snaps, never breaking eye contact with me.

"Just…be careful." Natalia's words lace with concern.

"I'd never hurt her." My tone is steady, my gaze intense, hoping Dinara understands the truth in my words.

"You already have," Natalia mutters under her breath as she walks away, leaving me to face the woman I can't stop wanting. The one I'm trying to win back.

"What the hell are you doing?" Her words cut like a blade, but I close the distance between us with a single step.

"What the hell were you about to do with him?" My hands reach for her jaw, gripping it with an almost desperate urgency, my lips hovering dangerously close to hers.

Every inch of me begs to kiss her, to make her mine again.

"That's none of your business." Every syllable is defiant, but I can see the flicker of something beneath the surface.

"Dinara…" I tighten my grip just enough to make her feel it. "Don't do that. You'll always be my business."

I drag my mouth down her neck, pressing a slow, possessive kiss against her skin. She fists my hair, holding me to her like she doesn't want to let go.

That's right, baby. You own me.

She can fight it all she wants, but we both know the truth: what we are together is inevitable. Unstoppable.

My fingers thread into her hair, twisting her ponytail around my wrist before I snap her head back, forcing her to meet my gaze. The fire in her eyes only fuels me. Her breath comes in ragged waves, her chest rising and falling in sync with the tension crackling between us.

I can't resist her. I don't even try.

"You're mine," I groan before slamming my mouth to hers, and she doesn't even fight it.

Desire surges through me, that same familiar fire—the one that's only ever burned for her.

My Dinara.

Hooking my arms around her, I lift her effortlessly as her legs wrap around my waist. Every step I take pulls us deeper into the haze of need, the noise around us fading into nothing. All I want is her.

Her mouth takes mine with wild urgency, fingers threading through my hair, nails clawing down my back like she's desperate to get closer—like even this isn't enough.

I push into the first empty room I find, kicking the door shut and locking it behind us. The music outside dulls to a distant hum, drowned out by the tattered sound of her breathing and the pounding of my pulse in my ears.

Then she stops, pulling back just enough to look at me. Her gaze cuts through me, deeper than I can take, sharp with something unspoken. Something that makes my chest ache. Slowly, she traces a finger along my jaw, her touch featherlight, before leaning in and pressing a soft, lingering kiss to my lips.

"Dinara…" Her name leaves me like a prayer, like a plea—one that doesn't need words to be understood.

I fucked up. And I don't know what to do or say to fix it.

"Don't say my name like that." Her voice breaks, her forehead falling against mine, her arms gripping me tight.

"There hasn't been anyone since you. There never will be," I whisper against her throat, mouth grazing up her soft skin while she holds me even tighter.

"Don't do that." She snaps her head back. "Don't fucking say that. You don't have that right."

Raw pain seeps from her gaze.

I did that. *Me.*

I hurt her so damn bad, and I don't even have a right to ask for her forgiveness.

"I've spent all these years without you, and I can't do it anymore." The confession slips free.

"I'm leaving." She sounds strong, but I see the crack beneath it—the flicker of pain, the war between resolve and longing. "I'm done with you."

My fingers curl around her throat, lips hovering just above hers. "But I'm not done with you. I never will be."

For a fleeting moment, emotions flash in her gaze—anger, longing, and heartbreak crashing together like a storm.

When my mouth captures hers, she fights it, pushing at my chest, resisting the connection she swore she didn't need. But the fight in her starts to fade until it shatters completely. And all that's left is the fire between us, burning too hot to ignore.

I walk us to the bed and throw her on top of it, my body lowering to hers, refusing to let her walk out of this room. Out of my life. Out of my head.

I want her everywhere. Permanently.

I devour her lips with a brutal kiss, yanking up her dress as my fingers find her clit, stroking with relentless intensity. She cries out, grabbing my cock and squeezing it painfully tight through my trousers.

"Let me go," she hisses while my fingers sink inside her, then back out, toying with her.

"You don't want to go, baby. You're just lying to the both of us because you hate it, don't you?" I thrust deeper, and her eyes roll back. "You hate knowing how good I make you feel. How in charge of your body I really am. That no man will ever make you do the kinds of things I can."

Her face strains with both pleasure and rage. "I hate you."

I let out a dry laugh, adding another finger, her walls rippling in waves around me. "No, you don't. You only wish you could. But no matter how hard you try, sweetheart, you'll never hate me."

Before she can say anything else, I flip her on her stomach and lift her ass in the air, dragging up her dress until the hem slips over and around her neck. I pull back both sides and choke her with it, working my palm over her wet core.

"Look at how soaked you are, and I haven't even fucked you yet."

"You're a bastard," she practically sobs, unable to stop herself from moaning.

"And you'll always be my whore, Dinara." My mouth drops to her ear as I work her deeper with my fingers. "Your heart may not belong to me anymore, but your body always will."

When I brush over her clit this time, her release crashes down hard and fast, her nails sinking into the bed beneath her. Undoing my belt, I work my zipper down, unable to stop myself from taking her with the savagery that fills my veins.

Breathlessly, she peers over behind her shoulder, her eyes turning to slits. "This changes nothing."

"Just a good fuck, right?" I work my crown into her opening, and she squeezes around me.

"Oh God, yes!"

"Then that's what I'll give you." I slam into her with a single vicious thrust, a strangled cry dying in her throat as she struggles to adjust to me.

But I don't give her the chance. I take her with unrelenting madness, our bodies colliding in a frenzy until the lines between us blur, until I can't tell where she ends and I begin. My hips drive harder, the sharp slap of skin against skin echoing through the space.

If this is all she's willing to give me, I'll take it. For now.

When she shatters around me, my own release tears through me, a guttural roar ripping from my chest as I spill inside her. The feeling of her bare, the way she molds so perfectly to me…it's something I'll never fucking get over.

"You feel too good in my arms," I whisper against her ear, pulling her closer, my cock still buried deep, refusing to let her go.

Not yet. Not even as she tries to slip out of my grasp.

Because whatever this is, it's not over. Not by a long shot.

And I'm not gonna let her forget it.

THIRTY-SIX

DINARA

Weeks drag into months, and somehow, despite everything, Cillian and I fall into the same pattern. We meet at the club, pretending it's nothing more than coincidence. Pretending we didn't come looking for each other.

But the truth is, we both know what's coming. We always end up the same way: lost in one another, surrendering to an all-consuming pull that neither of us can resist.

I tell myself it's just a fix, nothing more. A quick escape from the ache that haunts both of us. We're two bodies, tangled in passion, searching for something we'll never find again.

But who am I kidding? The moment I leave him, when I get home and the silence settles around me, the emptiness comes. It always does.

I want the man he used to be. The one who held me close and looked at me like I mattered. But now we're just strangers.

I know what's best for me. I know I should stop going to that damn club. I should walk away, save myself from this torment. But instead, I find myself falling back into bad habits, back into his arms, where it's easier to pretend that nothing has changed. That he hasn't broken my heart.

"Dinara." Konstantin's voice cuts through the fog of my thoughts.

The sound of his fork scraping against the dinner plate grates on my nerves, but his next words hit harder.

"You and Cillian seem to be enjoying each other's company again, I see."

I stiffen, aware of every gaze around the table shifting toward me.

My sister suppresses a smile, no doubt having heard what I've been up to from Natalia.

"It's nothing." I keep my tone neutral as I reach for my glass of water, hoping it'll cool the heat crawling up my neck.

"Doesn't seem like nothing." Aleksei's voice is rough, laced with dark amusement. "But I don't understand why you're still wasting your time with him."

Neither do I.

I don't have an answer.

Konstantin doesn't let it go, his focus unwavering as he turns to me. "So, there's no chance at reconciliation?"

I swallow hard. "None."

He chews slowly, considering my answer before cutting into his steak again. "Hmm. That's a pity. I was really hoping for an alliance between our families, but maybe Cillian isn't the right one." He glances at me, a sharp look in his eyes. "I think it's best we find you a more suitable match from the Quinn family."

What?! He can't be serious.

The words slam into me like a freight train, knocking the air from my lungs. A suitable match…from the Quinn family.

This can't be happening.

The room tilts for a second, my stomach twisting violently. I nearly push back from the table, but somehow, I stay seated even as my muscles coil tight, ready to spring.

"You've gotta be kidding me." My tone is sharp, but it doesn't even scratch the surface of the fury bubbling inside me.

Konstantin doesn't even flinch. He simply cuts into his steak, lifting the bite to his mouth with a maddening calmness, as if he didn't just rip my future from my hands and place it on a platter for someone else to claim.

He finally acknowledges me, dropping his fork with an infuriatingly casual clink. "What do you mean? Did you think I wouldn't arrange a match for you? It's what we do, Dinara. You know that. So does your sister."

His gaze flickers to Tatiana, who looks away quickly.

"And I still have every intention of making this alliance between us and the Quinns a reality," Konstantin finishes with an air of finality.

A pressure builds in my chest, like something too big trying to fit in too small a space.

How can he treat me like this? How is he the same man who once bought me my own place and told me I could date whoever I wanted as long as I was safe? Now he's deciding my future like my wants don't matter at all.

"Over my dead body." My hands curl into fists in my lap, nails digging into my palms so hard they might break skin. "I won't be some pawn in this family's game. If I choose a husband, it'll be because *I* want him, not because you tell me to."

"Eat." His lips curl at the corners, almost a smirk. "Your food is getting cold."

Cold? Everything is cold. The food, the air, the way they've already moved on to another conversation like my future hasn't just been decided for me.

I barely hear them as they discuss Gregory's upcoming birthday party, my mind spiraling.

There has to be a way out of this. There's no way in hell I'm gonna let this happen. If Konstantin thinks he can decide my life for me, he's about to learn just how wrong he is.

I will not be forced into marriage. Not to some Quinn. Not to anyone.

I need to find a way out of this if it's the last thing I do.

THIRTY-SEVEN

CILLIAN

Skipping this party for her brother's tenth birthday would've been smarter, but I couldn't stay away. I need to see her. I know she doesn't want me here, and I pretend it doesn't bother me, but it does. Fucking her at the club just isn't enough. I want more. I need more. And I want her to give it to me. Willingly.

I watch her, the wind stirring her dark hair, soft waves dancing in the breeze. My eyes drink in the sight of her, so fucking perfect in that pale blue dress that hits just above her knees, those long legs tucked into heels that make my blood simmer. She's perfection.

And when she sees me, I catch the fleeting panic in her eyes. She squeezes the hand of the woman beside her, a silent signal to escape, but she doesn't move fast enough.

"Dinara." Her name is like a command on my tongue.

I close the distance, my fingers snapping around her wrist before she can vanish into the crowd. The guests glance at us, curiosity written all over their faces, but I don't care. I pull her into a quiet corner of Konstantin's estate, away from prying eyes.

"What do you want, Cillian?" Her voice cuts through the air, stony and sharp. "I thought we agreed we don't exchange words unless your dick is inside me."

I can't help the chuckle that rumbles from my chest. "If that's the case, I'll take you upstairs right now. We can have a proper discussion."

Those cheeks flush, eyes narrowing with disdain.

"Not happening," she shoots back. "The club is all you'll have, and even that's more than you deserve."

I lean in closer, my thumb brushing under her jaw. "That's not enough."

"It'll have to be." Her brow lifts in defiance. "I told you, you and I are in the past. There's nothing left between us. Not anything that matters, anyway."

The words land like a punch. "Is that what you tell yourself when you're alone in bed, thinking about me?" I trail my knuckles up her arm, slow and deliberate, and she inhales sharply. "Tell me, Dinara. When you're touching that perfect pussy, are you pretending it's someone else in your bed, or is it still me?"

She huffs, her finger digging into my chest as if to push me away. "You don't occupy any of my private thoughts. And you never will."

I grab her wrist, yanking it toward my mouth. I kiss the pulse point, the delicate skin there, feeling the rapid beat under my lips.

"You're such a dirty liar, baby." The truth slides off my tongue like honey, thick with temptation. "I bet if I touched you right now, you'd be wet and greedy for me to make it better."

A sharp slap across my face cuts through the tension. I laugh, low and dark, because I've gotten under her skin, and she knows it. My hand slips toward the V of her dress, knuckles brushing down the flesh peeking through. Goose bumps rise in the wake of my touch, and my grin deepens.

"I love getting a rise out of you."

Her lips part, breaths quickening as if she's losing the battle against whatever's building between us.

"I heard Konstantin wants to find you a husband. You know I can't ever let that happen."

"It's funny that you still think you have some say in my life."

"It's funny that you're still in denial about it." I move in closer, my tone thick with possessiveness. "I can't let you marry anyone else. You're mine, Dinara. In whatever way you'll let me have you."

Her eyes turn hooded, dark and full of something else—something dangerous. And I'm lost in it.

"You're never gonna have me, Cillian Quinn." The words spill like venom from her lips, a challenge in them. "I hope you're okay with that."

She pats my face condescendingly, and I fight not to put her over my knee and give her the punishment she deserves for that.

"And I hope you're ready for the fight that'll come if you ever let another man touch you." My lips fall to her throat, lightly grazing her skin. "Or taste you."

Her hand crashes into my hair, fingers sinking, owning me in a way only she can.

I don't care what she says. I don't care how much she fights it. This woman's mine, and nothing will change that.

The clink of glass cuts through the noise, and suddenly the space is still. The music halts in an instant, and Konstantin stands at the center of the dance floor, a drink in hand, his voice booming through the quiet.

"My dear friends and family. It is a pleasure to welcome you all into my home. To share my food and my hospitality with each one of you for our dear Gregory's birthday is a gift to me." His gaze sweeps across the room, landing on Gregory. "Come, come," he calls, and the boy steps forward, joining him.

Both of us move in closer as Konstantin continues.

"Gregory and his two sisters, Tatiana and Dinara, mean a lot to me."

At her name, Dinara's smile tightens like she hates being the center of attention, her eyes flickering toward me before quickly turning away.

"I'm sure they know how much I love them," Konstantin goes on. "And it's why today is a special day. Not only because our dear Gregory is practically a man, but because today I announce something else special to me. Something that I have planned for a very long time."

Dinara's eyes widen, the color draining from her face.

What the hell is happening?

"Tatiana, may I please ask you to come here with me?" He outstretches his hand toward Dinara's sister. "My Tatiana turned eighteen not too long ago, and I wanted to find her a suitable match who would provide her with the same care I have provided her for these past years."

He pauses, his eyes meeting mine across the room. A sudden cold feeling strikes deep inside me.

"And who better than you, Cillian Quinn, wouldn't you say?"

My blood boils, fists curling tight at my sides as I fight to keep my composure.

"Are you crazy?! What are you doing?" Dinara shouts, drawing the attention of the guests.

Konstantin waves a hand dismissively, as if he hasn't just dropped a bomb.

"Is this a problem?" he asks, an amused tilt to his lips.

"Of course it's a problem!" Fury flashes in her eyes. "You know how I feel about him! How much I despise the man!"

I step forward, my jaw clenched, heart pounding in my chest.

Despises me, huh?

Konstantin chuckles, unbothered. "Of course I know that." He glances at Tatiana. "But Tatiana doesn't have to hate him. Right, my darling?"

She awkwardly nods.

"So, what do you say, Cillian? Will you accept this marriage arrangement so we can finally unite our two families?"

"Over my fucking dead body." My teeth grind. "I'll never marry her. Or *her*." My glare lands on Dinara.

Two can play that game, baby.

Her mouth curls into a sneer. "Ha!" She turns to me, features filled with disdain. "You think I'd ever want you? Maybe you think you're some kind of prize every woman wants to be with."

I smirk, stepping toward her. "You once thought so."

Her gaze turns hard as she stares me down. "I'm not that girl anymore. You're nothing to me, Cillian Quinn. Nothing!"

The bite in her words doesn't match the storm in her eyes, a storm that pulls me in despite the walls between us.

"Nothing, huh?" I step closer.

"That's right." She hits me with a defiant glint in her eyes.

"Say it again."

She laughs, a cold and lethal laugh. "You're. *Nothing.*"

The second she turns to walk away, I grab the back of her head, pulling her into me. Before she can protest, I crash my lips against hers, claiming the kiss she's been fighting so hard to resist.

At first, she fights me, hands gripping my jacket like she wants to push me away. But I don't let her. I pull her closer, and slowly, she unravels. Her resistance slowly fades and she melts into me, the years of pain, anger, and distance evaporating with every breath. This kiss—this raw, desperate kiss—wipes away everything we've been through. Or at least I'd like to believe it does.

When she finally pulls back, her lips are swollen from the intensity, breathing coming in shallow gasps. Desire flickers in her eyes, a fire

I've seen before. Undeniable. Uncontrollable.

She wants me. Just as much as I want her.

Konstantin's voice breaks through the haze between us. "Let's raise a toast to the new happy couple. Dinara and Cillian!"

She recoils. "What? No!" Her eyes dart between Konstantin and me, disbelief and fury flooding her features. "This isn't happening, Cillian. We're not getting married."

"For once, we agree." I cross my arms over my chest, enjoying this game.

Her eyes narrow, determination hardening her stare. "Great. So we'll both go to Konstantin and tell him this is not happening."

I chuckle. "I don't think he'd care what I have to say."

The amusement flickers in my eyes as I try unsuccessfully to hide my grin. She looks too damn cute when she's pissed.

"Fine," she huffs. "I'll go talk to him myself."

"Sounds good, baby."

"Don't call me 'baby.'" Her glare could melt steel.

I step into her space, my fingers brushing through her hair as I pull her closer, my voice rough with a challenge. "What would you like me to call you, hmm? Mine. Is that better?"

She grinds her teeth, eyes shooting fire. "Never."

I laugh softly, letting her go just as Tynan approaches, his gaze flicking between us with curiosity.

"Excuse me," Dinara mutters, slipping past me, her form graceful despite the fire in her eyes.

I watch her walk away, her every movement like a challenge I'm determined to meet.

"You okay?" Tynan asks, and I finally give him my attention.

I take a long breath, shaking my head, clearing the fog from my thoughts. "I don't know, man. Back then, I didn't want this. But the moment she walked away from me, I realized I couldn't live without her. Now I can't walk away from her. Not anymore."

He smirks.

I grip the back of my head. "You think Mom would be pissed?"

He shakes his head. "Nah. She'd be proud of you. She'd want you to fight for her."

I hope he's right, because I'm not letting Dinara go this time.

I've always wanted her. Always needed her. And now I'm gonna have her.

THIRTY-EIGHT

DINARA

"Are you out of your fucking mind?" I bellow, cracking with raw frustration as I glare at Konstantin in his study, needing privacy for this conversation.

He sits on the sofa, cool and collected, a smirk playing at the corners of his lips, as though he's enjoying the chaos he's created.

"Moya milaya, I love you very much, but if you speak to me like that again, you will meet the same fate as everyone else who dares speak to me that way." His calm, almost lazy tone makes the anger inside me boil hotter.

My chest heaves as I fight to keep my emotions in check.

"Sit, please." He gestures toward the sofa across from him. "Let's discuss this like civilized adults, hmm?"

"Civilized adults don't force each other into marriages they don't want." I run my fingers through my hair, trying to contain the hurricane of emotions threatening to spill over.

How can he do this to me? After everything!

"I thought we were on the same page."

Despite my best efforts to remain calm, the words tremble out of me. "You know how much the breakup hurt me. I left the country, for God's sake! And now you're doing this to me? After everything I went through?"

"Come on, Dinara. You know I've always wanted the best for you. I would never do anything I didn't think was right."

I laugh bitterly, my hands quivering as I clasp them in my lap. "And you think marrying *him* is what's right for me? No. This is about what's right for *you*, isn't it? You've wanted this alliance for years, and you're using me to get it."

Konstantin exhales dramatically, as if he's tired of this conversation already. I feel the heaviness of his gaze on me as he leans back, unfazed by my anger.

How can I marry someone who swore he'd never love me? Someone who chose to walk away from me the moment he found out the truth about my uncle?

I won't let him break me again. He didn't want me then. And now it's too late. He doesn't get to have me.

"Cillian isn't as bad as you believe." Konstantin smirks. "You two have a lot to work through."

"Work through?" I scoff, shaking my head. "And you think marrying him will fix that?"

"Absolutely." He grins like this is some kind of joke. "The man was crazy without you. Did he tell you that?"

"Sort of," I mutter. "But it doesn't matter."

"It does," he presses. "You think I'd let just anyone break into your house?"

My stomach twists. "You knew…"

"Of course. Everyone knew. That's why my men didn't treat him like an intruder. I wanted to see what he'd do. If things between you two would get better. But…" He shrugs. "Then you got into that accident and everything went to shit." He drags in a long breath. "So I thought you two needed some time off. If it was meant to be, you'd find a way back. It seems you did."

"That's bullshit, and you know it." I hit him with a glare. "I want nothing to do with him. And if you were me, you wouldn't either."

He raises a brow. "Perhaps. I'm not one to give love advice, but I can tell you this: a man who doesn't love you doesn't break into your house and lie in your bed while you're across the world."

"He did that?" My heart lurches.

"He did. Desperate. Stubborn. But he cares deeply." His chuckle is harsh. "He did come to me to ask where you were, but I didn't tell him. I wanted him to suffer, and he did." A sly smirk spreads across his face. "He deserved to be tortured all these years, don't you think?"

I stiffen, but I don't respond right away. I'm too filled with anger and sadness to speak.

"It doesn't make a difference. Cillian and I are in the past. I don't want to marry him. I don't want anything to do with him or his family. Find me someone else. I'll marry an ogre at this point. Anyone but a Quinn."

Konstantin laughs, mocking and dark. "How about I make you a proposition?"

"And what's that?" My brow furrows, but I already know I won't like it.

"You stay married to him for a year. And if, after that year, you still want nothing to do with him, I'll grant you a divorce."

I freeze, disbelief washing over me. "I have to live with him for a year?" Pinching the bridge of my nose, I try to gather my thoughts, forcing back the frustration bubbling to the surface. "God, you just want to make this day worse, don't you?"

"A year isn't a long time. You'll manage." He rises from his seat, clearly tired of the discussion.

"You're messing with my life." As I stand up, the tension in my body makes every muscle tighten. "You're forcing me to do something I want no part of."

"Sometimes we have to do things we don't want to do for the right reasons." He gives me a pointed look.

"Right." I snicker. "Well, like the vows say, 'til death do us part. Maybe I can make that happen sooner rather than later."

He chuckles as he walks me to the door. "You're starting to sound more like a true Marinov every day."

I've spent my whole life trying to be nothing like them. But maybe it's time I finally start acting like one.

"Din, I don't think this is a good idea," Natalia mutters the next day, grimacing as she tugs on her bottom lip.

"It's the only way to be done with him once and for all. I can't marry him, guys. Especially not in a week!"

A week. That's all I have. Seven days before Konstantin forces me into a marriage I can't escape. Seven days to figure out another way.

And this? This is my only shot.

Alisa shakes her head, her expression pinched with worry. "But Konstantin won't let it happen. He wants an alliance, and he won't accept this."

"He'll have to."

I shove my phone into my handbag, my stomach twisting. I won't marry Cillian only to have him hurt me in the end.

Natalia frowns. "But how will this even work? Won't Konstantin find out and stop it?"

"I have to try," I say as the limo rolls to a stop in front of the towering estate, hidden deep in the middle of nowhere, New Jersey. "The auction rules state that once I sign the contract, it's binding. Whoever wins my hand tonight will be my husband. So all I have to do is go first and make sure a winner is chosen fast, and then

Konstantin can't do shit about it."

I grin, proud of my plan. Sure, it could backfire spectacularly. Konstantin could ignore the rules, tear up the contract, and force me to marry Cillian anyway. But at least I'll be trying to do something to stop it.

Alisa exhales sharply. "Dinara, think about this. What if you end up with some asshole? What then?"

I turn to her. "Kill him."

Natalia groans.

Alisa throws her hands up. "I'm just gonna say it. I think this is a mistake."

"Maybe it is," I admit. "But marrying Cillian would be a mistake too."

She exhales in defeat. "Okay…if you're sure."

I nod. "I'm sure."

I'm also going to throw up.

Opening the limo door, I step out first, the girls following me as I head toward this weekend's location for Rzvrt. All I have to do is get inside, submit my name for the auction, and wait for it to start. Once the winner is called, I'll be his.

Of course it won't be that easy. So much could go wrong.

My heart cinches in my chest at the thought of finally saying goodbye to Cillian, to the things we once had.

But he's the one who threw it all away, not me. I'd rather be stuck in an unhappy marriage than go through Cillian's rejection ever again.

I'm not stupid. I know even the most beautiful fairy tales end in disaster, and that's what our marriage would be.

As soon as we head inside, our masks in place, we're let into the grand ballroom. The hypnotic music surrounds us, but I ignore it, having only one mission in mind: to get to where I need to be before either Konstantin or Cillian stops me. I have no doubt that Cillian will be here soon, if he's not already.

The girls and I weave through the space, heading for one of the women wearing a red collar, signaling that they work here.

"Hi. Can you tell me where the auctions are taking place?"

"Outside." She points behind her. "Are you looking to participate or watch?"

"Looking to join the wedding auction."

She removes a cellphone from the waist of her ultra-miniskirt. After pressing a few keys, she scans my mask.

"Read the contract and initial."

Before I can second-guess myself, I sign it. A jolt of adrenaline shoots through me, my stomach twisting, every nerve ending sparking to life.

I'm really doing this.

"In about thirty minutes, come back here, and one of the girls will get you ready for the stage. Do not be late. Understand?"

"Yes." I clear my throat from her cold tone. "May I go first?"

She laughs. "I will put in the request, but no promises."

"Thanks."

She nods, placing her phone back in her holster.

"This is crazy, Din," Natalia says as we start toward the bar.

I know.

THIRTY-NINE

DINARA

"Are you ready?" Tiffany, one of the staff members, pulls me from my thoughts as she inspects my outfit.

The sheer white gown clings to me, the veil draped over my face. Of course I'm not ready. This is insane.

"Yes," I lie.

She surveys me one last time. "I'll take you downstairs. Once you're on stage, the bidding begins." Checking her phone, she asks, "Dina is the name you want to go by, right?"

I nod.

"Good. We're all set."

The room suddenly feels too cold, like the walls are pressing in. A wave of anxiety climbs up my limbs, tightening around my shoulders.

What am I doing? What if this only makes things worse?

No. I'm not backing down. I refuse to marry a man who never wanted me.

"It's time." Tiffany interrupts my thoughts.

I nod, hands clammy, heels unsteady beneath me. "What happens after the winner's announced?"

"Didn't you read the contract?" She tsks. "You'll go home with the winner, marry him, and the boss requires a copy of the marriage certificate."

Oh, crap.

Anxiety sinks deep in my stomach.

"Right." I fight the fear clawing at me.

"We need to go now." She leads me toward the door. "It's time."

"Alright." My voice falters, choking on the word.

I step out of the room, tears threatening behind my eyes. Once, I wondered what it would be like to be his wife. To be loved by him. But those dreams died when he walked away.

Every step through the foyer leaves me shivering, goose bumps rising on my bare arms.

You can do this. It'll be quick.

As we step outside, all eyes turn toward me. The aisle is lined with spectators, and I feel the urge to run. When Tiffany feels my hesitation, she tightens her grip on my elbow.

"Keep walking," she whispers.

Is Konstantin here? Will he realize it's me? He's going to be furious.

At the front, a man in a black suit and demon mask takes the microphone. "Please welcome our first bride, Dina. She's twenty-three, speaks multiple languages, holds a business degree, and enjoys reading. Bidding starts at five hundred thousand."

"Five hundred thousand," a man calls.

Here we go.

The numbers climb higher, and I don't even glance at the people bidding.

"Three million. Do I have three million?"

"Three million," someone calls.

Can this be over already?

"Three million. Do I have four million?"

I glance at a man in a tailored gray suit, his arm around a woman.

My stomach churns. I can't do this. Every part of me screams to run.

"Three million going once, going twice…"

I shut my eyes, an ache in my chest. In this moment, I'd do anything to feel his arms around me again. To hear him tell me how much he wants me.

"Going three times…"

"Ten million dollars."

What the—

My eyes snap open. That voice. I know it.

My throat tightens as I search the crowd. It can't be him.

"Well…" The emcee chuckles. "That's one way to bid. Ten million, going once, twice…"

And there he is.

Cillian.

A gasp escapes me. Our eyes lock, the tension in his body unmistakable as he strides toward the stage.

"Going three times."

Cillian takes another step.

"Sold to this gentleman," the emcee announces, waving toward Cillian. "Come collect your bride."

He doesn't waste a second, marching up the steps and wrapping his arm around my waist as he leans in to whisper in my ear. "You've been a very naughty fiancée. I hope you're ready for your punishment."

"Go fuck yourself," I mutter, ignoring his fake smile for the crowd.

He pulls me down the stairs, and a woman scans our masks before allowing us to pass.

"I'd much rather fuck you instead."

"That's never happening again."

"It's funny how you say that every time, yet we always find ourselves in bed all over again."

We make it back into the house, and as soon as we do, he opens the first door through the foyer and drags me inside. The bedroom is empty, as though he somehow knew it would be.

He locks the door behind him, pressing his body against the wall as I instinctively step back, my pulse racing at the intensity in his gaze.

With a swift motion, he removes his mask. His eyes darken with anger and something else—desire. My body tightens in response.

"Take off your clothes." The command lands like a slow, sensual caress.

A shiver runs through me. He closes the distance between us, tilting my chin with the back of his hand, his gaze dark and hungry.

"You need to be taught a lesson." His thumb swipes across my lips. "I won't ask again."

CILLIAN

"Take off your clothes," I repeat, trying like hell to control the fury simmering in my blood.

When Konstantin called earlier to tell me she was joining the marriage auction, I thought he was fucking with me. I'd already planned on showing up to keep an eye on her, but when the call came as I walked into the mansion, I couldn't believe it.

How could she do this? Did she think I'd just let her marry someone else?

When I saw her on that stage with other men bidding for her, every part of me wanted to tear them apart. But I waited. Waited for the perfect moment to stake my claim.

My gaze wanders down her curves, every inch of her visible to prying eyes through that damn see-through nothing of a dress.

"You thought you could walk away from me and I'd let you go?"

Her arms round her body as she stands there, head held high.

A smirk curls over my face, my thumb brushing over her fuckable mouth. My lips lower, barely grazing hers.

"You're such a bad little wife. You know what happens to bad girls, right?" When she doesn't answer, I do it for her. "They get punished."

"I'm not your wife." The words are laced with vitriol.

A finger feathers between the swell of her breasts. "But you will be."

Her lips pull up. "What would you have done if you'd lost? If I'd become someone else's."

Gripping her chin, my teeth snap. "I'll kill anyone who takes what belongs to me. And you, leannan? You belong to *me*."

I back away, but the strength in her features is unwavering.

"Strip." I tug on the thin strap of her gown. "Before I do it for you."

Her hands drift to the straps of her dress, gliding them down her shoulders with agonizing slowness. The fabric slips lower, inch by inch, revealing the soft curves of her breasts, her nipples tightening in the cool air. Every glimpse of bare skin is a gift, a temptation I can never resist.

I'll never get enough of her.

The dress falls at her feet until she's in nothing but her heels.

My cock jerks.

Fuck.

"Mask off too."

She starts to slide it up, and when I see her, all of her, my damn heart just about rips from my chest. My fingers reach for her curves, gliding down from her sternum to her pretty cunt, her skin shivering under my touch.

"You were gonna give all this to someone else?" I cup her pussy, my eyes locked with her unrelenting gaze. "This is mine, Dinara. All mine."

"I don't belong to you." The challenge in her tone only makes me want her more.

Two fingers slide inside her, thrusting deep. When she moans, a dry chuckle falls from my chest, and I fist her hair with my free hand, pulling her head back.

"Oh, you do belong to me. For the rest of your life. I can guarantee it."

"How the hell did you find me?" She tugs on her bottom lip when I massage her G-spot, pressing deeper until her body quivers.

"Konstantin told me."

"Bastard. Both of you…" she grits. "Oh God!"

A feminine cry escapes her. So damn sexy and needy for it. I flick her clit, her core hot and wet for me. She gasps when I do it again, mouth parting, eyes filled with want.

"This is the last time I will say this, so you'd better listen, Mrs. Quinn."

At the mention of her new name, her jaw clenches, causing me to smirk.

"You don't so much as allow another man to look at you. This body is mine. If you disobey, there'll be no stopping what I do."

"You'd hurt me?" Her stare narrows.

Gently, I lift a loose strand of her hair and push it behind her ear. "I could never hurt you, baby. Now, him? Well, that would be completely up to you. Behave, and no one has to die. Don't, and his blood will be on your pretty hands."

"I hate you," she hisses, fighting the orgasm burning through her limbs.

My thumb strokes her jaw while I continue to drive her wild, thrusting harder and deeper. "That's okay. You'll learn to love me."

A raspy laugh escapes her lips. "Doubt it."

"We'll see about that." Without hesitation, I pull her toward the bed, tossing her over my knee with a force that leaves no room for argument.

My cock presses into her stomach, causing me to wince as my palm spanks her hard across her bare ass. She cries out when I do it again.

"You're gonna take your punishment like a good girl." Another hard slap hits across her flesh, her skin growing pink under my rough touch. "Because you deserve it, don't you, baby?"

When she doesn't answer, I tug on her hair, snapping her head back, and her eyes lock on mine.

"I asked you a question."

"Screw you." Her eyes flash with a fierce mix of wrath and desire. I can almost feel it radiating off her in waves.

When my fingers slide into her wet cunt, she groans, hips jerking off of me. I spank her again, stroking her in between each strike until she's dripping down my fingers, her orgasm so close, I can taste it.

Just when she's about to come, I stop, dragging her up to her feet.

"You're such an asshole." Her nostrils flare as I step back, adjusting my trousers to ease the strain of my arousal.

She shifts, pressing her thighs together, desperate for what I won't give her.

"Put your damn dress back on."

With a huff, she picks it up and slips it over herself.

I rip off my suit jacket, draping it around her body like it's the only thing that can shield her from the storm brewing between us. "You're coming home with me."

She stares, eyes wide. "What?"

I step closer, my voice low and strained. "That's right. You won't be living with Konstantin anymore. I'm taking you to Massachusetts."

She stiffens, her eyes flashing with rage. "Not happening."

I can't help the laugh that escapes, rough and unforgiving. "Good thing I'm not asking for your permission."

Her nostrils flare, that frustration echoing in the small space between us. Without another word, I wrap my arm around her waist, tugging her close as I guide her through the door. She heads to the room where she got ready, removing the dress she had on and sliding into the one she arrived in, the fabric clinging to her body like it's meant to be there. My gaze follows her every movement, not missing a single detail.

She knows I'm watching. I'm not going to let her slip away. Not again.

When she's ready, I take her hand, but she roughly slides out of my grasp. The chilly night air bites at my skin as we approach the car, her purse already waiting for her in the passenger side.

"When did you get this from the limo?" she asks as I help her in and clip the seat belt around her, because she's mine to protect.

"When I spoke to Konstantin."

She doesn't look at me as I settle into my seat, her eyes set forward, filled with a quiet storm of anger and something darker. Something that cuts deeper than any words could.

My hand finds her thigh, and I feel her tense, like she's bracing herself. She's not ready for this—for what's coming—but it doesn't matter.

I leave my hand there, letting the pressure of my touch sink into her, knowing it's just the beginning. The silence between us is thick, a barrier we can't seem to break.

But I can feel it in my bones: this is happening.

We're happening.

And she can either accept it or fight me. Either way, I'm ready.

FORTY

DINARA

We're standing in his house, and all I have to my name is this dress and my phone.

I can't believe this. Can't even wrap my mind around it.

I was given a week to brace myself for this, and now it's all up in flames.

"I'm calling Konstantin," I snap, already reaching for my cell, trying to keep my hands steady.

Cillian doesn't even look fazed as he casually slips off his shoes in the foyer, casting a glance my way, that infuriating smirk still playing on his lips. "Be my guest, but it won't change anything. I'm gonna be your husband, and you're gonna obey."

I can't help but burst out with a laugh—sharp, incredulous. "Oh, that's cute."

I pull off my shoes, my movements slow and deliberate as I walk closer. Even now, I feel so small next to him, so weak, despite every ounce of fury trying to build in me. I lift my chin, forcing my eyes to meet his.

"First off, we're not married yet. And second, I will never, ever obey you."

He leans in, his breath warm against my skin. "It's up to you. You're welcome to disobey." His rough knuckles skim down my cheek, and a shiver slides through me, sharp and unwelcome. "'Cause I remember how much you enjoy it when I punish you."

The words hit me with their truth. My stomach coils with irritation and lust, but that only seems to please him.

"Your cheeks get so pink when you're angry," he murmurs, watching me with a hunger that makes my skin prickle. "Almost as pink as your pussy."

Before I can stop myself, my hand flies through the air, aiming for the smug look on his face. But in a single motion, he catches my wrist, spinning me around and pushing me against the wall with a savagery that steals my breath.

"Do that again…" he warns, rough and low. "…and I'll have you over my knee. And I won't be gentle."

"Let go of me, asshole," I seethe, feeling the pressure of his fingers tightening around my throat.

His gaze narrows, the dangerous glint in his eyes making my chest tighten.

"If it was anyone else calling me that," he growls, "they'd be dead already."

My body stiffens with defiance. "I'm not afraid of you."

"I don't want you to be." His tone softens just a little too much.

His lips brush mine—barely a touch, yet it sets fire to my nerves. It's so tender that I almost want to lean into it, but I fight it with everything I have.

"I want this to be a happy marriage, Dinara."

"There's nothing happy about this." Bitterness and pain lace through every syllable.

"It can be. I'm willing to be the kind of husband you need."

"You don't want me. You're being forced into this just like I am. You've said it time and time again: I remind you of what my uncle did to your mom."

His jaw clenches.

"So let's be up front with one another," I continue. "We both don't want this."

"That might've been true then, but I've had a lot of time to think." His mouth curls just a little.

"Is this one of your hot-and-cold games? Sleep with me, make me think you've changed your mind about our past family history until you realize you can't?" My heart tightens. "Because I'm done with that."

Gently, he holds my cheek in his palm, staring right at me. "This isn't a game, Dinara. And I'll spend however long it takes to prove that to you."

"Whatever, Cillian. I don't want this, and I don't want you. Konstantin said I only had to be in this sham of a marriage for a year, and then I'll be done with you once and for all. But if you know what's good for you, I suggest you tell Konstantin you wanna divorce me now."

"Never." The word is firm. Commanding.

"Then I'll make your life hell."

He smirks, fisting my hair as he brings his mouth close to mine. "Go for it, baby. Do your worst."

"That seems like a challenge."

His chuckle is dark. "I like a good challenge."

"We'll just see about that." I quirk a brow, enjoying this little game.

"Things would go much easier if you stopped resisting." His voice is like a soft caress with jagged edges.

Lies. All lies.

I let out a laugh, shaking my head. "Stop resisting? You broke my heart, Cillian." The words are thick and raw. "And now you want me to believe that you've somehow changed your mind about hating my family? That all this time apart has made you realize what an ass you were and you regret it?"

I escape out of his grasp.

"Well, too bad. You haven't earned my forgiveness. You haven't earned a damn thing except my distrust. And that's all you're gonna get every day, every *hour*, that you're my husband." My mouth tilts up. "If that's not good enough for you, you know what to do. Walk away. You're good at that."

His hand tightens around my throat, his lips hovering dangerously close to mine. "I'll never leave you. No matter how much you hate me. Because I'd rather spend every single moment as your husband, even if you despise me, than be without you again."

My heart squeezes painfully, but I fight it, refusing to let him see the crack in my armor.

He steps back, letting me go, but his presence still suffocates me. "So suck it up, baby, because I'm not going anywhere."

"Then enjoy sleeping alone, because I sure as hell am not sharing a bed with you. Ever!"

"Never said I wanted you to." His arms cross over his chest. "In fact, I had a cozy bedroom made for you."

"Great." My gaze narrows. "Where? 'Cause the sight of you is making me nauseous."

"Right next door, wife. Where I can keep tabs on you."

"Still stalking me, I see."

"It's part of my charm."

"More like part of your abhorrence."

"That's not what you said the last time I was inside you."

My face heats up.

"Nothing to say?" The back of his hand feathers across my jaw, and that grin on his face deepens, as if he's savoring this twisted game between us. "If you get lonely or cold, you have my permission to crawl into my bed, love." That smug look on his face is begging me to erase it. "I'll always keep you warm."

"I'd rather freeze to death."

Then I'm storming off, not even sure where the hell I'm going.

"I can't believe you!" My frustration boils over as I pace back and forth in the cold, sterile laundry room I've found. "How could you let him bring me here? I have a life, Konstantin! I have stuff. My things aren't even here."

"Your things are being packed and sent as we speak." He's annoyingly calm, making my blood simmer.

"That doesn't change anything!" My pulse races, the walls closing in. "You told me the wedding was in a week. I should be home right now, not stuck here."

"Dorogaya, you only have yourself to blame. You thought you could marry another man and get away with it? You thought you could escape the reality of what's been set in motion?"

I feel the heaviness of his words sink deep into me, but it only fuels my anger. "I don't want to be here. I don't want to marry him. How many times do I have to tell you this?"

"I know he hurt you." His tone softens, but it doesn't make me feel any better. "But he's trying to make amends, Dinara. He cares about you. No man waits for a woman for so long unless he feels something strong."

A sharp pang hits my chest.

Maybe he's right. Maybe Cillian does care.

But it doesn't erase what he did. What he said. I can't trust him again, and trust means everything in a relationship.

"He could change his mind about me at any moment. What then?"

"Then we take care of it," Konstantin says, amusement clear in his tone.

I scoff. "Be serious."

"I am serious. If he ever hurts you, he'll answer to me. You know that."

I blow out a tired breath. "I do."

But it doesn't ease the fear clawing at my insides.

"There's one more thing you need to know."

I brace myself. "What now?"

"He asked to move the wedding up."

"What?! No!"

"It'll be a small, intimate ceremony at your new home in three days."

Three days.

My heart slams in my chest, each beat louder than the last. "No! You can't do this."

"It's already done. In three days, you're a Quinn." His words are final.

My world spins as the reality crashes into me. "I don't even have a dress!"

"He's arranged that too. You have an appointment in New York tomorrow."

"This is insane! I know no one here. I'll be alone."

"You'll make friends. The Quinns are friendly. You'll like them."

I shake my head, sarcasm dripping from my words. "Thanks for the happy news."

"This will be good, Dinara. You'll see."

I don't believe him. Nothing about this marriage can possibly be good.

CILLIAN

We head up the spiral staircase, stopping at the door next to the master bedroom, where she will eventually be. For now, though, I'll let her have the control. She can sleep without me, even though it'll kill me not to wake up beside her.

I take her hand, and for a moment, she tries to slip free, but I hold it tighter. Pushing the door open, I lead her into a large room with a king-sized bed at the center and pale blue walls surrounding it.

"This is your room."

She barely glances at the space, clearly uninterested. But now that I have her, I'll take my time proving I can be the kind of man who deserves her.

Turning toward her, I cup her face in both hands. "I know you don't believe me right now, but I am sorry for what I did. I don't expect forgiveness right away, but I swear I'll earn it."

For a moment, I catch a glimmer of softness, but she blinks it away quickly.

"Can you go? I need sleep."

I kiss the top of her hand. "If you need anything, just let me know."

She jerks her hand away, and I feel the sting in my chest.

Walking over to the dresser, I pull out one of my white t-shirts and hold it out to her. "This is for you to sleep in."

She scoffs, taking the shirt from me. "What am I supposed to wear to breakfast tomorrow?"

"Another one of my shirts." I smirk. "Until your things arrive. Konstantin said they should be here before you wake up."

"Great," she mutters, giving me her back.

When I turn for the door, her voice stops me.

"What am I supposed to do here all day when you're not around?"

I glance back. "I'll take you around the property tomorrow, introduce you to the horses, maybe teach you how to ride. Or you could spend time with my brothers' wives."

Now that Fionn is married too, she'll have both women to hang out with.

She exhales sharply, and I hate seeing her this way. I want her to be happy, and I'm determined to make that happen.

"I'll introduce you to my family tomorrow."

"Do they know about me?"

I chuckle. "Yeah, baby. They know *all* about you."

Her brows furrow. "What does that mean?"

I step closer, needing to be near her again. My palm finds her nape, her pulse racing under my touch. "You don't understand how crazy I was when you disappeared. They were there for the aftermath."

She looks down, biting her bottom lip, and I groan.

"Don't bite your lip like that." I tilt her chin up gently. "I'm trying hard not to throw you over my shoulder and take you to bed with me."

That mischievous glint in her eyes returns. "I don't recommend that. I might kill you."

I slip her hand into mine. "It'd be worth it."

She pulls away with a laugh—cold, sharp, and dripping with sarcasm. "We'll see about that."

FORTY-ONE

DINARA

The morning sun's rays hit my eyes, and I groan, throwing the pillowy-soft comforter over my face, unwilling to wake up and face this nightmare. But with a resigned sigh, I drag myself out of bed.

Crap, I don't even have a toothbrush. Yet when I head to the bathroom, I find everything I need, completely brand new.

I brush my teeth quickly, wash my face, and curse the fact that I don't have my moisturizer.

My stomach growls, reminding me it's been a while since I've eaten. But the thought of sitting next to that man, pretending we're a couple, makes my stomach twist into knots.

A soft knock at the door pulls me from my thoughts. I wipe my hands quickly before opening it.

And there he is, looking flawless as always. Hair perfectly styled, white tee, gray sweats riding low on his hips, teasing a glimpse of that V leading to the one place that drives me wild.

Nope. Can't be thinking that right now, Dinara.

"Good morning, baby. How'd you sleep?"

His smirk settles in my gut, sending a rush of warmth spreading through my body.

"Okay. Your bed is comfortable enough. Are my things here yet? I'd really like to take a shower and get changed."

I'm not even wearing any panties…

He holds out a hand for mine, but I don't take it.

He grabs it anyway, pulling me out the door. "Let's have breakfast. After your things are here, you can take a shower."

We make it down the stairs, entering an immaculate kitchen with a table already set up with plates and glasses. A woman places pancakes onto a platter.

"Good morning, Mrs. Quinn." She greets me with a smile, her salt-and-pepper hair tucked neatly in a bun. "I'm Mary."

I don't even bother correcting her calling me by that name. We're supposed to get married in a few days. What difference does it even make?

"It's nice to meet you." I extend a hand and she takes it in both of hers. "You're even more beautiful than Mr. Quinn said."

My face flushes as I remember the disheveled state I'm in. "You're too kind, but I look like a mess right now."

"Oh," she scoffs, throwing a dismissive hand. "You look great."

His mouth drops to my ear, his hand squeezing mine. "Just perfect. It's gonna be hard for me to eat knowing you're not wearing anything under my shirt."

I elbow him as she watches us.

"Go ahead and sit, you two lovebirds."

Lovebirds? I laugh to myself. If she only knew how many different ways I imagined killing him before getting out of bed.

"I've made all of Mr. Quinn's favorites," she goes on. "But if there's anything else you'd like, just let me know and I'll add it to the menu.”

“Anything you make is fine,” I say, trying to sound nonchalant.

“Alright, then.” She smiles, setting down strips of bacon and muffins before bringing over pancakes and croissants.

After pouring a pitcher of what looks like freshly squeezed orange juice, she heads out, leaving the air straining with tension. He pulls out a chair and sits, but before I can take mine, he pats his lap.

“This is your seat, leannan.”

I laugh and start to move toward the empty spot across the eight-seat table, but his gaze sharpens, his expression hardening.

“Dinara.” The single word is a warning.

With a smirk, I slowly drag the chair back, keeping my eyes locked on his, and finally settle into it. He shakes his head, his gaze intense, before rising to his feet. In one swift motion, he grabs me around the waist, and before I can react, he tosses me over his shoulder with a grin.

The cool air hits my ass as I fight him to let me down.

He spanks me hard across my behind. “You keep trying to get a rise out of me, baby, and it’s only making me want you more.”

He lowers onto his seat and takes me with him, one arm around my back, my legs dangling over his. That heated gaze drops to my thighs, a growl emanating from his chest. When his fingers roll up my knee, I quiver, releasing a pant. I can’t even control myself when he touches me. How am I supposed to resist him?

“I have something for you,” he says, his voice low and gravelly, each word carrying a husky rhythm that tempts me to want things I shouldn’t.

Sleeping with him at the club while pretending to hate him was one thing, but here, in his home, with the way he’s holding me so protectively, it’s different. And I don’t want things to be different.

My gaze drops to where his free hand slips into his pocket, and all the air evaporates from my lungs as he pulls out a small jewelry box. A tightness forms in my chest, taking me back to when he bought me the tennis bracelet. The one I stopped wearing as soon as I came home.

I didn't want him to know how much I still missed him, how much that bracelet meant to me. But the truth is, when I wore it all that time in Italy, it forced me to remember all the good times we had, and that only fueled the anger I felt over how he ended things.

I was a fool to beg him to stay that night when he told me he'd never love me. I won't be that girl again.

"What is this?" I force myself to come across indifferent.

He pulls me off his lap, and before I can even process what's happening, he drops to one knee, opening the box in front of me.

My heart stops.

"Dinara Marinova, will you marry me?" His eyes gleam, and a knot tightens in my stomach.

I know it's not real. We're both being forced into this, but still, in the depths of my broken heart, I wish it was.

I stare at the round solitaire diamond glistening in the light, nestled against a silver band. My impulse is to beg him to put it on my finger, to make it feel real, but it's also the last thing I want.

"I don't think I have a choice in the matter, now, do I?" I mutter.

"But what if you did?" The way he says it, so full of emotion, tightens my throat.

"We don't live in a make-believe world, Cillian. This is what has to happen. What I want never mattered."

He grinds his jaw, the tension between us palpable. "You're right. It doesn't matter, because you *will* be my wife, whether you like it or not."

He slips the ring on my finger, and everything inside me wants to cry. This should be a happy moment, but all I feel is a hollow ache.

Pulling me back onto his lap, he grips my thigh, while the ring on my finger is a reminder that I'm his now.

"What would you like to eat?" he asks, his gaze locked on mine, softening as the tension ebbs away.

His fingers lazily roll over the top of my left hand, the warmth of his touch spreading through my limbs like a comforting blanket. And I hate that it feels like that, like he's everything I need.

"Pancakes," I manage.

He fills his plate, never breaking eye contact as he cuts a piece and brings it to my lips. When I feel him harden beneath me, heat stirs between my thighs.

"Open your mouth, Dinara." His voice is smooth, yet rough—a deadly concoction of sin and seduction.

I part my lips, and he feeds me, watching me intently.

And the way he does, like he enjoys feeding me, has a shiver running down my spine.

The SUV pulls up in front of a high-end bridal shop in New York City, and Cillian steps out of the driver's side, opening the door for me. Two of his men remain in the backseat, their presence a constant reminder of his watchful eyes.

"I'll be around until you're done."

"Yeah, okay," I reply, not bothering to call the girls yet to update them on the new wedding date or my new living situation.

My sister, of course, knows. Konstantin told her, and she's not exactly thrilled about my sudden departure either.

Luckily, all my clothes arrived before our flight here, so now it's just a matter of getting my dress sorted. I know exactly what I want, so this will be easy.

When I step inside the store, I'm caught off guard to see my sister, Natalia, and Alisa already waiting for me.

"Oh my God!" I gasp, hand instinctively clutching my chest. "What are you guys doing here?"

"You really think we'd miss this?" Natalia shakes her head, a playful grin spreading across her face as she comes over to give me a hug, followed by Alisa and Tatiana.

"It's not like I'm exactly excited about it," I mutter just as a woman in a sleek pantsuit approaches.

Her teeth flash in a polished smile. "Mrs. Quinn."

I wince internally. Is he telling the whole world I'm a Quinn now? I force a smile and return the greeting.

"I know we don't have much time before your big day," she continues. "But I promise everything will be delivered on time. We just need to pick something today."

She's trying hard to sound confident, but even she seems a little nervous. They've probably promised her a lot of money to get this done quickly.

"I know exactly what I'm looking for," I tell her, outlining the specific details of the dress I have in mind.

Tatiana's gaze expands. Leaning in, she whispers, "Are you sure about that?"

"I am," I reply with a confident grin.

"Well, then I have just the perfect gown for you." The woman turns and disappears into the back.

Natalia laughs. "You're crazy, you know that?"

"If you can't beat 'em, join 'em, right?"

FORTY-TWO

CILLIAN

Fia sits perched on her father, Fionn's, lap, her bright, innocent smile lighting up her face as she watches Dinara intently across the dinner table.

She's a sweet, adorable four-year-old and has her father completely wrapped around her finger. But Fionn had no idea she even existed until just a few months ago. Neither he nor her mother, Amara, had any way of finding each other so she could tell him about their daughter.

"You're pretty," Fia says, grinning up at Dinara while my entire family is gathered around my father's dining table. "Do you love Uncle Cillian? Daddy says Uncle Cillian loves you."

I choke on my water, the sputtering cough catching me off guard. Dinara scratches her temple, her eyes flickering between Fia's earnest gaze and the silent room around us.

This is exactly how I imagined our family dinner would go. Total inquisition. Glancing at Fionn, I see the devilish grin tugging at his lips. Of course he's enjoying this.

Fia's gaze is still on Dinara, waiting patiently for an answer.

"That's not a polite question, baby," her mother says gently, giving Dinara an apologetic look.

Fia, undeterred, furrows her brow. "Why, Mommy? You have to love a boy to get married, right? Like princesses and princes?"

She looks at Amara for validation, the hope in her eyes clear and unguarded. I hate to break her little heart, but Dinara and I are no fairy tale, though a little lie never hurt anyone…

"That's right, sweetheart," I say, squeezing Dinara's hand and pressing a soft kiss to her knuckles.

And for the first time since we've reunited, my wife doesn't look like she wants to kill me. Her mouth twitches just a little as I go on.

"Dinara and I are very much in love. Aren't we, leannan?"

When she tries to slip out of my grasp, I don't let her, bringing our joined hands over my lap. She gives me a pointed look, one I meet with equal intensity.

"Um…yep. That's right. *So* in love." She clears her throat.

Maybe one day soon, she'll actually sound like she means it.

Fia's face lights up, her excitement palpable. "I can't wait to be a flower girl! Mommy showed me what to do! It's going to be so much fun! Right, Adora?" She glances over at Tynan's daughter.

Adora nods shyly. Unlike Fia, she's more reserved around new people.

Fia turns her gaze back to Dinara. "Do you like tea parties?"

Dinara narrows her eyes playfully, her lips curling into a teasing smile. "I've been known to throw a pretty awesome tea party or two. Just ask my sister."

Fia's eyes practically sparkle with excitement. "Can we have one together? You and Uncle Cillian?"

"Him at a tea party?" Dinara snickers. "I'd pay to see that."

I raise an eyebrow, pretending to look offended. "You think I can't hang with the girls?"

Dinara laughs, the sound light and carefree. "I guess we'll see."

Her smile widens, and it makes me wonder if this marriage, this life we've found ourselves in, might just work out after all.

"Are you nervous at all about the wedding tomorrow? I mean, we're a lot," Iseult cuts in, her tone playful as she takes a sip of her wine. "I wouldn't blame you if you needed to hightail it out of here. I'd even help you."

I shoot her an irritated look.

"Believe me, it's at the top of my priorities." Dinara's mouth curves.

I pull her closer, lowering my lips near her ear. "Don't you know by now, I'll never let you get away again?"

She shoots me a grin. "Try to stop me."

"Aw, aren't they just cute?" Fernanda chimes in, leaning her head on my father's shoulder.

My dad watches us with a fond smile, like he already accepted Dinara into our family as soon as they met. "I'm glad you all found someone to spend the rest of your lives with. It's important to have that one person you can always count on, no matter how old you get or what life throws at you." He kisses Fernanda's hand. "It makes this father very proud."

"Okay, Dad, cut it out with the mushy stuff," Iseult groans, quickly blinking away any sign of emotion as she grabs her glass of wine.

"Don't mind her," Gio says, wrapping an arm around Iseult. "She loves mushy stuff. It makes her cold, dead heart beat a little."

"I'll have you know my cold, dead heart is about to carve out yours if you don't stop talking," Iseult warns with a glare, though there's no hate behind it.

Gio laughs, pressing a kiss to the top of her head, while Dinara watches the exchange between them. Her gaze flickers to me briefly, and for a moment, I wonder if she's remembering the days when we used to have fun like that, before everything got complicated. I won't lie; I miss it.

And maybe, just maybe, we can get that back.

Waiting for her to walk down the aisle has to be the most nerve-wracking experience of my life. Every muscle in my body is tight, my thoughts racing in a dozen different directions. Part of me wonders if she's going to bolt, just turn and disappear like she did once before. I was on the edge of losing her for so long, and I'm still terrified of it happening again.

I scan the guests seated in front of the draped canopy: my family, hers, a sea of faces all watching me, all waiting for her. Never in a million years did I think I'd find myself here. A man who used to despise the Marinovs. Hell, I still don't like them—except her.

I want her more than I've ever wanted anything. It surpasses all my doubts, all the bitterness, all the things I used to believe. If only I could rewind time and undo all the hurt I caused her, maybe she'd be happy to marry me.

"You look like you're about to be sick," Fionn chuckles, breaking into my thoughts.

Tynan leans in. "He's probably afraid she's already run off, just like last time."

I throw him a warning glare, but it doesn't faze him.

If Dinara tries to leave, Konstantin will make sure she doesn't get far. I have no doubt about that.

"She won't run," Tatiana interjects from across the aisle, holding a bouquet of delicate white roses. Her voice is steady, confident, as though she knows for sure, and it helps settle some of the tension in my chest.

"But if you hurt her again…" Natalia cuts in, cold and stern, eyes gleaming with something darker. "I will personally kill you, and it will be painful."

I let out a dry laugh. "Trust me, I don't plan on ever doing that again."

I don't know if she realizes how much I mean it.

"Good." Her chin tilts upward in a gesture that says she's not messing around. "You'd better not."

The music shifts, and that's when everything starts to feel real.

The guests rise, the air humming with anticipation. My pulse pounds in my ears, every second stretching longer than the last. My gaze locks on to the end of the aisle…and then I see her.

I let out a laugh, unable to help myself.

Dinara isn't like other brides. While every other woman in this moment would be bathed in white, she walks toward me draped in black from head to toe. The black veil covering her face conceals her from view, while her strapless lace gown clings to her figure in a way that takes my breath away.

She's perfection. Strong, flawless, and every bit the woman I've wanted for so long.

Konstantin walks her down the aisle proudly, a smile curling at the corners of his lips. His eyes meet mine briefly before he stops in front of me, lifting her veil gently. He kisses both of her cheeks, whispers something I can't hear into her ear, then places her hand in mine.

"You take care of our girl," he says in a low, steady tone, filled with an unspoken trust.

"I will." My words carry the weight of all I've been through to get here.

Dinara looks up at me, her eyes locking with mine, and for a brief moment, I see something softer in them—a glimpse of the woman I used to know.

Leaning into her ear, my breath warm against her skin, I say, "Interesting dress choice, baby."

She meets my gaze with a coy little smile that makes me wanna kiss her right now. "What else is a girl supposed to wear to her own funeral?"

I can't help but laugh, shaking my head. "Tha thu bòidheach."

"What does that mean?" she whispers.

"It means, 'You're beautiful.'"

Her eyes widen for a moment before the priest gets our attention. But my focus remains on my wife, my heart pounding as I realize that everything—all the mistakes, all the years lost—has led me to this moment.

And no matter what happens next, I know this is where I'm supposed to be.

DINARA

"You may now kiss the bride."

As he lifts my veil, his eyes locking with mine, a flood of emotions rushes through me as I remember the time when I could have pictured myself marrying him without hesitation. Back then, the thought was a comfort, something I held on to. But now it feels like a chain, heavy and suffocating.

When his mouth captures mine, my hands instinctively grip the lapels of his jacket, desperate to hold on to something I've wanted for so long, even when it's the last thing I should do.

Cheers erupt around us as we pull away, but I'm still lost in him, in this quiet daze that surrounds me when he looks at me this way—full of longing. Even in this moment, as much as I fight it, he holds my heart.

Soon enough, we find ourselves on the dance floor, his arms pulling me close as we begin to sway, my hands resting on his shoulders.

"I can't believe they pulled off this wedding on such short notice." My attention momentarily sweeps around the elegant setting—the floral centerpieces of white calla lilies, the black tablecloths with gold runners—everything is just as I envisioned.

A soft melody drifts from the band, a song about love, about being open to it even after the heart's been broken. I can't help but wonder if Cillian chose this song intentionally.

"My stepmother has a gift for last-minute planning," he says with a half-smile. "Once she found out, she was all in to help."

"Well, they did a good job. If I wasn't marrying you, I'd actually say this is the nicest wedding I've ever been to."

"You're hurting my feelings, Mrs. Quinn."

"Wait, you *have* feelings?" I raise a brow.

His lips curl into a small smile. "I've missed this."

The back of his hand brushes softly down my cheek. A touch so familiar, yet laced with something bittersweet.

"Me too," I whisper, feeling a rush of warmth spread through me as the song fades into another.

As his gaze lingers on me, I want more than anything to trust him again, to believe in him. But the wound is still fresh, the fear too heavy.

Just as we're about to get swept up in another song, something catches my eye—a figure standing at the edge of the crowd. A cold wave of dread sweeps through me and I instinctively clutch Cillian's hand tighter.

"Dinara, are you okay?" His voice sounds distant, muffled by the rising panic clawing at my chest.

Through the sea of people dancing and laughing, I see him.

My father. His face is as cold and unforgiving as I remember as he stands alone, watching me with a chilling intensity.

"Dinara?" Cillian calls, sharper this time.

I snap my focus to him, trying to shake off the fear that threatens to swallow me whole.

"What's going on?"

"I…" My words falter as my attention darts back to where my

father was standing.

But he's gone. Vanished into the crowd, or maybe he was never really there at all.

The rational part of my mind tells me that I'm imagining things, that the years of fearing him have twisted my perception. But the lingering terror, the gnawing feeling in my gut, tells me something different.

I force a shaky smile at Cillian, trying to push the unease down. "Nothing. I'm fine. Let's go sit for a moment."

Cillian's brow furrows, suspicion flickering in his eyes, but he doesn't press further. He simply nods, leading me back to our seats. As we settle down, a nagging question burrows deep in my mind.

Was he really there? Is my father still lurking in the shadows, waiting for the right moment to strike? Or is it just fear playing tricks on me?

Either way, I can't shake the feeling that something isn't right. That this night isn't over yet.

Minutes pass before the clinking of a glass draws everyone's attention. The music fades, conversations hush, and all eyes turn to Konstantin as he rises to give a toast, a smirk tugging and a drink in hand.

"Ladies and gentlemen," he begins. "I'm grateful to see you all here, gathered to celebrate Dinara and Cillian. Now, I don't know if you all are familiar with the torturous history between these two— because believe me, it was torturous."

A ripple of laughter moves through the crowd.

"Especially for me," Konstantin continues.

Cillian exhales sharply beside me.

"But for those who don't know, let me sum it up: it took them *way* too long to get here. Honestly, I started thinking we'd all die of old age before they got their act together. And yet, here we are." He pauses, tilting his glass slightly. "So I, for one, sincerely hope this is the end of their problems, because the last thing anyone wants is a funeral." He grins. "Za zdorovye."

He raises his glass, and the room erupts in cheers, glasses clinking together.

Cillian mutters a curse under his breath while I struggle to contain my laughter. Because of course, it's just like Konstantin to end a toast with a thinly veiled death threat.

FORTY-THREE

DINARA

The noise of the evening fades into a quiet hum. The guests are long gone, leaving us alone.

The space between us feels suddenly endless. Even as the walls of my bedroom close in around me, I reach into a drawer to retrieve a nightshirt.

Glancing at Cillian, I want nothing more than to jump into his arms. To kiss him. To run my fingers through his hair while he looks into my eyes. To feel everything I should feel with my husband.

But instead, I find myself filled with nervousness.

"Do you need help with your zipper?" he asks, undoing his cuffs, his gaze locking on to me with an intensity that makes me flush.

I clear my throat, suddenly aware that there's no way I can reach the zipper on my back.

"Please." I turn to face him just as he steps behind me.

His mouth brushes against my throat while his fingers glide over my bare arms, sending shivers through me. "You were the most beautiful bride I've ever seen."

I'm hardly able to pull in a breath from his words, the gruff way he says them. Every inch of me wants him, needs him, but I won't let him have me. Not this easily.

"We don't have to do this. Okay?" I say. "We're married in name only. That's all this is."

When his mouth lowers to the space where my shoulder and neck meet, I let out a pant, dropping my head back against his chest.

"That's not what it is for me."

"Well, that's too bad," I whisper. "Because Konstantin and I made a deal, remember? We stay married for a year, and after that, if I still want a divorce, he'll give it to me."

He lets out a growl, flipping me around to meet his steely gaze. Roughly, he grasps my jaw, bringing his mouth close to mine. "I'll never let that happen."

"And how will you stop it?"

His thumb brushes my lips. "By making you fall in love with me."

My lashes flutter, body coiling as he pulls me flush against him.

"Come to bed with me." He kisses the corner of my mouth, while my body strains and throbs for him.

"I'm not just gonna jump into bed with you. You're gonna have to earn it this time." My skin prickles the more he looks at me with that lustful gaze.

"And how does a man get to earn this perfect body? Because I'll wait a lifetime if I have to."

Everything he says just makes me want him more, but I promised myself that I'd only sleep with him again if I feel I can trust him, and I'm definitely not there.

He spins me back around, unzipping the back of my dress and kissing my neck, his breath hot as the dress starts to fall. When I stand there in nothing but a white thong, he mutters a curse.

"How the hell am I supposed to just look at you and not want to bend you over and fuck you?"

With a curl of my lips, I slip a hand behind me and grab his cock, squeezing it tight. "Patience is a virtue, they say."

"I'm a desperate man." His voice is pained, almost pleading. He faces me, his gaze intense and full of something I can't quite place. "So tell me what to do, Dinara. Tell me how I can win you back." His hand gently cups my nape, his touch warm and familiar, yet it doesn't dull the ache in my chest. "What can I do to make you believe that I'll never walk away from you again?"

A sharp pang lances through me. I swallow the hurt, the heartache he caused.

"Beg." I quirk a brow, daring him.

His eyes flare with something close to desperation. "Please, I'll—"

I shake my head, cutting him off. "No. On your knees."

For a moment, he stands there, his expression a mix of disbelief and determination, before a smirk plays at the corner of his mouth.

Slowly, deliberately, he lowers himself to the floor. The sight sends a thrill racing through me. This powerful, ruthless Mafia man, feared by so many, is on his knees. For me.

His submission, the unspoken proof of how far he'll go to keep me, crashes over me like a tidal wave.

He reaches up, grabbing my hips, his eyes locking on to mine, steady and vulnerable.

"Please, Dinara Quinn," he says, thick with longing, tugging my hand in his. "Come to bed with me. Tonight, and every night after. Because sleeping without you has been pure torture."

The words hang between us, charged with everything we've been through and everything we still could be.

"What else?" I whisper, the strength I want to project slipping through the cracks.

"I fucked up." Every syllable is thick with regret. "I know I hurt you, baby. I own that. But not for a second did I stop caring. I'll drop to my knees every damn day if that's what it takes to bring you back to me."

A sting pricks behind my eyes, but I blink it away, refusing to let the tears win.

"And I need you to understand, wanting to share a bed with you isn't just about how much I want you. It's because I need to hold you, to wake up beside you. I need you next to me to feel whole."

Oh, God.

"I never moved on, Dinara. There was never anyone else. Only you."

Every inch of me battles against the emotions threatening to break through.

"But that's okay," he continues, and my heart stumbles as he slowly rises to his feet. His fingers tilt my chin up, guiding me to meet his stormy gaze. "Take your time. I'll wait, no matter how long it takes."

Then, with a tenderness that shakes me to my core, he presses a kiss to my forehead. It's soft, lingering, stirring something deep inside me. A battle I'm not sure I'm ready to face.

He pulls back, but his gaze stays locked on mine—intense, searching, as if trying to piece together the fragments of the girl he once knew.

His jaw twitches.

There's no way in hell I can walk away from him right now. All I want is to be in his arms, even if only for tonight.

"Okay." The word leaves me on a shaky breath. "I'll come to bed with you, but only to sleep."

His hands hold my face, thumbs sweeping over my cheeks with unparalleled devotion. "That's all I want. Just to hold you."

A lump clings to the back of my throat. I desperately want to love him, but I need to be sure.

I need to know he won't destroy me again before I risk handing him my heart a second time.

CILLIAN

I've been awake for hours, simply content to watch Dinara sleep. I meant every word I said to her, and having her here means at least some part of her believed me. That's enough.

Reaching out, I brush a stray strand of hair from her cheek. She stirs, a soft groan escaping her lips. I curse myself for nearly waking her and pull my hand back, forcing myself to settle. But just as I close my eyes, her voice cuts through the silence.

"Stop."

The word is faint, barely above a whisper, but laced with panic.

My body tenses.

She murmurs it again, louder this time, and my pulse hammers in my ears. Still asleep, she cries out, her face twisting in pain.

What the hell?

"Please," she begs. "Don't..."

Terror threads through her, and something inside me snaps. A switch flips, the violent need to protect her surging to the surface. Whoever did this—whoever put that fear in her voice   will pay.

"Mom! No!" she calls out.

My hand gently caresses her arm, trying to wake her, but the sound of her distress only intensifies.

"Shh." I move in closer, wrapping my arms around her, inhaling the floral scent of her hair as I tighten my grasp, letting her feel me, letting her know she's safe. "You're okay, baby. I'm here."

With a sharp gasp, her lids snap open, her chest rising and falling in frantic breaths.

She's not fully awake, not yet, and the confusion in her gaze only breaks me further. She doesn't even see me at first.

"Dinara?" I let her go for a moment.

When she finally faces me, her expression is full of fear, and tears are clinging to her lower lashes. "What happened?"

"You were having a nightmare."

She wipes her eyes quickly, as if just realizing she's crying. "I'm sorry if I woke you."

She sits up when I do, glancing down at herself as though embarrassed.

"Hey, no." I shake my head, my thumb brushing over her hand as I take it in mine. "You didn't wake me. And even if you had, I would want you to. I'm here, Dinara. I'm always going to be here."

She lets out a sob, and my chest tightens at the sound. I pull her into my arms, my chest warm and solid against hers and I hold her close. She exhales a weighty sigh, pressing her cheek against me, and for a moment, we're just here, together, wrapped up in the comfort of each other.

"Do you remember what the nightmare was about?"

She nods against me. "It's the same one I've had on and off for years."

"Wanna talk about it?" My fingers trace up her arm, the feeling of her skin making me come alive.

Her eyes meet mine, and for a brief moment, I see the trust in her gaze. Trust with whatever she has been bottling up inside.

"It's about my father…killing my mother." The rawness in her tone clings to every syllable, cutting straight through me. "I couldn't stop him."

"You were just a kid. You have to forgive yourself."

She tugs back just slightly, her tear-filled eyes searching mine. "Have you forgiven yourself?"

Her words land hard.

"No," I answer honestly, my throat tight. "But I wasn't as young as you were."

"That doesn't matter, does it?" Her fingers graze over my stubble, her touch light and electric. "We did what we could with what we had."

The truth stings, but it doesn't make the burden of our pasts any easier to carry.

"I thought I saw him," she goes on.

"What?" That instantly gets my attention. "Who?"

"My father." She visibly shudders.

"Where?"

"At the wedding." Anxiety settles on her features.

"That's impossible," I say, trying to reassure her, though doubt creeps into my own mind. "Everyone who came in went through security. But I'll have my people look at the footage. If he was there, we'll find out."

She exhales slowly, her body relaxing a little, but there's still an edge of fear in her voice. "Thank you."

"You don't need to thank me. As your husband, it's my job to protect you." My palm runs up her back, knowing I'd die for her before I let someone hurt her. "If he comes near you, Dinara, I'll kill him with my bare hands. I swear to God, I will. That goes for anyone."

She burrows deeper into my chest. "I know."

"You're not alone anymore. I'm here." I kiss her forehead, my lips brushing her skin. "Close your eyes, baby. It's okay to dream."

She smiles up at me—a real smile, the kind I remember from before. The ones that made everything feel possible.

Then she closes her eyes and I hold her all night, not sleeping a wink.

FORTY-FOUR

DINARA

I let out a groan, stretching across the soft bed. The remnants of the nightmare are now gone, leaving me with a sense of relief and ease. It's like the grip it had on me loosened as soon as he held me. Like in his arms, I was safe.

When I open my eyes, the spot beside me is empty, and a pang of longing tugs at my chest.

Did he have to work this morning? Does he even have a set routine?

I realize I have no idea what his days look like. He's still a mystery in so many ways.

I decide a shower is the best way to start the day, but as I step through the adjoining door to my room and pull open a drawer, I freeze. My clothes are gone.

"What the hell?" Frantically, I go through every drawer, then rushing to the closet. But nothing. None of my clothes are here.

Confusion stirs in my head. I quickly make my way back to

his bedroom, wondering if he decided to move me into his room permanently. Knowing my husband, I wouldn't be all that surprised.

When I open the walk-in closet door, a scoff escapes me. Of course he did. My things are here, filling an entire half of the closet. Neatly hung, organized, everything in its place.

When did he even have time to do this? It's so early.

I move toward his dresser, finding the right side completely filled with my clothes, carefully folded.

He really did this. Presumptuous as ever.

Grabbing a pair of leggings and a tank top, I head to the bathroom. When I turn on the shower, steam quickly fills the space. Stripping down, I step inside, letting the warm water run over me.

A minute later, the bathroom door creaks open, and through the misted glass, I see him. He strides toward me, and before I can react, he effortlessly slides the shower door open, his gaze dragging down my body with a heady grin.

"What are you doing?" I gasp, trying to shield myself. But it's no use.

"Conserving water." He smirks, casually slipping off his sweats and throwing his shirt over his head as I look away.

My face flushes as he pushes me aside playfully, letting the water pour down his glorious, tanned back. It's impossible to ignore the taut lines of his body, the muscles shifting as he reaches up, letting the spray hit his face.

"Don't worry," he says from over his shoulder with a twinge of amusement. "I'm not even looking at you."

But I'm definitely looking at you.

Heat rushes to my face as I quickly look away.

But when he turns toward me, that's when I see it…

My pulse stutters, and this time, I can't look away.

A tattoo stretches across his chest, bold and intricate, the black and red weaving together in a striking design. And it isn't just the artwork that sends my head spinning. It's what's written there.

My name. Wrapped in the coiled body of a snake, entangled with red roses, etched over his heart. The sight nearly knocks the air from my lungs.

My gaze snaps to his. "What's that?"

His lips twitch. "A tattoo."

A sudden lump forms in my throat, making it hard to speak. "When did you…why?"

He exhales slowly, his amusement fading into something deeper. Cupping my cheek, he tilts my face up, forcing me to see the sincerity burning in his eyes.

"After you left." His voice is low, reverent. "I needed you, and this was the only way I could have you. The only way I could carry you with me wherever I went."

A shuddering breath escapes me, tears burning behind my eyes. I reach for it, tracing the ink, feeling the steady drum of his heartbeat beneath my touch.

"I can't believe you did this." My gut tightens.

And then it dawns on me: I hadn't seen him shirtless since I came back. Not once.

He studies me, waiting, but I can't seem to find the right words.

Instead, he grabs the shampoo and squeezes some into his palm. "Turn around."

That commanding edge in his tone sends a jolt through my limbs, pulling me right back to the first time we met. I move before I even realize it.

The moment his fingers slide into my hair, massaging my scalp, my eyes flutter shut, a sigh slipping past my lips. His hands are slow, deliberate, working the lather into me. When he rinses me off, his touch lingers, gliding down my body, brushing over my breasts.

My breath catches.

This feels too good to stop. His hands are electric, fingertips skimming down my stomach before barely grazing my core. A sharp throb of heat jolts through me, leaving me breathless, frantic for more.

The ache turns unrelenting, so needy I crave him like my life depends on it.

"I thought you weren't looking at me," I whisper as his fingertips glide over my skin in a slow, tantalizing rhythm, like a dance of pure seduction.

"Never said anything about touching." His gravelly baritone sends a rush of heat through my body, igniting a chaotic mix of lust and temptation.

He picks up my sponge, lathering it up before dragging it over my skin with deliberate care. His pace is unhurried, almost reverent, as he washes me, then gently turns me to face him. Lifting one of my legs, he rests it on the edge of the shower, his darkened gaze locked on mine as the sponge slithers up my inner thigh, teasing, torturing, until it reaches the place I ache for him most. A breathless moan escapes me, my control slipping beneath his expert hands.

He takes his time, his expression hooded, drinking in every reaction as waves of sensation ripple through me, leaving me trembling.

"I think you're clean now." A mischievous smirk tugs at his lips, while my body screams for more—more of what I won't let him give me.

Not yet.

Placing the sponge aside, he pulls me under the cascading water, washing my hair clean, his hard chest pressing flush against my back. His strong hands roam my skin, igniting something deeper. Something dangerous. Something I may not be able to resist much longer.

"Why did you move my things?" I finally remember to ask as he shuts off the water and grabs a towel to dry me.

"You think I'd let you go back to sleeping alone after that nightmare?" His voice is low as he dries me slowly, his jaw tightening when his gaze flickers to my chest.

His words send a warmth spreading through me. He cared. He was worried about me. That's what this is.

A small smile trembles on my lips. "Thank you."

"Don't ever thank me for taking care of you. I enjoy it…" He grabs my jaw, his thumb brushing over my mouth. "Very much."

As his hand drifts downward, I find it hard to catch my breath, my gut coiling tighter with every passing second.

He finishes drying me off like he didn't just unravel me. I step out of the shower first, him close behind me. While I dry my hair, he's wrapping a towel around his hips.

"We should make this a thing," he says.

"Make what a thing?" I peer up at him as I slip into my clothes.

"Showering together."

I laugh, brushing right past him, while he follows me into our bedroom.

Our bedroom…

I hadn't realized how easily I thought of it as ours.

"You'd like that, wouldn't you?"

"Can you blame a man for trying?" His palms settle on my shoulders from behind, his mouth pressing against my neck, kissing me softly.

The longer he holds me, the harder it becomes to fight him. And I don't even know if I want to.

"By the way…" he says, his mouth dancing across my skin. "Fia called. She said we're having that tea party with her tomorrow at Fionn's."

A laugh escapes me, the heat of his body making it harder to speak. "So you have a four-year-old telling you what to do now?"

"What can I say?" He wraps an arm around my midsection, pulling me tightly against him. "The women in my life have me by the balls."

I peer over at him, cracking a smile. "Do you have to work today?"

"Just for a little bit. But Tynan did say Amara and Elara wanted to come by later if you're up for it."

"Sure. That sounds nice."

I didn't get much of a chance to talk to them at dinner, so maybe spending more time with his family will help me feel more like I belong.

A few hours later, the girls arrive, bringing food and drinks with them. The warm scent of fresh bread and savory dishes fills the air as Elara grins.

"We're so happy to be here," she says, dropping the bags on the kitchen counter.

Mary takes charge, gathering everything and heading outside to set up for us. We follow her, finding a table nestled beneath the shade of a tree. As we settle, Mary pours each of us a glass of wine before heading back inside.

A few bodyguards are stationed nearby, standing watch with quiet precision, but my attention is drawn to one in particular. He's been watching me for the past few days, his gaze too intense. At first, I brushed it off as my imagination, but now I can't ignore it. His eyes linger on me with a discomfort that I can't shake.

I force myself to push the unease down, trying to focus on the conversation as the women continue chatting. Their presence is warm, welcoming, and I quickly feel at ease in their company, like I've known them for much longer than just a few hours.

"So, how's married life going?" Amara asks, tossing her black hair over her shoulder, her hazel eyes sparkling. "I remember the slap at your brother's birthday," she adds with a soft laugh. "Have things improved since then?"

I take a long sip of my wine, trying to steady myself. "Well…" I trail off, my fingers tightening around the glass. "Maybe a little. But I'll be honest, it's hard for me to trust that he won't walk away from me again."

Elara nods in understanding. "Yeah, Tynan told me about what happened and that you left."

My throat tightens. "It was just too hard for me to stay after how much he hurt me."

"Trust can be a tricky thing," Elara continues. "Once it's broken, it takes time to rebuild it. But I'm sure you two can." She reaches over, her hand comforting as she gives mine a reassuring squeeze. "If you want to, that is."

I want to. God, I want to. But fear holds me back.

"I just don't want to get hurt again."

Sympathetic eyes greet me.

"I vote you make him suffer a little more," Amara says, a playful glint in her gaze. "Wouldn't want to make it too easy on him."

I laugh, shaking my head. "My cousin Natalia would agree with you. It's exactly what she told me to do."

We all chuckle, and for a moment, I forget about the fear and the past. It's easy to laugh, to feel like we're all best friends already. The warmth of their presence washes over me, making me feel lighter than I've felt in a long time.

"Um…" Elara leans in, glancing briefly toward the bodyguards and then back at me. "Is that guy checking you out?"

I follow her line of attention, and my stomach drops. The same bodyguard from earlier. His dark eyes are fixed on me, and when I meet his gaze, his mouth curves into a small, unsettling smile.

"I think so." My throat goes dry.

Elara's eyes narrow, and she fixes him with a pointed stare. He quickly shifts his focus elsewhere, but the discomfort in my chest lingers.

Why is he looking at me like that? Doesn't he realize that this kind of attention could get him killed?

At least it would if he worked for Konstantin. He'd never let something like this slide. But Cillian…maybe he doesn't handle things the same way.

I hesitate, unsure whether to bring it up to him. The last thing I want is to stir up trouble.

My gaze flicks back to the bodyguard, my thoughts spinning. It's possible I'm overreacting, but the unease refuses to fade.

FORTY-FIVE

CILLIAN

After wrapping up the business call with my brothers, I slide into the car, the weight of the day pressing down on me.

Without thinking, I dial a number I never thought I'd call again. The line rings for a few seconds before he answers.

"Cillian. What can I do for you, brother?"

I grind my teeth. Keeping my tone even is difficult, but necessary. "Can you teach me Russian?"

There's a long pause before Konstantin bursts into laughter. "I never thought I'd hear you ask me that."

"Can you or not?"

"Of course. But why?"

"Because I'm trying…with her, and I thought…" I trail off, not quite ready to admit how desperate I am.

A knowing chuckle follows. "Ah, you thought that if you speak her language, say something nice, something that makes you seem sincere, she'll believe you, huh?"

"Exactly."

"Well, I'm nothing if not a romantic at heart."

Right. The man who prefers to feed body parts to his pigs is *definitely* a romantic.

"I will teach you everything you need to know," he continues.

"I found some stuff online. Thought you could help me figure out if the translation's right."

"No, no. Don't waste your time with that nonsense. I'll teach you proper Russian."

"Alright," I mutter, feeling like I just inhaled glass. "Thanks."

Fuck, that was hard to say. But I'm willing to do anything, even swallow my pride.

"Anything you think I could do to win her over?"

"Did Dinara ever tell you about her mother?"

"A little."

"She was a good woman. Kind, gentle, loved her kids. She used to make this cake Dinara adores. If you bake it for her, you'll have her heart. I'll send you the recipe."

Baking isn't exactly my forte, but I'll try anything. "Alright."

"I've sent it to you. You know, I always said we'd be friends one day."

"Yeah, don't push it, Marinov."

He chuckles as I glance at my phone, relieved to find a text with a recipe attached—thankfully in English.

"After you share a meal and some cake, look into her eyes and say this: 'Moy teli mir v tvoikh glazakh.'" The words roll off his tongue smoothly, making them sound more poetic than I ever could.

"What's that mean?"

"My whole world is in your eyes."

Damn, that's good.

"Thanks for the tip. Hopefully it works."

"Listen," he continues. "I've always known you two would end up together, even when I wanted to kill you after she got into that accident."

Cold dread hits me. "What accident?"

He pauses. "You didn't know?"

"No. What fucking accident?" Rage fills my veins.

"The day after you left. She was driving to Natalia's, crying on the phone, and it was raining. A car hit her. Came out of nowhere. To this day, I can't find the bastard who did it. It's my biggest regret. But thankfully, we didn't lose her."

The words land like a heavy blow to my chest.

A fucking accident?

My hands tighten on the steering wheel, my pulse pounding in my ears.

I caused this. It's my fault.

The realization slams into me like a bulldozer. If I hadn't broken her heart, if I hadn't pushed her away…

"It was a long time ago." Konstantin cuts through my thoughts. "Don't beat yourself up about it now."

But I can't stop it. My mind reels with the weight of what he just told me.

"I've gotta go."

Ending the call abruptly, I drop the phone into the cup holder as I pull out of the parking lot, my pulse speeding just like I am.

I need to see her, to hold her, to apologize for everything over and over until I'm the one who forgives myself.

As I pull up to the house, I glance at the security monitors through my cell, finding Dinara out by the pool, reading a book, and it makes me wish I was right there beside her.

Then she shifts slightly, and her eyes flicker toward the left, where some of my men are stationed. There's a subtle change in her demeanor: her shoulders tense, her features tightening.

Why would the presence of guards make her nervous? She's been around this life long enough.

But then I see it. One of my guys…he's looking at her, and it's not the usual respectful glance. No, this is different. It's predatory. The kind of look that says he's thinking about taking what doesn't belong to him.

A cold fire ignites in my veins.

I don't know if he's stupid or just suicidal, but whatever it is, he's about to learn a lesson he won't soon forget.

No one touches what's mine and lives to tell about it.

DINARA

The sun warms my skin as I lounge in the chair. Amara and Elara are gone, leaving me to pretend I'm lost in the pages of my book. But I'm not reading. Not really. Instead, my attention drifts, side-eyeing the bastard stationed by the pool.

Conall. That's what I found out his name is. He's been staring at me again, like he's imagining things he has no right to.

I grip my book tighter, shifting slightly to make it clear I *do* notice. It doesn't deter him.

Maybe I should tell Cillian.

Just as the thought crosses my mind, the heavy doors to the estate swing open with a bang, and I nearly jump. Glancing behind me, I find my husband storming into the yard like a predator who's already locked on to his prey. And the second I see him as he looks at me—his sharp jaw clenched, his dark eyes burning with rage—I know.

He already knows.

But how?

I don't get a chance to react before he crosses the distance in a few long, furious strides. Conall barely has time to register what's happening before Cillian's fist grabs his shirt and yanks him forward.

"You thought you could look at my wife and I wouldn't find out?"

Conall stumbles, his hands rising in a feeble attempt at defense. "Boss—"

"Now you're gonna find out what happens when you forget who the fuck you work for." Cillian drags Conall right past the pool and slams him back against the stone pillar, his grip unrelenting.

The other guards don't move or speak. They know better. They know Conall just signed his own death warrant.

"Tell me," Cillian continues, his voice deceptively calm. "What exactly were you thinking while you stood there staring at my wife?"

Conall swallows hard, his gaze flicking to me for a split second.

Wrong move.

Cillian snaps. His fist collides with Conall's stomach so fast I barely see it. Conall chokes on a gasp, doubling over, but Cillian isn't done. He shoves him back again, his knuckles white from the force of his grip.

"You like looking at things that don't belong to you? Or were you stupid enough to think you could actually touch her?"

"N-n-no, boss, I swear—"

Another punch to his kidneys comes harder, and I gasp.

Cillian's grip tightens. "You weren't *what*?" he growls. "Gonna do something? Gonna try something?"

Conall shakes his head frantically, but it doesn't matter. Cillian's fist flies, and the sickening crunch of bone against flesh sends a shiver through me. Conall's head snaps to the side, blood already trickling from his nose as he stumbles, gasping, but Cillian doesn't let go. He grabs him by his shirt and drags him by the edge of the pool, and my eyes grow.

"Get on your knees!" He shoves him on the ground. "Get on your fucking knees and apologize to my wife for making her uncomfortable. Then you beg for my forgiveness for disrespecting me."

Conall rises on his knees, clasping his hands together, choking on a cry as he stares at me. "Please, Mrs. Quinn." He peers at me from his right. "I'm sorry. I was an idiot. I promise I'll never, ever look at you again."

"That's right; you won't." Cillian kicks him in the jaw, and a tooth flies out.

"Please, sir. I'm sorry. I-I messed up. I'll never do that again."

"Of course you won't."

What is he gonna do?

The hairs on my arms stand up.

"Now you're gonna find out what happens when you fuck with my wife."

In one swift, brutal motion, he drags him into the pool and shoves his face into the water, holding it there. Conall struggles, but Cillian is stronger. Faster. Angrier.

"P-p-please!" Conall chokes out when he pulls his head back. "I swear I—"

Cillian doesn't let him finish. He thrusts his face into the water again.

A violent splash echoes as Conall's body jerks, his arms flailing. Cillian holds him down without a word, his eyes on mine, his grip unyielding, unmoved by the frantic thrashing beneath him.

"Stop!" I get to my feet, rushing toward him.

But his eyes are distant, clouded with too much anger to calm down.

"You don't have to do this."

His mouth twitches. Not in a smile, but something colder. Darker. And it excites me.

"Let me make something clear, Dinara." His tone is low, but it cuts through the air like a blade. "You're my wife." He says it with unwavering certainty, a vow carved in stone. "And I will protect you with my life." His grip tightens, his expression hardening. "Anyone who hurts you will meet the same fate."

A shiver runs through me—not from fear, but from the undeniable sense of security he gives me. With him, I know I'm safe.

Bubbles continue to rise to the surface. Then fewer. Then none.

After a long moment, Cillian finally lets go, watching as Conall's lifeless form sinks, disappearing beneath the rippling surface.

He steps out, water cascading down his body, eyes fixed on the dead man as if he's just taken out the trash. Then, without hesitation, he stalks closer, gripping the back of my neck with a firm, possessive hold. His body presses into me, heat radiating between us, his hardness unmistakable.

"You're mine, Dinara Quinn." His voice is dark, absolute.

A vow. A declaration.

My breaths hitch as he backs me up against the stone pillar and pins me, the raw intensity between us igniting something primal.

"Yours," I whisper, the admission trembling past my lips.

The truth. The only truth that's ever existed.

A guttural growl rumbles from his chest before his mouth crashes onto mine, devouring, consuming, stealing the very air from my lungs. His hands are ruthless, pushing up my sundress and yanking my panties down in one swift motion. Then he spins me around, bending me over as heat floods my veins.

He shoves his pants down, and with one brutal thrust, he's inside me. A ragged moan tears from my lips as he fills me, stretching me, his hips driving into me with an unrelenting force that steals every thought from my mind.

I take it all—every punishing stroke, every ounce of his need—my body responding with desperate, reckless hunger. My heart clenches, aching for what we once had, what we could have again.

When my release crashes through me, it's explosive, shattering me from the inside out, but he doesn't stop. He thrusts deeper, harder, until my knees threaten to give out.

Only then do I realize the guards are gone. Not that it would have stopped me. Nothing would have.

With a final, feral growl, he spills inside me, his grip tightening as his body trembles against me. His hips slam into me like he wants to break me, consume me, ruin me completely.

As we both come down, his lips brush over my shoulder, his breath ragged against my skin. And for the first time in a long time, I feel whole.

Then his voice cuts through the haze. "Why the hell didn't you tell me you got into a car accident all those years ago?"

My eyes widen. Konstantin must have told him.

I shrug, peering over at him. "It was so long ago."

His nostrils flare as he eases out of me, pulling my panties back into place before adjusting his own clothes. But the tension in his body doesn't ease.

"Do you understand how much you mean to me, baby?" His words simmer with emotion. "The thought of something happening to you, knowing it was my fault…" He drags a hand down his face, his jaw tight.

"Hey…" I reach for him, tugging his arm down.

He lets me, his eyes filled with turmoil.

"I'm okay," I whisper. "I'm right here."

Pain flickers across his features before he clasps my face in both hands, his thumbs brushing along my cheeks. Then, silently, he leans in and kisses me. Deeply. Passionately.

And for the first time in forever, I want to believe that maybe, just maybe, we can have it all.

FORTY-SIX

DINARA

The next day, the chaos of Conall feels like a distant memory as I glance at Cillian just in time to catch Fia's wide-eyed expression.

She looks like she's about to set him on fire with her glare. My kinda girl.

"What did I do?" he asks, genuinely perplexed, while Adora pours tea into our bright pink cups—but really, it's just water.

I bite back a laugh as Fia crosses her arms, her little face scrunched with disapproval. "You have to pull the chair out for the princess before you sit down!"

Cillian shakes his head in mock regret, playing along as if this is the most serious offense imaginable.

"My apologies," he says solemnly, then steps forward and pulls my chair out with exaggerated care.

But Fia isn't satisfied. Her brow lifts, unimpressed.

"What did I do wrong now?" he asks, exasperated but amused.

She lets out a dramatic sigh, shaking her head as if he's utterly hopeless. "You didn't kiss her hand! Every prince kisses a princess's hand." To drive her point home, she smacks her forehead.

I pinch my lips, enjoying this way too much. Cillian exhales, then takes my hand, pressing a soft kiss to the top of it. But when his eyes lock with mine, something shifts.

The air around us thickens, my skin tingling from the warmth of his lips. The playful moment turns electric, and suddenly, I'm left frozen, caught in the intensity of his gaze.

Clearing my throat, I settle into my miniature chair, but the moment isn't lost on me. And when Cillian lowers his large frame onto a tiny hot-pink kiddie stool across from me, I can't hold back a chuckle.

Fia raises a brow at him. "Did you tell her how pretty she looks?"

He leans in toward her, lowering his voice to a dramatic whisper. "I'm really not good at this, am I?"

She shakes her head, mouth pinched in disapproval.

Cillian turns back to me, eyes dark and full of intent as he reaches across the table and takes my hand. "You're my every dream come true, Dinara Quinn."

My stomach does a flip at how genuine it sounds, like he means every single word. I can barely breathe. He doesn't let go of my hand, running circles over my skin, making my heart race faster.

"What would you like with your tea?" Adora asks, grinning as she holds up a tray of make-believe pastries.

"The chocolate cake, please," I manage to say, trying to sound unaffected, even though my heart is threatening to leap out of my chest under Cillian's hooded gaze.

"Coming right up." She places a plastic slice of cake on my plate before turning to her uncle. "And for you, sir?"

Cillian taps his chin dramatically. "I think I'll have whatever my wife's having."

"Good choice, sir," Fia adds. "But we only have one piece of chocolate. You get strawberry instead."

"Strawberry it is." Cillian chuckles, looking back at me with a grin as we both pick up our forks and start nibbling on our desserts.

As soon as his fingers release mine, a tiny part of me wishes he hadn't let go.

The girls pour more "tea" into our cups as we continue eating, the room alive with their laughter and the soft clink of plastic cups.

When we're done, Fia and Adora grab a small kiddie music player. A catchy little tune fills the room, and the girls turn to Cillian with one of those knowing looks.

"Oh, right…" Cillian clears his throat, standing and offering me his hand with exaggerated formality. "Princess Dinara, may I have the honor of this dance?"

I can't help but laugh at how royal he's being. As he stands there, hand outstretched, I wonder if this is what life would look like if we had kids. He's so natural with them, so tender and playful. My heart melts.

"You may, Prince Cillian," I tease, slipping into the role with ease as he helps me to my feet.

The girls giggle, their laughter bubbling through the air like magic, making the moment feel all the more special.

Cillian curls an arm around my back, holding me close, his other hand in mine as we begin to sway together, lost in the music. My head rests against his chest, and for a brief moment, it feels so right, like we've been doing this for years. A quiet sigh escapes my lips as I close my eyes, letting myself feel the warmth of his embrace.

The song changes, but we keep dancing, moving in perfect harmony, oblivious to everything but each other. The moment stretches on, peaceful and perfect, until the last notes fade away.

"We had a lovely time," I tell the girls as they start gathering their things. "Thank you for being such wonderful hostesses."

"Come back anytime!" Adora calls, her voice practically sparkling.

"Alright." I smile.

"Bye!" Fia waves as they start to head out, leaving the music player on, but in the last second, she turns around and says, "Thanks for the money, Uncle Cillian!" Then her little face freezes, eyes wide. "Uh-oh…"

"Wait, what money?" I glance between them with a narrowed stare.

"Whoops." Fia grimaces, covering her mouth. "Gotta go. Bye!"

And with that, she dashes off with Adora, leaving us behind in a trail of giggles.

I turn to Cillian, popping a brow. "Did you actually pay them for this?"

He scratches the back of his neck, a sheepish grin tugging at his lips. "Well…"

I shake my head, laughing. "You planned this?"

Cillian shrugs nonchalantly, his gaze intense and unshifting. "Is that so bad? It got you to dance with me, didn't it? You almost looked like you actually liked me again." He smirks, and my stomach flutters.

I've always liked you…

Did he really do all this just to be close to me? The thought makes my heart ache in the best way. He steps closer, his arm winding around me, pulling me flush against him.

His voice drops to a low whisper, stirring something deep inside me. "I'd do anything to make you see me the way you once did, Dinara. Moy teli mir, v tvoikh glazakh."

Air stalls in my lungs, and I almost can't believe my ears. "You learned Russian for me?"

He nods, looking at me with a mix of affection and determination.

"Who taught you to say that?" I wrap my arms around his shoulders, impressed by his effort. "You're not half bad."

"Konstantin," he admits, his lips curving into a half-grin.

"Are you two friends now?"

"Not even close," he chuckles dryly. "But he's…useful."

I scoff. "I'm sure he'd love to hear that."

"Are you gonna tell him?" he teases, dropping his lips close to mine.

"Of course not. I'm Switzerland." My tone grows raspy, butterflies spreading in my stomach.

"That's a good girl." He draws me into a soft kiss.

And when he pulls back, I feel an emptiness lingering where his lips just were.

"Oh, by the way…" he adds. "I had my people look into your father. He wasn't at the wedding. Not on any of the cameras, anyway."

I should be relieved. I want to be relieved. But I'm not.

I just nod. "Thanks for looking into it."

He notices the shift in me immediately.

Gently, he cups my face in his hands, his eyes soft with concern. "What did I tell you about thanking me for taking care of you? Don't do that. Understand?"

I nod, leaning into his touch, surrendering to the comfort he offers. With every passing day, he chips away at the walls I've built around myself, and I can't deny I feel that spark between us burning just as bright as it once did.

That evening, Cillian's dining room is transformed into a romantic oasis.

Candles flicker across the long marble table, a beautiful white floral arrangement in the center. Candlelight casts shadows over the rich dishes Mary has laid out. Every single one of them is my favorite. How he knew, I have no idea.

But the biggest surprise is that he made all of it. From scratch. I still can't wrap my head around that. When Amara asked to hang out after the tea party, I had no idea that she and Fionn were in on the surprise Cillian was planning.

I can't help feeling so adored as he takes my hand and leads me to my seat.

"The food looks incredible. How did you know what I liked?"

"A man has to keep some secrets to himself." He smirks, pulling out a chair at the head of the table, me on his left as he starts to fill my plate.

He watches me cut into the steak, like he wants to see my reaction.

"This is dangerous." I pop the piece into my mouth and groan. "If you keep cooking like this, I might expect it all the time."

He leans back in his chair, his whiskey swirling in his hand. "Maybe that's the plan."

There's something in his tone that makes my stomach tighten. A quiet confidence maybe, or the affection there. Because this is what he's been doing lately. Little things, thoughtful things, trying to win me over without forcing it.

After everything he put me through, I never thought I'd be sitting here, letting him.

And what scares me most? It's working.

We continue to eat, conversation and laughter filling the room. Before I can think too hard about how easy it's been to fall back into our relationship, one of the staff walks in, carrying something on a silver tray.

My breath stills the moment I see it.

A medovik: Russian honey cake. My absolute favorite, the one my mother used to make for us.

"It's your mom's recipe."

Emotion clogs my throat. It's been years since I've even seen this cake, since I've tasted the layers of honey-soaked goodness she used to make for me as a child. I lift my gaze to his, my vision blurring.

"You…" I swallow hard. "How did you…"

His expression softens with something deeper. "Konstantin shared the recipe. Figured I'd give it a shot."

My heart thumps louder in a way that feels dangerous. Because this isn't just some grand romantic gesture. It's intimate. It's proof that he cares. That he's trying, really trying.

I shake my head, forcing a watery laugh while he cuts each of us a piece. "You really made it from scratch?"

It's not easy. There are ten layers on this cake.

He nods, watching me carefully. "Took me a few tries," he admits, lips quirking. "But I got it right in the end."

I reach for the fork. The first bite is warm and rich, melting on my tongue, tasting like home. Like love. I exhale shakily, setting the fork down before meeting his gaze again.

"Thank you," I whisper. "This means a lot to me."

Something shifts in his expression, something unreadable, but I don't miss the way his jaw flexes, like he's the one struggling to keep it together.

Then his smirk returns, slow and deliberate. "Come here and bring your plate."

I blink at him. "What?"

He leans back in his chair, patting his lap. "Sit with me." His voice dips, smooth and commanding, and something tightens in my chest. "Let me feed you."

A slow heat creeps up my neck, but the look in his eyes—dark, unyielding—makes it impossible to say no. Biting my lip, I pick up my plate and move toward him, settling on his lap. His arm wraps around my waist, pulling me in.

"You've always felt right in my arms," he murmurs, reaching for the fork while my entire body prickles.

He cuts into the cake with deliberate slowness, lifting a bite to my lips. I part them instinctively, letting him slide the fork past them. The honey-soaked layers dissolve on my tongue, and a soft hum escapes

me.

Cillian's free hand skims along my thigh, his fingers brushing over the slit in my dress as he feeds me another bite. Then another. Each movement is unhurried, decadent, like he's savoring every second of this—watching me, feeling me melt against him.

By the time I've eaten nearly all of it, my body is thrumming with awareness, my chest rising and falling a little too fast.

Cillian sets the fork down, his lips ghosting over my ear. "Dance with me."

Before I can agree, he shifts, effortlessly lifting me as he stands. My hands grip his shoulders as he sets me on my feet. His thumb grazes my cheek, his gaze searching, completely unnerving me as he holds out a hand for mine.

And of course, I take it.

Music hums from his phone as he selects a song, then pulls me close, one hand resting at my waist, the other holding mine against his chest. The slow melody wraps around us, and we sway together in the dim light. His touch is warm. Grounding. Protective.

For a moment, I close my eyes, letting myself sink into him, into this. The safety of his arms, the quiet intimacy of it all. My cheek rests against his chest, my fingers curling against the fabric at his back.

When I veer just enough to look up at him, his gaze is already locked on mine, the tension between us thickening, crackling like a live wire.

Dark. Intense. Unrelenting.

His palm slides up to my nape, fingers threading into my hair, and he leans in, his mouth hovering just above mine.

A tremor runs through me, making it hard to focus on anything but the nearness of him.

And right before his lips touch mine, he murmurs, "Taim i ngrá leat."

I have no idea what it means, but the way he says it—low, full of passion—tells me it has the power to ruin me. And when his mouth finally captures mine, I let it. Because in this moment, I know for sure—I'm falling for him all over again.

And this time, I might not survive it.

FORTY-SEVEN

CILLIAN

I carry her into our bedroom, lowering her onto the mattress, my lips never leaving hers as I strip away her clothes, then slide out of my own.

The heat of her bare skin against mine is a fucking brand, scorching into me, making it impossible to think of anything but her.

Her hands are everywhere—gripping, pulling, desperate—as though she needs to feel every inch of me. I kiss her slow, like I've got all the time in the world to remind her that she's mine. Our bodies press together, fitting in a way that feels just right, like we were built for this.

Dragging back just enough to look at her, I skim my knuckles down her cheek, my jaw tight.

"I'm sorry." My voice is filled with everything I can't put into words. "I'll never hurt you again, Dinara. I swear."

"I know." Her gentle palm clasps my cheek, her touch like the antidote to the hell I've endured every day without her.

When her mouth strokes mine, I groan, sliding my fingers into her hair, holding her closer. My cock nudges into her, and I feel myself come undone.

"You're mine, always, for the rest of my life."

And with a single thrust, I'm inside her, my mouth crashing with hers, swallowing every gasp and every cry.

Her nails dip into my back as my hips drive into her, needing to claim, to own, to make her feel everything I feel in my heart. She tugs at my hair, kissing me with equal savagery.

I never thought we'd get here, to a place where she'd even consider forgiving me, but I'll spend the rest of my life proving I deserve this. Proving I deserve *her*.

I flip her onto her stomach, my body forcing her into the mattress as I sink deeper. Her soft curves mold against me, her back arching as she takes every inch.

"Fuck, baby," I groan, my hips pounding into her. "You take me so damn good."

Her body is so tight, so wet, sucking me in, clenching around me like she never wants to let go.

"I love you, Dinara."

She gasps as I tilt her chin with the back of my hand, needing her to see it, to know this isn't just a heat-of-the-moment confession. It's the truth.

"I didn't realize how much I loved you until you were gone. And I've loved you for too long now to wait another second to say it."

Her eyes gleam and her lips tremble, like she wants to say it too. But before she can speak, I shake my head.

"No." I slowly rock inside her. "Not yet. Not until you know you mean it."

Before she can say a word, my mouth finds hers, kissing her deeply, like it's the only thing keeping me alive.

I take her faster, my need taking over until her body starts to shake, and I know she's close. Her cries echo across my lips, her walls pulsing around me, milking me. But I don't stop. I go harder.

When I pitch back, I watch her come undone, the way her back bows, her mouth parting on a silent scream.

"Cillian!" My name rips from her lips, her body clenching around me as she shatters, taking me with her.

But I'm not done. Before she can catch her breath, I flip her over and move down her body, kissing along the path as I spread her thighs apart, her cunt pink and swollen. I latch my mouth around her, sucking her clit, and her nails dig into my scalp.

"Oh God," she gasps, shaking her head, her hands weakly pushing at my head. "I can't go again."

I smirk against her, gripping her thighs and drawing her closer as her legs tremble around me.

"You can," I murmur against her slick heat. "And you will."

With a growl, I pin her thighs down on the mattress, taking what belongs to me. My tongue sinks inside her while she pulls at my hair, her back bowing as she cries, desperate for another release.

This time, when I flick my tongue over her, she shatters, writhing beneath me, her release soaking me. Knowing I'm the one who made her squirt like that fills me with maddening possessiveness.

I climb over her, taking her lips in a fierce kiss before flipping her onto me. My grip tightens around her hips as I drag her over my cock.

"Ride me, baby. Take what's yours. Make me come inside that perfect pussy."

She lets out a shaky moan, grinding her clit against my length, teasing us both. My hand finds her throat, applying just enough pressure to make her eyes darken with need.

"So fucking beautiful," I groan, my hips arching up, her wet core making me insane. "Use me. Take what's yours, a ghra."

Her fingers grip my chest as she lifts herself just enough, the head of my erection breaching her entrance. Slowly, she sinks down, inch by inch, stretching around me, her gaze locked on mine as she takes every last inch.

"That's it. Take it all."

My restraint wavers, every muscle in my body coiled as she rolls her hips, riding me like she owns me. My fingers flex around her throat, my control slipping with every twist of her hips.

She chases her release, a wild look in her gaze. When it crashes over her, I flip her beneath me, hooking her legs over my shoulders. I drive into her, pounding roughly, lost to the madness of her. Our bodies move in perfect sync, until the pleasure consumes us both.

With a guttural growl, I give her everything, burying myself to the hilt, my orgasm surging through me as I fill her with it, my eyes fastened to hers.

And in this moment, nothing else exists. Nothing but the two of us.

DINARA

"I've never been on a horse before." I cling to him the next morning, scared shitless. "What if I fall?"

He tugs my hand into one of his, bringing my knuckles to his mouth. "I'd never let you fall, leannan."

"You promise?" I bite the corner of my mouth, emotions clinging to my throat as I get lost in the genuineness of his affection.

"Of course, baby."

And I believe him. The strength of his body is a safety net against my fear, his steady presence calming the nerves buzzing beneath my skin. Plus, it doesn't hurt how sexy he looks in a pair of jeans.

The beautiful white horse beneath us shifts, sensing my hesitation, but Cillian's grip remains firm over mine.

"Relax, Dinara. She won't hurt you." His words are rich with patience.

I exhale, slowly loosening my death grip on him. The late morning sun spills across the vast open fields, bathing everything in gold. Out here, it's just us—the cadenced sound of the horse's hooves against the earth, the rustling of the wind through the trees, the soft hum of nature embracing us in its stillness.

He nudges the horse forward, and I squeeze my eyes shut as we start moving.

"You doing okay, baby?"

I huff out a breath, my stomach flipping as if I'm about to plummet down a roller coaster. "Not so much."

He laughs, deep and rich, the sound vibrating through me. "You're doing great."

He guides us smoothly across the field, and little by little, I relax, trusting him. Trusting that he meant it—he won't let me fall. Soon, I ease into the rhythm, the tension in my muscles fading as we ride along the fence line. A rush of exhilaration courses through me.

"I think I like this."

Cillian grins, twisting slightly to glance back at me. "Told you."

We ride for what feels like forever, lost in the beauty of the open land and each other, until he finally slows the horse and dismounts, helping me down with ease. His hands settle on my waist, his touch lingering as his gaze deepens, pulling me into the quiet intensity between us.

"I have a surprise for you." He takes my hand, leading me toward a shaded spot beneath a towering oak tree.

A checkered blanket is spread out, a picnic basket sitting in the center.

My heart swells, warmth spilling into my chest. "You planned this?"

He tucks a loose strand of hair behind my ear, his touch slow and deliberate. "Wanted to do something special for my girl."

My girl.

The words wrap around me, setting my pulse into an eager pace. This life, these last few days…it's everything I once dreamed of for us. And now, it's really happening.

We lower onto the blanket, the sun kissing our skin as he pulls out food: slices of cheese, bread, fresh berries. Simple, yet perfect. He feeds me a piece of strawberry, his gaze steady, eyes brimming with something unspoken, something deeper. As I take it between my lips, my glance drifts to the bracelet he once gave me, now wrapped around my wrist, exactly where it belongs.

"I want to try," I confess as I gaze out at the peaceful stretch of land before turning to meet his eyes. "I want to trust you again. I want a life with you. A future. A family."

Each word carries a piece of me, raw and exposed, as if I'm handing him my heart and hoping he won't break it again.

"I don't want to run anymore."

I want to love you…

Cillian stills, something unreadable flashing across his face. Then, slowly, he cradles my cheek, his thumb stroking my skin as his lips pull into a genuine smile. "I don't wanna run either."

A lump forms in my throat, and I blink against the sting of tears. Leaning into his touch, I let myself savor the warmth of his arms wrapping around me like he has no intention of ever letting me go. I don't want him to either.

"I promise, I'm not going anywhere."

As his knuckles brush across my jaw, his mouth meeting mine, I let myself believe him. That maybe this time, we can have this. That his promises aren't just empty words, but truths he's carving into existence. Our kiss is slow, unhurried, steeped in devotion and quiet longing.

When Cillian pulls back, his green eyes flicker with a storm of emotions: love, passion, an unspoken determination to make this work. I can feel it in every fiber of his being.

His thumb gently strokes my cheek before a low groan rumbles from his lips. "Damn, I forgot I have to fly out for a meeting tomorrow morning." His expression tightens with frustration and regret. "I swear, I wish I didn't have to go, but Tynan needs me."

"Oh…"

The disappointment comes quicker than I expect, settling deep in my chest. It's not the end of the world. He'll be back. But after finally letting myself have him, the thought of waking up without him beside me leaves an ache in its place.

"A few days at most," he assures me, his fingers tightening around mine. "I wouldn't leave unless it was necessary."

I search his face and smile, kissing the corner of his mouth.

"Oh, Prince Cillian, I'm utterly disappointed," I tease, and he chuckles, flipping me until I'm lying across the blanket, his body conforming to mine.

He rolls his hips, his hardness pressing into me, igniting that dark and needy side of me. His hand skims down between us, tugging up my dress and sliding my panties to the side.

"How shall I ever beg for your forgiveness, Princess Dinara?"

"I can think of a way." Reaching between us, my palm presses against his cock.

He growls when I stroke him, but it doesn't last. Ripping my hand away, his mouth descends down my body until he's throwing a leg over his shoulder, hunger flashing in his eyes.

"So can I." His gaze meets mine, a finger hooking into my thong and pulling it to the side, exposing me to his greedy stare.

My hand tangles in his soft strands, and then his tongue slices through my core, circling around my clit, until I'm lost to him. Lost to the feelings only he can bring out in me.

And in this moment, as the sun warms our skin and his body worships mine, I realize something undeniable.

I don't just want this life with him. I *need* it.

FORTY-EIGHT

DINARA

Cillian left hours ago, and somehow, the house feels emptier without him, like he took its heart and soul with him.

I sit on the back deck, nursing my coffee, trying to shake the feeling of loneliness settling over me. Maybe I should visit my siblings and friends tomorrow. The thought of seeing them, of being surrounded by familiar faces, offers a small sense of relief.

With a sigh, I pull out my phone and quickly text Alisa and Natalia, letting them know I'll be coming over for the day.

Their replies come almost instantly, their excitement mirroring mine. A selfish part of me wishes they could find love close by so we can always be near each other.

As I finish texting Konstantin to let him know about my plans, Mary steps outside.

"Mrs. Quinn?"

For a second, I forget that's my new name until she repeats it.

"Sorry," I laugh nervously. "What is it?"

"You have a visitor."

"Oh?" I sit up straighter. "Who is it?"

"Mr. Quinn."

I frown. "Who?"

"Sorry, Quinn Senior." She laughs.

My heart jumps a little. Patrick Quinn is *here*? Why?

I set my cup down on the table and immediately stand, a rush of curiosity buzzing through me. I've hardly spoken to him, just a few polite words at the wedding. Given the history between our families, I never imagined he'd come to see me.

"He's waiting in the den," Mary adds.

I follow her through the double glass doors, stepping into the room where Patrick is sitting on the sofa, glancing at something on his phone. An envelope rests beside him on the cushion. He looks up as I enter, tucking his phone away and standing to greet me with a gentle kiss on the cheek.

"I'm sorry to drop by unannounced. But I know Cillian's gone, and I wanted to come say hello and check on you."

I'm taken at the unexpected concern. "Oh…thank you. I'm doing okay."

"That's good." He nods, as if considering his next words, his expression unreadable. Then, without warning, he takes my hand in his, his grip warm. "I know we haven't had any time to talk, but I wanted you to know that I'm happy Cillian has you." His gaze softens, his words catching me off guard.

"Thank you. I really appreciate that." My pulse stutters.

He nods, releasing a sigh. "I've gotta admit, I wasn't so thrilled with the idea of you two together at first, but I've come to realize that whatever problems our families had, it has nothing to do with you kids."

I blink back the tears clouding my vision. I can only imagine how hard this has been for him, losing his wife the way he did.

"I hold no grudges." I offer a small, genuine smile.

He stares fondly. "I also came to give you something."

Reaching for the envelope, he picks it up, staring down at it as though it weighs more than it does, while I grow with confusion.

"Before my wife was…killed, she wrote letters. One for each of our children." It's obvious he's struggling with what he wants to say. "And one for the people they'd end up with."

Oh…

A throbbing blooms in the center of my chest. I can't even begin to imagine the strength and pain it must've taken for her to do that. But I know how much it would've meant to me to have a letter, just one more piece of my mother.

He holds out the envelope for me, and I freeze, afraid of it somehow. My fingers tingle as I take it, pressing it close to my chest. I already know whatever is inside will break me.

"Thank you," I whisper. "I'm sure she was an amazing woman."

"She was." After a beat, he squeezes my hand. "I know Stella would've really liked you."

My throat tightens and I swallow hard, struggling to keep my composure.

"As I do."

The words land heavy on my heart, mattering more than he realizes.

"I want you to know that no matter what happened between our families, you will always have a place here. To me, you are my daughter now. No different than my own kids. You understand?"

A tear slips free, then another. I swipe at them, completely overwhelmed.

When I was growing up, my father would never have said anything remotely this sweet. He never even gave me love to begin with. And here is Patrick Quinn, a man who has every reason to resent me, telling me I belong. That I'm *his* family.

I throw my arms around him, and he holds me, letting me cry. A part of me never realized how much I've been missing this—a parental figure, people I can count on. Maybe Cillian's family will be that for me.

After a moment, he pulls back. "Why don't you come over for lunch? Fernanda cooked, and we'd love the company."

I sniffle, letting out a small laugh. "Okay. Yeah, I'd like that."

With one final glance at the letter, I tuck it safely into a drawer, returning to him.

Tonight, when I'm alone, I'll be ready to read it.

And even though we never met, I already know…I love her.

STELLA
TWENTY-FIVE YEARS AGO

This has been one of the most difficult things I've ever had to do as a mother. To write letters to each one of my children as though it's the last thing I'll ever say to them is like a knife to my chest. But it just might be the last time.

Our life is dangerous, and at times, I forget that. So there may come a time when I won't be here to hold them, to guide them, to love them. I want more than anything for them to know how much they mean to me even when I'm not there to show it. To tell them how special they are.

There is so much I could possibly miss out on. Their weddings, the first time they become parents, the sense of overwhelming love they will come to know as I did when I became a mother.

Tears fall down my cheeks, but I blot them away with my fingertips. I just have one more letter to write, this time to the person Cillian will hopefully one day fall in love with.

Whoever she is, I'm sure she'll be special, and he will cherish her with everything he has. Because that's who he's always been: a protector.

To the woman who will one day marry my Cillian,

I wish we were meeting under different circumstances. That I could sit across from you, hold your hands in mine, and tell you in person how grateful I am that you love my son. But life doesn't always give us what we want, and unfortunately, I'm not around to welcome you the way I should have been.

I hope that doesn't make you sad. And more importantly, I hope you don't let him be sad. Because if I know my Cillian, he's already found a hundred different ways to blame himself for my death, no matter the circumstances. He carries the weight of the world on his shoulders, even when it's not his burden to bear.

Please don't let him do that. Remind him that not everything is in his control, that fate has a mind of its own, and sometimes we don't get to rewrite the endings.

I have no doubt that he loves you with every piece of his soul. He's not perfect, no one is, but love like his is rare. And with love comes mistakes, comes hurt, comes lessons that will test the both of you. But I hope you always find your way back to each other. There is strength in forgiveness, in choosing each other over and over again, no matter how difficult life becomes. Believe me, I know that all too well.

Cillian is intense, stubborn, protective. He loves deeply, sometimes to a fault. But beneath that, he is still the boy I raised, the one with a heart too big for his own good. Love him fiercely, stand by his side, and never let him forget that he is worthy of happiness.

And for you—my daughter now too—I want you to know that you are enough. That you are worthy of the love he gives you and of every happiness life has to offer.

Hold on to one another. Cherish the good days, fight through the hard ones, and never forget that love, real love, is always worth fighting for.

With all my heart,
Mom

DINARA

I wipe away the stream of tears running down my cheeks as I clutch the letter against my chest. I don't know what I expected to find in her words, but what I found was peace.

Placing the paper on the nightstand beside me, I cling to the quiet sadness of knowing I'll never meet the woman who wrote those beautiful words.

I hate that. I hate that it was my family—my uncle—who took such a wonderful person away. She should have been here for our wedding, should've danced with her son. Instead, all he has left of her is these final words.

Staring up at the ceiling, I think about my own mother. What she would have said to me if she'd ever written a letter to me. She'd probably tell me to be strong, to never take anyone's shit, to not let the world beat me down the way my father did. She'd tell me she was sorry for staying, that she wished she could've given me a better life.

Or at least that's what I want to believe.

She was my rock. The only thing that kept me from falling into the same darkness that took her. And when she was gone, I didn't know how I'd survive.

But I did. We don't realize our own strength until we're forced to face the impossible, and that was what losing my mother felt like to me.

Shutting off the bedside lamp, I roll onto my side, willing myself to sleep. But it doesn't come. Not without him. As I lie alone in this massive bed, everything feels too big. Too empty.

My phone chimes on the nightstand, and I grab it quickly, my heart flipping at the sight of his name on the screen.

We talked earlier, right after I got back from his father's. I told him how Patrick had accepted me, and I could hear the happiness in his tone. But I didn't mention the letter. I don't know why. Maybe because I was afraid the reminder of her would shake the fragile foundation of what we've rebuilt.

But now, after reading it, I need to tell him. It was too beautiful.

"Hey, you," I answer softly.

"Hey, baby. Are you in bed yet?"

"Yes," I tease. "Why do you want to know?"

His laughter deepens. "Get your head out of the gutter, girl. I just wanted to hear your voice."

A slow smile spreads across my lips. "That's sweet of you, Mr. Quinn." I let out a yawn. "I miss you."

"Miss me, huh?" His tone lowers slightly. "How much?"

"Too much," I admit, closing my eyes and imagining he's right beside me. "When are you coming home?"

"The day after tomorrow."

I sigh dramatically. "I guess I'll survive. Oh, I was going to go over Konstantin's tomorrow to see Tatiana and Gregory."

"That's a good idea. I'll set up the plane."

"Thanks." I let out another deep yawn.

"You sound tired, love."

"Mm…yeah. But I just can't seem to sleep without you."

"How about this? Close your eyes, and I'll stay on the phone with you until you fall asleep."

I groan. It's exactly what I need, having a part of him even when he's not here.

"Thank you," I whisper.

A beat of silence passes.

"By the way, your father gave me something when he came by."

"What's that?"

I swallow past the lump in my throat. "Your mom…she wrote me a letter."

He pauses, and I'm almost nervous he'll get upset at the mention of her.

"What?" His voice grows more curious than mad.

"Your dad said she wrote letters to each of you and the people you'd end up with, so he gave it to me."

Silence lingers on the other end, thick and weighted. When he exhales, it's slow, almost hesitant. Like the memory of her still sneaks up on him, no matter how much time has passed.

"Shit. I forgot about that. What did she say?"

A small, bittersweet smile tugs at my lips. "Well…she said you'd probably be a pain in my ass, but that I should love you anyway."

His laughter makes me laugh too, the cadence warm, familiar. Home.

"Yeah…that sounds like my mother."

My grip tightens around the phone, my pulse picking up speed. I can feel it building inside me, the need to tell him how much I'm falling in love with him, to tell him just what he means to me, what he's always meant to me.

"Cillian?"

"Hmm?"

I swallow hard, my throat suddenly dry.

Just say it.

"I—"

But before I can, he stops me.

"No." That one word is thick and raw with meaning. "If you're about to say what I think you are, I want to see you when you do. I want to touch you." A beat of silence, then softer, rougher, "Think you can wait for me, baby?"

Emotions press hard against my ribs, so many of them I can barely count. I nod, even though he can't see it.

"Yes," I whisper.

"That's my good girl." Those words caress down my skin, sending warmth through me. "Now close your eyes," he murmurs. "I'm here. Not going anywhere."

"Okay." Another yawn escapes me, my body growing heavier with exhaustion.

I put the phone on speaker and pull the blanket tight around me, pretending it's him—his warmth, his presence, his steady heartbeat beneath my cheek. I can't wait to hold him again. To finally say the words out loud.

And as his breathing fills the silence between us, my body finally relaxes and I sleep.

With not a single nightmare to follow.

FORTY-NINE

DINARA

As soon as the plane touches down on the private airstrip, three of Cillian's men escort me out toward the SUV Konstantin sent. Just as I approach the vehicle, the tinted back window rolls down. At first, I can't see who's inside, but then a small face pops out.

"Hey!" Gregory waves excitedly.

I grin, pleasantly surprised. "Hey!"

Tatiana scoots closer beside him. "Hey, sis."

"What are you guys doing here?" I open the door and slide inside, immediately pulling them both into a hug.

"Konstantin said we could come pick you up," Gregory says.

His bodyguard, Vlad, starts the SUV, while Anatoly, Tatiana's guard, is seated beside him in the front.

"Well, I'm so happy you did."

Tatiana leans forward. "So…how's married life?"

Gregory smirks, and I see a little of the man he's becoming. "Yeah.

Is he treating you nicely, or do I need to have a talk with him?"

I chuckle, shaking my head. "Not so bad, actually."

Tatiana watches me for a beat, something softer in her expression. "I'm glad. You deserve to be happy."

My chest tightens as I reach for her hand and squeeze. "We all do."

As soon as I take my phone off airplane mode, a voicemail icon pops up. My heart gives a little kick when I see Cillian's name. Without hesitation, I enter my code, pressing the phone to my ear.

The moment I hear his voice, my lips stretch into a wide smile.

"Hey, baby, prasti menya."

He's speaking Russian. Oh God. Why is that so sexy?

"Ya idiot. Ya nakalenih budu prasit tvayo prasheniya telayu mayu jzin."

A full-bodied laugh escapes me now, drawing curious glances from Tatiana and Gregory, but I can't stop listening.

Cillian, my very Irish husband, has just declared himself an idiot and promised to beg for my forgiveness on his knees for the rest of his life. I like the sound of that, actually.

He continues, a little uncertain now. "I hope what I said was right. Konstantin told me that's how you say, 'I'm sorry I missed you before you got on your plane.' I probably butchered that. Anyway, I love you. Call me when you land."

The way he said all that—so serious, so utterly convinced he was saying something entirely different—only makes this funnier. Wait until he learns what he actually said.

Tatiana raises a brow, amused, as I lower the phone, intending on calling my husband and enlightening him.

"What was that about?"

I shake my head, still grinning. "Oh, you know…just Konstantin messing with Cillian. The usual."

Tatiana chuckles. "Of course he was."

As I'm about to press Cillian's name on my phone, the SUV jerks to a sudden stop.

My body slams forward, a cold wave of panic rushing through me as a wall of black vehicles surrounds us—four SUVs in front, two behind.

"Oh my God!" Tatiana cries while my stomach plummets.

Oh God. No, no, no!

"I'm scared," Gregory breathes out.

Me too.

"It's okay. Everything is gonna be okay."

But I don't even believe it myself.

The first shot rings out as a masked man in a backseat takes aim at us from the front. At the same moment, our bodyguards draw their weapons. This SUV is armored, but there are just too many cars out there.

Another shot fires, and my body jerks with absolute fear. Then—

Chaos.

Gunfire erupts from everywhere, bullets hammering against the SUV, the relentless ping of metal on metal filling the air.

"Get down!" Vlad shouts as he pops open the window just enough to fire into one of the vehicles.

I don't hesitate. I shove Gregory and Tatiana to the floor, shielding their bodies with mine.

"Stay low! Don't move!" I command despite the terror racing through me.

Through the window, I find masked men pouring out of the attacking SUVs, their weapons raised—guns, bats, crowbars.

They're coming for us.

"I'm texting Konstantin!" I tell them.

"He knows. He's sending backup!" Anatoly shouts back, firing and killing another man.

But we're outnumbered. How the hell do we survive this?

This has to be my father. No one else would be so bold. I can't let him take Tatiana and Gregory. They're my priority right now.

"Give me a gun!" I snap at Anatoly.

He doesn't hesitate this time. He tosses me a pistol, and I grip it tightly, my hands surprisingly steady. I shift just enough to peek through the shattered window, aiming for the closest target.

Bang.

One of them drops.

But it barely makes a difference. More take his place, swarming the SUV like vultures.

The vehicle rocks as someone swings a crowbar against the reinforced windows. Another fires at the tires, trying to disable us completely.

Vlad slams the gas, attempting to get away.

Boom.

An RPG fires, and the SUV explodes at the front, sending us flipping through the air.

A scream rips from my throat as we crash onto our side, metal groaning, glass raining down. Pain jolts through my ribs as I'm thrown against the door.

"Tatiana! Gregory!" I scream.

But I don't hear them. Their eyes are closed.

Oh my God. Are they dead?

No, they can't be!

I reach for them, needing to check if they're alive, to get them out so we can somehow get away. But suddenly, hands wrench open the door, two masked men dragging me out.

"Dvai suka." A man calls me a bitch as he pulls me out while I thrash, kicking and clawing my way out of the wreckage.

I see them doing the same to Tatiana and Gregory.

Nonono!

"Please, leave them alone!" I beg, but I know it's no use.

Gunshots ring out as one of the men points a weapon at Vlad and

Anatoly and blood starts seeping from their heads.

"No!" I scream.

But it's useless. They're dead.

A fist slams into my stomach, knocking the air from my lungs. Before I can recover, a rough hand grabs my hair and yanks my head back.

"Enough," another voice snaps. One I don't recognize.

Then…darkness.

A woven hood is placed over my head, and I'm shoved into a vehicle. My body slams against the seat as it speeds off, tires screeching.

I don't know where we're going. But I know who sent them: my father and brother. There's no doubt.

And I know one thing. This isn't just a kidnapping.

It's an execution. Mine.

CILLIAN

Something's wrong.

Dinara landed thirty minutes ago, but every call goes straight to voicemail. I've tried Konstantin too, and nothing.

What the fuck is going on?!

I just got off the plane in New Jersey, planning to surprise her after wrapping up business in New York early. But now all I can think about is finding her. Making sure she's okay.

I know she landed safely. My men saw her leave in Konstantin's SUV. But after that? Who the hell knows?

I try her again, pressing the phone tight against my ear.

Fuck.

Straight to voicemail.

I call Konstantin, and just like before, it just keeps ringing.

A cold weight settles in my gut. Every fear spins in my head. Anything could've happened.

I tell myself there's a reason she's not answering. Maybe she's busy. Maybe her phone died. But it doesn't sit right. Not when I know the threats against her. Konstantin told me everything.

My fingers curl at my side. I shouldn't have left her alone. I should've stayed with her. It's my job to protect her, to keep her safe.

I hit call again. Voicemail.

"Damn it."

Before I can try one more time, my phone vibrates in my hand.

Konstantin.

Fuck. Thank God.

I answer immediately. "Where the hell is—"

"She's just been taken."

The words slam into me like a bullet, ripping through my world until I can't so much as breathe.

I hit the gas, the car flying down the road. "What the hell are you talking about?"

"My men were ambushed. Her father's people took her and her siblings." His words are razor-sharp with fury.

Rage ignites inside me, hot and blinding.

"Where?" I demand, every goddamn awful thought of what they could be doing to her slamming into my mind. "I fucking hope you know where they took her!"

"We have an inside man. He told us where they're being held." He shoots off an address before his voice drops, low and lethal. "I'm bringing my army."

"So am I."

Silence.

Heavy. Deadly.

"Every man who touched my wife will die begging for her forgiveness."

FIFTY

DINARA

The pounding of approaching footsteps sends a jolt of dread through me. I struggle against the tight restraints biting into my wrists, the cold, unforgiving floor beneath me offering no comfort. The thick hood obscuring my vision keeps me trapped in darkness, unable to see anything but the emptiness around me. A muffled whimper echoes nearby.

Tatiana? Gregory? I can't tell.

The uncertainty fuels my panic, but I force myself to stay still. Fear is a weapon in their hands. I refuse to give them that satisfaction.

The hood is ripped away, and harsh light sears my retinas. I squint, blinking rapidly as my surroundings come into focus: an industrial warehouse, steel beams rising like prison bars, shadows swallowing the corners.

Then I see him: my father.

"Moya Dinarochka," he says, the mockery laced in his tone as chilling as the ice in his eyes. He pats my cheek with a cold hand, his expression twisted in disdain. "So good to see you again. You made beautiful bride."

I jolt back, the shock and knowledge that he was actually there hitting me hard.

I knew it! I knew I saw him.

"How? Cillian, he checked the cameras."

"I had help. Easy to sneak in with catering company. Your husband should do better job keeping you safe, lubimiya."

Anger coils in my stomach, the smugness in his eyes making me want to claw them out.

I glare, swallowing down the nausea curling in my stomach. "Where are they?"

Whatever he's done isn't important right now. Getting Tatiana and Gregory out of here is the priority.

"They're safe," he replies, his mouth thinning. "Don't worry about them."

I scan the space, desperate for a glimpse of them, but they're nowhere in sight.

He chuckles. "Is better you worry about you right now."

I meet his gaze without flinching. "I'm not afraid of you, Papa. Do what you want to me. You've always been a coward."

A cruel smile stretches across his face before he strikes, the butt of his gun crashing into my chin and snapping my head to the side. Pain explodes through my jaw, the metallic taste of blood pooling in my mouth. I refuse to make a sound, even as the sting radiates down my spine.

"Still so defiant. You never learn." He tilts his head, as if I'm some disappointing experiment. "That's not how you speak to your father."

"You were never a father to me," I spit, blood dripping onto my lap. "To any of us."

He laughs, dark and mirthless. "You were never worth my time."

The words should cut, but I feel nothing.

He's wrong about one thing, though: I've learned my lesson. I've spent my life knowing exactly what kind of monster he is.

His expression shifts, cold calculation replacing amusement. "Your siblings, however…still time for them. Once you're dead, I make them stronger. More loyal than you ever were. They won't be under Konstantin's thumb anymore."

"You never deserved our loyalty."

I don't even care if he hurts me again. What does it matter? I'm already dead, aren't I? Trapped in this nightmare, dangling on the edge of an end I can't outrun. Even if Konstantin knows where we are, it might not matter. He might be too late.

Then it hits me, sharp and unforgiving: the thought of never seeing Cillian again. Of never hearing his voice, never feeling his touch.

Of never telling him I love him.

The regret is a blade, cutting deeper than any wound my father could inflict. I should have said it. Should have given him the truth instead of waiting. But now…now, he may never know. I swallow back the sob clawing its way up my throat.

No. I refuse to let this be the end.

I force myself to breathe, to focus, to stay alive. If there's even a sliver of hope, a chance that someone—anyone—can save us, I have to hold on.

"That was always problem." My father crouches before me, slow and deliberate, his presence suffocating as he presses the cold barrel of a gun beneath my chin. His dark eyes gleam with cruel satisfaction. "You were never on my side."

"Never." I meet his gaze, refusing to flinch, though fear coils tightly in my chest.

I won't let him see it. I won't give him the pleasure.

"Go ahead!" My voice rings out, sharp and unwavering. "Shoot me. You've been waiting for this moment, haven't you?"

But instead of pulling the trigger, he curls his lips into a chilling smile. He straightens, rolling his shoulders as if shaking off the idea.

"No… I don't shoot you." His head tilts to the side as he gestures to someone just beyond my line of sight. "*He* does."

Confusion flickers through me. Until I see him: my brother Roman.

My stomach twists as he strides forward, dragging Tatiana with him, her sobs breaking through the heavy silence. Behind them, one of their men grips Gregory, my little brother's tear-filled eyes darting between us.

Terror slinks through my veins like ice.

"So, you brought your little lapdog to do your dirty work?" I sneer at Roman, ignoring the way my body screams in pain.

He grins, a twisted, mocking expression. "Moya sestra." His head tilts. "I was almost sad when I thought I killed you in that car crash."

The words hit like a freight train. My vision tunnels.

The accident. The weeks of recovery. It was him.

My stomach lurches, but I manage a cold laugh. "Of course you failed. You always do."

His smile vanishes. In an instant, he lashes out, his boot slamming into my ribs. Pain rips through me, white-hot and consuming, but I don't scream. Even as my siblings cry out for him to stop, even as he kicks me again and again, I stay silent.

"Hvatit," my father commands. *Enough.*

Roman halts instantly, panting, fists clenched. I struggle to lift my head, my vision blurred and spinning.

"Go on." I lock eyes with my big brother. "Shoot me, then. But it won't make you any more of a man."

Tatiana sobs harder. "Please, Papa, stop!"

But my father merely sighs, shaking his head. "Oy, Moya Dinarochka. You misunderstand. Roman does not kill you."

Dread curls through me, cold and sharp. "What?"

When he faces Gregory, my blood turns to ice.

My father places the gun in my little brother's trembling hands.

His small body shakes violently, his chest heaving with silent sobs.

"No," I whisper, my throat closing. "Don't do this to him."

"I don't do anything to my son. Unlike you, he loves his father. Has been on my side whole time. Haven't you?"

My head spins, unable to understand any of this. What does he mean?

A violent tremor rolls through Gregory's body as he looks at me, and I see the truth there.

No. No, this can't be true. He's lying.

"You know what to do, Gregory," our father says against his ear, the grip on his shoulder firm, possessive. "Now is chance to prove yourself. To show you are man, not boy."

I can't let this happen. I can't let him do this to Gregory!

Tatiana's cries grow louder, desperate pleas spilling from her lips, while my mind struggles to catch up, to piece together the nightmare unraveling before me.

My father's gaze shifts back to mine—dark, venomous. "She is traitor. You know what we do to traitors, don't you, my son?"

"No!" My head snaps toward Gregory, his shoulders shaking, his eyes cast downward as if afraid to meet mine. "Don't listen to him, Gregory! This isn't you. You don't have to do this. You don't want to be like them. I know you. I love you! Please, don't do this!"

Silent cries wrack through him, but our father only tightens his hold.

"Oh, he will. This has been plan all along."

I blink, heart pounding against my ribs. "What do you mean? What are you talking about?"

A slow, knowing smile spreads across his face. "You thought you could take my son from me? You thought you could keep him away?" He scoffs.

The room tilts, the walls closing in around me. Nothing makes sense.

"Gregory…what is he talking about?"

Laughter, dark and triumphant, echoes through the space. "I've always been one step ahead, dochinka." *Daughter*. "I had someone very useful helping," my father taunts. "It was only reason I was able to reach my boy and talk to him all these years."

A sharp inhale sticks in my throat. "Who?" My pulse pounds violently. "Who helped you?"

His smirk deepens. "You don't worry about it." Then he turns back to Gregory, his tone deceptively gentle. "Now, son. Do what must be done. End her."

A sob shudders through Gregory's small frame as he lifts the gun, his hands unsteady. And then his eyes find mine.

Everything inside me shatters.

Because the little boy I once knew, the one I swore to protect, is gone. And I don't know what he'll do next.

FIFTY-ONE

CILLIAN

"**P**lease!" Lenny cries out, blood dripping from the deep slash across his face as Konstantin idly spins a knife between his fingers.

Another wound splits his chest open, but we're still nowhere closer to the truth. I pace the length of Konstantin's den, my pulse hammering, fury burning through my veins. We need to find Dinara. Now. Every second wasted is a second too long.

But the thought I keep pushing away slams into me again: she could already be dead.

Konstantin's mole did give us a location, but by the time we got there, it was cleared out. Someone tipped them off. Konstantin believes Lenny is the rat, and honestly, I wouldn't be surprised. I remember overhearing that suspicious conversation in Dinara's room all those years ago. Told Konstantin as much. Now we just need Lenny to confess—to give us something, anything, to work with.

Konstantin leans back in his chair, unnervingly calm. "It's in your best interest to tell me the truth. You know what happens when I grow impatient, yes?"

Lenny shudders. "Please! I would never betray you. I'm not stupid. I know what you'd do to my family."

"Maybe." Konstantin tilts his head. "Then answer me. Why were you in Dinara's room that day? Who were you talking to?"

"That was a mistake, I swear!" Lenny pleads. "My wife, she called from Russia while I was looking for Sonya. I just stepped into the room for privacy because Dinara wasn't there. That's all! I didn't touch anything. I didn't do anything." His breath shudders as he sobs. "Check my international calls. It was my wife. She was fighting with her father back home, trying to drag me into it, but I told her I was not getting involved. That's the truth."

"Aleksei is already checking," Konstantin says coolly.

Right on cue, Aleksei walks in, his expression unreadable.

"So, what did you find on our friend?" Konstantin asks.

"It was the wife." A cruel grin stretches across Aleksei's face. "I just spoke to her. Lovely woman. Said she was trying to get Lenny to convince her father to stop screwing some mistress behind her mother's back. But Lenny didn't want to get in the middle."

Konstantin's eyes narrow. "And what about Dinara? Any leads on where they're keeping them?"

"Yeah. Surveillance picked up movement at an abandoned warehouse about twenty miles from here. We're sure that's where they took her."

"Then what the fuck are we standing around for?" I snap. "Let's move."

Once I get the address, my fingers are flying across the screen as I send the location to my brothers and the rest of our army waiting at my house here in Jersey.

Konstantin gives a sharp nod to one of his men.

"Leave him here. I'll handle him when I return. And you'd better pray I'm in a good mood," he warns Lenny, his voice cold, before following me out.

As soon as I slide into the car, adrenaline surges with brutal intensity. She'd better be there. And she'd better be unharmed.

If they touched one hair on her body, there's not gonna be an inch left of them when I'm through.

DINARA

"I…I can't, Papa." Gregory shakes his head, fresh tears welling in his eyes.

He's terrified. He doesn't want to kill me. Maybe whatever poison my father has been feeding him all these years hasn't worked as well as he thought.

Fury flashes across my father's face. "You told me where you would be, and now you are being coward!"

Oh, no… Gregory. No.

An ache slams behind my eyes. But I know it wasn't his fault. He's just a little boy who was tricked into doing something stupid.

"You—you said you wouldn't hurt Dinara. You promised!"

"Well, maybe that is lesson for you, my son. Never trust anyone. Now shoot her! Don't be disappointment like your sister. That is not way to make Papa proud. Look at your brother, Roman. He understands what must be done. You must also learn."

Roman grins, his expression one of twisted pride, sadistic amusement glinting in his eyes as he briefly meets mine.

"Don't listen to him," I tell Gregory. "He's trying to turn you into one of them, and you don't want that."

My father's glare snaps back to me, his words like venom. "You will kill the bitch."

I meet his gaze without flinching. He thinks he can decide how this ends. He's wrong. I have no intention of dying here. I will survive this. We all will.

And him? He's going to burn in hell.

I seize the moment. "Who helped you?" I need that information in case I make it out alive. "If I'm gonna die, what does it matter if I know or not?"

His eyes narrow. He's considering it.

Good. If nothing else, it buys me time.

"Fine," he finally says with a smirk. "I tell you. Not that it matters now. I have army. Loyal men who would die for me. I will take Konstantin's empire. His family. I will live in his house like king while he rots, knowing it's all mine."

Hatred surges through me, my hands curling behind my back. He has no idea what Konstantin will do to him.

Then, with a sharp nod, my father signals to one of his men, who quickly exits the room.

My chest tightens. What the hell is he doing?

Footsteps echo down the hall, drawing closer. When they finally drag someone into the room, confusion grips me.

Why is she here? What does she have to do with this? And then realization slams into me.

No…it can't be.

"Ludmilla?"

She clicks her tongue and rolls her eyes. "Leo, must you be so dramatic? Why you need to tell her?"

My father steps toward her, his gaze scrutinizing. "Are you ashamed for helping me?"

I trusted her. Loved her like family. And yet, this whole time, she was the enemy. She must have been feeding my father information this whole time. She betrayed us all.

But why? Why would she do this?

My hands shake as white-hot rage surges through me. My vision blurs, blood pounding in my ears.

If I had the chance, I'd kill her myself.

"No. Of course I am not ashamed, my love," she purrs.

My love?

My stomach churns.

He drapes an arm around her. "You see, Ludmilla and I have been together many years now. I met her when I learned she was working for that pig. I convinced her she'd have much better life with me. Then, of course, we fell in love." His grin makes me sick. "Isn't that right, my darling?"

"Yes, very true. Your father is good man." Her eyes settle on me. "You should always stand with family, Dinara."

"I do stand with family, and that's not him." Disgust twists my face. "You really want to be with a man who bashed his first wife's face in? What the hell is wrong with you?"

She lifts her chin defiantly. "I am not your mother."

"Yeah, that's obvious." My voice drips with contempt.

My father's expression darkens with rage. "You do not speak to her like that."

"Go fuck your—"

The words die in my throat as gunfire erupts beneath us.

My father freezes. Then, he realizes.

They've found us.

A quiet sob escapes me as relief floods my trembling body. Konstantin. Cillian. They're here. I know they are. We're going to be okay.

My eyes pinch shut as the tears fall. I can't wait to see him, to throw my arms around him and tell him how much I love him. Something I wish I could've said before all this.

"Go!" my father barks at Ludmilla, and she disappears from sight. He grabs the weapon he gave Gregory. "Let's go, Roman. We end this now. But Konstantin is mine, understand?"

Roman nods, cocking his gun.

"You stay with them," my father orders one of his men.

"Horosho." *Okay.*

As my father and Roman charge out of the room, I turn to my siblings.

My words are steady despite the storm inside me. "We're going to be okay. I promise this is over."

Gregory's face crumples. "I'm sorry," he whispers, thick with guilt. "I was afraid to tell you she was letting me talk to Dad. I didn't know he would do this, I swear!"

"It's okay. I know."

He tries to step toward me, but the guard blocks his path with an outstretched arm.

"Just stay there," I tell him. "This will be over soon."

And I hope more than anything that Cillian and the rest of them survive this.

FIFTY-TWO

CILLIAN

She's here. I know she is. I can feel it in my bones. The overwhelming need to find her, to touch her, to tell her how sorry I am for not being there to stop this, consumes me.

This is my fault. I will never forgive myself for letting her down again.

A bullet zips past my head, snapping me back into the fight. I force my focus onto the only thing that matters now: killing every last bastard tied to her father. There are dozens of them, but we have more.

I fire one clean shot straight between an enemy's eyes. He drops instantly.

"Behind you!" I shout to Konstantin.

He whirls, kicking a man in the chest before putting a bullet through his skull. Blood splatters, and the body crumples.

"Where are you, Leo?" Konstantin bellows, his voice cutting through the chaos. "Face me like a man! I cannot wait to rip you apart with my bare hands and feed you to my pigs!"

"He's here somewhere!" Aleksei calls, stomping a man's face into the ground before firing two more rounds into his chest for good measure.

I keep moving, cutting through bodies like they're nothing. I don't know how many men we've lost. Not yet. This is war, and casualties are inevitable. But if she's one of them…

No.

I'd trade my life for hers if it came to that. I just need to get to her first.

I grab one of her father's men, slamming him against the wall and pressing my gun hard into his temple. "Where is she?"

He spits blood, muttering a curse, then swings at me.

Wrong move. I pull the trigger and kill him instantly before moving on to the next. This one, I kick in the stomach, sending him to his knees.

I don't give him time to recover before I press my gun to his forehead. "Where the fuck is Dinara?"

The bastard lifts his hands, shaking. Before he can answer, a gunshot rings out behind me.

I pivot, my Glock raised, only to find Tynan standing over another lifeless body.

"Watch your damn back," he grunts before moving on.

I return my focus to the cowering man at my feet. "You have three seconds."

"Upstairs! Please, man!"

I nod. Then I put a bullet in his head.

As I reach the stairwell, something slams into my shoulder, fire tearing through my flesh. I stagger, but keep going, one mission on my mind.

Get her and her siblings out.

Pain rips through my arm as I reach the top, blood soaking through my shirt. I ignore it.

Then I hear her.

"It's okay. They'll be here. Don't worry."

Relief crashes over me. She's alive. My baby's alive.

I take a few quiet steps forward, peering inside. The second she sees me, her eyes widen. Just for a moment.

Her face, though…it's badly bruised.

Rage explodes inside me. Someone hurt her. And they're going to pay. Slowly and painfully.

Gregory sits slumped in the corner, while Tatiana is tied up on the floor.

That sick bastard really did this to his own kids. If Konstantin hasn't already ripped him apart, I'll do it myself.

Scanning the room, I spot a lone guard watching them, his back turned. I meet Dinara's gaze and press a finger to my lips.

The second he moves away from her, I fire. A single shot to the back of the head.

He drops instantly.

"Cillian!" she cries as I rush to her, cupping her face in my hands.

"Fuck, baby. I'm so happy to see you."

I kiss her, pressing my lips to her forehead, then pull out the flip knife attached to my keychain.

"Who hurt you?" My hands are steady, but my fury is a storm inside me.

"Don't worry about me," she says, but her expression shifts when she sees my arm. "You're shot!"

"Tell me who hurt you." My jaw clenches, muscles burning with the need for vengeance.

"My father. Roman. Take your pick." She tries to laugh, but winces, her pain twisting like a knife in my gut.

"Where does it hurt?"

She silently gestures to her stomach. As I lift her shirt just enough to see, a sharp, searing rage claws its way through me, tightening my chest and setting my pulse hammering. Deep, ugly bruises stain her flesh, a stark contrast against her pale skin. My jaw locks so tightly, it feels like my teeth might crack.

"It's okay," she says quickly. "I'm okay."

But it's not.

Gunfire rages beneath us. We can't leave yet, and that fucking kills me. She could have internal injuries. I need to get her out now.

"Are you two okay?" I glance at Gregory and Tatiana, having forgotten they were here for a minute.

Gregory nods weakly from where he sits, knees curled to his chest. Tatiana's eyes are filled with fear.

"When can we go?" Gregory asks in a shaky voice while I massage Dinara's wrists.

"We have to wait until your father's men are gone."

He nods, arms tightening around his knees.

I stand to free Tatiana, but before I can reach her, Dinara suddenly screams.

"Gregory!"

Everything happens in a flash.

One second, I'm kneeling beside Tatiana.

The next, I'm charging toward the door.

Roman is there, gun raised.

The shot fires.

I throw myself in front of Gregory without thinking.

Pain tears through my side, burning deep, but I don't stop. I raise my gun and fire.

Roman jerks back, collapsing onto the floor.

I fire again. And again. And again as I get closer. I want him to suffer. I want him to feel the agony she's felt.

But the sound of her cries rips through me, stopping me cold. "Gregory! No!"

I turn.

He's on the ground. Blood pooling.

And I know…

I was too late.

DINARA

I can't let him go. I won't.

Clinging desperately to my little brother's lifeless body, I hold him as tightly as I can, as if I can somehow will him back to me. His blood seeps through my shirt, soaking into my skin, but I don't care. My mind refuses to accept the brutal truth.

He's gone. This is how his story ends.

How is that fair? He was only ten.

"Dinara." Konstantin's voice cuts through the thick silence, and that's when I realize they're all here: my cousins, the Quinns.

The gunfire has stopped. The battle is over. While all I can hear is the pounding in my head, my own ragged sobs, and Tatiana's broken cries beside me.

"We have to get you and Tatiana out of here," he says gently.

"No." I shake my head, fresh tears spilling down my cheeks. "I can't leave him. I can't leave him here."

Cillian stands beside Konstantin, grief etched into his face. He reaches for me, a comforting palm on my shoulder, but it does nothing to soothe this agony.

"He won't be left behind," Konstantin promises. "We'll take him with us. We'll give him a proper burial."

My chest caves in on itself as a sob tears through me.

"I hate them," I choke out, my words raw with pain.

Konstantin's expression darkens, his jaw tightening. "I have your father. Believe me, he'll pay for this. I'll make sure of it before I end his miserable life."

It should bring me some relief. Some satisfaction. But it doesn't. Because no matter what he does to my father, nothing will change the fact that I've lost my brother.

That he's never coming back.

FIFTY-THREE

DINARA

The sky weeps with us.

A cold drizzle falls over the cemetery, soaking into the fresh mound of earth that will soon swallow my little brother whole.

My fingers tremble as I clutch the white roses in my hand, their petals soft, delicate. Too much like him. Too much like the boy who never got to grow up.

I take a slow, shuddering breath, but it doesn't stop the anguish caving into my chest.

It's been two days since Gregory died right in front of me. Since his blood stained my hands. Since his small body went still. Two days, and it still doesn't feel real.

It never will.

Cillian stands beside me, his arm wrapped tightly around my waist, grounding me, keeping me upright when all I want to do is collapse. His warmth is the only thing preventing the cold from consuming me entirely. But even that isn't enough to numb the agony tearing me apart.

I step forward, my boots sinking slightly into the damp grass. The coffin is there—polished black wood, lined with silver. Too small.

It shouldn't be this small. This isn't right. None of this is right.

With a shaking hand, I toss the flowers onto his coffin, watching them land softly against the surface. The finality of it crushes me, stealing what little breath I have left. My body trembles violently as I force out the words I should never have to say.

"I love you," I whisper, my voice shattering like glass. "I'm so sorry I couldn't save you."

Just like I couldn't save our mother…

Beside me, Tatiana chokes on a sob, her entire body convulsing as she falls to her knees, fingers clawing at the dirt as if she can pull him back from the grave.

"No, no, no," she wails, her grief raw and piercing. "I want him back. Please, just bring him back!"

Her screams rip through me, twisting the knife of my own pain deeper into my soul.

Konstantin crouches beside her, his hand on her back, whispering something I can't hear over the sound of my own heartbeat, the roar of my grief. He's trying to comfort her, but nothing will help. Nothing will make this better.

Nothing except vengeance.

I lower my gaze toward Konstantin, his expression grim.

"I want to watch him die." My words are hollow, stripped of emotion except for the deep, burning rage simmering beneath my grief. "I need to see it. I need to see him suffer."

Konstantin's lips curl into something that isn't quite a smile. It's crueler, darker—satisfaction and promise twisted into one. He kisses the top of Tatiana's head and rises to his feet, stepping closer.

"You will, dorogaya. I'll make sure of it."

A sharp gust of wind cuts through the cemetery, rustling the trees, as if the universe itself is bearing witness to his vow.

Gregory will never breathe again.

And soon, neither will the man who caused it.

The noon air is thick the following day with the stench of blood and filth. The distant grunts of pigs echo through the silence, their restless shuffling filling the space between the living and the dead.

I stand at the edge of Konstantin's pig farm, my fingers curled so tightly around Cillian's that my nails bite into his skin. He doesn't flinch. Instead, his grip tightens, anchoring me as I wait for the moment I've longed for.

The moment my father dies.

He kneels before us, wrists bound behind him, his cruel eyes locking on to mine with a twisted sneer. Even now, facing death, there is no regret in his gaze. No remorse for the wife he slaughtered. No grief for the son he led to death.

Only hate.

"Look at you," he spits, voice rough but dripping with contempt. "Standing there, thinking you're strong because they protect you." His eyes flick to Konstantin, then to Cillian. "You're weak, just like your mother. Just like that little bastard brother of yours."

Rage surges through me so violently, I take a step forward. But Cillian is already there shielding me, his body taut with barely restrained fury.

"You say one more fucking word about her, and I'll carve your tongue out myself," he growls.

My father smirks, but before he can open his mouth again, Konstantin steps in.

"Enough talking for you, Uncle." He rolls up his sleeves, exposing his tattooed forearms.

My father's expression flickers just for a second. A sliver of fear seeps through the arrogance, the realization settling in that this isn't just a death sentence. It's an execution. And it won't be quick.

Konstantin doesn't rush. He starts slowly, methodically, cracking his knuckles before delivering the first punch. My father spits blood, but laughs, even as Konstantin delivers another blow, then another.

The laughter fades when Konstantin pulls out a blade and drags it across his chest, carving slow, deliberate lines into his flesh.

The minutes stretch into eternity. My father's body is painted red, his screams mixing with the night air. He thrashes, but there's nowhere to go. No one to save him.

Konstantin steps back, breathing hard, his eyes cold and calculating as he signals to Aleksei, who grins and drags over a chainsaw. The sound roars through the night, a deafening, merciless noise that drowns out everything else.

My father's eyes go wide. He thrashes his arms harder, desperation finally taking over as the blade inches toward his leg.

"Nyet—podozhdi!" *No—wait!*

His screams are unlike anything I've ever heard. Blood sprays as Konstantin drives the blade through flesh and bone, severing his leg at the knee. His body convulses, agony twisting his face.

He tries to crawl, but Konstantin is already moving, taking the other leg. More screams. More blood.

I turn away and press my face into Cillian's chest, nausea churning in my gut. His hand slides to the back of my head, holding me close, shielding me from the worst of it. But the sound—the wet, sickening noise of flesh being torn apart, the fading gurgles of a man drowning in his own pain—it seeps into my marrow.

By the time I look again, my father is barely more than a torso. His body is slumped, his head rolling to the side. Blood pools in the dirt, thick and endless. His lips move, but no words come out. Just a pathetic, broken gasp.

And then…nothing.

He's gone.

I should feel relief. I should feel triumphant. But all I feel is empty.

Gregory is still dead. My mother is still gone. Nothing changes that.

But it's not over yet. Aleksei reappears, dragging two more figures into the dim light.

Ludmilla and Sonya.

Sonya snivels, her face streaked with tears, while Ludmilla stands tall, expression hard despite the bruises marring her skin.

Konstantin doesn't even hesitate. He grabs Ludmilla by the throat, shoving her to her knees.

"You betrayed me." His mouth curls ruthlessly, his voice deceptively soft. "You worked against me. You had to know what I'd do to you, yes?"

Ludmilla's lips part, but before she can speak, Sonya blurts out, "Please, sir, I didn't know anything. She made me think Lenny was the traitor! I didn't know she was working against you, I swear!"

Konstantin's gaze flicks to Ludmilla, who can't say a word to deny it. I heard it all from my father, and Konstantin knows the truth too.

"You were always easy to fool," she taunts Sonya. "So naïve."

Sonya's sobs turn desperate. "I thought she was my friend! I didn't know!" Her face crumples. "I-I didn't know. I swear."

Konstantin sighs, bored, and in one clean motion, slices Ludmilla's throat. The blood sprays. She gurgles. Then he severs her head with the chainsaw. It rolls to the dirt, eyes still open, lips still curled in defiance.

I barely flinch, while Sonya screams, recoiling in horror. Her knees buckle, but before she can collapse, Konstantin presses the gun to her forehead.

"You didn't tell me about Lenny," he says. "You should've told me."

She doesn't beg. Doesn't plead. She just cries.

A single gunshot echoes through the night, and Sonya falls.

Silence settles.

For a long moment, I just breathe, staring at the death before me. So much of it.

But there is no sense of victory. Just the pain of my brother's absence.

Cillian squeezes my hand, and I turn to him, searching for something—comfort, reassurance, anything to fill the void inside me.

"It's over now," he promises.

I shake my head. "No. It'll never be over."

Because Gregory is still gone. And that pain will never fade.

FIFTY-FOUR

DINARA
ONE MONTH LATER

I can't believe it's been a month since my brother's death. Since the pain and the betrayal hit me like a torpedo. It's been hard to move on, to escape this stabbing pain in my chest.

Everyone failed him.

No one knew what Ludmilla was doing behind our backs. How she'd been using her phone to make contact between my brother and my father since he was a little boy. It continued up until his death.

But it wasn't his fault. None of it was. He was just a child who wanted a father, and I can't blame him for that.

Konstantin was angry too, more at himself than anyone else, because like me, he knew he failed him too. And there's nothing any of us can do about it.

I kneel in front of his grave, the cool earth solid beneath my fingertips as I lay a bouquet of lilies down. The air is still, the heaviness of the moment pressing in on me. The headstone bears his name, forever etched into stone, a permanent reminder of a life cut too short.

He should've had a future. But my father stole that from him.

Tears burn in my eyes as I run my fingers over his name.

"I miss you," I whisper. "So much."

Cillian stands behind me, a quiet, steady presence—giving me the space to grieve, but letting me know I'm not alone. His warmth is a comfort against the cold reality that my brother is gone.

"I should have protected you better," I cry. "I should've known. Maybe if I had paid more attention…"

"Dinara…" Cillian kneels beside me and his hand finds mine, strong and grounding. "You can't do that to yourself. You did everything you could."

I shake my head, the lump in my throat nearly unbearable. "It wasn't enough."

He pulls me into his arms, holding me tightly as I let the tears fall, dampening his shirt. "You can't spend forever thinking about what you should've done. It won't bring him back, baby. All you can do is keep loving him and remembering him."

I clutch on to him, his touch anchoring me in a way I desperately need. He's been my rock these past few weeks. Patient, understanding, never pushing me to move on before I'm ready. He's just here, and that's what I need the most.

Riding with him has helped too. The horses have been like therapy, and he takes me every chance we get. Being out in the open, feeling the wind, the movement…it's the only time I can forget, even just for a moment.

"Thank you," I tell him.

And I know I don't need to explain, because he understands.

Cillian brushes a strand of hair from my face. "Always."

I manage a small smile, the first real one today.

"You're a pretty decent husband." Tears swim in my eyes.

He smirks. "I'd better be, or Fia would kill me."

A soft laugh escapes me, and it feels good to laugh.

He leans forward, pressing a kiss to my forehead, and I drop my head against his chest, glancing at the grave one last time. Then, because I know I have to, I let Cillian pull me to my feet. It hurts to leave, but with his hand in mine, the weight on my chest doesn't feel quite as crushing.

We walk back to the car in silence, but just before he opens the door, something inside me shifts.

"Wait."

He stills instantly. "You okay?"

His brows pull in, concern etched into every line of his face.

I nod, but my heart is hammering now, every beat carrying the words I've wanted to say. But with everything going on, my brother's death, both of us recovering from our injuries, I just…I don't know, I felt I needed to wait.

But in this moment, it's all I can think about.

My fingers graze the stubble along his jaw, my gaze searching his, drinking him in. He's been everything I've always needed, everything I never thought I'd have.

His eyes grow heavy-lidded as I rise on my toes, pressing a soft kiss to his mouth. He doesn't move, doesn't rush, just lets me take what I need.

"I love you, Cillian Quinn. I've loved you from the moment I met you."

He inhales sharply, clasping a palm around my nape, his jaw clenching as if trying to rein himself in.

"I've waited so damn long to hear you say that." His voice is rough, thick with something deep and unshakable. "And now I'm never gonna get enough."

"It's a good thing I don't plan to ever let you forget it."

With a growl, his mouth slants to mine, fierce and consuming, and I surrender to him completely.

Maybe I'll never stop hurting. Maybe this loss will never fade. But I don't have to go through it alone.

Because Cillian will always be right beside me.

FIFTY-FIVE

DINARA
ONE WEEK LATER

His fingers trace slow, soothing strokes up my back, grounding me in the quiet intimacy of the moment.

I keep thinking about the way he threw himself between Gregory and that bullet, unable to forget how he tried to protect my brother. How he took the hit without hesitation. It could've been worse. I could've lost him too.

A shudder runs through me at the thought.

I prop myself up on my elbow, gazing down at him, love swelling inside me so fiercely it's almost unbearable. My fingers skim the sharp lines of his face, unable to stop staring.

He groans, catching my wrist, his grip firm, as though my touch alone unravels him.

A spark ignites deep inside me, sharp and consuming.

"I love you," I whisper, the words a promise for all the days I didn't say it when I wanted to.

His eyes darken, hunger flickering through them. "Fuck, Dinara." His fingers thread into my hair, tilting my face toward his. "It makes me so hard when you say that."

A slow smile tugs at my lips. "Does it now?"

Sliding my hand beneath the comforter, I find the proof of his arousal, stroking the hard length through his boxers. A sharp curse escapes him as his hips jerk into my touch.

I lean down, slowly cutting the distance between us until my lips brush his. His grunt deepens, his restraint shattering as he grips the back of my head, and takes me in a fiery, intoxicating kiss.

In one swift move, he flips me beneath him, sliding between my thighs, his body pressing into mine until I can feel every rigid inch of him.

A needy moan escapes me as my body bows into him, aching for more.

His palm cups my cheek, his gaze locking on to mine, raw and intense. "When I look at you, it feels like my heart's going to give out. Because the way I love you, the way I need you…there's nothing else like it, baby. And no matter what hell we've been through, I swear I'll spend every day making sure you never have to face it alone."

My throat tightens, tears burning behind my eyes.

"You're never going to be alone, either. Not with me," I whisper, the depth of everything I feel for him evident in every syllable.

His forehead presses against mine, our breaths mingling, heavy and uneven. Then he kisses me, slow at first. But it doesn't stay that way.

Our clothes disappear in a flurry of hands and desperate need, until we're just skin against skin—two bodies, two hearts, made of one. Because this man, this love, it's infinite. Earth-shattering. Merciless.

He groans against my lips, his fingers slipping between my thighs, teasing, torturing.

"You're always so wet for me," he rasps. "And I haven't even tasted you yet."

Heat flares in my gut.

Before I can respond, he moves, flipping onto his back and dragging me with him. When I try to shift away so I don't press on the spot where he was shot, he tightens his grip on my hips, keeping me exactly where he wants me.

"Where the hell do you think you're going?" His voice is dark, laced with pure sin.

"Cillian, you got hit with two bullets. They may have been just grazes, but they were still friggin' bullets. You need to be careful."

Both of his wounds have healed, thankfully, but they're still red and raw, and the last thing I want is for him to somehow make it worse.

"I'm fine." His smirk is my undoing. "Now be a good girl and sit on my face."

A sharp pulse of need slams into me.

He sees it, feels it, and his grip tightens. "Come on, baby. You know I'm not gonna ask twice."

I barely have time to react before he pulls me up, throwing me over his mouth, his eyes gleaming with satisfaction. A gasp leaves me the second his tongue drags over my clit, hot and unrelenting.

"Oh God." My fingers curl into his hair as my hips roll instinctively, chasing the ecstasy only he can give.

His groan vibrates against me, possessive and gravelly. He licks, sucks, and teases, dragging me closer, drowning me in sensation. I cry out when he sucks me into his mouth, sending electric pulses of pleasure through my veins.

"I'm gonna come," I gasp, my body tightening, spiraling toward oblivion.

Cillian only growls, locking me in place, refusing to let me go until he's wrung every last drop of pleasure from me. And when I finally shatter, screaming his name, he doesn't stop. Not until I'm a trembling mess above him, utterly wrecked.

Slowly, he lowers me a little, his lips glistening, his smirk lazy and satisfied. "You taste like heaven."

I'm still trying to catch my breath when he flicks his tongue over my sensitive clit again, making me jolt.

"No, Cillian." I try to squirm away, but his hands tighten around my hips, keeping me exactly where he wants me.

"Yes, again." He sucks me into his mouth, and my cry fades into silence, drowned by the low rumble of his laughter.

When I squirm again, he grunts.

"How the hell do you say 'you're a pain in the ass' in Russian?" he asks, pulling back a fraction and spreading me open with his thumbs as he presses a lingering kiss to my clit.

"That's easy." I shudder. "Ya tebya lyublyu." *I love you.*

His eyes burn onto mine, heavy with desire, but deeper than that too. Fierce. Unwavering. Like I'm the only thing in the world that matters.

Without warning, he flips me onto my back, throwing one leg over his shoulder. The cool metal of his piercing grazes my core, a stark contrast to the heat rolling off him as he stares down at me.

"I can't wait another second." His chest rises and falls heavily as his gaze lines with mine. "I need you."

"I'm yours," I whisper, pulling him closer. "Always have been. Always will be."

A noise tears from his throat, tremulous and guttural, as if he's barely holding himself back.

And with one swift thrust, he's inside me—filling me, claiming me, taking my heart and soul with him. Our hands are everywhere, desperate, seeking, while our bodies move as one, perfectly in sync.

It hasn't always been easy. It hasn't always been beautiful. But this is our story.

Dinara and Cillian.

And I know, without a single doubt, that I belong here. With him. Forever.

And maybe, just maybe, this time, we'll get to live this life like we were always meant to.

THANKS FOR READING!

Want more Dinara & Cillian? Scan the code below for a bonus scene!

I hope you're ready for **Konstantin**, because he's been ready for his story for a while now.

Wondering if Iseult & Gio have a story? They do in **Twisted Promises**!

PLAYLIST

- "Dirtier Thoughts" by Nation Haven
- "Like You Mean It" by Steven Rodriguez
- "Too Late to Love You" by Ex Habit
- "No High" by David Kushner
- "Soul Tied" by Ashley Singh
- "Monsters" by Camilyo
- "You and Me" by David Kushner
- "Strangers Again" by Matt Hansen
- "He Loves Me, He Loves Me Not" by Jessica Baio
- "Hurts So Good" by Astrid S
- "Breathe" by Fleurie feat. Tommee Profitt
- "Heartbroken" by Diplo feat. Jessie Murph and Polo G
- "Shadow Preachers" by Zella Day
- "Fix It to Break It" by Clinton Kane
- "Hurts Like Hell" by Tommee Profitt feat. Fleurie
- "Dynasty" by MIIA
- "When the Party's Over" by Lewis Capaldi
- "That Girl" by Kenzie Cait
- "My Love Will Never Die" by AG feat. Claire Wyndham
- "Can You Love Me?" by Croixx
- "Someone to You" by Matt Hansen
- "Forget Me" by Lewis Capaldi
- "Empty Bench" by David Kushner
- "Камин" by Emin feat. JONY
- "Alive" by Austin Giorgio
- "All This Time" by Toby Mai
- "In Your Arms" by Croixx

- "Revolving Door" by Tate McRae
- "Breathe In, Breathe Out" by David Kushner
- "Angel" by Camylio
- "Autopilot" by memyself&vi
- "Nobody" by Toby Mai
- "I Hate That It's True" by Dean Lewis
- "Here We Go Again" by Psylosia
- "Don't Worry Babe" by Ex Habit
- "Scares Me" by Dean Lewis
- "The Best I Ever Had" by Limi

ALSO BY LILIAN HARRIS

Fragile Hearts Series

1. *Fragile Scars* (Damian & Lilah)
2. *Fragile Lies* (Jax & Lexi Part 1)
3. *Fragile Truths* (Jax & Lexi Part 2)
4. *Fragile Pieces* (Gabe & Mia)

Cavaleri Brothers Series

1. *The Devil's Deal* (Dominic & Chiara)
2. *The Devil's Pawn* (Dante & Raquel)
3. *The Devil's Secret* (Enzo & Jade)
4. *The Devil's Den* (Matteo & Aida)
5. *The Devil's Demise* (Extended Epilogue)

Messina Crime Family Series

1. *Sinful Vows* (Michael & Elsie)
2. *Cruel Lies* (Raph & Nicolette)
3. *Twisted Promises* (Gio & Iseult)
4. *Savage Wounds* (Adriel & Kayla)

Savage Kings Series

1. *Ruthless Savage* (Devlin & Eriu)

2. *Brutal Savage* (Tynan & Elara)
3. *Filthy Savage* (Fionn & Amara)
4. *Wicked Savage* (Cillian & Dinara - May 8th, 2025)

Marinov Bratva Series

1. *Konstantin* (September 8th, 2025)
2. *Aleksei* (Winter 2025)
3. *Kirill* (Spring 2026)
4. *Anton* (Winter 2026)

Standalone

1. *Shattered Secrets* (Husdon & Hadleigh)

For Lilian, a love of writing began with a love of books. From Goosebumps to romance novels with sexy men on the cover, she loved them all. It's no surprise that at the age of eight she started writing poetry and lyrics and hasn't stopped writing since.

She was born in Azerbaijan, and currently resides on Long Island, N.Y. with her husband, three kids, and lots of animals. Even though she has a law degree, she isn't currently practicing. When she isn't writing or reading, Lilian is baking or cooking up a storm. And once the kids are in bed, there's usually a glass of red in her hand. Can't just survive on coffee alone!